2009

To m... Y0-DOK-432 ...

Hope you enjoy.

Bob

ROAN'S REQUIEM

ROBERT L. HECKER

Hard Shell Word Factory

To my darling wife, Franceska.
And a special thanks to her sister, Jane Borrmann,
for all her encouragement and support.

© 2003 Robert L. Hecker
Paperback ISBN: 0-7599-4025-8
Published July 2004

eBook ISBN: 0-7599-4024-X
Published June 2004

Hard Shell Word Factory
PO Box 161
Amherst Jct. WI 54407
books@hardshell.com
www.hardshell.com
Cover art © 2003 Dirk A. Wolf
All rights reserved
Printed in the U.S.A.

Prologue

MAYBE IT WAS the country. Africa has a way of dulling your sense of outrage. You tend to become used to misery—and death. Even your own death would not come as a surprise.

Even so, Mbaraba prison was a shock.

During the two months I had been in Uganda, I had already developed a certain callousness toward brutality and death. I despised the feeling. But I hadn't realized how deeply it had penetrated until the day I found myself almost idly watching the torture of another human, and was not vehemently incensed. I should have felt a deep compassion for the man being whipped, and a bright burning anger directed at the monster inflicting the pain.

But I felt neither. Not now. Not in Africa. Certainly not here in Mbaraba prison. Here you rejoiced that it was happening to him and not to you. There was not even a sense of shame. You simply watched the torture and tried to keep your eyes and your mind blank, like the other prisoners. And God, it was becoming increasingly easy to do.

Ssss, thud!

Again the tooth-edging hiss ended with a sickening thud, the whip cutting like a sword through the pain-tensed muscles of the Buganda's sweat-drenched back. The man's head snapped back and a small sound ripped from his clinched jaw as a new trickle of blood coursed down the quivering skin, mingled with sweat, and spilled over the man's rope belt, soaking his sagging, ragged shorts.

Ssss, thud!

Mwanga grunted with effort each time he snapped the thin, limber whip, his own charcoal skin glistening with sweat and his wide lips were drawn back in a macabre grimace.

Mwanga was enjoying the hard work. He was a Nilotic-speaking Kakwa from Uganda's northwest corner and he had no love for the Bantu-speaking Bugandas, which was probably why he had singled out the man for such brutal punishment.

Beside me Jack Blucher whispered, "Kind of pretty, ain't it? Notice the way Mwanga cuts those diamond patterns. That son-of-a-bitch is an artist."

Tugawa, another Kakwa guard, turned his head and his small,

mean eyes focused on Blucher and me. We both stiffened, concentrating on the gruesome lesson all the prisoners were being forced to observe. Tugawa looked away, unable to forgo the certain pleasure of watching a Buganda being beaten unconscious for the possible joy of catching the two whites in an act of disobedience.

Without turning his head or moving his lips, Jack said, "Actually, it doesn't hurt that much. Cuts never do. Not at first. Not like a rubber hose or a flat strap. But tonight and for the next month that poor bastard is going to wish he'd never been born."

"So how come he just fainted?"

"Shock. Loss of blood." Jack chuckled, the sound like phlegm hacked up from his concave stomach. "And it do hurt some."

I couldn't take much more. A thin red curtain was slowly veiling my sight and a heavy surge of blood throbbed behind my temples, which I was sure had to burst under the awful pressure. We were standing in the huge open compound of the old Kabaka castle with the equatorial sun burning down on the crowns of our heads like a slowly descending furnace. It had to be close to ninety degrees even though we were in the Ankole region, close to 4000 feet above sea level.

After two months, I was heavily tanned but I could still feel the piercing rays penetrate the rotting material of my prison-issue twill shirt and sink into my skin. I could almost feel the melanoma tumors forming. My long, matted hair, already bleached to the color of oak, seemed to shrivel under the direct blaze. And from the red earth the heat radiated through the thin soles of my hide sandals until I was sure the blood in my feet and legs was boiling, rising to my head in a vapor of red steam. I closed my eyes, but the red mist only grew deeper. I couldn't stop thinking about ice—ice tinkling in purified spring water fortified with potassium and calcium and about a thousand mgs of vitamin C.

The image wavered and I swayed, glad that in a moment I would faint, and in the welcome blackness, would no longer be able to see or hear the torture.

Jack Blucher poked me hard with his elbow. "Belay that," he snarled. "They'd love to see you eating dirt."

I forced my eyes open, focusing again on the horror. Jack was right, of course. During the painful weeks I'd been in Uganda's notorious Mbaraba Prison, the Kakwa guards had pushed me hard, seeking an excuse for another beating with wrist-thick eucalyptus sticks. Thus far I'd been able to escape the wire whip. That was reserved for the serious breaches of rules, such as an escape attempt like the one made by the man now hanging limply from the blood stained post. But rules were often changed at the whim of a guard, or more likely, at the whim of Colonel Bakombo.

I looked up at the canopied balcony where the prison administrator stood watching the punishment, his broad face impassive. As usual, he was oblivious of the heat, wearing a heavy khaki uniform, complete with Sam Brown belt anchored with a pearl-handled 9mm Beretta pistol. Rows of decorative military awards he had given himself cascaded over his barrel chest.

Bakombo lifted his pugnacious jaw higher and popped his riding crop against his sharply creased pants leg. At the sound, the guards in the compound snapped to attention. Bakombo spat over the railing and went back into his quarters, which the thick lava rock and mud walls kept reasonably cool.

Mwanga shouted a command and the prisoners began shuffling across the sweltering compound toward the sliver of shade at the base of the 20' tall lava rock wall. The guards disappeared inside the prison barracks where they would sleep, play cards and drink beer made from bananas, sorghum, and millet or honey until some crisis like a fight or an escape attempt forced them back out into the heat.

Jack turned away and I asked, "Aren't you going to take a look at him?"

"What for? Not a damn thing I can do 'til they cut him down."

He kept on walking. I hesitated, then followed. There was no doctor at the prison and the role had fallen to Jack Blucher. During many years in combat, both in war and as a paid mercenary in half the back alleys and jungles of the known world, he had acquired a rudimentary knowledge of medicine. He knew his way around cuts and gunshot wounds. He was a fair surgeon when he had to be; a wizard at sewing up wounds with a leather-worker's awl and nylon thread.

Colonel Bakombo had allowed him the use of a small room in the barracks area as a hospital, although his medication was limited to aspirin and whatever native herbs he could threaten the colonel into providing. I'd seen him perform miracles with poultices and potions made from bark, leaves, roots, seeds and grasses. But I didn't see how he could do much for the poor bastard hanging from the post. He needed a hell of a lot more than an aspirin and tender loving care.

Jack led the way to a spike of shade formed by a deserted guard turret high on the wall, walking with his habitual, shuffling stride. A couple of muscular Bakigas were already settled in the patch of shade, and Jack nudged one of them in the side with his sandal. He jerked his head and the two men reluctantly got up and went to sit in the sun. Either of them looked as though he could have torn Jack Blucher's head off, but they simply hunkered down on the burning ground and stared at us.

I'd seen it happen before. It wasn't only that they looked upon Blucher as a kind of shaman or witch doctor. They also knew he was capable of killing both of them. Even the Kakwa guards did not push Jack Blucher too hard. He wasn't big, maybe 5'10" and weighed around 160. And he must have been close to 60 years old. But everyone knew he was a death machine.

He was American from somewhere in Texas or Arkansas. He'd fought with a commando group in the Viet Nam war. After the war, he spent a few years with the French Foreign Legion. When the Legion had come apart at the seams he'd resigned with his feet and headed for Angola where he'd been a paid mercenary without being too particular whose side he was on if the pay was right. From the little I'd been able to get out of him, he'd been caught with some group trying to pull a coup in Uganda. Most of the others had been executed, the lucky ones. But President Museveni, for some unfathomable reason, apparently thought he could find some use for Blucher, so he'd stowed him away here in one of Idi Amin's old prisons.

According to Jack's calculations, that was more than two years ago. In that time, the prison inmates, and the guards, had discovered that the old man with the graying hair was capable of doing great bodily damage with either his hands or his feet. And because he knew, he was relaxed, unconcerned, secure in his own knowledge.

I wondered how many of these men he'd had to kill or maim before the others had gotten the message. If he'd picked his target, which I was sure he had, it probably only required one. Like the lesson exemplified by the man hanging from the post, Jack Blucher's lessons would also be harsh but effective.

I sat down next to Jack and tried to find a spot on the hard ground that didn't feel as though I was sitting on a stove. Jack watched my squirming with amusement. "Relax," he said. "You're just raising a sweat."

"How can you relax in this place? It's like trying to relax in hell."

"When you can't do anything about something, go with it until you can."

"Not me. I prefer to make it happen, not just wait for God or somebody."

"Yeah," he chuckled. "Let's see you make it cool."

He was sprawled on the ground with his eyes closed, ignoring the heat as though it did not exist. I wondered if I would ever be able to shut out the world like that. I looked above the towering rock walls at the heat-washed blue of the African sky. Maybe I could learn to ignore the heat and flies and the putrid odors, even thought I was sure I was incubating every disease in Africa, but I would never learn to ignore the walls. Depressing. Hot and depressing. A psychiatrist could make a fortune here, if he didn't mind taking his pay in an incredible assortment of flies, bugs and lice.

"There's got to be some way out of this place," I muttered. "I can't spend the next twenty years in this hole."

"What's your hurry? You're not married. No kids. You said you're an orphan, so you've got no folks. Here you've got no worries, no problems. So relax. Look at it as a twenty-year vacation."

"No worries? I'm rotting away. Look. My hair is beginning to fall out. My teeth are coming loose. I'm getting spots on my hands as big as the cockroaches. My liver must be one big ball of worms. I don't even want to think about my gall bladder. I've got to get out while I'm still a shadow of myself."

"You're healthy as a horse. Where else are you gonna get natural food like here? No additives; no preservatives. Unless you count weevils and rat droppings."

I fought back a compulsion to regurgitate. My body needed the little nourishment it could absorb from the swill they called food. "If I don't get some breathing room, I'm going to have a heart attack. I've got to get out."

"You think you're hurting now?" He nodded toward the man hanging from the post. "You'll end up like him—or worse. You won't just think you'll have a heart attack. You'll pray for one."

The man had regained consciousness and was standing, trying to take the weight off his bound wrists and the lacerated muscles of his back. Flies from miles around had scented the blood and were already clustering around the open wounds. I couldn't stand to think about what they might be doing there.

Could I stand maggots on my own skin without going insane? But I was going insane. "I can't stay here. I'd rather be dead."

"You should've thought of that before you got mixed up with this cockamamie country."

It always amazed me how difficult it was to make the truth believable. Lies are easy to make clear and logical. But then, thinking about what had happened, it was difficult even for me to understand. At night I would still awaken in a sweat with the screams of the wounded and dying in my ears along with the gut wrenching sound of bullets thudding into bodies.

They're shooting! My God! They're actually shooting!

My body arched backward, twisting away from the automatic weapons fire, my hand clawing for the S&W .38 in my shoulder holster. It'd happened with incredible speed. One second, I'd been standing on the loading platform of the Kampala railway station while an Ugandian customs inspector checked the labels on the crate containing the VAX 11/780 computer while the three Uganda guards nervously fingered their Soviet AKM-47 rifles.

The next second, the inspector snapped a command. The guards must have been expecting the order because instantly they swung their rifles toward me and began firing. A too-hastily fired burst ripped past my head and hit a group of people standing behind me. Their screams were more nerve shattering than the sound of bullets thwacking into their flesh. I spun away, clawing for my gun. Then a round ricocheted off the concrete and my head suddenly exploded in a brilliant white flash.

My trial was short, lasting less than an hour. And most of that time was spent listening to the government prosecutor's harangue about how I had tried to steal government property. The most damning evidence was that the customs inspector had been killed—during the fight they said—and the bullet that killed him had come from my gun.

It didn't take a genius to see I had been set up. Someone had paid the inspector and the guards. A lot of people would do almost anything to get their hands on a late model computer, which was why I had been hired to escort it to the Uganda capital city of Kampala. I'd relaxed when it had been unloaded at its destination. Now the computer had vanished and I was in prison for God only knew how long.

"Even if you got out," Jack Blucher was saying, "where the hell would you go? It's fifty miles to the border of Rwanda or Tanzania." He jerked a thumb toward the man standing at the whipping post. "With no transportation, they'd catch you in a day, just like him."

"Getting out is no problem." I'd studied the rough stone blocks that formed the compound walls so I knew they would be easy to climb. "But you're right about transportation. We'd have to have a car or truck."

"You'd play hell getting one. Any vehicle comes through those gates gets treated like gold."

"Yeah." I sighed. "It doesn't look good." I scratched at a particularly vicious louse in my beard. Why was I concerned about escaping? I was surely going to die of sleeping sickness or the African version of Rocky Mountain Spotted fever long before I could put a plan in operation. "Maybe they'll let me write a letter. I've got people who'd help if they knew where to find me."

"And maybe you'll sprout wings." Jack eased back with his hands behind his head, staring up at the burnished sky, dismissing the subject.

I shifted to a position that would be more comfortable for about thirty seconds. "How about another lesson when it gets cooler?"

Jack had been instructing me in hand-to-hand combat, and in the use of knives and improvised weapons. We had to substitute sticks for knives, but in Jack Blucher's skilled hands, even a six-inch twig was deadly.

"Too damned hot," he muttered. "Wait'll December or January."

"That's months."

"So what? You going somewhere?"

"Yeah," I said. "I've got to."

He did not answer. The forced inactivity didn't bother him; he appeared to enjoy it. But it was driving me crazy. My body demanded exercise or it would begin to disintegrate. I was already beginning to feel dull and lethargic. A few more months of inactivity and I'd be able to sleep in the middle of the day, just like Blucher.

But then, he didn't have my motivation to escape. With him it wasn't a consuming passion. He'd told me that he had no family on the outside; no friends; nothing. If he did get out, he would get right back into somebody's dirty war. It was a far simpler and safer life here in the prison as long as you kept your nose clean.

But for me, everything was out there beyond the walls. There was my security agency in Newport Beach, California that was just beginning to pull in the really big money after four years of sixteen-hour workdays, six and seven days a week. Sure, Herb Stax, my partner, would keep it going. But I wasn't sure he could handle it alone. Herb was a salesman, not a manager.

Damn! The entire business might be coming unwound while I was sitting in this armpit they called a prison. And there was Helen. Funny I should think of her so much. We were close. But not that close. Not for some time. It was my fault. For the past four years, I'd put most of my time and energy into making the agency work. How many beautiful women could, or would, play second fiddle to an all-consuming mistress like that? So the fires had begun to cool.

But now, with nothing to do but think, the passions had all come back, hotter than ever. For the thousandth time I told myself that when I got back I was going to tell her how much I loved her, and we would be married and live in a bay-front house on Balboa Island with a red tile roof and a sail-boat just like everybody else. And every night I would make her put on shoes with six-inch heels and a see-through nightgown and dance for me while I lay in our big king-sized bed and watched. She would move slow and sexy, easing the straps off her shoulders before letting the filmy garment slowly slide—

Honk! Honk! Hooonnkkkk!

The sound of a horn yanked my thoughts back to reality. Outside the prison's main gate, a truck with a broken muffler bellowed to a stop and its driver pounded on the horn again.

Honk! Honk!

I pushed myself to my knees, passion driven from my mind by the interruption. It could not be the supply truck from Masaka. It wasn't due for another week. The other prisoners also knew the truck was out of schedule and they got to their feet, moving warily. In Mbarara prison, any change in routine would more likely be the harbinger of bad news instead of good. Even Jack Blucher propped himself up on one elbow and stared toward the gate. No one spoke as two guards swung the thick wooden gate open. Except for the creaking of the ancient hinges and the rumble of the truck's idling engine, there was no sound. The air was charged with a tense silence.

The truck's engine roared and it lurched through the gate and into the compound. The gate was quickly closed. The truck's engine died with a rattling overrun and silence closed in. Nobody moved. The bed of the truck was surrounded by sagging wooden siding, which could be hiding anything from crouching soldiers with machine guns to tons of explosives. It was wise to keep your distance from an intruder until he, or it, was proven to be harmless.

Colonel Bakombo came out on his balcony and snapped his riding crop against his leg, and guards moved to surround the truck, their AKM-47s ready, their fingers on triggers. Colonel Bakombo popped his riding crop again and all eyes swung to stare at him as though pulled by a single, invisible string. He shouted a brief speech in Bantu and the eyes swung back to stare at the truck. The colonel popped his leg again and went back inside.

Mwanga yelled a command and the prisoners slowly shuffled into a ragged line. Jack and I went to join them. Jack did not appear nervous. But he was the only man in the line who wasn't sweating. Whatever Bakombo had said had not been particularly reassuring to the others.

"What's going on?" I whispered. "We can't all get in that truck."

"Presents. Courtesy of President Museveni."

"Presents?" I felt a surge of anticipation. Maybe the truck had brought some wholesome food. Maybe I wasn't going to get beriberi after all. I had learned to stomach the swill of maize, beans and rice that was our standard fare twice a day, but I knew that my body had to be suffering. Even a little fresh fruit and vegetables would help ward off total disintegration—for a time.

"Clothes," Jack said, shattering my euphoria. "He wants us dressed up for visitors."

The hinged tailgate of the truck was loosened by two guards and it fell open with a bang revealing a huge pile of new twill shirts and shorts. Mwanga and one of the other guards climbed into the truck and began throwing a shirt and a pair of shorts to each man as the line slowly inched forward. There were no concessions for size. It was strictly one-size-fits-all. But then, most of the prisoners were about the same size—walking skeletons. For most, it was necessary to use a piece of rope or string to cinch in their shorts so they would not fall off. Almost all were barefoot. The only way a prisoner got sandals was to have a member of his family bring them. Jack got those we wore as barter for treating wounds or illness.

After receiving his new clothes, each man stripped off his old shirt and shorts and threw them in a pile near the truck. I wouldn't have been surprised if the entire filthy pile hadn't walked away.

I hated looking at the other prisoners. I could see myself in a few months. I still retained much of my body weight, but my reserve was going fast. It was a question of which one would go first, my body or my sanity. I had to get out!

While Jack and I were changing, I asked, "What kind of visitors? Must be damned important to rate this."

"Didn't say. But I suppose it's Red Cross."

"Red Cross? Do they come here?" I held my breath, waiting for his answer. This might be a chance to get a message out.

"A couple of people did about six months ago. But if you think you can work anything through them, forget it. One move and Bakombo'd have your balls."

"Did they give you new clothes then?"

"Shit, no. All they did was make us stand in the sun so those two assholes would see we were alive."

"So it probably isn't Red Cross. Who else had been here? Museveni?"

"Christ, no. He wouldn't come to this hole."

"How did the Red Cross guys get here? In a car?"

"Helicopter. But don't get any ideas. They watched that thing like it was full of whiskey. A dung beetle couldn't have hidden in that chopper."

A helicopter. My heart had sunk as soon as Jack said the word. I knew how to fly a light plane, but a helicopter was out of the question.

Still, I couldn't give up. There might not be another opportunity in months—years. There had to be a way I could use this situation.

When the last of the prisoners had received his allotment, Mwanga forced four of them to pitch the old clothes into the empty truck bed. Once loaded, its driver ground the engine into life and it swung around and went out the gate where it stopped. Before the gate was swung completely shut, I saw guards peering into every orifice of the truck to make sure they weren't hauling away a prisoner. Then to my surprise, the truck cut its engine.

"He's not leaving," I told Jack as though he had not heard.

"Too late in the day. These guys don't like to drive at night. He'll get drunk with the guards tonight and head back to Masaka or wherever the hell he's from tomorrow when his head stops hurting."

A truck. I couldn't get the thought out of my head. There had to be a way to get my hands on that truck.

Sitting in the shade, Jack looked up and saw me staring at the gate. "Forget it," he said. "Every bastard in here has the same idea. Colonel Bakombo's laughing up his shitty sleeve."

But I couldn't push aside the thought that this might be my only opportunity to escape. There had to be a way. Damn!

"Could you talk to some of these guys? See if they know anything about who the visitors are going to be. And how they're going to get here."

Jack grinned and shook his head. "You dumb bastard. They don't know any more than we do."

"The guards then. Mwanga. He must know something."

"So you find out. What the hell good will it do?"

I sat down beside him and tried to put some optimism in my voice. "Listen. There just might be a way we can use this thing. I don't know yet. But what the hell have we got to lose?"

Jack looked at the man who had been whipped. He had passed out again and was hanging limply from the post. Fly-blackened, congealing trickles of blood dripped to the sodden ground. "You have to ask?"

I stared at the man and some of my enthusiasm waned. Then I thought of the long years ahead and weighed them against the torture of a whipping, or even dying. It was no contest. "Don't worry," I said. "If I try anything, I won't get you involved."

"I'm white. They'll think I'm involved."

I rubbed a hand across my dirty face and beard. As the only two white prisoners, we were linked by a racial chain made stronger by the fact we were both Americans. If one got into trouble, the other just had to be involved. Everyone in the prison would assume so, whether it was true or not. Still, it might be my last chance. Blucher would understand that. Hell, he was a soldier, wasn't he?

"I'll try to find out myself," I said, and moved to get up.

Jack put a hand on my arm. "I'll do it. Shit. You don't even speak the language. And they sure as hell aren't going to speak English even if they know how, which they probably do."

Uganda, along with Kenya and Tanzania, or Tanganyika as it was once called, had been under British rule for almost a hundred years before achieving independence. Most of the natives understood some English and many could speak it. Colonel Bakambo could. When they'd sent me here he had told me clearly enough what kind of treatment I could expect. He also had an evil laugh.

Jack got up and slouched toward Mwanga who was watching intently as the man he'd whipped was cut down by another guard. He saw Jack approaching and hitched up his AKM-47. Jack stopped with plenty of distance between them and nodded toward the unconscious man. He said something and Mwanga laughed. Jack stayed well clear of Mwanga as they talked, apparently telling jokes about the Bugandas because Mwanga laughed harder and some of the nearby prisoners glared at Jack as though they didn't think it was so funny.

Mwanga yelled to two of the guards who finished cutting the bloody man down, leaving him sprawled in the hot dust. Mwanga turned back to the barracks and Jack sauntered back to sit beside me.

"Amnesty International," he murmured. "Who the hell ever they are."

"I've heard of them. Some kind of an organization operating out of London or Switzerland. They check into the torture and mistreatment of political prisoners. They must carry a lot of political clout for President Museveni to take them seriously."

"Whoever they are, it won't do us any good. They're coming by chopper. Unless you can fly one, you're under a volcano without an umbrella."

Damn! A sickening depression made the sun unbearably hot and I had to press my fingers against my aching eyes. What was I thinking? Instead of trying to find a way to get myself killed, I should be thinking of ways to survive. Maybe the next political regime would give me a pardon. If I lived that long.

I shook off the malaise. I had to get that truck! "What time are they due?"

Jack gave me a bemused look as though I was a backward child to be humored. "Why? You've been torpedoed."

"Not yet. I'll think of something. What time?"

He sighed. "He didn't say. But I'd guess they'll fly in from Masaka or maybe Entebbe. That'll put them here about noon or a little later, unless they start awfully damn early."

A sliver of an idea was beginning to form and I let it grow, allowing it to choose its path, giving it a nudge of possibilities when it appeared to get stuck. What the devil was that phrase?—if you can't lick 'em, join 'em. "These amnesty guys. They've never been here before?"

"Not since I've been here."

"So the colonel won't know exactly who to expect. You think they'll be European?"

"Sure. I guess so."

"Maybe from London. With British accents."

"Yeah, could be."

"Wearing what?"

"In this weather? Shirt and shorts. What else?"

"And boots. They're going to be hard."

"Hard to what?"

"Hard to get. Who around here has got boots?" Jack sat up and stared at me, his pale blue eyes narrowed in a sidelong glance. "What have you got in mind?"

I had it now, if I could only pull the pieces together. "It's hard to explain. But if I can get a razor and some boots, I think I can pull it off. And I know just the place."

"Yeah? Where?"

"From Colonel Bakambo."

Jack looked away and combed his fingers through his matted hair in a gesture of frustrated resignation. "Shit," he said softly as though to dismiss the entire idea as too preposterous to warrant further thought. He turned his back and settled down for his afternoon nap.

But there was no napping for me—not today.

THAT NIGHT, UNDER a starry dome, I scaled the compound wall. The heavy blocks of lava had rough edges and wide cracks that made the climb easy. Even in the dark of the moonless night, I was able to work my way to the top of the compound wall silently. Only one guard was on the rampart and he was asleep, slumped over his rifle. I edged behind him to the wall of the barracks where it butted into the main palace wall, and climbed across to the colonel's balcony.

I paused on the balcony to listen. The night was still, sullen with heat. I turned to the slatted French doors that closed off the room from the balcony. As I expected, they were partially open to allow any stray current of air to find a way inside.

I cautiously inched my way through the opening and into the room. It was almost pitch black, the stale air heavy with an oppressive heat. I paused just inside the doorway to allow my sight to adjust.

In a moment, objects began to take shape. I was in a study. There was an ornate but battered desk in the center of the room, and a scattering of heavy chairs upholstered with thick leather. Several small rugs muffled my steps as I crossed to a door and eased it open. It opened onto a hall, dimly lit by small-wattage bulbs in corroding ceiling fixtures. At the far end of the hall, a guard was sleeping in a chair, his rifle across his knees, his chin resting on his chest.

There were three more doors in the hallway and I wondered which led to the colonel's bedroom. Probably the one nearest the guard. Trying to open the door without waking the man was too much of a long shot. It would be better to neutralize him.

I went back into the colonel's office and wrapped a heavy stone paperweight in one of the small throw rugs. Returning to the hall I tiptoed to the sleeping guard and smashed him behind the ear with the makeshift blackjack. I caught his rifle as he slid to the floor. The rifle wouldn't do me a bit of good no matter what happened so I left it.

Carrying the rug bludgeon, I edged open the door to what I hoped was the colonel's bedroom. I felt a draft of cool air and heard the labored hum of an air conditioner. So the colonel wasn't so tough after all. Inside the room, I discovered he also slept with a night light that spilled through the partially open door of a bathroom. The colonel was lying nude in bed, his massive arms around two equally nude girls. They looked as though they were about twelve or thirteen with small, budding breasts and slim childish hips. I could understand why he needed the cool air.

The sound of the air conditioner hid any noise I might have made as I moved past the huge bed into the bathroom. The toilet was an ornate stool with no water, and the stink was almost overwhelming even though my nostrils were used to the stench in the compound. There was a bowl of murky water on a sink and next to it a straight razor with a mother-of-pearl handle. I put the razor in my pocket and eased out of the room.

One of the girls moaned in her sleep and rolled over and I clutched the bludgeon, hoping I wouldn't have to use it. She relaxed with a sleepy murmur and I began searching for a pair of boots.

Under an open clothes rack that doubled as a wardrobe, I found what I was looking for—thick-soled hiking boots with an odorous pair of socks thrust inside. Lifting the boots slowly and carefully, trying not to touch the germy socks, I carried them into the stifling hot corridor and eased the door shut.

The guard was still unconscious. As long as the colonel was unharmed, he would be afraid to report anything. If the colonel wondered what had happened to his razor, the guard certainly wasn't going to give him any answers that might get his own head removed.

There was one other item I needed and I found it on a shelf in the colonel's office—a full bottle of Gilbey's gin. There were several identical bottles on the shelf so I doubted he would miss one. I figured the colonel might be very occupied in the morning.

I did not return to the compound. After replacing the rug and paperweight, I walked down the stairs past another sleeping guard, and out the front door. Before trotting off into the scrubby acacia trees and elephant grass, I stopped at the truck parked outside the big gate. As I expected, the ignition keys were gone. I might have been able to hot wire it, but even if I got it started, I wouldn't get far. They'd be after me before I was a mile down the road. By running cross-country they could easily cut me off. No, I needed a head start without pursuit. I left the bottle of gin in the cab and ran into the African bush.

I kept moving until I found a stream. When I stopped, I was panting for breath. Two months ago a mile run wouldn't have made me breath hard. I was surprised at how quickly my body was betraying me. I'd probably picked up some vicious African protozoa which was slowly attacking my debilitated tissues. I knew that if I didn't get out of this blasted country I'd be dead in weeks—months. Or, with my luck, years.

I resisted an urge to keep running. Without that truck and a good head start, I'd be dead in hours. At the stream, I gingerly washed the colonel's stinking socks, keeping a wary eye out for crocodiles. I didn't know if they inhabited this area, but I sure didn't want to find out the hard way. The socks might not dry before I needed them, but even if I had to wear them wet, pneumonia was preferable to leprosy.

I walked another ten minutes, then climbed the tallest acacia tree I could find and settled for the night, hoping I was high enough to escape any night marauders. Wedged in a fork of the tree, I listened to the unfamiliar sounds of the African night. If this thing worked, I'd be home soon.

I wondered what had been happening since I left Newport Beach. Everybody probably thought I was dead. I couldn't blame them. This was a land of death. I'd felt it all around me from the minute I'd set foot in Africa. All kinds of death. Death by any of a dozen strange diseases; death by starvation; death by government soldiers or police; death by creatures that slithered, crawled, walked or swam; or death by sheer fright. They were all out there waiting. Tomorrow I would either be a victim of one of them, or I could kiss them all goodbye.

I slept little during the long night, and even the brief snatches of sleep were punctuated by bad dreams, dreams of body surfing in the clean curl of a breaking wave at Huntington Beach or board surfing at Malibu. Only the wave would turn into a tunnel and suck me into a black vortex where Mwanga was waiting, his white teeth flashing in wide-mouthed laughter.

Just before dawn I crawled stiffly from the tree. After washing my hair, I used the colonel's razor to trim it into what I hoped would pass for a British cut. Using a pool of water as a mirror, I painfully scraped off my beard, revealing a dead white patch of face with many nicks and cuts, surrounded by deeply tanned areas and highlighted by a sunburned and peeling nose. I was a walking invitation to skin cancer.

I covered the worst of the white areas with streaks of mud, and rubbed some into my hair. With the aid of the razor, I tore a generous number of rents in my new shorts and shirt and splashed on a spatter of mud.

The colonel's socks were still damp. But they were reasonably clean and they helped fill out the boots which were at least two sizes too big even for my size twelve feet.

The sun was high in the sky when I stumbled out of the bush and painfully limped toward the prison gate shouting and waving my arms. A guard at the wall saw me and yelled something before he disappeared. Passing the truck I saw the driver slumped inside the cab, the almost empty bottle of gin dangling from his slack fingers.

So far, so good.

At the gate I pounded and yelled "Help! Help!" and in a moment the heavy panels creaked open and Mwanga came out flanked by two guards with leveled rifles.

When I saw Mwanga, my heart leaped. I hoped that my look of near panic would add to my masquerade. God, if he recognized me now....

Using my best British accent, I said harshly, "I say! You've just got to get help immediately, old chap. I think Paul is dead and Bertie's on the bloody edge."

"Who dead?" Mwanga rumbled, his small eyes cold and mean. "Who you?"

"Lance!" I blurted. Lance? Where the hell had I gotten that? I hoped it sounded British. "Lance Carruthers. Amnesty International! There's been a horrible accident."

At the mention of Amnesty International, Mwanga's expression changed to one of alarm. "Accident? Where accident?"

"I'm not sure." I waved vaguely toward the bush. "Back there. The helicopter. It crashed. I've been walking for hours."

Mwanga stepped back and motioned me inside. "In. In. We get Colonel."

With increasing confidence, I followed him inside. If Mwanga hadn't recognized me, the colonel certainly wouldn't. I'd only been face to face with him once and that was the day almost three months ago when they'd prodded me off the truck with the other incoming prisoners. And his inspection had been brief. The Colonel did not like standing in the hot sun. Except for noting with a tight smile that I was white, he'd ignored me. So I was sure he wouldn't connect this muddy, beat-up Englishman with the sullen, bearded American. Unless, of course, he recognized his boots.

I held my breath when he stomped into the anti-room stuffing his shirt into his pants and buckling his Sam Brown belt. He said something to Mwanga in Nilotic and Mwanga snapped an answer containing the words 'Amnesty International.'

I took the initiative and stepped toward him. "Colonel, you've got to get help. Quickly."

Colonel Bakambo threw up his hands in horror. "Oh, what is happening to you, sir?" he said in good English. "Mwanga says there has been an accident."

I put my hands to my head, partially shielding my face, and slumped against an ornate table. "We really must hurry. It's—" what the hell was the name I had used? "—Bertie. He's terribly hurt. And I'm sure the pilot's dead."

Colonel Bakombo snapped an order and Mwanga ran out of the room. The colonel shouted over his shoulder at someone and I heard the word 'whisky.'

"A car," I grated. "You've got a Rover, of course. We can reach them in a Rover." I knew there wasn't the slightest possibility he could find a Land Rover within a hundred miles. But I wanted him to start thinking about transportation. I also didn't want to give him time to dwell on the situation

"No, no," he said, waving his hands in agitation. I could understand his alarm. President Museveni would not be pleased if the Colonel caused a bad report from the highly important visitors. After the problems that Uganda had with Adi Amin, their international reputation was low and the country could use a few favorable reports. Which was probably why Museveni had allowed the representatives from Amnesty International to enter the country in the first place.

"A truck perhaps," I cued him. "I believe I saw a truck."

"A truck?" The colonel's face brightened. He asked something of one of the guards and the man replied in the affirmative. The colonel's eyes lost some of their apprehension. "Yes, yes. We have a truck. It was due to return to Masaka this morning, but it has not."

"I say, that is a stroke of luck." I turned to lead the way out, not wanting the colonel to have any time to think about the situation. And also I wanted to be well on the way before the authentic visitors arrived. At the door I paused and turned back as though I'd just thought of an important point. "A doctor! We're going to require your best physician."

"Doctor?" Again the colonel's eyes took on a harried look and the patches of sweat that had begun to stain his shirt grew larger. "There is no doctor."

"We've got to have medical aid. Don't you have anyone here? A prisoner perhaps? Anyone?"

Again the Colonel's face cleared and he held up a trembling finger. "Yes, yes. We do have such a one. A very good doctor. One of the prisoners." He turned to the guard and yelled a command in the man's face. I caught the word 'Blucher,' and as the guard turned and hurried away, I wiped a hand across my face to hide a smile.

"Come," I snapped. "Let's see this bloody truck."

"This way. This way!" Colonel Bakambo waved to the remaining guard to follow, and he almost ran out the door and across the dusty ground to the truck. I followed, moving rapidly, not wanting to take any chances on the colonel suddenly thinking about making a phone call to Masaka or Mbarara to check on my story.

If things got out of hand I could grab the guard's rifle and take the colonel hostage. It might work if we could get clear and cut the telephone line before Mwanga or one of the other guards could get a message out. But it would be better if we could get a good start before the deception was discovered. With any luck that wouldn't be until the real people from Amnesty International arrived. By that time, we should be well on our way to the Tanzania border.

The truck driver was still slumped over the wheel. Colonel Bakambo opened the door and shook the man so hard his head banged on the steering wheel and the bottle slipped from his hand and fell on the ground. Colonel Bakambo picked it up and recognized the brand. His face contorted in fury, he grabbed the man's shirt and yanked him from the truck cab, slamming him on the ground. He kicked the man in the side and shouted at him.

But the driver only moaned and drew his legs up in a fetal position. With a shrill scream of rage, Colonel Bakambo grabbed the AKM-47 out of the guard's hand and fired a long burst into the driver. The body jerked and writhed as it disintegrated, gouts of blood and bits of flesh and clothing exploding away, torn from the body by the savage leaden teeth. The colonel stopped firing and hurled the gun into the guard's chest who caught it with such an expression of relief I was sure he thought he was going to be next.

Colonel Bakambo, his face dripping with sweat and his shirt almost completely soaked, turned to me with clenched fists. "A thief. He was a thief!" he snarled as though that condoned the execution.

To him, it probably did. But I was sick with guilt. I hadn't meant to get the man killed. My only thought had been to cause him to delay driving the truck away. I stared at the slowly settling mass of flesh and oozing blood, hardly recognizable as having been human. I hoped to hell the man didn't have a wife or family.

"You will drive," the colonel was saying. "It is better. You know the direction."

"Yeah, okay," I said dully. Suddenly realizing what I had said, I snapped my head up and said again. "Of course, old boy. Perfectly justified. Beggar was a thief, you say?"

"Yes, yes. He is fortunate to be dead."

I couldn't agree more. I didn't like to think what Bakambo would have done to the poor bastard if we'd left him alive. Jack Blucher had told me that in the old days in this part of the world, it was a common practice for thieves to have their lips, cheeks, nose and ears cut off, leaving only their eyes. And it was not uncommon to cut off a person's arms or legs for the most trivial offense. Now there was the bloody post in the prison compound or the dank rooms under the old palace.

I told myself again that if anything went wrong, I would not be brought back alive. I could well imagine what Bakambo would do to me.

I heard hurrying footsteps and turned to see Mwanga and Jack

Blucher trotting toward me. Jack was carrying a haversack that contained his limited supply of medicine and medical equipment. When he saw me, he almost stopped and his eyes widened. Then he regained his stride, but I could tell he was having a hard time keeping a straight face.

Damn! He was going to blow the whole thing.

Then Jack saw the body of the driver and his eyes lost their humor. Again, I could be grateful to the driver. I wished his soul good journey to wherever Bugandas went.

"What is it?" Jack said, looking at me. "What is this?"

"Accident," I said in my clipped accent. "Bloody awful. We'd better hurry."

Without waiting for a reply, I climbed into the cab of the truck and looked for the ignition key. Fortunately, the driver had put it in the ignition. I didn't think I could have gone through his pockets.

While I coaxed the truck's ancient engine into life, Jack ran around and climbed in beside me. Colonel Bakambo shouted to Mwanga and the guard to get in back and they climbed over the side panels, not looking too happy about riding on top of the filthy clothing that had been discarded by the prisoners. Colonel Bakambo clambered in beside Jack, making it a tight squeeze in the narrow cab. The engine caught and I gingerly worked the gas pedal until it coughed into a shuddering roar.

I checked the gas gauge. Three-quarters. That should be enough to get us to the border. The oil pressure was low, but the old wreck probably hadn't felt a full crankcase since it left the factory.

I yanked it into gear and gave the engine full throttle. It bellowed with a staccato roar, spinning the startled tires in the dust and we shot forward onto the tarmac road. Between gears I speed shifted, keeping the gas pedal on the floorboard, and we roared down the narrow road, leaving the dreaded prison farther and farther in the distance.

When it was safe to take my eyes from the narrow, winding road, I glanced in the rearview mirror. Jack was sitting in the middle so I looked directly into his eyes. His eyebrows lifted as though to ask, "What now?"

Looking back at the road, which twisted through the scattered acacia and eucalyptus trees, I gestured toward the colonel's pistol. Jack nodded and flexed his hands. The colonel was about to get a karate lesson.

A couple of miles from the prison, we crested a rise and rounded a sweeping curve that pressed Jack hard against the colonel's side. He put his two hands on the colonel's sweating neck and dug in his fingers. The colonel opened his mouth and his eyes glazed. When Jack took his hands away, the colonel's head lolled with the jouncing of the truck and Jack had to hold him upright.

"Is he dead?" I had to shout to be heard above the rattle and bang of the speeding truck.

"No. But he'll be out a couple of hours. You'd better stop as soon as you can."

Alarm flooded my body. "Stop? What for?"

"We've got to cut the telephone line before they figure out what's going on."

"Mwanga'll see us."

Jack pulled the colonel's pistol from its holster and checked it. "We'll have to take him out."

"That won't be easy. He's a suspicious bastard. If we stop, he'll be ready."

He nodded toward the colonel. "When you're ready, I'll dump him. They'll turn to look at him."

I saw he was grinning. The old bastard was happier than I'd ever seen him. He seemed to thrive on the prospect of getting shot or of shooting somebody.

He waited until we hit a particularly rough stretch of road, then opened the door and shoved the colonel out. The rush of air past the open door alerted Mwanga and the guard, and in the rear view mirror I saw them peer over the side at the colonel's body which rolled and flopped behind the truck.

By the time they realized what had happened, Jack was half out the door and hanging over the truck bed. Mwanga, moving faster than I would have thought possible, got off a burst from his AKM-47, but his haste and the jouncing truck bed caused his shots to go in the air. Before he could correct his aim, Jack shot him twice.

The guard made no attempt to use his weapon. He hung onto the side panel with one hand, his eyes popping in fright. Jack motioned with the pistol and the guard dropped his rifle. I slowed and stopped. Jack climbed into the truck bed and picked up the two rifles. The guard moved to the rear of the truck bed, where he crouched in fearful anticipation, certain Jack was going to kill him. Then he straightened slowly, the fear going from his face. He stared at Jack, his face calm, ready for death.

My mouth was sour as I asked, "Are you going to kill him?"

"No," he said. "There's no point now."

"If we let him go, he'll be back at the prison in an hour."

To my surprise, he said, "We'll take him with us, and drop him near the border."

I would have to reevaluate my opinion of Jack. I'd thought he could kill with the same emotion I would have swatting a fly. Could it be there was empathy under that shell? "Okay," I said. "But we'd better get rid of Mwanga. The Tanzanians might not lose any love for Bugandas, but they'd take a dim view of bringing bodies into their country."

"You're right about that. Get him out. I'll be right back."

While I concealed Mwanga's body in the tall grass, Jack walked across the road to a pole that supported three strands of electrical wire. The one on top was the telephone line and he shot it down.

When he came back, I was waiting in the truck. As Jack climbed in beside me, I asked, "Why didn't you shoot the other wires?"

"If they were all down, it might look suspicious back at the prison. If only the telephone is out, they won't pay a hell of a lot of attention."

"That's true," I agreed. "Nobody but the colonel uses the phone much anyway unless they get a call."

I jerked my thumb toward the guard in the back who was sitting dejectedly on the pile of clothes. "Maybe we should tie him up."

"No need." Jack patted the rifle in his lap. "If he jumps out, he knows he couldn't get more than twenty feet. Back there he's safe."

I put the truck in gear and drove down the narrow road at a slightly less frantic pace. I had to resist an impulse to put the pedal on the floor. The objective was to make it to the border, not blow the cylinder heads off the engine. It was just beginning to hit me that we were actually going to make it when Jack shook his head in disbelief.

"God damn!" he muttered. "You did it. You crazy son-of-a-bitch. You did it."

We rode in silence, savoring the ecstasy of freedom. It was a total euphoria most people would never know. Such elation could only be experienced after deep despair, after a realization that the prison you were in, whether physical or mental, was all that the future held. Then, suddenly, you were out. Free! But powerful as it was, it was an emotion I never wanted to experience again. The price was too high.

"Ever been to California?" I asked.

"No. What's there?"

"Everything. The best weather, the best beaches, the best women. You'll love it." I pushed harder on the accelerator. California was waiting.

Chapter 1

YOU'D THINK that when you've been on intimate terms with death, you'd be able to sense its presence like a subliminal specter. But when Herb Stax drove his Cadillac convertible into the parking lot next to our office building, any hint of pending disaster was lost in a tide of joy at being home.

Herb and Jack Blucher got out and started toward the office, but I sat for a moment savoring the sound of traffic on Balboa Boulevard and the dull boom of Pacific surf breaking on the beach behind the beach houses. I drank in the tangy smell of the sea mixed with the aroma of gourmet cooking wafting from the many nearby restaurants.

After being away almost three months, even our small office building looked beautiful. It was little more than a two-story wooden box, but we'd tried to give it a little class by painting the clapboard a pale blue with white trim and by putting colorful blue and white awnings over the entrance and the front windows. The bronze plaque beside the door that stated S&R SECURITY was highly polished but discreet. Maybe you couldn't buy class out of a paint can, but after experiencing the hot breath of hell, I wouldn't have traded the old frame building for the Taj Mahal.

When I followed Herb and Jack through the door into the outer office, I was startled by a chorus of voices shouting "Welcome home, boss!"

The staff had rounded up a bunch of metallic balloons and ribbons, and red-white-and-blue bunting so the office looked as thought somebody had forgotten to clean up after a New Year's party. Kim Fuji, my secretary, ran over and threw her arms around me and lifted her five-foot body high enough to give me a quick kiss on the cheek.

"Oh, I'm so glad you're not dead!" she cried and I was surprised to see tears glistening on her cheeks.

Mrs. Davis, our accountant, came over and gave me a quick peck on the cheek, and Judd Procter, the dispatcher, pumped my hand as though to reassure himself it was real.

I looked around for Helen, but she wasn't there. My sharp disappointment made me realize just how much I wanted to see her. Why wasn't she here? If she had been the one returning from a long trip, I'd have moved heaven and earth to meet her. Perhaps the old adage was wrong and absence did not make the heart grow fonder. Maybe she had already found somebody else.

Herb Stax whacked me on the back. "Hell," he said, "if I thought I'd get a welcome like this, I might try disappearing myself."

Herb was the 'S' in S&R Security. I was the 'R'. If I'd had a father, I wouldn't have minded if he'd been like Herb Stax. He was 54, but he looked younger. He was considerably overweight, most of the weight concentrated in his stomach and in his round, shiny face, which was without the trace of a wrinkle. His hair was light brown, fine, tinged with gray, but it was full and flowing.

Everyone said that if Herb only had a long beard, he would make a perfect Santa Claus. Except for this clothes. Herb dressed for the youthful image, favoring turtle-neck shirts that hid his double chins. His jackets were usually cashmere, and his cowboy boots were lizard or snake skin. He even had a pair made of ostrich skin that I knew had cost him at least three hundred dollars. I think the real reason he favored boots was because they added a little height to his 5'6" frame.

"They must not have had anybody to sign their checks," I told him and Kim punched my arm.

"That's not the reason," she said. "I can forge your name better than you can."

Jack Blucher was hanging back near the door. I raised my hand until I got a little quiet and said, "Everybody, I want you to meet the guy who saved my life—Jack Blucher."

They turned to stare at Jack who was leaning against the door jamb with his arms folded, his pale eyes taking in everything. They probably thought I was putting them on because Jack didn't look as though he could save the life of a kitten. He was now wearing a white shirt with a button-down collar, a maroon necktie, and a dark blue suit so new the pants still had knifelike creases. But he still retained an air of bemused sangfroid that made one believe he didn't give a damn whether anyone said hello or not.

Kim Fuji grabbed my hand and led me to her desk just outside my office door where there was a big square cake with 'Welcome home' scripted on the icing. I winced at the thought of all those empty calories, but I didn't want to disappoint the staff so I cut the cake while Herb Stax opened a magnum of champagne that had been chilling in the office refrigerator. I quickly came to the conclusion there are few things that taste worse than champagne with sickeningly sweet marzipan.

Looking at our small but very special staff, feeling their genuine happiness, I had to blink back tears. It was so easy to work with people year after year and never know for sure what they thought of you. It took something as traumatic as coming back practically from the dead to discover true feelings.

In a way, we were all strangers. Herb and I had only started the company four years ago. When we got our first really big contract, providing security for Colton Labs, we'd been able to hire an accountant. That was Mrs. Davis. Helen Cotrell had come on board as our first secretary. Later, for reasons I'd never been able to understand, Helen decided she wanted to be a uniformed guard. And she wanted to work the night shift at Colton Labs.

The remainder of our small office staff and our force of guards had been accumulated as we got more contracts, most of them during the past year. It was gratifying to think they were glad I wasn't fertilizer for elephant food in some remote corner of Africa

Herb said he wanted to bring me up to date on company projects and we went into his office. But I had something more urgent to talk about. Trying to sound unconcerned, I asked, "Where's Helen? I hope she's not sick."

"She's fine," Herb said. "She really went to pieces when we got word you'd been shot. I called her first thing when I got the message you were on your way back."

The warm glow returned. She did care! "Thanks, Herb," I said. "I, uh, kind of thought she'd be here."

"I asked her. She said she'd rather see you alone." He indicated his telephone. "She's waiting for your call."

I let the wonder of it wash over me. Could we—could she—rekindle the feeling she once had for me? Maybe—just maybe all my dreams, all my fantasies could come true.

My hands were trembling as I punched her number. When I heard her soft "hello" my throat closed like a fist.

"Hello," she said again, and at the sound of my strangled gasp, she asked. "Ben? Is that you, Ben?"

"Helen," I choked. "Yes. It's me."

"Oh, my God, Ben. What happened? Where have you been? We thought you were dead."

Her voice flowed through me like strong wine. I managed a strangled laugh. "Not so fast. Why don't we get together for dinner and I'll tell you all about it."

"Are you all right? They said you were shot."

I reveled at the anxiety in her voice. "No, no. I'm okay. What about dinner?"

"Can't I see you before that? What about right now?"

I drew a deep breath. It was coming true—my craziest fantasy. I would rush to her, take her in my arms, kiss her soft, willing lips. Damn!

With an effort, I closed off the memories. Underlying my euphoria like a mattress of nails was the fear she might only be feeling sorry for me.

"I'd like that," I said. "But... I've got to stop by my place first."

"You stopped by the office first," she said with what sounded like a pout. "I'd hoped I was more important than that."

"You are. You know that. They only get the tip of the iceberg. You get the whole thing."

"Just what I need—an iceberg."

"I'll let you thaw me out."

"When?"

I glanced at my watch, making a fast estimate. "What about seven?"

"Can't you make it sooner? I have to be at work by eight."

"Tonight?" Disappointment clouded my elation. How could she even consider going to work tonight? "Take the night off."

"I can't," she said, and I could hear the pain in her voice. "I haven't been able to line up a substitute. We're kind of short-handed."

I felt a stab of annoyance, not sure I believed her. We had several guards on our staff who were bonded and had the experience to work as substitutes. Guards' salaries were far from large and most were usually happy to make extra money. But maybe the company really was short-handed. A lot of changes could take place in a few weeks.

"Okay," I said. "I'll come by as soon as I can get away. Probably about five."

"All right," she breathed as she hung up. "I'll be waiting." The way she said it in a low register with a little catch in her voice made a chill of anticipation shoot through me.

I slowly placed the phone back in its cradle, unwilling to break the spell. Somehow, the time away from Helen, the distance, had brought us back together. I felt a powerful inner joy I hadn't experienced for a long time. I wondered if Helen felt the same incredible sensation about me. Or was she simply being kind to an old friend who had come back from a long and dangerous journey? I would soon find out.

Chapter 2

HERB STAX DROVE us to my house on Lido Isle. During the short ride, I stared at the familiar sites of Newport Beach with new eyes.

The Newport/Balboa Peninsula is roughly five miles long and a quarter mile wide. It's connected to the city of Newport at the north end, with Newport Bay on the north-east and the Pacific Ocean on the south-west. Balboa Boulevard saunters down the middle of the peninsula until it ends at the Bay entrance on the south end.

Until the 1970s, Balboa had been a sleepy hideaway community of wood-frame beach houses facing the ocean, and small shops and stores on the bay side. Two large islands inside the bay, Lido and Balboa, were chock-a-block with small homes, mostly California stucco built in the '30s and '40s with red tile roofs spangled by flaming bougainvillea and fronted by huge Washingtonia and Cabbage palms. Most island houses are still decorated with sailboats tied to small docks in their back yards.

On the mainland, along the edge of the bay, the Pacific Coast Highway provides a main artery to take people from LA and Long Beach through Newport, south to Laguna Beach and on to San Diego. About the only place visitors stop is at the Balboa Bay Club or one of the marinas to get reacquainted with their yachts.

Back in the good old days, high school and college kids would swing off the main highway to hit the Balboa Pavilion where Stan Kenton used to reign and where rock groups now made irregular appearances.

However, in the '80s, the burgeoning of Orange County—brought about in large measure by the commercialization of the giant Irvine Ranch—property values escalated exponentially. While many of Newport's old bungalows still remained, primarily on Lido and Balboa Islands, they were gradually being replaced or remodeled to reflect the community's affluence. The beach front houses had almost all been remodeled into two stories to make room for a flood of relatives and friends.

Most of the old shopping area at the wide end of the peninsula had been bulldozed and rebuilt into California chic, known as Lido Village, with charming little shopping areas and modern restaurants and brick-paved streets. The boat yards around the turning basin, instead of being home to miscellaneous dinghies, dories and small sail boats, now repaired and outfitted sleek customized sloops, schooners and power yachts. On the mainland, the towering buildings and opulent shops of the nearby Newport Town Center explained why there were no vacancies in any of the marinas or homes.

When we crossed over the Via Malaga bridge from the peninsula to Lido Isle, we left the glitz behind. My house is situated next to the water on the south side of the island.

After we'd parked on the narrow, palm-lined street, I was pleased to see my gardener had kept my small yard looking neat and that there was no 'for sale' sign hanging on the door.

Jack got out and stared at the house. "This yours?"

"Yeah. It's small and old—built in the '30s—but it's big enough for me."

"Every kid's dream—a house in California with a boat dock in back and a couple of palm trees waving in a breeze right off the ocean."

"Right. Until they have to pay the taxes."

"Couldn't be much. You've got that Prop thirteen in California."

"Yeah," Herb Stax said. "Thank God for Howard Jarvis."

"Howard who?"

"Jarvis," I said. "He got the proposition passed. Dead now," I added, "but I still bless him every night."

Jack gave me what he probably considered a smile. "Still say your prayers?"

"Hey, they worked in Africa."

He nodded. "You've got to let me in on your pipe line."

Before Herb drove away, I told him I'd see him at the office the next day, and he suggested I take a few days off. "Maybe a vacation, somewhere like Hawaii."

I thought about it for about five seconds. The business had done all right without me for almost three months. It could survive a couple of weeks more.

"I don't think so," I told him. "I'd like to get back to work."

"Okay. I understand."

I was not sure he did understand. It was not just the work itself. I wanted the routine. Before I'd made the trip to Africa, I had my life under control, all my icons in a row. I knew what I was going to do each day, each week and each month. Some people might crave the excitement of the unpredictable, but I preferred order in my life. I like to feel I'm in control of the future, of watching each event fall into its predetermined slot. That was why Herb and I made such a good team. He provided the sizzle; I provided the steak.

This did not mean I couldn't be flexible. No plan is ever perfect; nothing ever works out exactly as planned. So I had learned to adjust. California's depressed aerospace industry had made S&R Security scramble for business. High-tech electronics and telecommunications were filling in the gap but they didn't require as much security as had the military-oriented companies.

Fortunately—at least fortunate for the security business—crime and the fear of terrorism continued to grow, so security was a growth industry. But my stomach did not produce so many flutters when things went according to plan, even a contingency plan. And if that made me a bore, so be it. Economic stability was more important than a flashy personality.

Jack Blucher watched with amusement as I dug my spare key out of the azalea pot. "You must have stupid burglars here."

"That's Newport," I said. "They prefer to hang out at the beach."

"Don't they ever get hungry?"

"You forget. This is the good old U.S.A. Food stamps. SSI."

He rolled his eyes. "Jesus. I'm gonna like it here—for about a month."

I opened the door, but did not go in right away, savoring the moment. I hoped Jack thought it was to let some of the stale air out.

On the floor below the mail slot was a mound of magazines and mail. Jack helped me stack them on the glass-topped coffee table. He looked at the names on some of the magazines and reports and cocked his head at me. "Harvard Medical News Letter? Fitness and Health? Muscle?"

I'd forgotten about the magazines. But it was too late to hide them now. "I like to keep up with developments."

"Yeah, well," Jack said, his expression amused, "whatever works."

There were also several computer magazines and I handed one to him. "Here. Move into the twenty-first century."

He took it and studied the cover. "Pentium Power. That a Greek supremacy group?"

"Sure. You'll enjoy reading about it."

When we'd finished stacking the mail, I showed Jack around, pointing out a few earthquake cracks in the plaster that gave the place a certain California ambience. He silently looked at my Swedish contemporary furnishings, at the gymnasium I'd made out of my spare bedroom, at my 1967 Corvette convertible in the garage and at my Santana-20 sailboat which I'd put on its trailer behind my garage before I left on my trip.

It wasn't until we'd returned to my living room with its picture window facing the bay that he said, "The security business must pay well."

"Better after the September attacks. But I'd go broke if it could change things."

"And all I've got to show for forty years of getting my ass shot off is a fifty-dollar suit and a gold tooth. Shit, I've got the brains of a migrating lemming. I should have a place like this."

I turned away to hide a smile. The idea of Jack Blucher settling down in a bay-front cottage failed to fit. I wondered if his choosing to be a professional soldier had anything to do with a rejection of his background. Perhaps his entire life was a rejection. He'd let it slip that his parents, somewhere in Ohio, were relatively well off. He'd grown up with a full belly and no real problems when a lot of people were struggling just to get enough to eat. He must have carried a heavy burden of guilt.

When he'd run away from home to enlist in the army during the Viet Nam conflict, he had probably been motivated as much by a rejection of his family's life style as he was by patriotism. Apparently, his aversion to affluence had never changed. As a professional mercenary he'd probably spent few nights in a real home.

The shaping of my values had been just the opposite. My house meant a lot to me. It was the first thing I'd bought when I began earning a little money. A psychiatrist would say it represented the security I never had as a child. And he would probably be right. My formative years had been spent in orphanages such as LA County's MacLaren Hall, and a long series of foster homes.

About the time I was able to convince myself that the current foster parents were actually my own, they would do something to end their role like moving or having a child of their own, so they didn't need an extra kid. I'd be sent back to some orphanage, adding another layer to the bitterness, another layer of longing for a real home.

How could I expect Jack Blucher to understand my passion for material things any more than he could expect me to understand his reasons for rejecting them? At the moment he was filled with regret for not putting down roots. But that would pass. The Jack Bluchers of this world would program themselves not to have lingering regrets about anything.

"I'm sorry I've only got the one bedroom," I said. "You take the bed. I'll sack out here on the couch."

Jack shook his head. "I don't trust beds. That's where you go to die." He checked the springs on my twelve foot long Madigan couch, upholstered in a heavily grained, hand-woven cotton fabric and positioned to face a fireplace set in the middle of a long picture window that looked out on the bay. He dug the toe of his shoe into the deep pile of my Aubusson-patterned oriental rug.

"I wouldn't even sleep well on this. It's softer'n a whore's ass."

"Pull up the rug and sleep on the floor if you want." I chuckled. "Or sleep outside. There's a patch of lawn between the house and the bay."

"The floor'll be okay. I've got to start adjusting."

"Fine. *Me casa, es su casa.*" I headed for the bedroom, peeling off my shirt on the way. "If you don't mind, I'll take a shower before the two-bit tour."

I heard him mutter. "A shower? In the middle of the day? Jesus."

I shaved off my fourteen-hour beard and took a blistering hot shower. I wished there was some way I could wash away the memory of those men who had died in Africa. I knew I wasn't responsible, but it still bothered me. I kept running the event through my mind as though it were on tape, wondering if there was something I could have done to prevent what had happened. Each time I came up blank.

I was just lucky I hadn't been lying on the concrete beside them.

When I came back in the living room after dressing, Jack said, "You know, I'm only staying 'til I can get a place."

"You're welcome as long as you want. You know that."

"Sure. But I've got some living to catch up on. I need a place of my own for what I've got in mind. So will you."

"I thought you were going to come to work for Herb and me."

"I'll think about it. I need to get my heat down some. Catch up on a few things."

"Sounds like a plan. Well, any time you're ready."

I wanted to ask about his finances, but Jack Blucher wasn't the kind of man you asked about something that personal. The pay might be good, but mercenaries were not the type to save their money. And why should they? Their life span was probably very short. To hear him tell it, he should have been dead many times over. His philosophy was eat, drink and be merry for if you couldn't party, you had to be dead.

I knew about living on the edge, but not for the same reason. I'd grown up with nothing. Now my big worry was that my good fortune would come crashing down and I would again be on the street with nothing. Living hand-to-mouth might not bother Jack, but I never wanted to be both old and broke.

But at the moment I was the one with a source of income, while Jack might be broke. I'd have to keep an eye on him.

Chapter 3

AS I DROVE in the soft light of a setting sun to Helen's apartment complex near Jamboree Road, I marveled at the growth that had taken place in the area during the last few years. Much of the rolling country inland from Newport Beach and for miles to the south had once been part of the giant Irvine Ranch. The ranch had been part of a Spanish land grant that occupied practically all of eastern Orange County. When old man Irvine had died, the heirs had taken a hard look at the southward march of the L.A. suburbs and elected to turn large chunks of the estate close to Newport into shopping centers, high-priced residential areas, and high tech industrial parks.

Helen's apartment complex was in an area of expensive apartments and condos not far from the University of California, Irvine. It was so new, the brilliant red bougainvilleas had not as yet swallowed the buildings.

When she opened her door and stepped back, I felt as though a fist had been slammed into my gut. Helen is tall, almost matching my 6'1" when she wears high heels, like now. Her dark blue eyes, widely spaced under thick light-brown eyebrows, gave her a look of cool intelligence. The coldness was given a lie by lips that had the kind of pouty fullness movie stars were taking collagen injections to acquire. Her hair was a gold-blonde cloud of curls and ringlets that tumbled across her shoulders and cascaded down her back.

Her narrow waist accentuated the flat plain of her stomach and the long sweeping curves of her hips. She was wearing a thigh-length, sleeveless cocktail dress of some stretch material that hugged her like a stocking. The decollate was low and scooped, revealing the valley between her breasts. Around the perfect column of her neck she wore a fine gold chain which suspended a three carat heart-shaped diamond that had been my birthday present to her last year.

She stood silently, allowing me to stare, her lips lifted in a gentle smile of understanding. "Well," she said after a moment, "if it looks that good, don't you want to hold it?"

I kicked the door shut and took her in my arms, frightened that this might be another dream. I didn't simply kiss her. I drank from her soul, absorbing her warmth, savoring the reality, desperately needing the feel of her in my arms. Without releasing her lips, I reached up and traced the outline of her face and trailed my fingers across the curve at the nape of her neck, giving myself to the wonder of her and the feel of her warm, soft body.

I moved my arms to lift her, our lips still clinging, but she placed her hands on my shoulders and gently pushed me away.

"No, Ben," she whispered. "Not now. I want to know what

happened. When they said you were dead, it almost killed me."

Reluctantly, I stepped back, the spell broken. "I'm sorry. You don't know how much I thought about you."

Her lips curved in a mischievous smile. "What did you think?"

I felt my face redden as the memories sprang full blown. "Just say that without them I think I'd have gone crazy."

I moved to put my arms around her again, but she was already turning to take her purse and a sequined jacket off the back of the couch. She handed me the jacket and I helped her put it on.

"No more than I thought about you," she said. "What on earth happened? All Herb told us was that there'd been shooting. He thought you were dead. He was almost as upset as I was."

I took her by the shoulders and turned her to face me, letting the hunger show in my eyes. "Are you sure you want to go out? Why don't we talk here?"

For answer she moved to the door. "I got dressed so you could show me off," she said lightly. "Remember, I need some therapy, too."

"But therapy was what I had in mind."

"My kind first." She opened the door and I followed her outside. "I'm a little overdressed for this early, but I thought you might like it."

"I love it," I admitted. "To hell with convention." I tried to keep the disappointment out of my voice. Was it my imagination, or was she avoiding close contact? Maybe I was simply expecting too much too soon. She needed time. After all, I'd been gone quite a while. I was practically a stranger.

A short time later, sitting in a candle-lit corner of Arpeggio's, I told her everything that had happened. "I feel kind of responsible for what happened."

"Hey, you were the victim, not the criminal."

"I know. But if I hadn't taken the job, it might not have happened."

"You did all you could. You could have been killed."

"Yeah. I was lucky. The round that hit me was probably a ricochet."

She stared at me, tears in her eyes. "I don't want you to go away ever again."

She leaned her head against my shoulder and grabbed my arm with both hands in a strong grip as though she were going to protect me from all the powerful and evil forces trying to carry me away. I could see the other men in the room surreptitiously staring at us, envy in their expressions, and I felt a surge of pride. They could look, but she belonged to me.

"That's a promise," I said. "Besides, I've got to spend a lot of time in the office. Herb is a great salesman, but I'm going to have my hands full straightening out those projects and schedules. That's going to take at least—" I grinned at her "—a month."

She straightened and looked at me, suddenly very serious. "Ben, I'm not fooling. Promise me you won't go anywhere. Not for a long, long time."

Again the feeling of warmth swept over me. I just could not believe that someone as beautiful and wonderful as Helen could be in love with me. But I was willing to try. "All right," I told her. "No more trips without your approval."

"Promise?"

"Cross my heart."

"And, Ben, be more careful. I don't want anything to happen to you."

She was so serious that at first I thought she was trying to warn me of some impending doom. Then I realized it was only a reaction to my close brush with immortality. "Okay," I answered. "I'll watch myself. I've got too much to lose."

She licked her lips as though they were suddenly dry. "I don't mean only on a trip. I mean—here."

She was serious. "Here? I don't understand."

She suddenly moved back and brushed at her hair nervously. "I guess I'm just worried. I thought I'd lost you. I don't want to go through that again."

Nor did I. I'd never really understood why we had drifted apart before I'd made the trip. Could it have been my fault? I'd been working fourteen-and fifteen-hour days trying to keep S&R Security profitable. But that was not unusual. I'd been putting in those kinds of long hours from the day Herb and I had started the company. Somehow, there'd always been time for Helen.

Looking back, it seemed it was she who had begun avoiding me. We'd never talked about it. There had always been tomorrow. Then, abruptly, there almost were no more tomorrows.

I put my hand on top of hers. "Helen, what happened to us? I was really in love with you. I still am."

She avoided looking at me when she said softly, "I don't know, Ben."

"It seemed like one minute we were crazy about each other, and the next..." I shrugged, still not understanding. "Maybe I was just too intense."

She took her hand from beneath mine. "Please, Ben," she whispered. "Let's not talk about it. Not now. Not tonight."

Throughout dinner she was strangely silent, scarcely touching her food. I had also lost my appetite. Something had come between us and I couldn't figure out what it was. I wanted to recapture the spell that had been there when I had taken her in my arms at her apartment. Love had been there. I was sure of it.

So why was she now acting as though this was our first date?

A possible explanation intruded into my thoughts with such dark malevolence it caused me to jerk out the words, "Are you in love with somebody else?"

Her quick smile was genuine. "You're the only one I love."

Vastly relieved I grinned at her. "You'll have to prove it."

Her smile hung in the air like a ghost. "All right."

Her words were right but the tenor of her low murmur brought back the specter of doubt.

Even when we were lying in bed in the familiar darkness of her bedroom and my hands were slowly savoring the smooth warmth of her skin, I was still wondering why she had sounded more resigned than excited. Even now I sensed an unexpected tenseness in her body, an underlying tightening of the muscles, as though she expected some kind of physical assault.

"Relax," I whispered, my lips trailing across the taut muscles of her shoulder. "I haven't turned into a cannibal."

"I know," she said, and I could sense an odd catch in her voice. "I'm sorry."

She put both arms around me and pulled me against her fiercely. I could feel her trembling. I tried to turn my head to kiss her in the hollow of her throat and she said, "No, Ben. Please. Just hold me."

I cradled her gently, waiting out her strange reticence. We'd made love in the past, many times. And she'd said she loved me. The evening was young. All I had to do was take it slow and easy.

I was enjoying the warmth of her body, breathing in the perfume of her breath while I nuzzled the hollow beneath her breast-bone when she rolled away and got up.

"I'm sorry, Ben," she said, and I knew she was crying. "I'm really sorry. But... I have to get ready for work."

I lay on my side, too surprised to speak. How could she reject me so abruptly? She had plenty of time. She didn't go on duty until 8:00. What had I said? What had I done? Questions spun through my head;

questions that triggered other questions, other doubts. But the one that kept pushing to the top was: Did she care for me at all? Had she ever cared?

She was standing in the half-open bathroom door, her back against the jamb, tears streaking her cheeks. She put her hands up to cover her face, pressing her fingers hard against her eyes as though to dam the salty tears.

I got up and went to her, almost afraid to touch her. "What is it? What's going on?"

"Nothing," she answered, her voice muffled by her hands. "I'm...just not ready. I...thought you were dead. Then all of a sudden you're here and...I can't handle it." She went into the bathroom, leaving the door partially open.

So I had been right. It was too soon. She needed more time and I was being an insensitive clod.

"Okay," I said. "I'm sorry I came on so strong. It's just that I'd been thinking about you so much. Needing you. Then all of a sudden, it wasn't a dream any more. I guess I can't expect you to go along with my fantasies."

She came to the door. She had wrapped a long towel around her luscious body and she clutched it together with one hand. She kissed me softly and quickly. "I'm sorry, darling. Just give me a little more time. I'll make your fantasies come true. I promise."

She turned and I caught her arm. "Just one question." She looked back, her head cocked, her expression worried. "Do you love me? Is there somebody else?"

She smiled and put her finger tips to my lips. "That's two questions. But yes, I do love you." Suddenly there were tears spilling down her cheeks again and she whispered, "I do love you, Ben. You don't know how much."

Then she went into the bathroom and turned on the shower. I slowly dressed and went out into the warm California night wrapped in a glow of happiness. She did love me. It wasn't until I was driving home that I realized she never had answered the second question.

Chapter 4

THERE IS SOMETHING about California sunshine that makes death hard to believe, especially violent death. Helen could not be dead! Not when the skies were blue, the sun bright and the temperature made for living.

Besides, if she really was dead I would be feeling something more than a stunned surprise, an overwhelming desire not to believe. It couldn't possibly be true. Only a few hours ago she had been with me, in my arms; warm, pulsing with life, too much alive to be dead now. She had to be out there somewhere in the sunlight, laughing at the joke.

But why would Herb Stax lie about it?

I stared numbly out the window of my office at the September sun glistening brightly off the calm waters of Newport Bay and tried to deny what Herb had just told me. If my refusal to believe was strong enough, would it make it all a lie?

In the deep water at the center of the bay a sloop moved slowly, heading out of the marina to the blue Pacific. A girl in a bikini stood leaning out over the bow, her long blonde hair streaming in the breeze. She looked so vital, so alive. She reminded me so much of Helen I couldn't stand to look at her. I turned away, torn between cursing and crying.

Herb Stax came around my desk to stand beside me. "Judd Proctor told me about it when I came in. I told him I'd tell you." Judd was one of our guards at Colton Labs.

"Why didn't he call me at home?" I let a rush of anger wash out the pain. "What the hell was he thinking about?"

"They only found her an hour ago. You were already in the water."

I swallowed a protest. An hour ago I would have been half way through my morning swim around Newport Pier. I remembered how good it had felt to renew the routine of morning exercise, then run to the beach and plunge into the chill Pacific water.

From the beach I only had to walk across Balboa Boulevard to reach the office where I kept a closet of clean clothes.

I'd always loved the water, which was why I'd picked this office site. But now the sparkling bay and the picturesque buildings of Lido

Island seemed unreal, like badly done computer graphics. I turned my back to them. By holding hard to the belief that it was all a mistake I could discuss it coldly. My hands weren't shaking as I continued buttoning my shirt.

"Where is she?" I asked, my voice low and controlled.

"At the lab," Herb said. "That's where it happened."

"How what happened?"

Herb gave me a puzzled look. He was surprised I could be this calm. But, come to think of it, he'd never seen me in a real crisis— ever.

Herb moved past my computer with its blank staring monitor and sat heavily on the large couch that stretched completely across one end of the room. For once words did not come easy for him.

"She was supposed to go off duty at six this morning." His voice was so low I had trouble hearing him.

"I know. Last shift." I was the one who had granted her request to be assigned to Colton Labs, which failed to make me feel any better now.

"When she didn't check out, they went looking for her. They found her out on the radar test range. She'd been dead three or four hours they think."

"From what?"

Herb rubbed his hands together. They looked as dry and old as his face. "They told Judd it looked like electromagnetic radiation, what the hell ever that means."

"An accident?" I knotted my necktie and quickly ran a comb through my hair.

"They don't know. It looks that way." He followed me out the door. "What else could it be?"

"I don't know," I told him.

Kim Fuji was just settling herself at her desk and she looked up at me with those startlingly big almond eyes when I said, "Kim, call Clint Hemet at Colton Labs. Tell him I'm on my way."

She said, "Okay, boss," and reached for the phone. She didn't ask any questions. She knew me well enough to know when I was in no mood to talk. Mrs. Davis and Judd Proctor were silent as they watched me stalk out the door, their faces set in sorrow. They had, of course, heard about Helen before I did. As in most small companies, everyone knew everyone else, so they all knew Helen and liked her. But there was a big difference between liking someone and being in love.

It was a fifteen minute drive—if you ignored the speed limit.

Colton Labs was situated in one of the older industrial parks between Jamboree Road and MacArthur Boulevard. Sprawling over several acres, the buildings had been designed to give the research and development facility the appearance of a modern university. The buildings were all two floors, constructed of combed and fluted concrete with huge opaque windows of black and amber glass.

The grounds were contoured into decorative mounds carpeted with vivid green lawn and meticulously groomed banks of brilliant flowers. The trees, mostly clumps of Madagascar and coconut palms, smoky olives and Australian willows, had been artfully planted near reflecting pools to enhance the illusion of quiet solitude. The only sounds were the quiet hum of cars on the highway and the shrill warbling of mocking birds.

In the main parking lot all places in the visitor's section were taken, but I forced the 'vette into a minuscule place between a Mazda RX7 and a shiny new Mercedes. I was more concerned about saving time than about parking tickets or being towed away.

Inside the spacious lobby, I gave my name to a girl behind a waist-high security counter who could have been a fashion model. She telephoned Clint Hemet, then told me his secretary would be out in a moment. I signed the visitor's register and she handed me a red badge. I stood by the inner door, waiting impatiently.

Huge windows on two sides of the lobby displayed a vista of green grass and trees. Light from a reflecting pool shimmered on the walls. On one wall was a metal sculpture made of hundreds of thin metal rods welded together. Whoever had created it had a good eye for composition. It looked as though it had cost a bundle.

The door to the interior opened, and instead of his secretary, Clint Hemet himself came toward me. He was wearing gray slacks with a white shirt and striped necktie, and a dark blue blazer with the emblem of the Balboa Yacht Club stitched onto the breast pocket. His head was almost totally bald, and like his craggy face, was tanned to a dark maroon. I knew Hemet was in his late forties, but like so many people who are dynamic and actively athletic, he looked years younger. Today his face was solemn as he shook my hand with a grip that made me wince.

"Hello, Ben," he said. "I'm damn sorry about Helen."

I nodded in reply. Hemet was aware of my relationship with Helen, so he knew the news would hit me hard.

"I can't believe it," I told him.

"Yeah," he said. "Me, too."

"What the hell happened, Clint? She was okay last night."

Hemet glanced toward the receptionist. "We'll go out there. We can talk on the way."

He signed my pass for the receptionist, then led me into the building.

"I heard about what happened in Uganda," he said. "Sounded like you had a close call."

"Yeah, I'm glad to be back."

He gave me a swift glance from head to toe. "You don't look any the worse for it. A little thinner maybe. But you'll get that back in a hurry."

"I feel okay," I said. I didn't want his sympathy. "I hope my being gone didn't cause any problems here."

"No, no. Your people have got things running well." He paused. "Until now."

I held back questions that crowded my mind as we hurried down a long corridor. I tried to shut out the reality by concentrating on the surroundings. We were moving along a corridor lined with two-man offices. Almost all had their doors open and inside I could see engineers working at computer terminals or at blackboards scrawled with incomprehensible symbols and numbers.

We left the office area and went through double doors into a shop area where machinists were using banks of computer-controlled machines to contour metal components.

Farther on we passed glass-enclosed, antiseptically-clean rooms where women wearing short nylon smocks and with their hair covered by nylon caps were peering through microscopes, putting the final touches on printed circuit boards. All the rooms were flooded with cold blue-tinged fluorescent light which reflected from polished asphalt tile floors.

There were no harsh factory sounds. Even in the machine shop, there was only the muted sound of humming electric motors and the dull whir of carbon-steel biting into metal or plastic. It all had an unreal look about it as though everything was happening in slow motion.

"We could take a vehicle," Hemet said as we walked, "but it would take longer. This route will take us straight to the test range."

"Fine," I said. "Walking's fine." Then I voiced a thought I could no longer contain. "They told me it was electromagnetic radiation. Is that right?"

"That's what it looks like." The way he said it, flat and noncommittally, reminded me that even though Hemet had been a cop in L.A. and a couple of other places, he was now head of security at Colton Labs, and he wasn't about to make any positive statements that might be used in a law suit. "I notified the Newport police as soon as I found out about it. They're out there now."

We were passing through an area where rows of women were installing printed circuit boards and other components in black boxes when I noticed Harry Deen, Colton Lab's photographer. He had an Ikegami color camera set up to video tape an assembly operation. Naturally, the girl he had picked for his shot was stunningly beautiful. He was being assisted by a young fellow who looked as though he had just come off a university football team. He had a sweeping blonde mustache and a tangle of longish brown hair. He was wearing the pseudo-artist's de rigueur blue jeans and tennis shoes and a black tee shirt printed with the words 'A single picture is worth a thousand bucks.'

I hoped to pass by without being noticed, but Harry Deen looked up and called, "Hey, Ben."

He left his camera set up and strode over to intercept us. Deen was about forty, small and wiry. In contrast to the suits and neckties usually worn by Colton engineers, Deen was wearing worn jeans, an old plaid shirt and broken-down hiking boots. His thinning hair was shaggy and he sported a full beard that made his face look buried in hair. He'd told me once that this get-up was to show the world he was a non-conformist, and therefore, an artist.

He had done a few photography jobs for me before he hooked up with Colton Labs. At that time he was trying to bang out a living taking cheesecake pictures for girly magazines. While his camera work was adequate, he was a long way from being an artist. But maybe it didn't take much artistic talent to crank out videos and still pictures of black boxes and radar displays. If it did, Harry Deen wouldn't have lasted long.

"Good to see you," Deen said as he walked toward us. "I heard you were dead."

"Almost," I answered.

I started to hurry on, but Deen grabbed my arm. "You need any help, let me know."

"Thanks, Harry," I said, and was about to turn away when the girl they had been using in their pictures, said, "Hey, Harree. *Que pasa?* Jou finish with me?"

The guy with the t-shirt said, "How about it, Deen? This a wrap?"

"Yeah, yeah," Deen said. He rolled his eyes at Hemet and me.

"Eddie Hooker. Come on. I'll introduce you."

"Later, Harry," Hemet interjected. "We're in a hurry."

I was already moving away as Deen said, "Everybody's in a hurry. Okay. Catch you later."

Walking out to the back range we passed several buildings with radar antennas mounted on their roofs or on nearby towers. A few of the antennas were covered with fiberglass weather shelters that made them look like oversized golf balls.

Hemet saw me staring up at them and said, "We do a lot of radar work."

"I know. That's microwave—electromagnetic radiation—isn't it?"

"Right." He saw what I was driving at and shook his head. "Some of those antennas put out enough megahertz to cook anything that gets too close in front of them. I've seen birds get knocked all to hell. But those types are situated up high to get away from ground clutter. There's no way you could walk in front of them. Besides, we don't do any range work at night."

I assumed he was correct. Radar and high-tech electronics were not my fields. So I kept my mouth shut as we left the complex and moved into Colton Lab's outdoor radar range. This was a cleared area on the edge of Colton's hundred-acre industrial site. Out here the land was undeveloped, crossed by shallow arroyos created by generations of California rain, and covered with dead, wheat-colored grass and tangles of scrub oak, stunted eucalyptus, mesquite and brush.

On the near side of the range, several people were milling around an area of trampled grass cordoned off with yellow plastic ribbons. There was also an ambulance with its rear doors open. The county coroner's station wagon was off to one side. Two of my uniformed guards, Ed Emblem and Ted Olds, were watching the local police investigation team work the area. The coroner, old Doc Martin, had finished his preliminary and his men were preparing to slide a body bag off a gurney into the ambulance.

I hurried over to stop them. I wanted to see Helen, no matter how much it might hurt.

When I said, "Excuse me, Doc," the coroner turned, his round face troubled. He ran a veined and liver-spotted hand through his thick gray hair and looked uncomfortable.

"Hello, Ben," he said. "Good to see you back. I—I'm sorry about this."

He had a soft voice that made him sound perpetually sad so it was hard to tell how sincere he really was. But he'd been around a good many years and had known Helen even before I did so I supposed his empathy wasn't a professional put on.

"Let me see her," I said.

Doc hesitated. He was probably trying to decide whether he could spare me unnecessary anguish if he said no. Then he saw the expression on my face. "Okay," he said.

He nodded to the two attendants and one of them unzipped the body bag and pulled the edges open and there was Helen. She could have been sleeping. Her eyes were closed and her features were smooth, composed. Her long, honey-colored hair, which she usually wore coiled under her uniform cap, was loose and fanned out behind her head. She was not a small person and her body looked strong and healthy, the muscles firm, filling out the tan uniform. It seemed impossible that she could be dead. Except for a slight redness of her skin, like a mild sunburn, she looked the picture of health.

I half-expected her to open her eyes with that heavy-lidded sleepy look and the small smile she always had when waking from a satisfying sleep.

I turned away and tried to close my mind to the ugly sound as they yanked up the zipper of the body bag and slid the gurney into the ambulance. Doc again said he was sorry and turned toward his station wagon. I put a hand on his arm.

"Doc, are you positive it was microwave radiation?"

His eyebrows pulled down in a negative slant. "That's what it looks like."

"You've had cases like this before?"

"Well, no. I've heard of people being injured by radiation, but this is the first fatality as far as I know."

"Then you can't be positive."

He ran his hand through his hair again. "The symptoms look right and the means was certainly available. As far as I know, her health was good. It's the logical explanation at this time."

"Will you be able to tell by the autopsy?"

Doc sighed. "I'm not sure. Like I said, I never had anything like this before. I'll let you know."

He climbed into his station wagon, closed the door gently and drove away, followed by the ambulance.

I watched them go, feeling as though I was involved in an awful dream. The morning sun was unbelievably brilliant. Everything seemed to be etched in sharp relief. I hated the harsh reality. I desperately wanted to make it a dream. If I could somehow soften the image, perhaps it would change to a different time, a different place.

It took real effort to turn away and walk over to join Clint Hemet who was talking to Cal MacDonald. Cal's name was really Clarence MacDonald and he was a lieutenant with the Newport Beach police. But nobody called him Clarence. He didn't even look like a Clarence. He was built like a nose-guard and his face looked as though it had caught too many fists. His eyes, under shaggy brows, were tough and shrewd, just like his thinking.

I'd known MacDonald since one of my first foster parents had brought me to Newport. I'd taken a job delivering *The Balboan* and the old police station had been on my route so I'd gotten to know some of the NBPD officers.

"Oh, Ben," MacDonald said when he saw me. "Sorry this happened. Especially to Helen."

"Thanks," I replied. "I know." Today, if measured by its industrial and population base, Newport Beach might be considered a large metropolis. But it used to be a small town and to the long time residents, it still was. As in most small towns, everybody knew the affairs of everybody else. Cal MacDonald was both a native and a policeman, so he knew all the gossip about Helen and me. Hell, everybody knew.

"How the hell could she have gotten that much radiation?" I asked.

Clint Hemet glanced toward the police technical people who were taking pictures and poking around the matted place in the dry grass where Helen had been found. "Let's go to my office. We can talk there."

I considered telling him I wanted to look around here, but I didn't really believe I'd find anything they couldn't. The Newport Beach police department was small, but they were efficient. If there was something to be found, they would find it. Judging from the clear trail left in the grass and weeds, she'd stumbled out here and died. It looked as though she had been alone. If there was more to it, it would be in MacDonald's report.

I was in a daze during the walk back to Hemet's office. My mind was a caldron of memories, of Helen, of the good times—only the good times—swimming in the chill waters of an April sea, a long ago candlelight dinner in the restaurant at the top of Sandia Peak in Albuquerque, skiing the beginner's slope at Mammoth, the feel of her arms around my neck and the sweetness of her breath when we made love—events and places I'd probably never think about if she was alive. Now the memories were washed away by the image of Helen lying in the ugly body bag. I just couldn't believe I'd never see her again.

I came back to the present when we reached Clint Hemet's office. It was in the front section of the main engineering building on the second floor. We passed through a large outer office, where a secretary was talking on the phone, into Hemet's larger inner office. His dark oak desk was angled in a far corner leaving space for a glass-topped coffee table in the middle of a thick, pale blue carpet. The table was flanked by several deep, leather chairs. The only thing on the table was a telephone with banks of buttons and a built-in conference speaker.

The walls were decorated with colorful tapestries from South

America and the Middle East. It made me curious about Hemet's salary. If his office was any indication, Hemet was making very big money. Perhaps our security contract with Colton Labs could stand reappraisal.

I immediately felt guilty for the thought. I'd just seen Helen's body and I was thinking about money. I wondered how long it would be before I felt the impact of knowing she really was gone forever. Probably not until the funeral. Except for the episode in Uganda, the only time I'd seen a dead person was when I was six or seven.

My foster mother at the time had died unexpectedly. I think they'd said it was a thrombosis that had hit her heart. She was only fifty, but to a six-year-old that was ancient. So I was not surprised she had died. It was the suddenness that was a shock. But her abrupt death also made it easy for me to deny it. I'd convinced myself that she was simply taking longer to do the shopping than usual. It wasn't until I saw her lying cold and dead in the open casket at her funeral that I accepted she would never return.

It would probably be the same with Helen. And I dreaded it. I would much prefer to believe, childishly, that she was only away on an extended trip and one day there would be a knock on my door; I would open it and there she would be, smiling and beautiful.

Hemet lit a cigar, and for once, I did not mind the foul odor. It kept my mind centered on the present. He offered one to MacDonald who took it with a gruff thanks. He knew better than to offer one to me.

He said through a cloud of putrid smoke, "I haven't notified the security people at the DOD Industrial Security Office." He looked at Macdonald. "No need to unless you can convince me it wasn't an accident."

"Why should it be anything else?" MacDonald asked.

"No reason I can see. How about you, Ben?"

"Why would anyone want to kill her?" I hated the words, hated to admit she was really dead.

Cal MacDonald dug a notebook and pencil out of his inside jacket pocket. "Does S&R provide all the guards here?"

"Yes," I told him. "Colton contracts for its security personnel. A lot of companies do."

"How many guards?"

"Fifteen during the day shift. Five at night."

"Only two shifts?"

"Yes. The overtime is less expensive than hiring a third shift."

MacDonald noted this in his notebook before he turned to Hemet.

"So what does that leave for you to do?"

"I'm in charge of overall plant security. That includes badges, passes, clearing personnel, debriefing, security inspections, handling and storing classified material, all the related functions. S&R supplies the guards, but they're under my jurisdiction."

"Don't you give people a safety briefing when they come to work? Tell them not to walk in front of a high powered radar?"

Clint Hemet's face tightened. "We brief all our personnel. We're extremely safety conscious here. We fully comply with the CAL/OSHA Safety Program. Last year we were awarded—"

"Okay," MacDonald interrupted with a wave of his cigar. "I just wanted to be sure." He turned his pale eyes to look at me. "How about S&R? Do you give your people special briefings for this kind of job?"

"Yes. We've got our own safety program. Besides, all our guards are experienced. The various companies provide any special instructions that are required."

Hemet reached for the telephone on the coffee table. "I can have her file sent in. It'll tell you exactly when she attended our training program."

MacDonald shook his head. "I won't need that now. Maybe later."

He meant that since it was an accident, he would not require the information. If the coroner said it was something else, he would be back for that and a lot more.

"When did she come to work here?" he asked.

"A year ago last November," I said. "I can get you the exact date."

"Okay. You want us to notify the next of kin?"

The question came as a shock. Until now, I hadn't thought of Helen's family. She hadn't lived at home for a couple of years, but I knew she and her parents were close, especially she and her father. Lou Cotrell was going to take this hard. I can't think of anything rougher than losing an only child. It would leave life so damn pointless.

My first impulse was to let MacDonald give them the news. It was a task any sane person would avoid if at all possible. Just as quickly I realized I had to do it myself. I was not only her employer, but her parents knew we'd been very close. They probably knew we were lovers—or had been. Lou Cotrell would really hate me now. He had been furious when Helen had dropped out of the university to come to work for me. The idea had been hers, but her father never believed that. I could image what his feelings toward me would be after this.

"She worked for me," I said. "I'll take care of it."

MacDonald nodded, relieved. "Good." His eyes shifted to Clint Hemet. "How could radar kill somebody?"

Hemet leaned forward and moved the telephone a couple of inches. He wiped a spot of dust off the glass table top. "It never has before that I know of. There have been a couple of cases of people dying allegedly because of chronic exposure to microwave transmissions. I believe there was one such case ruled on by the New York State Worker's Compensation Board. But I'm not aware of any deaths attributed to a single exposure."

"But it could happen?"

"Studies regarding the biological effects of EMF have been made by several agencies," Hemet said carefully.

"EMF?"

"Electromagnetic fields," I said. I'd read a little about EMF because I was concerned about radiation from the microwave oven we had at S&R. But there was very little definitive information on the subject. "I understand Sweden is the leader in EMF research."

"We're also doing work in the field," Hemet said. "The American National Standards Institute, the Environmental Protection Agency, the Navy, they all have electromagnetic environmental effects divisions. They set standards for the industry. I believe that biological damage begins at around ten milliwatts of exposure per square centimeter. I can check on that figure."

"Make it simple," MacDonald said. "Theoretically, could the beam from a megahertz radar kill if the person was close enough to the radiating antenna for a long enough period of time?"

"How close?"

"Say—a few feet."

Reluctantly, Hemet said, "Yes, it's possible."

"But all your antennas are on top of buildings or towers."

"The ones being range tested, yes."

"They could kill somebody who walked across the range?"

"No. The beam's energy would be dispersed or attenuated by the distance."

MacDonald paused and I asked, "So where could somebody get that kind of heavy radiation dosage?"

"Probably in the environmental test lab."

"You conduct tests at night?"

"Sometimes. Specifications call for certain Mean Time Between Failure capabilities—MTBF. We sometimes operate systems continuously for hundreds of hours to make sure they can meet the specs."

"Don't your engineers supervise those tests?" MacDonald asked.

"Not continuously. They monitor or take readings during the shifts. They leave it to the computers and recorders when they're not there."

A tiny nagging alarm began in the back of my mind. "These experiments would be clearly indicated as dangerous, wouldn't they?"

Clint Hemet hesitated. "I think this might be something for our attorneys."

"Come on, Hemet," I told him. "Forget the lawyers for a minute. Could she have accidentally walked in on a test?"

He rubbed a hand across his forehead shiny with sweat. "Anything is possible, I suppose. I mean, obviously she did. But why would she go into a test chamber? Those chambers are clearly marked. The only way anybody could be hurt is if they weren't paying attention. Or were high on something."

"My people don't get high," I said. "Not when they're on duty."

"Of course not," he answered quickly. "I'm not implying any such thing. I'm only stating a possibility."

"The autopsy will settle that," MacDonald said.

"Could we have a look at that environmental chamber?" I asked.

Clint Hemet pushed himself out of his chair as though he welcomed an end to the discussion. "Sure," he said. "That's a classified area, but we won't be discussing specific parameters. Besides, we've got your clearance on file, Ben. Mac, I'll have my secretary write up a visit request letter for you."

Walking through the shop and the electronic assembly areas, I thought about what Hemet had said about somebody needing to be high on something before they would stand in front of a radar beam. With Helen, that was impossible. The only alcohol I'd ever seen her take was a glass of wine with dinner and maybe a cocktail or aperitif afterward. Even the times we'd hit a couple of piano bars, she'd only had one drink. If she wanted another, it was always Coke or Perrier water.

I think that was one reason why I fell in love with her—she respected her body. Like many California women, she valued her health too much to abuse it with a lot of booze. And using drugs didn't square with her daily two miles of jogging and her aerobic workouts. Of course, there was the possibility that our drifting apart had pushed her in a different direction, opened some dark doors. Even so, it just didn't sound like Helen to get high while on the job.

So why was she dead?

Clint Hemet led us to an area in a huge building with a cement floor where several engineers and technicians were working at computer consoles and studying an array of recorders and CRT displays. Thick cables snaked from the electronic equipment to environmental chambers that ranged in size from microwave ovens to free-standing structures large enough to hold a couple of good sized trucks.

"This entire area is used for environmental testing," Hemet began. "The temperature and humidity chambers can be heated to several hundred degrees or cooled to below zero." He pointed to a large, steel-walled room. Its open doors revealed a radar system mounted on an Army truck chassis. "This one is a temperature shock chamber. It can go from high to low temperature in a matter of seconds."

"It doesn't look to me like anything could have happened to her around here," MacDonald said.

"You're right," Hemet agreed. "These are mostly for component testing. But let me show you one of our electromagnetic shielded rooms."

We followed him to one of the structures, with gray-painted metal walls, that was free standing in the spacious test area. Hemet slid aside a large metal door and we followed him inside.

I stopped to stare, thinking for a moment we had entered some sort of medieval torture chamber. Every square inch of the 30-foot square room, including the high ceiling and most of the floor, was covered with foot long, charcoal-colored spikes. Looking closer I saw the spikes were made of blocks of foam material. Lights buried in the foam lining of the ceiling spread a soft, even glow throughout the area. Some of the spiked blocks on the floor had been removed to create a narrow corridor, and in the rear of the room, two engineers wearing white smocks were checking a large metal box sitting on a low pedestal.

"This is one of our anechoic chambers," Hemet said. "We have more full-scale electromagnetic test chambers than any one in the world. We can handle—"

"We're not tourists," MacDonald said dryly. "You can skip the sales pitch."

Hemet gave a short coughing laugh. "Sorry. I guess I get carried away." He waved to the men at the end of the room. "Bill, could you hold up there a minute?"

One of the men straightened and walked toward us. He was young, about 24 or 25, with longish dark brown hair and a close-cropped beard and mustache.

Hemet introduced him as Bill Holtz, one of their best engineers, and asked if he would mind telling us about the work they were doing. Holtz had undoubtedly heard about Helen and he gave us a speculative look before he began.

"Well, this chamber is used for EMI-Tempest tests."

"Tempest?" MacDonald snorted, echoing my own thoughts. "What's that?"

Holtz's voice had an impatient edge. "EMI stands for electromagnetic emissions. Tempest isn't an acronym. It's simply a name referring to investigations or studies of compromising emissions."

"Compromising, huh?" MacDonald said.

"Only an expression," Hemet said quickly.

Holtz pointed out strips of copper on the edges and the frame of the sliding door. "You can see the room is sealed against emissions. The walls are double layers of steel and copper. None of the holes for conduits or cables go straight through."

"Is it designed to prevent emissions from getting in or getting out?" I asked.

"Both. When we run tests in here, we want our results to be pure."

I pointed to the spikes of foam material. "What are those for?"

"Absorption of emissions. They're pointed to prevent echoes. The waves get trapped between the points where they're absorbed."

"You mean radar emissions."

"Yes. Right now, we're running sideband tests on a hardened antenna—"

"Hardened? What's that mean?" MacDonald asked.

Again Holtz looked at Hemet before he answered. "Hardened against nuclear blast effects. And EMP—that's electromagnetic pulses. That's what we're working on. But sometimes, we use this facility for acoustic emission testing."

I stared at the black box mounted on the pedestal. It was about six feet square and four deep. Solid. Monolithic. The front was pierced with slotted openings where I supposed the radar emissions came out. I could almost feel the radiation striking through my kidneys and reproductive organs.

"It isn't on, is it?" I asked.

Holtz stared at me as though I was out of my mind. "No," he said. "Of course not."

I felt my internal organs relax.

MacDonald asked, "The tests you're running, could the radiation kill a person?"

Holtz again glanced at Hemet. He wasn't sure whether to answer or not.

And if he did answer, would he tell the truth?

Hemet realized his dilemma and gave MacDonald a tight smile. "I doubt the testing going on now has that much power. Isn't that right, Bill?"

Holtz took the hint. "That's right. A person would have to be in here a long time with the system at full power before it could have any adverse effect."

"How long?" MacDonald demanded.

Holtz apparently realized he had opened a door he would have preferred remain closed, but he couldn't sidestep the question. "More than an hour, I'd guess." Drops of sweat appeared on his forehead and he wiped at them with the back of his hand. "Of course," he added, "I'm only guessing. We've never had such an injury. We're very safety conscious."

I moved down the narrow aisle between the rows of foam spikes toward the radar antenna. I scanned the floor, but there were no signs of disturbance among the forest of spikes which looked delicate enough to break or crush easily. "Do you leave this aisle open when you're running a test?"

"No," Holtz answered. "While we're setting up, we store the floor material outside the chamber. We put it back before we secure the area."

"This is just the antenna," Hemet explained. "The radar system itself is outside the chamber."

"The controls?"

"Yes," Holtz said. "We install the detection equipment or the simulated target when we're ready for testing."

"Was the system left on last night?" I asked.

"No," Holtz said shortly.

"Could it have been turned on last night?"

"Not without us knowing about it. It'd show up on the recorders."

MacDonald said, "Was the door locked?"

"No. No need for it."

"So somebody could wander in here?"

Holtz shrugged. "Not exactly wander. They'd have to open the door."

"Unless it was left open."

Holtz did not answer.

"How many more of these chambers do you have?" MacDonald asked.

"This is the only Tempest chamber this size. We have two smaller ones. Here, I'll show you."

We left the chamber and checked out the other two. Clint Hemet wasn't walking as fast as he had been and his face beneath the heavy tan was a pasty white. He was thinking the same thing as MacDonald and I. If Helen had been radiated in that Tempest chamber, it could not have been an accident. Nobody in their right mind was going to turn on the system, then walk into the chamber and take a nap. It had to be murder—or suicide. And there were a lot better, and surer, ways to kill yourself.

But if it wasn't an accident or suicide, there should be some evidence. Nobody was going to allow himself to be placed in a death trap without putting up a struggle, especially Helen. She would fight a bulldozer if she had to.

Except that there was nothing; no sign of a struggle in any of the chambers. None of the spiked foam material looked as though it had been damaged. And every test engineer stated his equipment hadn't been operating during the night. They showed us their recorders and graphs which would have picked up the results of any test emissions.

A couple of the exterior systems, which had their antennas on towers pointing out at the test range, had been run throughout the night. But to receive a fatal dosage, a victim would have to be close to the radiating antenna for hours. And how could that happen? It was impossible. Except that Helen was dead and I was already beginning to miss her.

Chapter 5

LOU COTRELL owned a management consulting company with offices on Pacific Coast Highway in the middle of Newport Beach. He'd started the company when he retired from the Navy in the '90s. People who wanted to do business with Cotrell and Associates called him 'Commander' Cotrell. He hated being called 'Mister'. He said it made him feel like a stupid ensign.

When I first met Helen, her father's business was situated out on the ratty end of the peninsula where he was struggling to pay the rent on a small building that had been converted from an apartment into an office. But with the influx of electronics and aerospace companies into the Newport area, his business had increased until now he had about a dozen employees operating out of a modern office building he owned on the north side of the Pacific Coast Highway.

He'd planned for Helen to come to work for him when she graduated from U.C. Irvine, where at his insistence, she'd majored in business administration, although I knew she'd have preferred being an art major. He blamed me for ruining her career. Actually, he should've blamed Herb Stax.

Herb had known Lou Cotrell and his wife Claire before I ever came into the picture. In fact, when Herb and I had begun developing Stax and Roan Security, it was Cotrell who'd helped us set up the corporation. He'd liked me then; said I had great potential. That was before Herb introduced me to Helen. I admit I'd taken it from there. I'd fallen hard and I guess she had too because there'd been no hesitating when I'd first asked her to dinner. I was surprised though when she quit college and asked for a job. I'd given it to her, naturally. By then, I wanted her near me as much and as long as possible.

When they found out about it, her parents were furious, especially her dad. Claire Cotrell never had much to say. Lou Cotrell did all the talking for the family. Even Helen tightened up when he was around. He never spoke to me again after Helen came to work. I guess he and Herb Stax remained friends because I'd seen them together once having dinner at the Tuxedo. At the time I'd made it a point to stay out of their sight. I didn't want a big scene in the most expensive restaurant on the bay.

But there was no avoiding this meeting today, and my forehead was covered with cold sweat. During the drive I'd rehearsed what I was going to say, except that there were no words I could think of that would ease the shock and the pain. And coming from me, it would only sound worse because he hated my guts. I should never have agreed to be the one to tell him. I hoped he didn't have his big Mexican chauffeur with him when I broke the news. He might tell Juan to break my neck.

I'd never been inside Cotrell's new headquarters and I was immediately impressed. Obviously, he was doing very well indeed. The reception area was big and richly carpeted. You had to walk a long way to get to a chrome desk where an extremely handsome girl was typing away at a computer keyboard.

I figured the long walk was designed to give a visitor time to be impressed by the beautifully bronzed elevator doors in the right wall, the massive crystal chandelier dangling about fifteen feet below the vaulted ceiling, and the brocade wallpaper that formed a perfect backdrop for a series of oil paintings, mostly big, brilliant canvases of contemporary mindless baroque. Only an American artist would have the gall to make art out of acrylic cacophony and only somebody who insists on being called 'Commander' would buy it. Another time I would have detoured to check the name of the artist, but not today.

The receptionist looked up and smiled a greeting when I asked for Mr. Cotrell. She asked if I had an appointment. I said no and her mouth changed into a suppressed smile of amusement.

"Tell him it's Benjamin Roan," I said without trying to hide my irritation. "And it's about his daughter. An emergency."

She was extremely efficient. Without another word she picked up a telephone and punched one of the buttons. "Commander," she said.

Cotrell's familiar grating voice was so loud I could hear him snap, "Damn it! Yes!"

"Sir, it's an emergency. About your daughter. A Mr. Benjamin Roan is here."

There was an infinitesimal pause before Cotrell said something so quietly I couldn't understand the words.

She hung up the telephone as she nodded toward the elevator. "He'll see you, sir."

I took a step toward the elevator, then turned back. "Which floor?"

"The penthouse, sir. I'll take care of it."

She reached toward a set of buttons on her desk, and as I walked toward the elevator, its doors opened with a subdued sigh. Inside, the button marked PH was already illuminated.

Because of Newport Beach zoning restrictions, the building only had three floors plus the penthouse, but the elevator surged up as though it meant to put me in orbit. I guess everyone who came into this building was in a hurry.

The doors opened directly into Lou 'Commander' Cotrell's office which occupied the entire room. The three walls facing the bay and the ocean beyond were composed of some kind of smoked glass that reached from floor to ceiling. The fourth wall, facing inland, was paneled in a dark wood that looked like burled walnut. His private bathroom had to be behind the paneling. I wondered if it had floor to ceiling windows so he could enjoy the view while sitting on the john.

There was a spiral stairway in one corner of the room, probably leading up to a roof deck and down to the working offices.

Cotrell was standing at a big conference table near one side of the room talking to a man in shirt sleeves. Juan, Cotrell's chauffeur, was just coming up the stairs. I figured either Cotrell or the receptionist had summoned him.

When I walked in, the man with Cotrell stared at me with hard eyes until Cotrell jerked his head, then he quickly gathered up some papers and went down the stairs. Juan crossed to a chair in the far corner and sat down, his black eyes fixed on me in an unblinking stare.

Cotrell moved so the conference table was between us. I wondered what the devil they thought I was going to do, attack him in his own office?

He hadn't changed much since I had last seen him almost two years ago. He was still tall and thin, but he wasn't as ramrod straight as he had been. He had retained his penchant for double-breasted sky-blue blazers and gray slacks with white shoes and blue striped neckties. I was sure he chose the colors because they made his eyes look intensely, almost piercingly blue. His fine blonde hair had thinned a little more and he had begun to comb it across his forehead to disguise his receding hairline. His mouth and jaw, however, looked as grim as ever.

He took a cigar from his jacket pocket and lighted it with slow deliberation while he stared at me silently with those hard blue eyes that reminded me more than ever he was Helen's father. He knew damn well how much I hated cigar smoke. It was his way of saying he hoped I choked.

Well, the hell with him. After today I'd never have to see him again.

"Well?" he said. "Let's have it."

As much as I disliked him, it was still difficult to break the news. "I don't know exactly how to tell you this," I began, "but—there's been an accident."

His face sagged and he took hold of a chair back. "How bad?"

"Very. It happened at Colton Labs."

He put the cigar in a gigantic ash tray and came around the table, heading for the elevator. I noticed he still limped slightly from what he claimed was a wound he'd sustained in Viet Nam. "Where is she?" he said shortly. "What hospital?"

"Wait," I said, and he stopped abruptly. I think he realized what I was going to say because his face drained of color even before I added, "I'm sorry, but—it's too late."

His eyes went dead and he walked woodenly to a big leather-covered chair and sat down. He bent forward and put his face in his hands. "Oh, my God," I heard him breathe. "Oh, Jesus God."

Juan's face had not changed expression, his eyes continuing to stare. Hell, it wasn't his daughter.

"It was an accident," I repeated. "They found her this morning."

His head came up slowly and he stared at me through brimming tears. "You son of a bitch!" he said, his voice flat and hard. "It's your fault. You put her out there. You son of a bitch."

"I'm sorry." I turned to go. What else could I tell him? That she was the one who had insisted on leaving office work for field work? She'd even asked to be assigned to the Colton night shift so she could break in before she transferred to the tougher day shift. But in his state of mind, Cotrell wouldn't listen to any defense from me. He wanted it to be my fault.

At the elevator, I poked the button before I turned to him. "Talk to Lieutenant MacDonald or Doctor Martin. They can give you the details." He'd put his head back in his hands and his shoulders were shaking. "One thing," I added. "I want to go to the funeral."

I was going anyway, no matter what he said. But I thought it best to warn him I'd be there. If he knew in advance it might avert a scene, maybe a scene of Juan tearing my arms and legs off.

I was waiting for the elevator doors to close when I heard him say, "I'll have to tell Claire. Oh, dear God. What am I going to tell Claire?"

Mercifully the elevator doors slid shut and I dropped swiftly away from Lou Cotrell and his pain. But there was no way I could escape my own.

Chapter 6

USUALLY I ENJOY having lunch with Herb Stax. I like to hear him talk about some of the problems involved with marketing, although I'm not crazy about his choice of restaurants. He prefers the windowless bar/restaurant combinations typical of California, with deep red leather booths and lighting so dim that to read the oversized menu you had to hold it to the light of a small candle flickering in a glass pot on the table.

It wasn't so much the atmosphere that bothered me as it was the food. Herb liked his fatty red meat and greasy French fries, and high cholesterol salad dressings and sauces. I preferred health food. My favorite restaurant was a little place on the lower end of the peninsula that specialized in lettuce and fruit with pita bread and the best soy bean hamburgers in the world.

The one time I'd been able to talk Herb into going there, he had taken one look at the bare steel tables and all the sunshine spilling in from the huge windows and had refused to enter. "Where the hell is the bar?" he'd asked incredulously, and when I told him there was only a juice bar, his eyes had rolled so far back in his head I thought he was going to faint. Needless to say, we did not stay for lunch.

Today I ordered the seafood plate figuring it would do the least damage. As depressed as I was, I only picked at it anyway.

Helen's death did not adversely effect Herb's appetite. After he polished off the last of the French fries, he lifted a finger and a cute waitress in a short, flouncy skirt and low-cut blouse automatically brought him another margarita on the rocks. When she put his drink on the table, she lifted an eyebrow at me. I resisted the temptation to order a double scotch. Instead, I ordered a slice of cherry pie. It should have enough sugar in it to give me an energy boost, however brief.

Herb took a swallow of his drink, and sat back. "I'm going to have to take a look at the liability clause in our Colton Contract," he said. "Helen's accident might be grounds for litigation."

I'd been thinking about Helen also, but not because of any law suit or insurance. "I don't buy the accident theory."

Herb stared at me before he took another sip of his drink. "Oh? Why not?"

I wasn't sure I could explain. I had no proof, only the same uneasy feeling I'd had last night that something was wrong. It was like signing a contract and having the feeling you'd missed something in the fine print. You didn't know how you knew it; you just did.

"Helen'd been working out there more than a year." I spoke slowly, trying to articulate my suspicions. "She knew her way around. She wouldn't get in front of an operating radar."

Herb put down his napkin as though he was prepared to indulge me. "I think you're making a mistake. If we can prove it was an accident, we might be able to make a substantial recovery. If it wasn't an accident, that leaves murder or suicide."

He stared at me and I was surprised at the hardness in his eyes. This was a side of Herb I hadn't encountered. "I don't buy murder. And if it was suicide... Well, the Cotrells are old friends. And if you had anything to do with it, if you said or did something to make her want to go off the deep end, maybe we should take another look at our partnership."

"If I did," I said, "I'm not aware of it."

"You're sure of that?"

"I was with her last night. If she had suicide on her mind, it didn't show."

"How could you tell? What did you talk about?"

"About me mostly. What happened in Uganda."

"Did she seem...overwrought?"

I hesitated, remembering the disquieting way she had changed from warm to cold. Something had been troubling her. But then perhaps it had simply been my imagination. Perhaps I had expected too much too soon. Why wouldn't she feel apprehensive about making love to somebody she hadn't seen in weeks? That had to be the explanation. But it wasn't something I wanted to share with Herb.

"It couldn't have been suicide," I insisted. "Certainly not because of me."

Herb let his breath out and slumped back in the booth, his face once again smooth and soft. "I'm glad to hear that. I'd hate to think we'd lose this set up."

I very much agreed. S&R Security was making a very nice profit for both of us, even with Herb's overblown expense accounts. Or maybe they weren't overblown. Herb got results.

When we'd first met, Herb was in charge of public relations for Rex Electronics in Costa Mesa. I was working at Rex as a guard while I studied for my master's degree in Business Administration at U.C.

Irvine. After graduation I'd thought about starting some kind of a business. When Herb suggested a partnership in industrial security, I jumped at the chance. I was certain that soon this entire area would be filled with small and medium-sized corporations and many would need security services. So we'd both quit our jobs and started Stax and Roan Security Services, which we'd soon shortened to S&R Security.

From the first, I was the organizer and Herb was in charge of marketing. He had a flair for nosing out the right contacts, and although sometimes in those early months I sweated de-ionized salt trying to make our meager assets pay his bar and lunch bills, it had paid off. Now S&R provided security services of one kind or another to a large percentage of the high tech companies in the Newport/Costa Mesa area. Occasionally, one of our operators would be injured while on duty, but none had been killed—until now.

"We've got to find somebody to take her place tonight," Herb said. "Who have we got available?"

I was glad he'd interrupted my morbid ruminations. Dwelling upon Helen's death was too damn painful.

Who do we have available to take her place? My mind began pushing buttons like a computer input terminal. Names and faces of available personnel flashed into view and were discarded for one reason or another. Some of them might have been acceptable, but for one reason or another, I kept rejecting them.

"I'm not sure," I said. "It has to be somebody with at least a 'confidential' security clearance."

"How about that fellow Cole? He has a clearance from when we used him at Aerojet. He might be available."

An idea I'd been trying to brush aside kept coming back, nagging through my ambivalence. Something had been bothering Helen. The answer might be at Colton Labs. Which meant I didn't want Cole or anybody else. I had a better, and probably a more stupid, idea.

"I'm going to do it."

Herb's eyebrows lifted. "Why should you? We can get somebody."

"It'll give me a chance to look around out there. Maybe I can get a line on what really happened."

"For Christ's sake, Ben. The police are working on that. Hemet's working on it. You'll just screw up the investigation."

"I'm not going to do anything. Just look around."

"You can't walk off and leave the office now. You just got back. They need you."

"I'll be at the office every afternoon. The staff can hold it together for a few more days." Herb started to form another protest and I added, "Herb, I've got to."

Herb's pale eyes took on a look of resignation and he shrugged. "Yeah, okay. It's probably the end of S&R Security. But what the hell. Easy come, easy go." He took a last swallow of his margarita, then his eyes chilled. "But watch yourself, amigo. If there's anything in what you say, it could be dangerous. All we need is for you to disappear again."

"Don't worry. I'd hate to think what would happen if you really took over the office."

Herb's laugh was not loaded with humor. He motioned to the waitress to bring another drink and another piece of pie. But I was already feeling the surge of energy from the sugar in the last piece. I wanted to get moving. Unlike Herb, I couldn't sit for hours going over the same ground again and again. Maybe that was the secret of his success—patience. He could run a client up and down through a gamut of options for hours, playing him like a hooked marlin, waiting for his victim to tire so he could reel him in. He never lost his pleasure for the game.

But I didn't have that kind of patience. After a subject had been covered, however desultorily, I was anxious to move on, like now.

Leaving Herb at the restaurant, I drove by my home to pick up my key to Helen's apartment. She'd given it to me when our relationship was halcyon, but I'd never used it. Never had to. We'd always been together when I went to her apartment. I was still having trouble realizing it would never happen again.

I was rummaging through my dresser trying to locate the key when Jack Blucher came in. He was wearing his baggy shorts and sandals. One of my beach towels was draped around his neck.

"Back already?" he said. "You had a short day."

I told him what had happened, and he stood silently gripping the ends of the towel, but not looking surprised. I suppose when you've been intimately involved with death for most of your life, it would not hit you as hard as it would most people. And, except for my endlessly talking about Helen during the plane ride from Africa, he did not know her. To him, she was simply a name.

"Anything I can do?" he asked.

"No, I guess not. I'm going over to her apartment to look around."

His expression did not change, but his eyes developed a new sharpness. "Look around?"

I stopped looking for the key and put my hands flat on the top of the dresser. Without looking at him, I said, "I don't buy the accident or suicide. When I saw her last night, she wasn't the Helen I knew. Something was wrong. Maybe I can find out what."

"You think she was murdered?"

I started to give him a flat yes, but I pulled back. Why should I believe someone would kill her? Just because she had seemed tense and nervous last night? I had to have more evidence than that.

I relaxed and continued my search for the key. "I don't know," I said. "Right now, all I want to do is look around her apartment."

"I'll come with you."

I started to say no. I wanted to be alone in the apartment with my memories. Maybe searching for something that would explain her death was only an excuse to be there. Except that the memories were now all pain and guilt. It might be better if I took Jack along to help prevent the ghosts from crowding in.

"Okay," I said. "Hurry up."

He pulled a tee shirt on and announced he was ready. "I started looking at apartments down by the beach," he said. "Nothing available. So I went for a swim. Never saw so many gorgeous bodies in my life. Doesn't anybody work around here?"

"Seems that way," I answered. "Keep looking. There's a lot of mobility here. You'll find something."

"Oh, I've already found a few things. You'd be surprised."

I assumed he meant women, and I wondered what type he would go for. Then I found the key and forgot to ask.

Driving the familiar route to Helen's apartment in the hazy midday sun gave me plenty of time to think about our relationship and what it might have been. Strange how you tend to remember only the good parts, the good dreams. The guilt begins to pile up when your mind inevitably turns to the selfish things you'd done—the unintentional neglect; the places you'd planned to go, but never did; the things you'd planned to say, but never did. The recriminations would be around for a long time even if you knew you didn't deserve them because there was always the suspicion that you did. How much more should you, could you, have done?

Helen's apartment was in one of those sprawling mega-unit complexes that seemed unique to the southwest. Only two floors in height, it covered acres and encompassed two big swimming pools, a sauna and landscaping that was all perennial flowers and palm trees.

Parking was in open car ports at the rear of the complex. I was going to park in Helen's assigned parking stall, but it was already occupied by her little Mustang.

"That's strange," I said. "Her car is here."

"What about it?"

"So how did she get to work last night?"

"Bus maybe."

"No buses near here."

"Taxi?"

"Taxies cost an arm and a leg. Why didn't she just take her car?"

"Maybe it's out of action. She'd have to pay the freight on a taxi."

"That must be it. It's a mile to a bus line. She wouldn't walk that after dark."

I made sure nobody saw us when I unlocked her door. I could explain why I was there if I had to, but why get into that kind of a hassle if I could avoid it?

I went in first, stopping just inside the door to stare at the familiar surroundings. The drapes were drawn and the room was in semi-darkness. I had the strange sensation that if I stood there another minute she'd walk out of the bedroom with that long, swinging stride and wrap her arms around me for a lingering kiss.

I shook off the feeling and moved inside with Jack following. I pulled back the drapes and the room flooded with sunlight.

"What are we looking for?" Jack asked.

"I don't really know. Anything that might suggest suicide, I guess."

"What the hell would that be? A rope with a knot in it?"

A surge of anger shot through me. Helen's death was not a joke. If he'd known her... But he hadn't. And to a man like Jack Blucher, death had to be a joke. It was necessary it be held at bay with gallows humor. Otherwise, how could you look in the hooded, skeletal face day after day without going insane?

Quickly my anger drained. "Something like that. Maybe a note."

"Okay. I'll start in the kitchen."

He went into the kitchen and I took a slow turn around the living room, trying not to look at the many objects that brought back unwanted memories. I had to remember why I was here now, not the good things of the misty past. It shouldn't be so difficult. I'd gotten plenty of experience in trying to block out the past when I was a kid.

For what seemed like the millionth time in my life, I thrust bitter memories back into the darkness by focusing on the present. I slowly swept the room, looking at every article with an analytical stare. What should a suicide's place look like? Would it be unusually clean so the people left behind would not think of you as a slob? Or would it be left dirty because you would be beyond caring what anybody thought? I guess it depended on the personality. This room looked just as it always had—no more no less.

I began moving around the room. letting thoughts flow in free association, hoping something would come that would make sense.

Why did her furnishings look so expensive? Were they really expensive? Or did she have an ability to make them seem out of the ordinary?

Those serigraphs on the walls. Were they done by famous artists? Were they originals or copies?

I peered at the signatures, but they meant nothing to me. I had some original art in my own place, but it was inexpensive, created by unknowns—oils and sculptures I'd picked up at shopping center galleries and outdoor festivals. Naturally, I could recognize a Van Gogh or a Picasso, but that was about it.

But if these were originals by artists with name value, where did she get the money?

The answer was not in the living room. Maybe not anywhere.

I went into the bedroom, not wanting to go, but unable to stay away. Memories born in that bedroom should not be violated with anything ugly I might find today.

Helen was a messy sleeper. She hadn't made the bed before leaving for work and the rumpled bedding was half on the floor. I found myself staring at the far side of the bed, looking for the impression left by my body. It was there. A faint suggestion, a wrinkling of the lower sheet.

Could it have been made by someone else after I'd left?

Jealously slashed through my mind like a knife thrust. Maybe that was why she had wanted me to leave so early. Maybe that was why she had been so unresponsive. Maybe there was someone else!

Well, hell! It was her privilege. I had no right to feel one way or the other about it.

From the top of the dresser a picture of Helen smiled at me. How could all that beauty be gone? A thought intruded again as it had so many times in the past. Goodness and beauty only survived a short time, but cruelty and ugliness seemed to last forever. And when beauty did survive, it was only through constant nurturing, while ugliness multiplied spontaneously, crowding out the beauty like weeds in a garden or graffiti on a statue. Helen's death was one more reinforcement of the depressing thought.

I turned away. Then stopped. Something was missing. A picture. There should be a picture of her father and mother on the dresser. It was a wedding picture of Commander Cotrell in his Navy uniform and her mother in a bride's gown with the veil thrown back. I remembered that her mother at that age looked very much like Helen, but more fragile as thought her beauty would crumble at the first wintery wind of adversity. Why should that one picture be missing?

I was looking through the drawers of her dresser, feeling like a ghoul, when I found it. The picture was face down under a neat stack of sweaters on the bottom of a drawer and the glass in the silver frame had been broken. Perhaps it had fallen which would account for the broken glass. But why hide it? And from whom? Herself?

The glass did not look as though it had been broken by a fall. It looked more like it had been shattered by a blow. It didn't make sense; she adored her father. Maybe she was angry with her mother. If so, it was no longer relevant.

"Find anything?"

I almost dropped the picture. Jack was standing in the doorway, his hands on either side of the frame. I put the picture face down on the top of the dresser. For some unknown reason, I didn't want anyone to see it. It was too much like looking into an intimate part of Helen's mind. There was no reason to invade that private part of her world. "No," I said. "Nothing out of the ordinary."

"Me neither. Except that if it was suicide, she decided after she left here."

"Why do you say that?"

"Too many things left half done, like she was coming back."

"That's the feeling I got too."

"Which means it was an accident—or somebody killed her."

"I can't believe that. There was no reason."

"How would you know? You've been gone almost three months."

I turned away, unwilling to examine the thought. Just how well did I know her anyway? Mark Twain once said that every person is like the moon, with a dark side they show to no one. Did Helen have a dark side she had kept hidden? Did I really want to find out?

"Are those car keys?" Jack pointed to a set of keys on the dresser.

I picked them up. "Yes. I guess they're Helen's."

"Let's see if her car is running."

I followed Jack outside, closing the apartment door softly and carefully.

When I used her ignition key, the Mustang's engine started easily. I backed it up and ran it forward to check the transmission and brakes. Everything worked. There was even a half-tank of gasoline. I shut off the engine and sat staring at the dead instruments. Maybe she hadn't taken the car because she knew that she was going on a one-way trip.

"So why didn't she use it?" Jack asked.

"I don't know," I whispered, not wanting to express what I was thinking.

"Maybe she knew she wouldn't be coming back." Jack's voice echoed my thoughts.

I brushed the unwanted idea aside. "She could've left it at the lab. What difference would it have made?"

"Depends. There's one other thing."

I turned my head to stare at him, afraid. I desperately didn't want it to be suicide. I wanted someone to be responsible. Someone I could make pay. "What's that?" I asked.

"How did she get there? You already said she wouldn't use the bus and a taxi was too expensive. So what's left?"

"Somebody gave her a ride."

"Yeah," he said. "I wonder who."

I thought of the impression someone had made in her bed, and suddenly I didn't think I wanted to know any more.

Chapter 7

I KNEW I should take the afternoon off and get some sleep before going on duty at Colton Labs. But I wanted to check with my night shift guards, so I had Kim call and ask each of them to be in my office at 5:00.

They drifted in one by one and sat quietly in the outer office sipping coffee from the Mr. Coffee machine, not even talking to each other. They knew the meeting was related to Helen's death and was not likely to be pleasant.

When all four had arrived they came into my office, moving uneasily. They sat staring at me expectantly. I was unsure how to begin. I knew MacDonald had already talked to them and they'd told him all they knew about Helen's accident. So how could I ask more questions without sounding as though I didn't trust them? And with whom should I begin?

Maybe with Ed Emblem. He was the oldest; 6l, if I remembered correctly. His gray hair was closely trimmed and he wore a military mustache that made him look like a benevolent grandfather. As with many ex-policemen who now lived a relatively sedentary life, he had allowed himself to put on too much weight and his stomach overhung his belt, straining against his uniform shirt. I'd have to talk to him about that again. S&R did have an image of sorts.

Ron Renbourne was our James Bond. Whenever we had a visiting female celebrity to bodyguard, or a fancy party to work, I always tried to send Ron. He was 6'2", slender of hip and wide of shoulder. He had curly dark hair and deep-brown eyes that gave him a dangerous devil-may-care look. His teeth were almost unnaturally white and his lips had a cruel, amused twist, that for some reason, seemed to intrigue women.

Hanna Carbo considered herself a tough cookie. She was 37, short and blocky. In her uniform, she looked like a Russian prison guard, and in fact, at one time she had been a guard at Chino State Prison. Before her husband died, he'd run a little bar over in Costa Mesa and I'd been told that when he'd needed a keg of beer hooked up at the spigot, he waited until Hanna came in to lift the heavy keg into place. The way she looked at Ron Renbourne when she thought he wasn't watching made me think she'd like to throw him over her shoulder and carry him off to a cave.

Ted Olds was a 35-year-old ex-Marine. Everybody seemed to think if you were a Marine, you were some kind of superman, but Ted didn't fit the image. I think he'd left the Corps because he was so terribly uncoordinated. He looked fit enough, medium in size and solid, but he couldn't step off a curb without falling. He was a good guard, however, conscientious and reliable. Everybody liked to work with Ted.

I moved around to the front of my desk and sat on its edge to help ease the image of speaking from the position of an employer. I didn't want to make it sound like an inquisition, so I kept my voice as impersonal as possible.

"I want to thank you for carrying on while I was gone," I began. "And also thank you for coming in now." My throat and mouth were terribly dry. Asking personal questions was not only embarrassing, they probably thought I didn't trust them.

I swallowed painfully and began again. "There's nothing official about it. I'd just like to know if any of you noticed anything unusual last night."

"You mean about Helen?" Hanna Carbo asked.

"Well, yes. Or anything else."

There was an awkward moment of silence. Ted Olds finally said, "Nothing I could see. Everything was normal on the main gate."

"Me, too," Ed Emblem said. "Of course, my beat is way over on the other side of the plant and most nights I don't even see Helen."

I looked at Hanna Carbo and she shook her head. "I talked to her when she came on duty. She seemed okay then."

"How about you, Ron?"

He hunched his broad shoulders. "Nope. Everything seemed okay to me."

"I thought it was an accident," Hanna Carbo said. "Wasn't it?"

"That's what it looks like," I told her. "I have no reason to believe anything else really. It's just that... Well, it seems a little odd to me that Helen would be so careless. She's been around those radars for months. She knew what they could do. Why the hell would she stand in front of one?"

"Maybe she didn't know it was radiating," Ted Olds said. "That's something you can't see."

"And there's no sound," Ed Emblem added. "You could get cooked before you knew what was happening."

"I suppose it could happen," I conceded. "But there was nothing else? Nothing unusual?"

"*Nada*," Renbourne said. "Everything was normal as far as I could see."

The others nodded in agreement.

"I know the lab doesn't have a swing or a graveyard shift any more," I said. "But there must be a lot of people around anyway—janitors, delivery trucks... Who else?"

"Engineers, technicians, mechanics, maintenance men. Lots of people work overtime," Olds said.

"Don't forget secretaries," Ed Emblem smirked. "Some of them put in a little overtime, too."

"In any case," I cut in, "you've got a lot of people coming and going."

"Up until about midnight," Olds said. "But after six, they all have to use the main gate and we log everybody in and out."

"Who keeps the records?"

"Plant security. If you want to take a look at the log book, check with Clint Hemet."

"Okay. I'll give him a call. But I'm sure both Hemet and Cal MacDonald have already checked them."

The four sat staring at me, waiting for the next question. But my mind was as blank as my throat was dry. I knew if they had noticed anything suspicious that night, they would tell me, which meant that there was nothing to report. I was about to let them leave when I remembered Helen's car.

"Do any of you know how Helen got to work? She didn't take her car."

"Sure," Renbourne said. "I gave her a ride. We've been car-pooling."

"Car-pooling? You don't live anywhere near her."

Renbourne's teeth flashed. "Well, it wasn't exactly a car-pool. We always used my car. I'd go over and pick her up and bring her back."

Jealousy tightened my stomach into an indigestible knot. "All that distance? Why?" It was a stupid question, and I wished immediately I hadn't asked it.

To give him credit, Renbourne did look uncomfortable when he replied. "I was., uh, trying to make brownie points. I hope I wasn't out of line."

I forced myself to my feet and stood with my back to the picture window so my face would be in shadow. I didn't want any of them to see I was disturbed at the thought of Helen and Ron Renbourne being together.

"No," I told him, every word yanking tight another knot in my gut. "You weren't out of line." I moved to the door and opened it. "Well, thanks for coming in."

As they filed out, I added, "Oh, I'll be taking her place for the next couple of nights until we can line up somebody else. Ted, you can show me the ropes."

Ted Olds nodded. "Sure, Ben. Come to the main delivery gate at about seven-thirty. I'll show you how to log in."

As Renbourne went past, he said, "You're not uptight about it, are you? I never put a hand on her."

I generated a weak smile. "No, I had no claim on her."

He walked away looking as though he didn't believe me. Why should he? I didn't believe it either. I wanted to fire him, to get him out of my life so I'd never have to face the truth—that Helen had found someone else.

Hanna Carbo was the last to leave. She stopped and gripped my arm so hard it made me wince. "I'm glad you're okay, Ben," she murmured. "And I'm sorry about Helen. She was a good kid."

I closed the door and slumped in my chair feeling tired and depressed. It all added up to an accident. So why didn't I believe it? I had no real proof, only a suspicion based on what I knew of Helen's personality. Which was a stupid rationalization. What did her personality have to do with an accident?

I remembered the time I'd been in a home where my foster parents had three kids of their own. I'd fallen off a skateboard and scraped a hole in my pants and a lot of skin off my knee. My foster father was furious because he had to pay for a new pair of pants. He'd let me know without saying it that if I hadn't been a stupid foster child, it wouldn't have happened. As though that had anything to do with it. His own kids fell off all the time and they were a hell of a lot more stupid than I was.

Maybe I'd find something at the plant. Tonight there would be plenty of time to look around.

By the time I went to my office closet and took out my old uniform, the pain in my stomach had subsided to a dull ache. I hadn't worn the uniform in three years, but it still fit reasonably well, courtesy of the diet at Mbaraba Prison, which if you ask me, was a lousy way to lose weight.

I THOUGHT CLINT Hemet would laugh when I walked into his

office. But he only smiled. "You look pretty good in a uniform," he said. "You should've stayed a guard or joined the Army or something."

"Or been a doorman." I took off my hat and flexed my shoulders. "Anyway, it still fits."

"If anything, it's a little baggy. They must not have served gourmet meals where you were."

"All natural food. Great if you're a goat."

"You'll get it back. You've never had a weight problem. Lucky bastard." Hemet kept himself in good shape, but he had to fight to keep his weight under control. He patted his stomach and sucked it in. "Wait'll you get old—or married, which ever comes first. You'll explode—boom! Just like everybody."

"Maybe." I smiled, although I didn't really believe him. Even as a kid, I'd been skinny. When I was fourteen I'd found some old weights in back of Juvenile Hall and I'd worked hard to build some real muscle. I hadn't gained an ounce. But the few muscles I did have became hard as rocks.

But it wasn't my weight that interested me at the moment. "Were you able to get the gate log?"

Hemet turned to his desk and picked up a loose-leaf notebook. He flipped the pages and handed it to me. "This is the log for Tuesday night. After you called I went over it, but I couldn't find anything out of order."

I took the notebook to the big couch and sat checking through the list. There were careful entries in Ted Old's' meticulous handwriting logging people in and out from 8:00 p.m. to 1:00 a.m. when he'd logged himself out for lunch and Ed Emblem had taken over the gate. Olds had picked up again when he came back, and except for coffee breaks, had worked the gate straight through until 8:00 a.m.

I checked through the list of people who had worked overtime. There were quite a few. Then a name jumped out at me—Bill Holtz, the engineer. He'd worked until almost 10:00. I wondered why he hadn't mentioned that.

Farther down the list I came across the name of Eddie Hooker, Harry Deen's photographer assistant. He'd worked until 10:30.

None of the other names rang a bell and I handed the notebook back to Hemet. "Could you hang on to this a while? I might want to check it again."

"No sweat. Just let me know. I already made a copy for MacDonald."

I excused myself by telling him I wanted to look around the plant before going on duty, which was partially true. There is a big difference between walking through a busy plant with people all around and actually patrolling the place when it was deserted and quiet. You had to learn to look with different eyes. Of course, there was always some activity around a company as large as Colton Labs—overtime work, deliveries, equipment being installed, removed and undergoing repair, offices being renovated or shifted, janitorial work. But those activities were known in advance.

For a guard, the trick was to pick the unauthorized activity from the authorized. Memorizing night activity reports helped, but a lot of it came from instinct alone. After you had been around a place long enough you got a feel for its ambience and its people. Your instincts then told you if the pattern was broken.

Why hadn't Helen's instincts warned her? She certainly had the experience and she'd been around Colton Labs long enough to have the feel of the place. Unusual activities or strangers would have alerted her, I was sure of that. So whoever or whatever had killed her could not have been that unusual.

Provided she had been killed. And provided it hadn't been suicide. And provided I wasn't wrong about her instincts. Provided a lot of things. Hell. I was probably all wrong and being here was a waste of time. Just like checking with Eddie Hooker would be a waste of time.

But that was the one thing I did have—time.

I knew generally where Harry Deen's photo studio was located and by asking a couple of directions I found a door in the corner of the machine shop area marked 'Photo Group.'

The door opened into a deserted office area furnished with a couple of cluttered steel desks with Formica tops. Against the walls were several four-drawer filing cabinets and large steel equipment cabinets secured with combination locks. Odds and ends of photographic and video equipment were scattered around—tripods, camera cases, video tapes, slide film holders, light boxes, an old 16mm B&H movie projector, and numerous books and magazines about photography and video taping. Several certificates and plaques awarded by audio-visual festivals were gathering dust on the walls. Two or three were awards from an organization I'd heard of called Association of Visual Communicators, so maybe Deen was a better film maker than I'd thought.

The phone on one of the desks rang and Deen came from a door in the back to answer it. When he saw me he broke his stride long enough to say, "Oh, hi, Ben. Be with you in a minute."

He grunted a few times into the phone before he hung up. He made a note on a pad.

"Fuckin' nuisance," he grumbled. "I hate video. We not only have to shoot the damn things, we've got to do all the projecting. I've got to yank Hooker off whatever he's doin' and send him way the hell and gone to the idiot board room to run a tape.

"Christ! Why can't they do it themselves? Lazy bastards. All you've got to do is shove a cartridge in the machine and push a button. Even a half-assed executive could do it." He focused on me as though he'd just become aware of my presence. "Hey, Ben. Why the uniform? What brings you around?"

I watched his expression while I explained that I was taking Helen's place, but he appeared completely disinterested. "I stopped by to see what kind of a setup you've got here."

"Yeah? Not too shabby. I hope you haven't been waitin' long. I was in the editing room. That's another damn thing. With video, you got to do all that friggin' editing. You got to make sound tracks an' release copies and all that shit. Then everybody turns into a friggin' critic. I wish the hell they'd farm out the damn stuff. I wish I'd stayed with stills. What can I do for you, Ben boy?"

If Harry Deen got three wishes he'd complain because it wasn't four.

"I'm afraid to ask," I said.

Deen laughed, his breath exploding in short barks. He jerked his head toward the door. "Come on in. We're getting set up for some damn rush project. We can talk while we're workin'."

"No hurry. If you're busy, I can come back"

"No, no. Let the bastards wait. Come on."

He led me through a small room that contained Avid and EMC video editing systems with extra monitors on the walls. Judging from the racks of tapes, it was also a storage room. Another door opened into a surprisingly large studio. Several photographic lights on stands were scattered around and more were rigged overhead on a metal grid suspended from the high ceiling. The walls were padded to make the room sound proof. In one corner an expensive-looking Horseman still-camera was aimed at a wall-mounted stand designed for producing photocopies. A big Ikegami video camera was on a wheeled camera stand. A teleprompter was on a stand next to it.

For the current production, the studio had been rigged to look like an office. One of the two intersecting wall flats had a real window without glass. The fake view showed plastic flowers and bushes against a painted landscape. In front of the window was a huge walnut executive desk, complete with a high-backed leather chair and a thick carpet that could be genuine Moroccan. Against one of the fake walls was a tall bookcase filled with engineering manuals. On the other side was a closed cabinet containing a refrigerator bar. Next to it was an oversized couch upholstered in a pale-gold tapestry that must have cost fifty dollars a yard or more. The walls were decorated with framed still pictures of company products. All in all, a very plush setup.

Eddie Hooker was fiddling with one of the studio lights trying to manipulate the barn doors on the front of the lens to eliminate shadows. From time to time he moved to squint through the eyepiece of the camera pointed at the couch. He had changed his tee-shirt to an orange creation with words in front reading 'Stop All Abortions—except mine.'

I wondered how much the set had cost. Enough to pay a lot of guards' salaries that was for sure. Deen saw the incredulous expression on my face and waved his hand to indicate the set. "Executive office. Pretty authentic, right?"

"Yeah. If you're president of General Motors."

"Hell, today all the big shots have offices like this. One of the fringe benefits. Sure, we lay it on a little. Nobody wants their clients to think they're dealing with a penny-ante business. You've got to spend money to get money."

"You're going to use this in a company video?"

"Sure. Sales picture for a new digital communications system. We open in the office of the vice president—that's what this is—and he tells the audience what a terrific place we've got here and why they should buy from Colton. Then we cut to scenes of design and testing, using the off-screen narrator, a pro. Then we come back here for a talking-head closing. I only hope the bastard doesn't freeze up and take all day."

I looked at my watch. It was already seven. "You're shooting tonight?"

"*Manaña*. First thing in the morning."

"You do many of these?"

"No, thank God. They're a pain in the ass. Most of our work is with stills." He motioned to the big studio camera in the corner. "We do some microfiche for record keeping, but most of that shit is on computer chips. We only handle the sensitive stuff."

"Sensitive stuff? You mean classified?"

"No. We do a little of that, but not as much as we used to. Freedom of information, you know. Got us away from a lot of that crapola. I'm talking about company classified stuff. Proprietary, state-of-the-art crap we wouldn't want anybody to see."

I could appreciate that. Colton Labs, like just about every high-tech electronics company, was conducting research out on the edge of the power curve. Today the company that made the breakthrough was the one that reaped the profits, and at the rate electronics was taking over functions ranging from the kitchen stove to electric cars, you had to play fast but tight.

Even when you were out in front in an area as highly advanced as fiber optics, microchips, artificial intelligence, microwave technology, virtual reality and high energy lasers, you couldn't afford to let down your guard or you'd lose your competitive edge. It was a business where a company could reap a fortune, especially when you looked at the future of electronics and light spectrums. But it was also one in which you could lose everything overnight if a new invention by a competitor made your product obsolete.

"Looks like a nice setup you've got here, Harry," I said. "I'm surprised you've got a studio this big."

"This is nothing. Some in-plant outfits have got thirty or forty people doing audio-visual work. That's not counting still work. Eddie and me have got to run this whole damn thing ourselves."

"Speaking of Eddie—" I turned to look at him "—I notice you worked late Tuesday night."

Eddie Hooker looked up and moved away from the camera. "That's right." He glanced at Deen. "I was processing those printed circuit shots for the newsletter."

"Yeah. That's right," Harry Deen confirmed.

"Is that the one I saw you shooting?"

"With the broad. Yeah. We were shooting video and stills."

"What time did you leave?"

"Around ten, ten-thirty, I think it was."

That checked with the time entered in the gate log book. "Did you by any chance see Helen Cotrell on your way out?"

"That guard who got zapped? Nope. Didn't see her that night at all."

It had been a long shot at best. And even if he'd seen Helen, it might not have meant anything. Guards were supposed to be seen. "Okay, thanks," I said.

He grunted and ambled back to his camera, moving with the

peculiar heel lift of an athlete who had gone to seed. Harry Deen took a half-step toward the set and paused, making it clear he'd like to get back on the job if I'd stop asking questions. "Sorry we weren't much help," he said. "If there's anything else..." He let it hang there as though he hoped there wasn't.

"Not now," I said. "I'll let you know if there is."

"Any time," he said and walked away.

I was passing back through the editing room when I noticed another door with a sign over it that said 'Dark Room. Keep out when red light on.' The red light wasn't on, so I opened the door and went inside. To get to the dark room you had to negotiate a couple of S-turns designed to block any stray light from entering.

The room itself was fairly large and lighted by overhead fluorescent lights. It was a typical photographer's darkroom with processing tubs, enlargers, dryers, and storage cabinets. The place smelled strongly of developer or whatever the stuff was that gave darkrooms such a stink.

I noticed two rolls of 35mm negative were hung up to dry after processing. Handing them carefully by the edges, I could see they were pictures of the gorgeous brunette Eddie Hooper had shot yesterday. Most of the frames were extreme close-ups of the PCB she was holding.

There were no other pictures so I left, closing the door after me. I hoped I'd left soon enough to escape being saturated with the chemical odor.

It took only a few minutes to walk to the environmental test area and locate Bill Holtz. He was peering at a waveform pattern on a CRT display outside the Tempest chamber and talking to a couple of young, intense looking engineers. I moved into his line of sight and waited patiently for him to acknowledge my presence. When he pointedly ignored me by half turning away, I move up to stand almost against him, peering over his shoulder.

He turned, irritation pulling at his face, his eyes stony. "Yes?" he said. His voice was polite, but hard and impatient. "Can I help you?"

"I don't know," I told him. "I just had a couple of questions. You got a minute?"

He wanted to say no, but he could see by my body language I was not going away. He made a clearly understood groan of exasperation and told the two engineers to watch the waveform for negative changes and moved away a couple of steps. "I hope this won't take long," he growled.

"No," I assured him. "I just noticed on the log book that you worked late Tuesday night."

"That's right."

"Alone?"

"Yes." He motioned to one of the other engineers. "Jim was here 'til about seven, then he had to leave. I stayed 'til about ten."

"Did you see the guard, Helen Cotrell?"

"She came by. She usually does. I didn't talk to her."

"What time was that?"

"I don't know. I don't look at my watch when I'm working."

"Make a guess."

He glared at me, the color mounting in his face. "Look, I told all this to the police."

"All right. I'm sorry." I put on my most distressed look. "But she meant a lot to me. Could you please tell me, too?"

He made a gesture of irritation. "I don't know. Eight. Eight-thirty. Nine. Some where around there."

"Did she look okay to you?"

"How would I know? She didn't stop. She just walked through the area. That was it. If you want to check my notes for that night—"

"No, no," I said. I was wasting my time. He wasn't about to take his mind off his work and concentrate hard on some dumb guard who got herself cooked. It wasn't his concern. The experiment he was running was more important.

"Okay," I said.

He turned so abruptly my thanks bounced off his back. I watched him and the engineers for a minute. Maybe their world of advanced electronics was so consuming they just did not have room for little human touches like courtesy. I wondered if they turned themselves off like one of their computers when they went home. Maybe their wives and kids were on the same frequency and were able to communicate in some secret code that left outsiders like me wondering what their narrow world was all about.

It was almost 7:30, and as I walked through the plant toward the main gate, I was passed by people hurrying out. In the guard room adjacent to the gate Ted Olds, Ed Emblem, Ron Renbourne and Hanna Carbo were talking to the day crew guards who would go off duty at 8:00. Ted Olds had come in early to brief me on my route and procedures, but Ed Emblem, Ron and Hanna had no reason to be here this early unless it was to give me moral support.

They looked up when I walked in and Hanna Carbo gave a low

whistle. "Hey, Chief," she said. "You should wear that uniform all the time."

Ed Emblem waved his hand in front of his nose. "Jesus, I hope not. The moth balls'll kill us."

"That isn't moth balls," I said. "What you smell is gun powder. I was wearing this uniform when I captured all those spies."

"Spies?" Renbourne said. "I heard they were four guys playing gin rummy."

"Well, a kibitzer is kind of a spy."

Hanna Carbo smiled and started to pick up on the line. Then her smile vanished as though yanked off with a string. "Ben," she said. "You be careful."

Ted Olds nodded. "She's right. I don't buy that accident shit. And I don't think Cotrell was acting like a suicide."

"You really think somebody killed her?" Ed Emblem asked with a note of strain in his voice. "What the hell for?"

"I didn't say that," Olds said quickly. "I said it didn't look to me like an accident."

"If it wasn't suicide either," Renbourne cut in. "What's left?"

Ted Olds rubbed the back of his neck. He had tried to sound like an authority and they had backed him into a corner. "I didn't say it couldn't have been an accident. Hell, I stay the hell away from those radars when I work out there. Maybe she never learned."

"Maybe horses can fly, too," Ed Emblem growled.

"Motive," Hanna Carbo grunted. "You find the motive and you can find the killer. That's what you've got to do."

"Now who said she was killed?" Ted Olds said with satisfaction.

"All right," I interjected. "The police are looking into it. They'll find out what happened."

"Bull," Ted Olds said. "If you thought that, you wouldn't be here."

I had no answer. They were aware I could've hired another experienced guard or transferred somebody from another job. The fact that I'd taken the job myself was proof enough I wasn't satisfied with the 'accident' theory. It also made it look as though I didn't trust the police to find out what had happened. Which was partially true. MacDonald had been very quick to accept the idea that Helen's death was an accident. I didn't think MacDonald was lazy, but if it was an accident, it would certainly save him and everyone in the department and at Colton Labs a lot of trouble. It was only human nature that he wouldn't push the investigation unless there was some hard evidence she'd been killed.

Well, maybe I could do something about that.

"Ted," I said. "You were going to show me Helen's route."

"I know her territory," Hanna Carbo said quickly. "I'll show you around."

I looked at Ted Olds, and he shrugged and spread his hands. "Fine with me."

It was close to 8:00 when I added my name in the log book and fastened a radio unit to my belt. Ted Olds was working the main gate as usual, so he stayed behind while I followed Ed Emblem, Ron Renbourne and Hanna across the macadam expanse that stretched from the gate to the delivery docks in the rear of the main buildings. Emblem and Renbourne headed off toward the manufacturing buildings, and I followed Hanna into the building where most of the R&D engineering work was conducted.

Inside, the vast buildings were strangely quiet. The only sounds were the occasional whir of a machine operated by someone working overtime or the echoing footsteps of a lone workman moving through the network of corridors. In a distant corner somebody dropped a metal trash can and the loud clang echoing from the high ceiling made me jump.

Hanna chuckled. "You think this is quiet. Wait until about two o'clock in the morning."

"I can hardly wait," I said dryly.

Maybe it was my imagination, but as Hanna walked with me through the area, pointing out exits, fire alarms, fire extinguishers, and potential hazards, I thought she was walking much closer to me than was necessary. From time to time our hands brushed and several times when we stopped and she pointed something out, she stood so close I could feel the soft resiliency of her breast through the heavy material of her uniform jacket. I felt awkward in moving away from what I assumed was an accidental contact because her manner was strictly business.

I felt a surge of relief when she left me at the far end of the building and proceeded to her own patrol area which included the office buildings in the front of the lab complex. Hanna was not a bad-looking woman, if you liked the stocky type with a thick waist, heavy boobs and a wide, Slavic face.

At one time, I might've been susceptible to her body language. Not now. I wasn't sure how long it would be before any woman would be able to erase thoughts of Helen from my mind. Why is it we most long for the things we've lost or can't have?

Walking through the plant I found myself thinking Helen had walked this same corridor just last night; Helen had checked this storage area; Helen had touched this same light switch; Helen had—

I snorted. This was accomplishing nothing. If I was going to find out anything at all I'd have to look at my surroundings through my own eyes, not hers. And the place to start was that environmental test chamber. But not now. I'd wait until everybody had gone.

I was getting a drink at a fountain when I heard a soft sound behind me and turned abruptly, my nerves jangling. But the sound was only the thump of a broom being pushed by a janitor as he moved down the corridor toward me.

"Hi," I said.

"You the new guard?" the man asked in a heavy, thick voice that matched his body. I judged him to be about forty. He wore baggy brown pants and a very clean light-brown jacket over a turtle-neck sweater. A painter's hat, pulled down almost to his eyebrows, covered a heavy thatch of black hair. His skin was dark and his round, closely-shaven face was shiny with a thin sheen of perspiration.

"Temporarily," I answered. "How's it going?"

"No big deal. Sorry to hear about that guard, Cotrell. She was okay."

Of course he'd have known Helen. They must have passed from time to time while she was making her rounds. "Thanks," I said. "Did you see her last night?"

"Sure. We almost always passed each other about here." He squinted at me and cocked his head. "Not supposed to smoke in here, but she never said anything if I took a drag or two."

I wondered whether I should begin enforcing the No Smoking rule that was so important in the manufacture of high-tech electronics. I'd been told that molecules of smoke residue could foul up circuits whose electrical impulses had to travel along paths several times narrower than a human hair. In this area, however, it was mostly machine shops, so smoking shouldn't do any harm except for cancer, emphysema and heart failure. And it was possible the man could give me some information.

I shrugged. "What I don't see, I don't know."

"That's a good way to be."

He pulled a pack of cigarettes from his pocket and extended the pack. I shook my head. The damn things even looked like coffin nails. "No, thanks," I said hastily. "I don't smoke."

"Yeah, well, don't start. It's a lousy habit. Costs a bundle. I could be driving a Porsche with what these damn things've cost me. I figured it out one time. A buck-and-a-half a pack average, three packs a day. That's four-and-a-half bucks. Three hundred sixty-five days a year. That's more'n sixteen hundred bucks a year. Times twenty years, that's damn year thirty-three thousand bucks. That's a hell of a lot of dough."

"Sure is," I agreed. And, I thought, that wasn't counting doctor bills.

"Now they're talkin' about addin' another buck in some friggin' tax. Jesus, I've got to quit." Abruptly he shoved out his hand. "I'm Joe Welts."

"Ben Roan." His hand was hard and calloused, the kind you find on people who've spent a lifetime at hard work—or lifting weights. "Last night, Joe, when you saw Helen, did she seem okay to you?"

"Yeah. I told that to that detective, MacDonald."

"Oh, you talked to him already?"

"He came by my place this morning. I couldn't tell him nothin' though. Looked quiet enough when I left at eleven."

"That your usual quitting time?"

"Yeah. Unless I leave early."

I had the feeling he wasn't holding back. If he had seen anything unusual, he'd have told me. "Okay," I said. "Thanks."

"You gonna be here from now on?"

"I'm not sure. The next couple of nights anyway. If you think of anything, I'd appreciate it if you'd let me know."

"Sure." He leaned on the boom and stared off into the far reaches of the building. "She was a nice lady." He turned to look at me and his voice hardened. "The next guard'll most likely be a son-of-a-bitch. No offense."

"No big deal."

"If you got any pull with the boss, try to get one in here who don't think she's a damn Nazi storm trooper like that broad over in the headquarters section."

There was no doubt he was referring to Hanna Carbo. "I'll do my best." I considered asking more questions about Helen, but my gut reaction was that he had little awareness of anything outside his job. A lot of people were like that. If something did not affect them directly, they had no idea what was going on, and most likely didn't want to know.

He began to push the broom down the corridor, then twisted to look back. "Hey! What'd you buy with the money?

"What money?"

"From not smoking. The thirty thousand bucks you saved?"

"Oh. I got a Corvette."

"Shit! I'm gonna stop" His thick eyebrows pulled together in thought. "But what the hell. In twenty years I'll be too damn old to give a damn. I might as well live it up. Right?"

I shuddered, imagining what his lungs would look like in twenty more years. "Right," I agreed.

He began to whistle as he moved off down the corridor, trailing a plume of cigarette smoke. I'd have to find a way to tell him he'd have to knock off the smoking indoors. But at the moment, I wanted him on my side. He was in a perfect position to observe everything that went on in the area until he went off duty. Who paid any attention to the janitor? Except me. I'd be talking to Joe Welts every chance I got.

I was passing the area where PCBs were assembled when I heard the sharp rap of heels on the concrete floor and a voice said, "Hey, jou. Mister guard."

I turned to see the girl from Eddie Hooker's pictures coming toward me. Even under the harsh fluorescent lights she looked exotically beautiful. She was wearing a pale blue sweater and tight pants. She had changed her soft-soled work shoes for shoes with three-inch heels. The way she filled out the sweater it was easy to see why Hooker had picked her from the assembly line for the shots.

"Yes?" I said.

She stopped in front of me, her dark brows furrowed in lines of worry. "I hear that girl guards get herself killed." She pronounced the word 'kill-ed'. "Is *verdad?*"

"There was an accident," I said.

"But she dead, no?"

I nodded slowly, hoping my pain was not evident. "Yes. She's...dead."

She was silent, staring at the floor, her luscious lips pouted in thought, her hands clasped.

"Oh," she murmured.

Her brow was still furrowed when she turned and began walking rapidly toward the distant exit. I called to her, "Aren't you working kind of late?"

She slowed and called back over her shoulder, "Damn right. Overtime. Good, huh?" She continued walking, her back rigid, her heels punctuating the air with staccato shots.

As I resumed my rounds, it occurred to me that Helen's death had probably created a storm of gossip and speculation. Many of the employees must have known her so her death had to mean more than the passing of a stranger. I'd have to talk to Clint Hemet about releasing some sort of bulletin to quell any pejorative rumors.

It didn't take long for the job to become boring. I had forgotten how time could drag late at night, even when you thought you had plenty to occupy your mind. Around 11:00, I got very sleepy. It's strange the way the body develops habits, and when those habits are changed, the brain forms a tremendous resistance. My body wanted its full eight hours of sleep, especially since I was still suffering from residual jet lag, and at 11:00 p.m., some small group of cells began telling the others it was time to start shutting down the factory.

But I couldn't let that happen. Not tonight. I rarely drink coffee, but I found a vending machine and bought a cup of the stale but hot liquid they called coffee and gulped it down.

In a short time the sleepiness passed and I knew I wouldn't have any more trouble staying awake the remainder of the night. Once habit was overcome, the well-tuned body was capable of responding to an emergency. It would also help to stay awake if I kept reminding myself to look for signs the police might have overlooked.

It was nearing 1:00 a.m. when I checked the monitors on Bill Holtz's test equipment to make sure the radar wasn't operating, then turned on the lights at a switch by the door and went into the big Tempest chamber.

The foam material designed to absorb microwaves also absorbed sound waves and it was incredibly quiet in the room. Only in such absolute silence was it possible to realize how much ambient noise there was outside in the deserted shop.

I had no concrete reason to believe Helen had been in the chamber, except it didn't make sense that she'd have voluntarily remained in front of an operating radar antenna long enough for it to kill her, unless she wanted to die, and I'd ruled that out. And you could hardly force anybody to stand in front of one of the tower-mounted antennas, so the radiation must have occurred inside a test chamber. This was the only chamber currently in use that was large enough to house a person. If I was right, there might be some evidence she'd been imprisoned here.

I began my search near the far end of the chamber. Except for the black box of the hardened radar antenna on the pedestal and the blocks of Styrofoam radiation absorption material, the room was totally bare, so anything unusual should be easy to spot.

There was nothing. After an hour of going over the room practically inch by inch, lifting and replacing each block of foam material that covered the floor, I hadn't found a thing out of the ordinary. None of the spikes of foam material were broken or bent. There were no scuff marks on the exposed surface of the painted concrete floor, no shred of cloth or a button from Helen's clothing, nothing.

I was more disappointed than surprised. Besides, who was I to think I could do better than trained detectives? The time I'd spent as a security guard hardly qualified me as an expert.

I walked out and slid shut the thick metal door. I carefully turned off the lights before I securing the door latch the way I'd found it. I was suddenly conscious that the dead silence inside the chamber had brought the building's ambient noise into sharp relief; the hum of an electric motor, the muted purr of a car or truck outside, even the gentle brush of wind against the roof high overhead seemed strangely loud.

I shook off a feeling of uneasiness, wondering how Helen must've felt here alone every night. The thought made me smile. She probably thought less of it than I did. She was a realist who rarely let her imagination linger on anything more complicated than sex or art. Even the quiet shadows would not frighten her. She knew how to take care of herself. And yet, she hadn't.

A few minutes later, after using my radio to check in with Ted Olds at the main gate, I was walking past a large trash container when I noticed the edge of a Styrofoam block sticking up above the top. At first it didn't register. Even when I realized what it was, I almost ignored it. Those pointed blocks would be easy to damage and were probably being discarded all the time.

Then it dawned upon me that there weren't any anechoic test chambers nearby. So where had the foam blocks come from? Why would anyone carry them all the way over here when there were plenty of trash containers near the test chambers?

I carefully lifted out the block and placed it on the concrete floor. I found three more blocks in the container. Each block was about three feet square at the base. They appeared to be identical to those used in the Tempest chamber, except their foam spikes were bent or completely broken off.

I was on my hands and knees examining one of the blocks when I heard a sound behind me like the scrape of a shoe on the concrete floor. I twisted and leaped to my feet, ready to resist an attack. But there was no blow, only a laugh.

"Hey, you can really move," Hanna Carbo said, and she chuckled again. "Who did you think I was? A bogeyman?"

My hat had fallen off and I picked it up and hid my embarrassment by brushing the knees of my pants. "I guess I'm out of practice," I said. "I didn't used to be so jumpy."

"Your procedures are kind of funny, too. I never heard of anybody patrolling on their hands and knees."

"It's a new technique. It's called falling asleep in easy stages."

"Yeah?" Hanna stared at the blocks of foam material spread out on the floor. "You think those are out of the Tempest chamber?"

Hanna was just as capable as I at putting two and two together so there was no point in trying to hide what I was doing. "Hard to tell. They look the same, but I don't know if they use these anywhere else."

"Let's see. They pick the trash up in this area every couple of days, so they couldn't have been here long."

"The trouble is I don't know if these get broken in normal use."

"If they don't, it could mean Helen was in that chamber. Maybe in a fight. Right?"

"It could've happened that way."

"If she was, there might be some of her hair or something caught in the material. That what you're looking for?"

I nodded.

"Find anything?"

I shook my head. "I was just starting to look when you scared the holy hell out of me."

Hanna smiled wolfishly. She'd put on fresh lipstick and her thin lips glistened. "Sorry about that." She began unbuttoning her uniform jacket. "I'll help you look."

I didn't want her help; I wanted to go over every inch of the material myself. "Shouldn't you be on your patrol?" I said, hoping she would take the hint.

"I've got it covered. My boss'll never find out." She took off her jacket and laid it on a nearby shop foreman's desk. Without the bulky jacket, her figure looked a hundred percent better, which she obviously knew because when she bent over to examine the foam material her heavy breasts strained against her shirt.

"Was she a natural blonde?" she asked. "Or should I be looking for dark roots?"

Any erotic thoughts I might've had vanished. I felt a sharp anger at her insensitive remark. "Forget it," I snapped. "I don't need any help."

Deliberately I moved around to the other side of the squares of material and began my search. Hanna stood looking down at me, but I continued to ignore her, keeping my back toward her so she'd take the hint.

"I'm sorry," she said softly. "I didn't mean that. I guess this thing has got me on edge, too."

I didn't want to give her any encouragement, so I simply muttered, "Okay" and continued my inch-by-inch examination of the material.

She hesitated, then sank to her knees on the far side of the material. "I liked Helen. I want to help. I want to do something. We all do."

I couldn't ignore the appeal in her voice. Her remark might have been flippant and unfeeling, but I knew she really felt awful about saying it.

"Yeah, okay," I said. "I'm looking for anything that would link these blocks to Helen and that environmental chamber."

Silently she began examining the foam material, using her fingers, as I was, to probe the crevices. I saw metal chips, filament glass fibers, and an accumulation of dust and dirt the material had apparently picked up in the trash bin, but nothing that would link it to Helen's death.

"This stuff is nice and soft. Make a nice bed."

Hanna had worked faster than I and she'd worked her way around so she was kneeling beside me. She was caressing one of the foam spikes whose tip had broken off, moving her fingers sensuously over the foam material. "Wouldn't you like to have a bed made of this stuff?" she said softly. "It feels like a woman's breast."

Her words disgusted me. Her crack about 'dark roots' might have been unthinking, but this was a deliberate wedge. I checked my rising anger; I didn't want to put her down again. Maybe she simply had the sensitivity of a flea.

"Yeah," I said with a forced laugh. "I suppose so."

She looked straight at me with her eyes half-closed and her teeth nuzzling her wet-looking lower lip. "I doubt you'd have trouble getting someone to share a bed with you," she said from deep in her throat.

I had no desire to get caught up in an office intrigue with Hanna Carbo, so I ignored the obvious invitation and stood up. "Wouldn't work," I said lightly. "I've got a single bed." I began piling the blocks of foam material on the floor next to the trash container where MacDonald could have them picked up.

The rejection failed to bother Hanna. "I haven't," she said.

When I didn't respond, she stood up and began helping me stack the material. She paused, a block of the foam material cradled in her arms, and gave me a hard, direct look, her eyes bright. "Ben," she said. "How serious were you about Helen?"

I could've lied to her, or simply told her it was none of her business. But the courses I'd taken in employee relations said that you didn't do it that way. If you wanted to keep your employees happy and loyal, you engaged in dialogue. So I told her the truth.

"I'm not sure. Before I went on this last trip, we'd kind of drifted apart. But when I got back... I don't know. I guess absence doesn't make the heart grow fonder."

"I had the feeling she wasn't that serious about you."

I must have given her a strange look because she quickly added. "We used to talk out here sometimes. It can get pretty lonesome. I—I'm not so sure you really knew her."

I felt a hot indignation that this woman should try to tell me how Helen felt. How would she know what went on between the two of us? She had evidently hypothesized something from her conversations with Helen; something that was a lie. My voice was cold when I said, "We used to talk sometimes, too. I believe I knew her as well as anybody."

Hanna studied my face, debating whether to continue the subject. She knew she was probing an open wound. But I didn't move away. Maybe she really did know something of importance. Helen might have confided things to Hanna that she wouldn't tell me. I began to wonder just what they had talked about.

As though she could read my mind, Hanna said, "Why don't you come by my place this afternoon. I might be able to fill you in on a few things."

A knot of alarm began to form in my stomach. Was there some mystery involving Helen? Or was Hanna merely trying to get me to pay more attention to her?

"If you know anything about what happened," I growled, "I'd like to hear it—now."

She smiled with her lips tight and shook her head. "I've got to get back on my beat." She picked up her jacket and slipped it on. "Make it about four. That way we'll have plenty of time to put our heads together. I'm sure you'll find it interesting."

I watched her walk away, her wide hips moving with the smooth precision of pile drivers. I didn't want to go anywhere near her home. It could very well start something I was certain would be full of regrets. But if she and Helen had been friendly, she might shed some light on

Helen's strange behavior. Whether or not I could cope with Hanna's own behavior was beside the point. I had to accept her invitation, whatever strings might be attached. I just didn't like the idea of her pulling them.

Chapter 8

THERE WAS NO way I was going to get any sleep. I'd set the alarm for 2:00 so I could get in some time at the office before going back on duty at Colton. I could survive on around five hours of sleep, if I got it. It was going to take a long time for my metabolism to adjust to going to bed at 9:00 in the morning. I'd assumed that jet lag from my sojourn in Africa would help, but I was wrong. The muted pounding of the distant surf and the sound of cars on the boulevard were no longer soporific. Instead, their sound seemed to penetrate every cell in my brain. It was the same with sunlight. I had pulled the drapes, but brilliant shafts of light seeped through every crack like laser beams, all aimed directly at my bed.

But what was really keeping me awake was my subconscious. It would not stop going over Helen's death ad nauseam. Now I had insomnia to add to all my other problems. I'd probably never sleep again.

The fluttering beep of the alarm jerked me awake. I looked at my watch. 2:00. So I had fallen asleep. Thank God the insomnia was cured.

By the time I finished dressing I smelled bacon frying. In the kitchen, Jack was sorting through plastic carrying bags from Ralph's Market. He looked up when he heard me. "'Mornin'. How'd it go?"

"All right." I looked at the bags. "You walked all the way to the market."

He shrugged. "It wasn't far. Not more'n a mile. You were clean out." He nodded to the gas range. "Dinner's about ready."

I stared at the straight up eggs sputtering in the deep grease of the frying bacon. My God. The cholesterol level had to be astronomic. I dared not even think what was in the bags. Jack's idea of good food would put an ordinary person in the grave by the time he was forty.

But I didn't want to hurt his feelings. "Thanks," I murmured. "But I'm not very hungry. Did you get any orange juice?"

"Hell, yes. I know you like that junk food. So I got both."

I had to ask. "Both?"

"Orange juice and—" he lifted a half-gallon of whole milk from one of the bags "—milk. I got the kind that's fortified with vitamins."

I gasped. "They didn't have any non-fat?"

"Shit, you might as well drink water."

"That's fine," I lied. "What about the juice?" Thank the Lord there wasn't any way he could make a mistake with the orange juice. I was wrong.

"Got it." He went to the refrigerator and opened the door. He pointed with a triumphant grin. "Three cans."

"Cans? Frozen?"

"Yeah. Hell of an invention."

More like an invention from hell, designed to rob food of its natural juices. But this morning it would have to do. I had to take something or Jack's feelings would be shredded.

While I was sipping the watery orange juice and Jack was putting away an awesome amount of potential carcinogens, he said, "I was hanging out at the beach this morning. I figured some of those yo-yos might know where I could find a flat or something."

"Any luck?"

"Naa. But I found out something else."

"You mean it's loaded with pretty girls?"

"Yeah. There is that. But I also found out that all those guys aren't what they seem. If you want to know anything about this town, that's the place to go."

Remembering my own days on the beach, I said, "That's one thing about surfers. They're democratic. You get a real cross section."

"Yeah. In those sloppy shorts, you can't tell a rich kid from a dirt biker."

I looked at Jack's baggy British-style shorts and khaki singlet. "You should fit right in."

"Yeah. They like war stories." He took another bite while I wondered what his stories might be doing to the adventure-oriented minds of the surfers. "I found out something interesting about Colton Labs."

I froze, glass half-raised to my lips. "Colton? You found out something?"

"Maybe. Nobody seems to know much, except that something was funny. That's all I got."

Something funny? Could they be referring to Helen's mysterious death? The news must have hit the beach like a tsunami. They'd be talking about it for days. Or was it something else?

Jack said if I'd drop him off at the beach on my way to the office, he'd see if he could find out anything more.

"All right," I said. "But don't push it. I've already lost one friend.

I don't want to make it two."

I dropped Jack off near Newport Pier and drove back to the office. On the way, I stopped at The Vegi Restaurant and Health Store and grabbed a walnut burger with apple juice. Jack's jungle-conditioned metabolism might be able to cope with greasy food, but it would be acid time for me.

When I walked into the office, it was like walking into a church. Everyone was working, but it was a grim performing of the necessary. If someone had to talk on the phone or ask a question, their voice had the subdued quality of hard depression. Even Kim's elfin face was drawn into a mask of quiet grief. Her expression changed to concern when she saw me.

"Hi, boss," she said. "How'd it go last night?"

I tried to think of an answer that'd put a little more life in the atmosphere without sounding callow.

"Okay," I said. "My big problem was the same as Judd's—staying awake."

Kim and Mrs. Davis smiled. Judd Proctor turned from his switchboard and peered at me. Judd was tall and thin, and wore thick glasses. He disguised a receding chin with a short beard, and he smoked cigarillos, a combination he hoped would make him into a macho man.

He picked up on my cue and said, "You don't look too bad. I was afraid a little hard work might do you in."

"Wait'll tomorrow," I said. "A kid like me can miss one night's sleep. But I'm not so sure about two."

Kim said, "That detective, Mr. MacDonald, called a couple of times. I told him if it wasn't urgent to let you sleep. Did he?"

"Yes. Thanks."

"Any time."

"Would you see if you can get him for me?" I started to go into my office, then stopped. "Is Herb in?"

"At lunch time? Are you kidding? This is wheeling dealing time."

"Lunch? It's three o'clock."

She lifted her eyebrows. "So?"

I shook my head. I should know better. Herb's lunches could easily last an entire afternoon.

In my office I pulled the drapes across the picture window to cut down some of the sunlight bouncing happily off the waters of the bay. Today my psyche wasn't up to it.

I checked through the mail Kim had placed on my desk. It was surprising how much could accumulate in a few weeks. No surprises here—easily discarded junk mail or business-related correspondence. I caught myself reading a mail order catalogue for garden supplies and realized I was procrastinating. I didn't want to meet with Hanna Carbo. Whatever she had to say could only lead to trouble.

Still, if Helen's death was an accident, why did Hanna want to see me? She'd started to tell me something last night, then stopped. I had to see her. If all she wanted was a lover, I could always say no. And if it was only information she had in mind, I had to find out what it was.

I clicked on the power to my computer terminal and requested the data bank for Hanna Carbo's address. I could've asked Kim to look up the address in our files, but I was a little embarrassed about how my going to her home might look, and I preferred to skip the explanations.

I printed out a copy of the address. The street was familiar—on the north side of Costa Mesa. Not too far away.

The phone buzzed. When I picked it up Kim said she had Lieutenant MacDonald on line one. I punched the button and said hello.

"They tell me you took over her guard work," MacDonald said for openers. "You trying to prove something?"

I ground my teeth against mounting irritation. "I'm not trying to prove anything, I just wanted a chance to look around without going through a lot of red tape."

He surprised me by saying, "Good idea. Find anything?"

I told him about the foam material and if he could check it out. There was a tiny pause before he said, "I don't see much point to it."

"You still think it was an accident?"

"More than ever. Your guard was drunk."

I almost dropped the phone. I sat down so heavily the glass of the picture window shook. "You're sure?"

"Yeah. The blood tests showed a heavy concentration."

"That's hard to believe. She wasn't a drinker."

"Once was enough."

I had no answer. If Helen had turned into an alcoholic, she could have kept it hidden. Maybe that had been her secret. "Did the autopsy show exactly what killed her?"

"Electromagnetic radiation. A very heavy dose. She must have passed out in front of one of those high powered antennas."

"How? There's no way she could climb up to those antennas on the towers. Not if she was drunk. And there's no sign she was ever in that big test chamber."

"Nobody can answer that except her," MacDonald snapped. "So, unless you can come up with something to the contrary, it goes down as an accidental death."

"Don't worry," I said. "I'll damn well come up with something."

After I hung up I began to lose confidence. Could heavy drinking be why Helen had changed? If she was an alcoholic, how long had it been going on? I thought I was the one who might be changing. But now....

Had she really loved me? Was her withdrawal a means of protecting me, or of reaching out for help? Could I have done anything if I'd known?

Hanna Carbo. Did she want to tell me about Helen drinking? Or was it something else?

The questions kept piling up, each one leading to another like a maze with no beginning and no end. And that led me to yet another question. Would I ever know the truth?

I told Kim I wouldn't be back until tomorrow and drove out to the address the computer had given me. Hanna Carbo's house was an old frame bungalow with peeling paint on a quiet side street. Both sides of the street were lined with extraordinarily tall Washingtonia palms, their fronds motionless in the afternoon heat. A narrow cement walk led from the sidewalk between two patches of parched grass to a small concrete porch. Hanna's new Honda Civic was sitting on a badly cracked cement driveway beside the house.

At the front door I pushed the rusty door bell and the building erupted with a shattering roar. The blast hurled me back down the walk like a disjointed tumbler. I hit the ground heavily, my breath driven out by the impact. I tried to see, to hear, but my eyes were seared with a pure white ball and my ears rang as though my head was imprisoned inside a huge bell someone was beating with a jackhammer. I sucked in air and tried to move but my arms and legs refused to obey.

Searing heat brought me to my knees; heat and the ugly crackling sound of fire. Shielding my face with my hands, I stared at the house through a red haze. It was wrapped in flames, the roof already sagging into the inferno. My God! Hanna was in there!

I struggled to my feet and groped toward the source of the heat, straining to see. Heat, intense, burning heat stopped me just as a secondary explosion hurled me to the ground. Then I felt hands grabbing me, pulling me back. I struggled to break free and I heard my voice shouting that Hanna was inside. But the hands would not let me go and they forced me to the cool concrete of the sidewalk where tears washed my burning eyes.

Chapter 9

SUICIDE! GOD, how I hated that word. The fire fighters said Hanna's death was either suicide or an accident. They wouldn't know for sure until their investigators examined the debris. It appeared that the house had been full of natural gas that was ignited by a spark from the doorbell. The way they explained it, people who attempted suicide by gas generally turned on every burner they could find—stove, oven, heaters, everything. Neither the explosion nor the fire would destroy that kind of evidence. An accidental gas leak would be harder to pinpoint.

But, hell, anybody could have turned on the gas. And if it was an accident, there was the question of why Hanna failed to notice the telltale fumes.

"Maybe she was sleeping," Clint Hemet suggested. "She'd been working all night."

"I doubt it," I said. "She was expecting me."

It was now 5:00 p.m. and I was in Hemet's office where I'd come to tell him about Hanna before I went on guard duty. At the hospital they'd given me an examination and certified nothing was broken. My eyes had taken a couple of hours to recover from the flash, but they'd washed them out with something that felt like Visine. They'd wanted me to stay in the hospital for observation, but I just didn't have the time. At the moment, my health was not important.

Something strange was going on at Colton Labs and the only way to find out what was to be there. I'd explained my suspicions to MacDonald when he'd stopped by the hospital. As usual, he'd said he would look into them, which I interpreted to mean that he had cases with higher priorities.

So I checked out of the hospital, put on my uniform and went to see Clint Hemet.

I paced the carpet of his office, ignoring protests from my aching body. Things were happening over which I had no control, no insight. I detested the feeling. I wanted to do something. I wanted to lock my hands, my thoughts, on something concrete. But there was nothing, only a malaise that could be caused by my unwillingness to accept the truth.

Hemet sat on his couch drinking coffee and watching me with a speculative pursing of his lips as though I was a problem he wished would go away quietly.

"Hanna Carbo," he asked abruptly. "Did she drink?"

The thought had crossed my mind. Hanna might have been too drunk to have smelled the gas. Instead of sleeping, she might have been unconscious. I avoided answering because I wasn't sure. On her security clearance form she'd said she wasn't a drinker, but she could've lied. After all, Helen had also said she didn't drink and we knew that was a lie.

"The autopsy will tell us," I said. My uniform felt tight, hot. I unbuttoned the jacket. "They might be able to determine if she was unconscious at the time of her death—like Helen."

Hemet put down his coffee cup and made a steeple of his fingers in front of his face. He tapped his fingers together which I suppose was to make me think he was giving his words a lot of deep thought. "Are you suggesting her death was in any way connected to Colton Labs?"

"I'm not suggesting anything," I said. "Only it seems a heavy coincidence that two of my guards should die so close together."

"It's possible."

I had the feeling that Hemet, like MacDonald, was avoiding a really hard look at what had happened. In a way, I could understand Hemet's reluctance to face the issue. If there was something going on here at Colton, it was his job to know about it. And if he'd failed, it could cost him his job. It was in his best interests not to dig too deep.

But if he did know of something and was covering it up, I meant to find out what it was.

"You know as well as I do," I said, "what lengths a lot of countries would go to for the kind of technology you're dealing with here. Or your competitors, for that matter."

"We're well aware of that. We run a highly secure operation. If you don't believe it, talk to the GAO and Defense Investigative Service inspectors. You know how that works."

That was true enough. Since all our guards had to have DOD security clearances, S&R Security was subjected to a mandatory DIS security inspection every three months. If there were any irregularities, the system was designed to catch them. Except that the system didn't always work. The Walkers had been trusted and cleared employees of the Navy. And there was the Bell case at Hughes. And Esterhaus at AA&E. And Aimes, the CIA turncoat. And the F.B.I. agent, Robert Hanssen, lead a double life for years.

I was reaching for straws and I knew it. Colton Labs had recently received a commendation from DIS for their security. And after the fervor caused by the rash of security breeches at Los Alamos, all companies had tightened procedures. It would be virtually impossible to conceal any sort of security breach. If something was going on at the lab, it'd be stupid to draw attention to it by killing somebody.

"How about non-classified projects?" I asked. "The government doesn't get involved with those."

"True. However, in a sense, we have no non-classified projects. Our customers wouldn't be interested in anything that wasn't way out at the edge of the state-of-the-art. All our data is either classified or proprietary. Hell, the electronics business is so competitive today you've got to play your cards right up against your buttons. We're vulnerable. We're into microchips, nano-technology, electro-optics, digital signal processing, HPM weapons, communications—really advanced technologies. We're dealing with submicron electronic gate widths in millionths of millimeters.

"Right now we can etch lines so fine we can put more than a thousand on a human hair. Eventually, we'll be able to put all the books in the world on a crystal less than two-hundredths of an inch square."

All the books in the world? I was stunned. I couldn't grasp those kinds of numbers. I'd been working with computers since high school, but like most operators I never gave much thought about what went on inside the machine. "That kind of research would be worth a fortune to somebody, even if it isn't classified."

"Making sure they don't get it is my job. Hell, if we thought there was anything funny about the death of Cotrell or Carbo, we'd be turning the building upside down. We've got to protect our research."

I dropped into a chair feeling as though a door with a glimmer of light on the other side had been slammed in my face.

"Personally," Hemet said in a lower tone. "I think Helen's death was an accident or it was something personal. I don't see any connection between her and Hanna Carbo. In any event, it had nothing to do with company security."

I wiped my face with both palms. He was probably right, and I was wasting my time. What did I have except a nagging suspicion— and an insight into Helen's personality that even her parents didn't have? You couldn't possibly spend as many hours just talking as we had without getting to know something about a person's values.

But Hanna Carbo was another matter. All I really knew about her I had learned from her resume. She'd said she had something to tell me.

Was it something about Colton Labs? If my guards were off base, I'd better find out what the hell was going on or we wouldn't just lose the Colton contract, we could lose them all.

"I'm going to stay on here a couple of more nights," I said. "If there was anything going on involving either Helen or Hanna Carbo, I should be able to get a lead in that time."

Clint Hemet stood up as though he wanted to bring our discussion to a close. "I know these accidents have hit you hard," he said. "Especially with one right on top of the other. But don't forget, you're not alone on this. You've got all the help you want from MacDonald and from me and my staff. We want this thing resolved as much as you do."

"I know," I said. "I'm probably swinging at shadows."

He walked to the door and held it open. "In a couple of months all this unpleasantness will be cleared up. We can all get back to doing our jobs. You'll see."

I moved to the door. "Well, thanks anyway. I've got a substitute coming in for Hanna. I'd better go meet him."

"Hold on a minute." Hemet crossed to the coffee table and picked up a copy of the company newsletter and handed it to me. "Here. You might want to read this. There's a good story about Helen."

I took the newsletter, wondering if I wanted to read the article. Why irritate wounds that had not even begun to heal? But Clint Hemet wouldn't know that. He thought he was being helpful.

"Okay," I said. "Thanks."

As I walked away he said, "Let me know if anything develops."

"Okay," I said, but in reality, I had no confidence in my ability to know if anything did develop. I didn't even know what I should be looking for.

Besides, there was no way I could analyze the situation objectively. My mind was a jumble of unrelated thoughts, painful memories, and suspicions. Could I really be wrong about Helen, about Hanna Carbo, and about the way each had died? Nothing seemed to tie together and yet, everything seemed to be related, like a cryptographic puzzle. When you appeared to solve one aspect, it screwed up the remainder.

The only time I remember having had such a feeling of confusion was when I was twelve years old and my foster parents had taken me camping in the Angeles Forest up by Lake Arrowhead. I figured it was a good time to run away again and I had headed into the hills, thinking I could find my way down to San Bernadino where I could get a job or something.

Except I'd gotten lost. I'd wandered through the woods for hours looking for some sign of a trail that would take me to a highway where I could catch a ride. But every turn seemed to take me deeper into the woods or ended in a dead end. As the hours went by and I was no closer to finding my way, I gave up trying to find a highway. All I wanted to find was a way out.

And when I could not even do that, an unfamiliar feeling of panic began to grow. It was an ugly sensation, bordering on fear and childhood nightmares. I fought to shake it off. For the first time in my life I was unsure of my next move, unwilling to make any move for fear it might be another dead end.

During the years following, I'd often wondered what would've happened if darkness hadn't come and I'd seen the lights of Arrowhead Village. Would I have broken and run screaming through the woods? It had worried me for a long time, and I swore I'd never again have to experience that awful feeling of total disorientation.

The solution was careful planning and preparation. My paths now were always well blazed and plotted. Even with Helen, I had held back, unwilling to abandon my intellect to pure emotion. Each time I'd sensed myself slipping into a realm of uncharted emotions, I had subconsciously retreated. Don't be hasty. Make sure the trail is well defined before plunging ahead. If Helen had really been in love with me, my caution must have been frustrating as hell.

But now my mounting confusion was not due to a lost love. It was because I didn't know which way to turn for answers. Every time I seemed to have a grasp on something, it slipped through my fingers like quicksilver. The thing to do was take my time, keep my eyes and ears open, and try to sort through the tangle. Patience. It was all I had.

Walking between the buildings on the way to the main gate to check in, curiosity overcame aversion and I glanced at the newsletter Hemet had given me. On the front page a picture of Helen in her uniform brought a stab of pain. The story was a brief account of what was considered an accident. There was no mention of alcohol in her blood.

As I finished reading, I noticed in an adjacent column a picture of a strikingly beautiful, dark-haired girl soldering a printed circuit. She looked familiar. Then I recognized her. She was the girl Harry Deen and Eddie Hooker had been photographing the morning Helen had been found; the one who had asked me about Helen.

The caption beneath the picture said her name was Samantha

Cazzoli. For some reason her name was also familiar.

Why did I know that name?

She hadn't told me. And when Harry Deen had stopped me that morning, he hadn't introduced her. No. I hadn't heard it; I had seen the name written somewhere. That was it.

Where?

What had I been reading that contained a list of names? The log book. Her name had been in the log book, meaning she had worked overtime the night Helen died. Now why would an assembly line worker be working overtime when the line was shut down?

Suddenly the tangle had another loose thread, and maybe pulling it would loosen the entire puzzle—or create more knots. I would probably feel better if I took the advice of Hemet and MacDonald, and forgot the whole thing. All I had to do was accept the accident report and allow everything to slip back to normal as though nothing had happened. I could go back to my uncomplicated, uncluttered, predictable existence, the way life was supposed to be if you worked at it. That would make a lot of people happy, especially, I was sure, Herb Stax. Herb didn't like rapids in the smooth stream of his life any more than I did.

But I could never resist untangling snarled lines. Chaos bothered me. That seemed to be ingrained in most orphans. The desire for stability, for a permanent home, for parents who would always be there was reinforced with every rejection until the search for order was almost an obsession.

By the time I located Samantha Cazzoli in the PCB assembly area it was almost time for the shift to end and she was clearing her workbench. As usual, she was wearing an eye-popping sweater and tight pants. I was again struck by the healthy look of her dusky skin. She couldn't have been sick a day in her life.

When she saw me she stiffened slightly and I thought a quick look of fright appeared in her dark eyes. I wondered whether it was because of me or my uniform.

"Miss Cazzoli?" I asked.

"Yes?" She said the word with a slight twist to the sibilant.

"Have you got a minute?"

"For what?" Her tone was belligerent and guarded.

"Nothing important," I assured her. I showed her the story about Helen in the newsletter. "Remember. You asked me about this?"

She nodded, but refused to look at me. "Everybody knows. Everybody talk about it."

"Did you know her?"

She looked at me as though I was accusing her of Helen's death. "Me? Know her? How I know her?"

I smiled as warmly as I could. "Just asking. I've been asking everybody. A girl as beautiful as you... I thought you'd probably know everybody."

Her face smoothed. This was familiar ground. She probably got propositioned several times a day. She turned back to her workbench and continued packing her test instruments into a small storage case.

"She friend of jours?"

The uncertainty had gone from her voice. I was just another jerk trying to make a hit on her.

"Yes." I let my feelings come through as I added, "A very...close friend."

"I'm sorry." She looked at me for an instant as though she was going to add something, then silently continued her work.

"I just thought that, since you were working late that night, you might've seen her."

This time when she looked at me, the fear was back in her eyes, and there was no mistaking the way her shoulders hunched into a hostile set. "Why jou think I work late?" she practically snarled.

"Your name was on the sign-out log book. You were here until after ten o'clock."

"Oh, jou mean that night," she said and the relief in her voice was so apparent I wondered if it was real. "That night Mr. Deen and Eddie Hooker taking pictures. They make me stay late. They say I get overtime."

"Oh? I saw them taking pictures of you the next morning."

"Next morning, too." She smiled, her face radiating pleasure. "They like me for the pictures."

They'd made a good choice. She was clearly the most photogenic of the women on the line. When she smiled her sultry, surly beauty came alive. Her skin was an olive gold, unblemished, tinted with a faint blush of pink in her cheeks that made me think of a dusky rose. Her eyebrows were thick and black, arching in a natural curve that highlighted her liquid brown eyes and slender nose. Her lips were wide and full with a petulance that matched her suspicious gaze. In repose, they gave her face a defensive, sullen look. But when she smiled, it was as though she had suddenly swallowed a rainbow.

From the way she moved, the way she responded to my tonal inflections, I knew she was very much aware of her effect on men. And apparently enjoyed their admiration, which might be her vulnerable point.

"You should be in the movies," I told her. "You're wasting your talents here."

She paused in clearing her workbench and looked sideways at me, her eyes suspicious, as though she'd heard that line many times, but still liked to hear it. "Jou think so?"

"Sure. You're better looking than Julia Roberts or J. Lo."

She turned to face me, flashing her smile. "Maybe I am in movies someday. Hollywood is not too far from here."

"That's right. Maybe I can help. Some of my best friends are producers."

She stopped smiling and her eyes frosted. Her voice reeked of suspicion and her lips curled as she said, "Who? Who these producers jou know?"

"Oh." I tried desperately to remember some names that would impress her. "Nobody really big. John. John Cameron. Ah, Mike— that's Mike Douglas. Steve Spielberg a little." When I saw the disbelief in her face, I hastily added, "I'm a member of the Balboa Yacht Club. They come down to sail with their friends. I crew for them all the time."

"Oh." With my credentials established, the smile came back. But now it was different. Now there was a calculated look in her eyes. "Maybe jou remember my name when jou talk to these producers. Cazzoli. Samantha Cazzoli."

"Sure, Samantha," I said. "But do me a favor."

Her face went blank and her voice hardened. "What kind favor?"

"Helen... The girl who was...who died... If you can think of anything that might help me find out what happened to her, will you let me know?"

The suspicion cleared from her gorgeous face, but the smile failed to return. "Sure. But I don' know nothin'. I never see that girl."

"Okay. Thanks anyway. And next time I see Mike or Steven, I'll mention you."

"I have pictures," she said as I turned away. "If they want, I got. With clothes. No clothes." She pulled her shoulders back to display her incredible bust line as though to insure I would keep her in mind. It was a wasted gesture. I could not have forgotten her under torture.

But there was one thing I could not forget. I retained an indelible image of Harry Deen taking pictures of Samantha Cazzoli—in the day time. Harry Deen would not work five minutes overtime for anybody unless it was the company president. And then they'd have to threaten to take away his cushy job if he didn't

So she was probably lying about working with Harry Deen that night. I wondered why.

Chapter 10

GROWING UP, I'd been lonely much of the time. This would have been a surprise to most of the people in my life because I usually wore a smile and bad things didn't appear to bother me much. They didn't know I was covering up bitter resentment and hurt because I felt that I'd been denied the good things of life.

When I got older, the loneliness had stopped hurting, but it hadn't gone away—not entirely.

Then I'd met Helen and the pain had vanished. I had a friend who would not desert me; someone who cared about my life, my hopes and my dreams.

Now the loneliness was back.

God, but this place was lonely at night. Inside the huge building, it was like being isolated inside a giant, living entity, sleeping now, waiting to come alive with the rising sun. By eleven o'clock, I could almost hear it breathing, almost feel its slow coursing pulse.

I was glad when I arrived at the storage bin where I'd left the foam material for MacDonald. Giving it another careful examination would get my mind away from the emptiness of the building and the emptiness in my life.

The material was gone. But so was all the trash in the bin. Had the trash collectors picked it up, or had MacDonald? Maybe he hadn't believed that checking it was worth the effort. If he was already convinced Helen's death was an accident, there would be no reason to check the material. In the morning I'd call MacDonald and find out if he was still on the case—if there was a case.

Moving through the manufacturing areas, past the silent machines, I tried to visualize what Helen might have seen that had cost her life. Clint Hemet had said there were secrets to be guarded. But nothing I saw looked ominous. There only complex-looking display consoles and control panels in various stages of fabrication and assembly. And how could a black box be made to give up its secrets to anyone less than an electronics engineer? I was not capable of deciphering the secrets of the silent electronics, and I was sure, neither was Helen.

Only in the environmental test area were any of the machines alive. On computerized control panels, lights glowed and blinked; automatic pens silently scribbled lines on recording paper— electrocardiograms of a machine's fight to stay alive inside one of the torture chambers. Some of the smaller chambers had windows in the thick doors, and I could peer through at the test subject inside. It was usually a small module or component, endlessly repeating electronic or mechanical tasks. There were no sounds except, occasionally, the low hum of an electric motor.

But I had little interest in the small environmental chambers. I moved past them to the big EMI-Tempest anechoic chamber. Bill Holtz and his crew had departed and their test equipment was shut down. I examined the devices carefully. To an electronics engineer, something might have seemed out of place, but I could see nothing that looked even vaguely suspicious. I had the feeling Colton's engineers and scientists were working so far into the future that even an EE with a Ph.D. would be unable to simply walk in and tell what they were doing. So what could a person with a B.A. in Business Administration expect to find?

But I also possessed a hard determination, so I ignored my instincts, clicked on the lights and slid aside the heavy metal door leading into the big chamber.

The chamber looked exactly as I had last seen it, with a narrow path through the foam material leading to the black box containing the radar antenna sitting on a pedestal at the far end. To me, the metal box looked ominous—dark, massive, ugly. Maybe it was only because I knew it could kill. But it was dead now.

I walked down the aisle and put my hand on the dark metal in front of the slots in the face of the antenna. The metal was cold and had a slight slippery feeling. I wondered what it was made of. Titanium, maybe. They'd said it was hardened to withstand the blast of an atomic bomb. I suppose that meant if it wasn't hit directly.

Suddenly my hand began to tingle. I jerked it back. The damn thing was on! But that was impossible. I had seen the controls before I came into the chamber and they'd all been off. Something was wrong as hell!

Behind me I heard the heavy door slide shut with a soft thud. I sprinted down the narrow isle in growing panic, but before I could reach the door the lights went out and I was in absolute, total blackness.

Still, I knew the location of the entrance and I was able to move quickly to the door. I groped and found the handle and tugged. The door wouldn't budge. I braced one foot against the frame and, using both hands, strained against the door. The edges of the handle bit painfully into my palms and the muscles of my shoulders creaked. It wouldn't move!

I was trapped in the chamber and the antenna was spewing deadly electromagnetic radiation. I felt nothing—no heat, no burning. But I knew the radiation was penetrating by body like atomic bullets, rending the tissues, lodging in my spinal column, plowing through my brain!

Oh, God! I strained against the door, ignoring the pain, willing all my strength into my hands and arms. It had to open. It had to!

Suddenly the handle ripped away in my hands. Now, there was no way to get the door open short of a crowbar. And the lethal radiation was ripping through my body.

I put my back against the door and tried to think. Was there another way out? I stared into the blackness and tried to form a mental picture of the chamber. There was no other door. The ceiling was too high to reach and was probably steel also. Calls for help probably could not be heard through the walls even if someone was passing by, which was not likely.

Then I remembered my radio. Quickly I took the unit from my belt and keyed the mike. "Ted. This is Ben. Can you hear me? Come in, Ted."

Except for a faint crackle, the radio was silent. Of course. This room was electromagnetically sealed. If high energy radar transmissions could not get out, neither could the far weaker radio waves. Besides, the strong radar signal was probably jamming them.

I put the radio back on my belt, fighting mental shock. I had to do something before the radiation destroyed my ability to think at all. I could visualize the powerful rays burning through my skin. Microwaves cooked by exciting water molecules. And the human body was 80-percent water.

So how long would it take to die? Ten minutes? An hour? Two? Even if they came searching for me when I failed to check in, how long would it take them to find me? Would I still be alive? If I was, would the radiation I had absorbed cause a slow, lingering death? Were my blood cells even now being destroyed by the billions? If they didn't find me soon, maybe it would be better if they didn't find me at all.

Damn! I couldn't just stand and wait. I had to find some way to shut down the radar. Maybe I could unplug the cables.

Dropping to my hands and knees, I felt my way along the narrow aisle to the massive antenna. The closer I came the more I was sure I could feel the radiation tearing into my flesh, penetrating deep under my skin and into my brain. Thus far, there was no pain, no feeling at all. It was an invisible, silent killer. But I knew it was happening and that made it worse.

When I reached the pedestal I felt for input cables. The only ones I could find were two that came from the back. I trailed them to a receptacle in the wall. By feeling the connectors I could tell that they were cannon-plugs with screw retainer rings. I unscrewed the rings and pulled the plugs. Immediately I felt better. With the radiation cut off I could stay in the chamber until I was missed and someone came looking for me.

I crawled back to the antenna and, just to be sure, I put my hand in front of the slots.

My God! The thing is still alive! I could feel a strong tingle and the hair on my hand and arm stood on end. The plugs I'd pulled were probably instrumentation cables. The power cables and radar wave guide from the transmitter must come through the floor under the antenna.

I put my back against the heavy box and dug my fingers under its edge and heaved with all the strength in my back and legs. They say that panic gives you superhuman strength, but it wasn't enough. The antenna housing probably weighed hundreds of pounds, and in addition, was firmly bolted to the pedestal base. I might as well try to topple the Empire State building.

Fighting panic, I willed myself to think. Okay. I couldn't turn it off and I couldn't break it. I'd have to find some way to live with it. If it only wasn't so damn dark. Maybe then I could see something I could use—some tool, some weapon. Stupid thought. There was nothing in the room but the antenna and the foam material. The material! Of course! It was supposed to absorb electromagnetic radiation. Maybe if I used enough of it....

There should be less radiation at the rear of the antenna. Probably only side lobes and reflections from the walls. That would be the safest place. I began gathering the blocks of foam material and stacked them against the rear wall. When I had a huge pile, I burrowed under and worked my way to the wall. I tore a square of blocks off the wall, then began beating on the metal with my radio in a measured cadence: bang, bang, bang, pause. *Bang, bang, bang,* pause. The sound wasn't loud, but maybe outside it would echo in the silent building. With about three feet of foam material covering me, the radiation probably wouldn't get through. And if it did, it would be very weak—probably.

I kept up the pounding. When one arm got tired, I switched to the other. I had no idea how long I had been working when there was an answering bang from the other side. I hit the wall with a quick tattoo, then paused to listen.

I heard a faint call. "Who's in there?"

"The guard," I yelled. "Let me out."

"Okay," the voice called. "Hang on."

I heaved upward, flinging aside the foam material and waded through the stuff until I bumped into the antenna. I was feeling my way around it when I heard a clang and the door slid open, letting in a flood of light. Silhouetted in the doorway was Joe Welts, the big janitor.

He peered into the darkness, and when he saw me stumbling toward him, he said, "Hey, man. How'd you get locked in there?"

Which was a question I also had in mind.

Chapter 11

"IT'S NOT LIKELY you could receive enough ER the short time you were in the chamber to do you any harm," Clint Hemet said. It sounded reassuring, but hard to believe. I could practically feel my red and white blood cells withering and dying in the onset of leukemia.

It had been almost an hour since I'd been rescued and I was standing outside the test chamber explaining to Cal MacDonald and Clint Hemet what had happened. The watch officer at police headquarters had rousted MacDonald out of bed when I told him the trouble was at Colton Labs. Ted Olds had called Clint Hemet for me.

Now, one of MacDonald's men was dusting the hasp on the door for fingerprints while another took pictures. The Colton Labs night supervisor was hovering around the radar system's controls checking to make sure I hadn't wrecked the damn thing. It was he who had shut it down after I'd managed to reach Ted Olds.

Joe Welts watched the man dusting the door for prints and clucked disapprovingly every time some of the fingerprint powder fell on the floor.

"You feel up to answering some questions?" MacDonald asked me.

I felt worse than I looked. My uniform was streaked with dust and flecked with particles of foam material and my face and hands felt grimy. My muscles ached. I hoped it was only from the unaccustomed strain I'd put on them. I was sure that at any second my skin was going to break out with large patches of melanoma and my hair would fall out by the handful. But it was what was happening on the inside that worried me. I felt as though my body had been shot through and through with invisible bullets of neutrons and protons.

One good thing—If I had worms, it had probably killed them.

"Yeah, I'm okay," I lied. "But I'm not going to be much help. I was in there looking around when somebody closed the door and locked it. They turned on the system."

"You didn't see anybody?"

"Not a soul."

"We can check to see who was working late," Clint Hemet said. "It had to be an employee."

"Which gives us a couple of hundred suspects," MacDonald said dryly. "If he was crazy enough to sign out when he left."

"Everybody is supposed to sign out," Clint Hemet said.

"If they left," I interjected. "It would be simple to hide around here somewhere until morning. Then he could just start work as usual. We'd never find him."

"You've got a point," Hemet admitted, and his forehead wrinkled. "That's a security problem we should look into."

Cal MacDonald beckoned to Joe Welts. "Mr. Welts."

Welts walked over to join us, shaking his head. "That's not gonna work. There must be a million prints on that door, just like everything around here. 'Sides, nobody'd be stupid enough to leave a print if they was tryin' to kill somebody, now would they? Not if they ever went to a movie or watched some of them detectives shows on TV, or even read a book." He looked at MacDonald. "Hell, I bet I know as much about your job as you do. I used to watch NYPD all the time and them guys knew their jobs. Then there was that old guy, what was his name? Matlock. Yeah. And them guys on Law and Order. They're the best."

"Fine," MacDonald said. "Then you know what I was going to ask you."

"Sure. You wanna know did I see anybody. And the answer is no. I wasn't near this place 'til I happened to go by an' hear this bangin' noise. I figured it was one'a them tests. But I never heard no test like that. I figured somethin' musta come loose and was floppin' around and maybe I better see what before it broke somethin'.

"When I gets near the wall there, I know it's comin' from inside. Sounds like somebody poundin'. So I holler and somebody hollers back. Right quick I know somebody got hisself locked in. So I runs aroun' and opens the door and that's it. Good story tellin', huh?"

"Precise and to the point," MacDonald acknowledged. "You'd make a good detective."

"Yeah, I would," Welts said with a wide grin. "You got any openings?"

"Not at the moment."

"That's what I figure. Hell, I didn't want it anyway. You guys keep crazy hours. I got me almost a month here. Some day I'm gonna get me one a them twenty-five year pins, and I'm gonna retire with a good pension. 'tween that an' my social security I got it made. Right?"

"Right," MacDonald agreed. He handed Welts his pad and pencil. "Would you please write down your name, address and phone number for me?"

"Sure," Welts said, taking the pad and pencil. "I'd make a good witness." He cocked his head to look at Clint Hemet. "Hey, Mr. Hemet. Do I get paid if I have to be a witness or do I have to witness on my own time?"

"I don't know," Hemet said. "I'll look into it."

MacDonald turned to me. "Ben, if it hasn't occurred to you, you'd better have a doctor check you over. You might be all burned up inside like you were in a microwave oven."

My face must have gone white because MacDonald almost smiled. I refused to give him the satisfaction of knowing how worried I was.

"I feel fine," I said cheerily. "I'm sure I'd feel it if I wasn't."

Actually, I did feel it. Every microbe in my body was probably growing at an exponential rate because of the radiation and would soon come bursting through my skin like miniature Godzillas. As much as I hated going to doctors, I'd have to see Doc Blanchard. "But I'll take your advice right away," I added. "I'll have Ed Emblem cover for me here."

"No need for that." He glanced at his watch. "It's after midnight. We'll be here the rest of the night."

I left them and walked out to the gate where Ted Olds was nervously waiting. I gave him a quick run down on what had happened. I asked him to call the office when it opened in the morning. "Tell them I might be a little late getting there."

Then I drove home and checked the mirror to see if any telltale melanoma blotches had begun to form, or if my skin was starting to peel away from my bones. To my immense relief, everything looked normal. If there was tissue damage, the deterioration had not yet begun or the destruction was all taking place on the inside.

I woke up Doc Blanchard with a phone call and told him what had happened and he said he would see me whenever I was ready. I wanted him to meet me at his office immediately, but he pointed out that there was no treatment known for radiation effects, so there was no point in rushing in. The best thing to do was go to bed and get some rest.

Rest? With my entire body disintegrating? After I went to bed I must've tossed and turned for five or ten minutes before I was able to drift into sleep.

I was struggling to hold my disintegrating body together while its cells slowly evaporated when the cheerful chirping of the telephone jarred me awake. For once, I did not feel resentment for being disturbed.

I glanced at the LED readout on my bedside clock/radio. 1:45. Who would call me at this time of the night, especially when everyone expected me to be working all night at Colton Labs.

"Hello?" I croaked.

"Ben? Is that you?" The voice was muted, almost a whisper.

I almost slammed the phone back on the cradle. "Jack? For God's sake, it's the middle of the night."

"I'm sorry, Ben. I've been trying to reach you. I might have something if I can get out of this place alive."

I sat up in bed. "Where are you?"

"At a club. Stoney's."

I climbed out of bed, switched on the lights and began struggling out of my pajamas while holding the phone to my ear. "Stoney's?" Stoney's was a strip joint and pickup dive. "What are you doing in that joint?"

"I don't have time to explain. Just get your butt over here."

"I'll pick you up in fifteen minutes."

"Okay. I'll work my way out."

"What do you mean, 'work your way out?'"

"I'm in the women's dressing room. They'll try to stop me."

"Who will?"

"For Christ's sake, I can't talk now. Those two broads'll hear me. Just get the hell over here. Knock three times on the freight door around in back."

He hung up and the jarring click sent shock waves through my ravaged body. Who was after Jack? And why? Broads? What did he mean by that?

I finished yanking on my clothes in the bathroom and splashed water on my face. A surreptitious glance in the mirror still did not reveal any visible signs of rotting skin, which made me feel a lot better.

On the way out the door, I thought about calling the police, then realized it might be a mistake. I had no idea what kind of trouble Jack was in. If he'd wanted the police involved, he'd have called them instead of me. I only hoped we wouldn't both end up in jail. I'd prefer to spend my last few days of life enjoying the sunshine.

I made it to Stoney's in eleven minutes. The club is in the newly created center city mall, practically in the shadow of city hall. I parked a block away, surprised at the number of cars still in the area this late. Like most clubs in California, Stoney's closed at 2:00 a.m. Three or four young men were standing in front of the building, but there was no sign of Jack. My eye focused on a sign that had been plastered across the facade above the Door: Female Mud Wrestling.

Mud wrestling? What the devil was Jack doing here?

I sidled down an alley to the rear of the club. There was a small loading dock and a sliding door I thought might lead to the kitchen or to a food storage room. I wasn't sure whether this was the door Jack had meant, but it was the only one I could see.

I climbed up on the loading platform and rapped softly, three times. When nothing happened, I knocked again, louder.

There was a clicking sound as the door was unlatched and I helped slide it back, which turned out to be a mistake because I was confronted by a girl whose magnificent figure was barely covered by a bikini and a glistening layer of mineral oil.

"So you're the other one!" she snarled and launched a fist at my nose.

I ducked and grabbed her arm before she could pull it back. I twisted her around, pulling her arm up into a bar lock. I didn't want to hurt her, but I also didn't want her punching me out.

With the speed of a cat she leaned forward away from my pressure on her arm and grabbed my ankle between her wide spread legs and yanked. I fell flat on my back, pulling her down on top of me with a thud that knocked the wind from my lungs. I tried to hold her, but the coating of oil made her as slippery as an octopus and she squirted away.

Then she had my leg in a half cradle and tried to twist my foot off.

"Hey," I yelled. "Stop that. What the hell are you doing?"

For an answer she gave my foot a vicious yank. I bent the fingers of my hand at the knuckles and jabbed her in the kidney, trying not to make it too hard.

She yelped and fell down holding her side, screeching, "Foul! Foul!"

I knelt beside her. "I'm sorry," I said, ready to move fast if she recovered before I could explain. "I didn't want to do that. But you were breaking my leg."

"I'll break your balls," she gritted. She tried to get to her feet, but I grabbed her hand, the least slippery part of her, and bent it into a wrist lock that made her arch her back, causing her incredible breasts to point at me like twin cannons. She had marvelous trapezoids and pectoral muscles. She had to be into body building.

"Why?" I asked. "What the hell is going on?"

"What do you mean, what?" she yelled, getting her voice back to full volume. "You bastards wrecked our show!"

"Who did?" I said, knowing the answer even before I spoke. "I wasn't even here."

She opened her eyes wide and stared at me. Under the coating of oil I saw her lovely muscles tense. "You're with him. I heard him call you."

"No, no," I said quickly. "I came to get him. I'm on your side—I think."

"Not if I get him first." In one fluid motion she broke my grip on her wrist and was on her feet, moving with the grace of a dancer. She stood with her feet spread and her fists on her hips, glaring, as I struggled to my feet.

"Where is he?" she demanded.

"Look, I don't know what he's done, but let me talk to him. I'm sure we can work this out."

"Jill!" Another gorgeous, oily girl in a bikini had appeared from a hall doorway. "You found him."

She advanced in a half-crouch, her hands curved into claws. The first girl, Jill, half-turned to her. "It ain't him, Rosy," she said, disgust plain in her voice.

Rosy straightened her splendid body and I stared in awe at the way her muscles rippled.

"Shit!" she said. "So where is the bastard?"

"I think he knows," Jill said nodding toward me.

"So—we make him tell us." Rosy began circling to get behind me. Jill crouched for an attack, unsure whether to follow the other girl's lead.

"Wait," I implored. I had no desire to fight two large, enraged females. They looked as though they had plenty of experience at dismantling hopeful men. "I'll help you find him," I volunteered. "But no fighting."

Rosy hesitated, her bikini top straining. "You're not shitting us?"

I pressed my slight advantage. "No. I don't know what he's done to get you so mad, but I'm sure—"

I was interrupted by Rosy's growl, "The son-of-a-bitch ruined our act." She had beautiful teeth, incredibly even and white. I was staring at them in awe as she added, "I'll tear his heart out."

I believed her. With those canines she would have the killing power of a saber-tooth tiger.

"Act?" I said. "You mean mud wrestling?"

Jill looked down at her body. "Oil. We do oil."

"You never been here? You've never seen the show?" Rosy

sounded as though she thought I was some kind of freak.

"Nope."

"You don't know what you missed."

If these two amazons were examples, I had some regrets myself. "Women wrestling," I said. "That can't be too entertaining."

Jill suddenly giggled. "Boy, are you gonna be surprised."

Rosy smiled, her wonderful teeth highlighted by her glistening face. "Ain't that the truth." She looked at the open door and shivered, hugging her arms around her. "Jesus, I'm freezing. Close the damn door."

I slid the big door shut, cutting off the chill ocean breeze. Rosy said, "Ah, the hell with it. We'll take care a that snuff-bag if he ever comes back. I'm gonna take a shower."

"Me, too," Jill echoed. She turned to follow Rosy, then paused. "If you want to wait, I'll be ready in about half an hour. You can buy me supper."

She was silhouetted in the doorway with her weight on one lovely leg, her hands high, grasping the door frame, her amazing biceps distended, her deltoids writhing. Staring at her beautiful body made it very difficult to weigh the fun we could have against the work I had to do tomorrow. And I still had to find Jack. Why hadn't he met me at the door? There had to be a stronger reason than fear of these two women. So, like a fool, I shook my head.

"A rain check," I gasped. "Give me a rain check."

"Come back tomorrow," she said. "Ask for Jill."

She turned and stalked away, moving like a stately gazelle. I moved into the hallway and tried to decide where to begin searching. Jack had said he was calling from the woman's dressing room. If Rosy or Jill found him before I did, Jack was in big trouble.

I was turning to follow the girls when I heard a muted cry of alarm. I paused, listening. It seemed to have come from the floor above. It was quickly followed by the crash of breaking glass.

I raced down the corridor, searching for stairs. When I found them, I went up three at a time guided by sounds of angry voices and splintering furniture.

The stairs ended at a short, second floor hallway. The commotion was coming from the open door of a room on my right and I charged toward it. At the door, I paused. I wasn't about to leap into a room where all indications were that I could get my skull crushed. If Jack wasn't involved, I certainly didn't want any part of the fracas.

When I peered around the jamb, I saw that the room was a large, sumptuous office. There were five men in the room, three of them standing. One was lying on his side vomiting on an expensive carpet. Two huge and ugly men, who I assumed were club bouncers, had Jack by the arms while a smaller third man wearing a three piece suit and brass knuckles was driving his fist toward Jack's face.

I knew I was too late even before I leaped through the door. Except that the blow was diverted by Jack's kick to the man's throat. The man crumpled, clutching his throat and gagging. The bouncer holding Jack's right arm let it go to clamp his thick forearm around Jack's neck while he drew back his other arm to smash at Jack's face. I charged across the room, yelling and reaching for the man's arm.

But Jack was faster. His right hand, fingers rigid, was already powering up between the man's legs. The man grunted with anguish and his swinging fist faltered. He mewed with a high pitched keening sound and sank to his knees. The man pinioning Jack's left arm started to lever the arm up behind Jack's back, but Jack leaned forward, relieving the pressure on his arm as he stomped hard on the man's instep with the heel of his shoe. The man grunted and his leg sagged.

As Jack twisted away, he slammed his elbow into the man's jaw. Then he took the dazed man by the throat with his thumb and fingers. The man's yelp of pain was cut off in a strangled gasp. Jack squeezed and pulled and the man came over in a flopping dive, smashing into the side of a huge desk. Before the man stopped rolling, Jack drove his knee in the man's kidneys, then clubbed him in the temple with a calloused knuckle. The man sighed and relaxed, his eyes going blank.

Jack crouched and swung to face me, his left hand up and half-curled, his right held low, the fingers board stiff, his eyes like small blue rocks.

I held up my hands. "Hey, Jack. It's me."

The flint went out of his eyes and he straightened. His smile was like a death's head. "Welcome to the party."

I stared at the men on the floor. Two were motionless. The other two were writhing slowly and moaning. "Why did you call me? You didn't need any help."

"Not here. These guys are goons. It's those women. They were gonna kill me."

"You could've handled them." The two Amazons were big and probably very tough, but they certainly wouldn't be any trouble for Jack.

"They were women," Jack said as though I should be smart enough to figure it out for myself. "I couldn't hurt them."

I thought it was a strange code of ethics that would allow him to cripple or kill a man with no compunctions, but wouldn't allow him to protect himself against two marauding females bent on tearing him into small pieces.

"So?" I said. "Don't tell me you've never fought any females. Some of those Viet Cong were women."

"They were soldiers. These were in bathing suits, for Christ's sake. How can you fight somebody with boobs like balloons?"

We heard the sound of a telephone falling to the floor. One of the men was up and calling for reinforcements—or the police.

"Come on," I said. "Let's get out of here."

We charged down the stairs and were hurrying along the narrow hallway toward the rear entrance when a door opened and one of the Amazons, I think it was Rosy, stuck her head out.

"I hear sirens," she called over her shoulder. "Maybe..." She saw Jack, who was ahead of me, and her feral teeth bared in a snarl. "Hey! You're the guy. Jill," she yelled. "It's him! Come on!"

She surged out the door and blocked the hallway, her legs wide. I could tell, however, that her fighting was not going to be its most efficient because the top of her bikini was unfastened and she had to use one hand to keep it from falling off.

Jack froze. His eyes were fixed on Rosy's chest where she was waging a losing battle to keep the most critical portions of her breasts covered.

"Come on, Jill," Rosy shouted. "I've got 'im cornered."

"I can't," Jill shouted from inside the dressing room. "I'm naked."

"Oh, Jesus," Rosy muttered. She glared at Jack. She was so intent on keeping him from escaping, I didn't think she even saw me. "Come on anyway," she called harshly. "He can die happy."

Jack held up one hand. "Never mind. Tell her we'll come in there. We'll have a party."

The invitation stunned Rosy. He was volunteering to be dismembered. I could see confusion roiling her thought process. She backed a step, her features working, alternating between rage and a growing fear she might be dealing with a madman.

I took advantage of her confusion to pull Jack aside while holding up my other hand palm out in the universal sign of peace. Or stop. Which was just as good in this instance. "Look, ah, Rosy," I said. "This whole thing has been a mistake. I'm sorry Jack got carried away. I'll see that he gets punished for it and—"

She leaped on the word. "Punished? How?"

"Well..." I searched for some diabolic punishment that would appease her wrath. Then I grinned at her, disarmingly. "I had in mind a sex change operation. Let him find out what it's like on the other side."

Jack sucked in his breath with a sharp hiss. "Like hell," he snarled. "Don't even joke about it."

Rosy's beautiful eyebrows pulled into a frown as she let the thought percolate. Then they lifted. She looked at Jack and her splendid lips twisted into a sneer that flashed her sharp incisors. "No. No woman should be cursed with that miserable body. Just get him the hell out of here."

Jack growled and took a step toward her, but I got a firm grip on his arm and turned him toward the rear door. "Come on, Jack. Forget it. You've struck out here."

He glanced back over his shoulder at Rosy's Junoesque silhouette and muttered, "Regrets, regrets. What could've been." He lifted his voice in a sad farewell. "Try to forget me, Carlotta. It'll make it easier with the others."

"Up yours," Rosy shouted. "And don't come back." She went into the dressing room and slammed the door. An instant later it opened and she stuck her head out. "And I feel damn sorry for Carlotta, whoever the fuck she is."

Then her head disappeared back inside and the door slammed again. This time it stayed shut, which was fine with me. I had no desire to linger. If the men upstairs had been able to call for reinforcements, they could be arriving any second. I hoped not. I'd seen enough of Jack's reaction to threats. He was typical of those with utmost confidence in their ability to defend themselves, not instigating violence, but refusing to back away from those who had an equal confidence in their ability to make him back down.

The result for men like Jack was a momentary suspension of reason, an injection of adrenaline that blacked out that small part of the human brain conditioned to logic. It was an atavistic reaction, designed to save a troglodyte's life when confronted by Sabertooth Tigers and wooly mammoths. Such an instinct did not surrender easily to evolved social mores, not when it had been deliberately resurrected and honed to perfection. No, I did not want Jack to be challenged by any more antagonists.

Outside, the air was chilly, smelling of the sea. The pavement was wet from a delicate mist that sifted down from a low marine layer brought inland by the night's onshore breeze. I shivered and pulled my jacket tighter. Our steps echoed from the facades of deserted shops and stores. The sound of an approaching siren mingled with the fog. When we got in my 'vette, I started it and drove away quickly, wondering how a car could be so silent in the daytime, but sound like a jet taking off in the middle of a quiet night.

The danger that we might be followed by the bad guys didn't bother Jack Blucher. He was slumped in complete relaxation, his eyes closed, his body slack like a panther that had made its kill and filled its belly on the prey.

I was the one who broke the silence. "What the devil was that all about?"

Without opening his eyes, he said, "The word around is that club is where the action is. I wanted to see if there was any connection to Colton Labs."

"Action? What does that mean?"

"Dope. Guns. Whatever you want."

"In Newport Beach? You've got to be kidding."

He turned his head to stare at me. "Shit. Half the guys on the beach are between jobs."

"I know that. Some of them are actors, musicians."

He barked an explosive laugh. "Actors! Shit!" He relaxed back against the seat. "Anyway, they turned me on to that club. If something dirty was going on, they'd know about it."

"Helen wouldn't have anything to do with those creeps," I said. "I know her. It doesn't make sense."

"Maybe not. But the one who wanted her dead might. I heard they sell contracts."

"Contracts? To kill people?"

"If your girl was hit, somebody had to do it."

I recoiled from the thought. Not because Jack might be wrong—he was right—but because my mind rebelled at the idea that this town where kids still delivered newspapers on bright sunny streets and earned Boy Scout merit badges, and where people still dressed up to go to church on Sunday mornings, could harbor murder for hire. What the hell was going on in that dark, shadowy world? Had I been living in my own little ivory tower all these years, blind to what was happening in my town? Was there a connection between those creeps at the club and Helen's death?

The thought made me bitterly angry. The bastards would not get away with it, whoever they were. "Did you find out anything?"

"Didn't get much chance." Jack chuckled faintly. "I didn't want to get that heavy right away. I was laying the ground work, sort of, when I got carried away. Jesus, you should've seen it. Did you know they bid to wrestle with those women?"

"They what?"

"They bid on 'em." He saw my look of incredulity and added, "To wrestle. In some kind of oil. They come out and strut around, and the guys bid."

"So you bid."

He lifted a shoulder. "Some son-of-a-bitch kept toppin' me. We were up to thirty bucks and it was all the money I had."

"So?"

"So when they got to wrestlin', it looked like a hell of a lotta fun so I peeled down to my shorts and kind of hauled the other guy out and told him to get lost."

"Told him?"

"I, uh, threw him out and, uh, started to take his place. Everybody got mad. Started a damn riot. Those two broads tried to kill me—them an' everybody else."

I was dismayed, but not surprised. I only hoped this was not an example of Jack's adjustment to urbanization. For many years he'd lived at the forward edge of the battle area where might made right, both in and out of the combat zone. To suddenly drape him with a mantle of gentility might be more than he was capable of accepting. Maybe I'd turned a half-tamed tiger loose on Newport Beach with no leash.

"What happened upstairs? How'd you get into that?"

"Oh, that. Well, I was looking for a place to keep from getting my nuts busted. When I saw those guys in the office, I figured I'd have a talk. Well, shit, they're the ones I came to see."

"I sort of gathered they didn't have much to say."

"Maybe if I went back tonight I could turn up something," Jack added hopefully.

"No," I said quickly. "I think you've worn out your welcome."

"Yeah, I guess you're right. I might have a job lined up anyway."

That was good news. A job would keep him occupied and could greatly improve his adjustment to the community. "That's great," I said. Then a chilling through struck. "What kind of a job? Is it legal?"

"That's what I was going to ask you. I don't want to get in any trouble with the gendarmes. Is making porno movies legal in this state?"

"Porno movies? You?"

Jack looked hurt. "Well, why not? I got a good body—

considering."

"Yeah, okay." The thought of Jack Blucher as a porno stud opened entirely new vistas of comedy. Then my smile faded. "Where would they be making these films?"

"Right here someplace."

My stomach churned. Boschian cubby holes had been opening around me with frightening rapidity. Now it was pornography.

"Are you sure they're made around here? They usually make those things on the fringes of Hollywood."

"Yeah, I think so. On the beach yesterday, a guy was asking if anybody wanted to. He said the pay was good if you could produce."

"What guy? What'd he look like?" If I could get a description, maybe I could alert Mac or some of the guys who patrolled the beach area. They could pick the guy up and find out what was going on.

"Young guy. Big. Brown hair, kind of long. He was wearin' a t-shirt with some funny stuff printed on it."

A picture leaped into my mind—a big guy with longish brown hair on the set of Colton Labs. A photographer. Eddie Hooker? "What did the words on the t-shirt say?"

"Can't remember for sure. Something about abortion."

So it had been Eddie Hooker. Apparently, he'd found a way to make some extra money. He was probably even using Colton Labs' equipment. If Harry Deen found out, Hooker would be an ex-Colton employee.

"You'd better forget that," I said. "I think that guy is going to be out of business in a hurry."

"Shit," Jack snorted. "I could've been a star."

AS I GOT ready for bed, I kept a keen awareness for any new aches or pains. I had no idea about the complications of microwave radiation. Maybe it would start with your hair falling out like with chemotherapy. I checked my hair using two mirrors so I could see the back. Everything looked normal.

I thought worry about my health would keep me awake, but when at last I slipped into bed and snapped out the light, I found that my thoughts were about Helen. In the distance, I could hear the dull boom of surf and its pounding seemed as unrelenting as my feelings of guilt.

Would Helen still be alive if we'd never met? What dark secret had she harbored that had made someone want to kill her? I had to know, not simply because it might lead to the her killer, but also, so I could turn back from my own walk through hell.

Chapter 12

I FOUGHT MY way out of a drug-like sleep, blinking in bright sunlight. I turned and pain wrenched my muscles. Alarm flooded my body with adrenaline. Could the soreness be due to the unaccustomed strain when I'd tried to force my way out of that test chamber? Or was it a harbinger of something worse? I didn't like to think about what worse could be.

I toiled through my morning workout despite the fear I might be doing my tortured body more harm than good. To my intense relief, as I warmed up, the pain diminished. So it was, after all, only a case of strained muscles and tendons.

Strangely, I was feeling fine when I got to Doc Blanchard's office. It was a good thing. All he did was take blood samples which he said he'd send to a reliable lab for analysis. It would be several days before he received the results. Maybe he was just trying to make me feel good. He did say I should come in every week for a few weeks so he could see if the radiation had caused any progressive deterioration of cells or abnormalities in the cell structures.

I expected him to prescribe some medication, but he said that short of a bone marrow transplant, there wasn't much that could be done. And who was I going to get matching bone marrow from? The best chance would be from a blood relative, but if I did have any living relatives, I had no idea who or where they were.

At the thought, I felt the familiar mixture of despair and anger. Why couldn't my parents have left me some indication of my heritage? How could I ever rid myself of this burning resentment when my lack of heritage was continually coming back to taunt me?

Leaving the doctor's office, I used my cell phone to call the office and asked Kim Fuji to get me the address of Samantha Cazzoli. "She's an employee of Colton Labs," I explained. "But I don't want them to know about this. So check her out through the credit bureaus. I want everything they have on her."

In ten minutes, she called me back with the information. Samantha Cazzoli was not her maiden name. That was Samantha Lopez. She had been born in Mexico. She was now a U.S. citizen. She'd obtained her citizenship after her marriage to Lorenzo Cazzoli when she was sixteen. She'd divorced him when she was nineteen, four years ago. No children. She was buying a house out near Orange Coast College, which was a very nice neighborhood.

She bought heavily on credit, but always paid her bills, even though she was sometimes a little late. She drove a new Mercedes which she was also paying for. When I totaled up her house payments with her car payments and other things she was buying, she was putting out five hundred a month more than she was taking in. I wondered where she was getting the extra money.

Her house, when I got there, looked as though it was worth a fair chunk of money on today's market. It was new, or nearly new, in a recently developed area. The lawn and the trees had a raw look as though they hadn't been planted more than a few months.

The garage was built onto the house, California-style, and I parked in the driveway. I knew she wouldn't be home from work for a couple of hours, and if any neighbors were watching I wanted to look as though I belonged. I assumed that the garage would have a remotely controlled door so I took a variable-frequency remote control unit from my glove compartment and played with it until the door opened. I drove inside and closed the door behind me.

She hadn't bothered to replace the original cheap key-in-knob locks with good deadbolts so it was no trick to jimmy open the door from the garage into the house.

The door opened into a laundry room connected to a modern, sunny kitchen decorated in rich golds and yellows. It was pretty, but smelled of stale food and dried urine from a cat box in the corner. Under my feet the floor was gritty. There was a stack of dirty dishes in the sink. She hadn't completely shut off the faucets and a stream of water ran over the dishes with a sound like a miniature brook. The kitchen table still wore the remnants of a solitary breakfast which I took to mean she was living alone.

Even so, I paused to listen. The only sound was the soft murmur of the running water.

Moving cautiously, I went into the living room. It was beautifully draped and furnished, although the furniture looked as though it was Gold Key special.

I slowly pushed open the bedroom door and two huge cats leaped off the unmade bed. One of them sprang up onto a TV sitting on a VCR and arched its back with its tail rigid and its teeth bared. The other escaped past me in a scramble of fur and claws

I like cats, but not this one. I couldn't very well search the dresser with that cat looking as though it wanted to leave incriminating evidence on my body in the form of claw marks, so I moved out of the doorway to the far side of the bed, giving the animal plenty of room to escape. When it made no move to do so, I lifted a corner of the bedclothes and gave it a shake and at the same time hissed, "Scat!"

The cat launched itself in a dive at the open door. He was already running when he landed, and he shot around the corner and out of sight.

I began checking the drawers of the dresser. Samantha Cazzoli was as sloppy as she was beautiful; clothes were jumbled in the drawers as though they'd been tossed in directly from the dryer. I pawed through the mess knowing she'd never be able to tell if a search had been made. But all I discovered was that she had a taste for exotic underclothing and nightgowns, mostly red and black.

Her walk-in closet looked as though a gorilla had been searching for bananas. Clothes that weren't strewn on the floor were clutching desperately at hangers and nails. Dozens of colorful shoes, none which seemed to match, were interspersed with the clothes on the floor. All the clothing and shoes looked new or nearly new. Balanced precariously on a shelf that ran around the upper part of the closet was a mishmash of hats, hat boxes, more shoes, scarves, sweaters, skirts, steam-irons, hair-curlers, perfume boxes and bottles, and assorted unidentifiable objects.

But one of them I did recognize. A photograph album! Next to it was a topless shoe box holding video tapes.

I worked loose the box and the album from the tangle of shoes and clothing and carried them to the bed. There were no chairs so I sat on the bed, picking a spot on the rumpled bedclothes which I hoped the cats hadn't occupied. Before I opened the photo album, I sat staring at its cover.

Did I really have the right to pry into this girl's personal life? Just looking at the album made me feel unclean. Looking through it was tantamount to becoming a peeping Tom. But Helen was dead. And so was Hanna Carbo. And, perhaps, I was on the road to a lingering death. Hell, in a month I might be a vegetable.

I opened the album.

Most of the pictures were professional four-by-fives of Samantha Cazzoli, nee Lopez, in her sexy clothing or underclothing. Her sweater hadn't lied. She had one hell of a figure.

By the middle of the album, she had discarded the clothing and was posing in the nude. The last few pages were straight pornographic pictures showing Samantha making it with one man, then with two.

There were long shots and close ups. The faces of the men could sometimes be seen, but except for Samantha, all the participants were strangers. Most of the time the camera was focused on the genital areas or Samantha's face.

When I finished the album, feeling as though I needed a hot bath in Lysol, I looked through the box of video cassettes. Some had titles penciled with a black felt-tipped pen on the tape boxes, such as 'Me and one dude,' 'Me and two dudes,' and 'Me giving head.'

Then my fingers froze and I felt as though a powerful hand was squeezing my heart. The writing on one box read, "Me and Helen with Bill."

I stared at the cassette, overwhelmed by a desire to see what was inside, and at the same time, frozen by a chill of apprehension. Something inside me screamed, Throw it away! Helen is dead. Let her go in peace. Let her go with dignity. Don't open the lid of this Pandora's box. Don't put any more demons in your brain!

It wasn't true. How could I even be thinking such vile thoughts? There were hundreds of women named Helen. It couldn't be my Helen.

Clinging to the thought, I turned on the VCR and the TV. When I put the tape in, my hands were trembling so badly I almost missed the slot.

I sat clutching the comforter and waited while the video's leader flashed on the TV with descending numbers. There was no sound which was probably a blessing.

Then there in full color was Samantha Cazzoli in an office pretending to be a secretary. Helen—my Helen—came in. I wanted to claw my eyes.

Oh, God, don't go on with this! Stop it! Stop it now while you still have your soul!

But I couldn't stop. My eyes were fixed on the scene with the rigid intensity of hypnosis. I saw Helen walk behind Samantha, reach over her shoulders and unbutton her blouse, then begin playing with Samantha's full breasts. She was smiling, looking as though she was enjoying the lesbian role.

Could that be it? Could that be why she had changed? Oh, God, no!

Samantha got up and unbuttoned Helen's clothes and helped her take them off. Then she quickly stripped and the two of them began making love on a big couch, their bodies entwined, their mouths eager.

Oh, God in heaven! Was she acting? Was she being paid for this? Could anybody do such a thing for money?

I reached to shut the VCR off, ill with an overwhelming grief, when I saw a door behind the women open and two men come in. My hand froze on the controls. One of the men was the engineer, Bill Holtz. The other man was Ron Renbourne. They registered surprise when they saw the two naked women, acting with the stilted self-consciousness of amateurs. The girls jumped up happily and pulled the two men to the couch. The men's faces split into leering grins as the two women tore off their clothing and began to——

I yelled in rage and smashed the VCR's power button and the screen went blank.

I sat trembling, fighting back a rising tide of bile, my mind refusing to accept what I'd seen. The single thought that kept pounding through my mind was not why—it was when. When had Helen been forced to make such a filthy movie?

She couldn't have done it while we were going together. I'd have known. I'd have sensed that something was wrong. She'd never do such a thing unless she was forced to.

Blackmail! It had to be blackmail. But for what? And who?

Eddie Hooker! Jack had said he was into porno movies. And he knew Samantha! Oh, God, he also knew Helen....

He was dead! I'd kill him with my bare hands.

Oh, Jesus! How had he done it?

What terrible thing had he been able to hold over Helen's head that would make her perform like a prostitute in front of his filthy camera. If he'd used coercion, the threat of physical harm, she'd have told me. Except that I'd been thousands of miles away, rotting in a Ugandan prison.

But she could have gone to the police. They'd have put a stop to Eddie Hooker and his porno set-up in a hurry.

So why hadn't she? Something had kept her silent; had not only kept her silent, but had forced her to perform in the filthy movies.

I felt a shock of pain. Movies? Could there be more than one?

My hands trembling, I checked through the titles on the remaining tapes, but there was only the one with Helen's name on it. That didn't mean she couldn't have been in others, only that Samantha Cazzoli didn't have a copy. And if there had been others, who had she been with? Bill Holtz? Ron Renbourne? Or one of the men I'd seen in the still pictures with Samantha? It could've been any one....

God in heaven, could it have been more than one?

My memory burned with the words written on one of the boxes: 'Me and two dudes.' Could Helen, my Helen, have been forced to submit to assaults from two men? Or more?

I ground the heels of my hands into my burning eyes while my mind screamed for release, anything to stop the pain.

Ron Renbourne! I'd kill the bastard! But first I'd make him tell me what he knew about Eddie Hooker and his operation. How deep did it go? Who was involved? And was that why Helen had been killed? Or was it to prevent her from telling the terrible secret being used to blackmail her?

Did I want to know what it was? Did I have the right to know? She might've given her life to prevent its disclosure. Was she protecting someone? Who? And why? And at such a price. If so, did I have the right to make her sacrifice meaningless?

Then I suddenly felt as though I'd been touched by a leper. Maybe I was simply fooling myself. Maybe there was no blackmail, no threats.

Maybe Helen was no better than Samantha Cazzoli, willing to do anything if the price was right. How well did I know her anyway? How well can you really know someone? Was it possible that she had participated because she had wanted to?

She was a very sensual woman. The times we'd made love had left no doubts about her sexual capacities. I had assumed her total surrender was because she loved me. But maybe she was the complete hedonist, able to extract pleasure from sex with anyone? I'd heard of people who enjoyed making love with all the dispassionate pleasure they experienced in riding a roller coaster. Pure excitement. A tremendous thrill. Especially if it bordered on an out-of-control flirtation with death. Pleasure without love, a simple abrasion of the exposed roots of sensuous joy.

Could making love really be that casual? No involvement, no commitment? Just a mind-blowing diversion. Why not? After all, you didn't have to be in love with a roller coaster to enjoy the ride. Was it necessary to be in love with a sexual partner to enjoy the highest thrill of all?

Had it been like that it for Helen? Maybe if love wasn't necessary, then sensual people like Helen and Samantha were right. Do it with anybody. Cater to the temporary thrill. It was only a game. And if you were in love, it was simply a greater thrill.

Damn it, Helen wasn't like that. She was not!

I got up and leaned against the dresser, my head down, my temples throbbing. Samantha Cazzoli might be happy to get it on with anybody if the price was right. But not Helen! I knew her better than that.

I lifted my head, clinging desperately to the thought, trying to think of something that would block such ugly intrusions. Eddie Hooker. Ron Renbourne. Bill Holtz. Concentrate on those bastards. Let the hate and rage build until it wiped out all other emotions.

I turned to stare at the TV. How could Eddie Hooker afford that elaborate office set? And why did the thought of it pick at some dim memory? It was something in that film.

Could I stand to see it again? Could I afford not to?

Reluctantly, I turned the VCR back on and rewound the tape. I hesitated before I started it forward again, steeling myself for the shock, like a man in front of a firing squad waiting for the wrenching impact of the bullets.

Almost savagely I punched the play button and the tape began its insane parody. As I watched, I tried to divorce my mind from the two women and their macabre illusion of joy and tried to concentrate on the background.

It was the couch that triggered my memory. It was the same pale-gold couch Harry Deen was using in his movie set at Colton Labs. In fact, the 'office' in the film was the office set I'd seen.

The films were being shot right there at Colton Labs.

That meant it wasn't just Eddie Hooker. Harry Deen had to know.

With a sense of relief I didn't have to see more of the awful scene, I ejected the tape from the VCR and slipped it into my pocket. My hands felt unclean from just touching it, but I'd need it to convince MacDonald that Helen had been murdered. God, I dreaded having to show it to him.

I carefully replaced the other cassettes in the box and replaced it and the photograph album under the jumble of junk in the closet. I didn't want Samantha Cazzoli to know I'd discovered how she got her extra money. She might tell Eddie Hooker or Harry Deen, and I didn't want that to happen. Not yet. Not before I was finished with them.

The toughest part was getting the two ugly cats back in the bedroom where I'd found them. I tried to herd them in through the open door, but they refused to go, instead crouching away from me, their backs arched and their eyes filled with fear and hate.

After several minutes of charges and skirmishes, I began to really hate cats. Dogs were so much better. You could deal with dogs. You could talk to them and they would at least do you the courtesy of listening.

Cats, I began to realize, were like some people—they couldn't be made to do anything unless there was a reward at the end. These two worked cheap. All it took after I got my brain focused on the problem, was a piece of cheese from the refrigerator tossed on the messy bed When Samantha got home there would be nothing left but an ugly stain, which would fit right in.

By the time I climbed into my car the burning anger had returned. I was no longer simply trying to find who had murdered Helen. Now I wanted to watch someone die!

Chapter 13

THEY SAY WHEN an animal is killed by a predator, the animal doesn't feel pain because it immediately goes into shock. I used to believe that. Then I saw a picture of an antelope being eaten by a pride of lions while it was still alive. Its head was raised and it was bleating, its eyes stark with pain and horror. That's how I felt.

At first I was in deep shock, my body wooden, my senses deadened to all feeling, unable to think coherently. But the shock quickly wore away and bitterness flooded my brain like acid. My initial refusal to believe was replaced by black shadows of doubt.

To hell with the evidence. Pictures had been known to lie. I absolutely would not allow myself to believe Helen could've been involved in that cesspool. And if the person I saw had been Helen, she could not have been involved willingly.

But what really gnawed at my guts was the ugly suspicion that I might be wrong, that I might have meant no more to her than any of those other 'johns.'

I dreaded meeting with Clint Hemet, Cal MacDonald and Herb Stax. What I really wanted to do was crawl in bed and pull the sheets over my head. But the memories would be under the sheets with me and I would, in the end, go raving mad.

So I went to the meeting in Hemet's office at Colton Labs and sat in agony while they looked at the tape, my eyes burning and my stomach knotted. When Hemet at last shut off the VCR, they sat silently staring at the blank TV screen, their faces closed like fists, cautious.

I held my own face stony and wooden. But my blank expression hid nothing. They knew how I felt. That's why they were silent. They didn't want to hurt my feelings. They couldn't know it was too late. My feelings would bleed forever.

Cal MacDonald broke the silence. "They've got a sweet little setup going for them. No overhead. All the equipment, the electricity, all the sets charged to Colton."

"Yeah," Herb Stax agreed. "I'll bet Harry Deen even charged the tapes to the company." He was talking slower than I'd ever heard him, and his voice was low and gritty as though he, too, was suppressing a mounting anger. "And that son-of-a-bitch Renbourne... I'll kill the bastard. I'll bet he's the one got her involved in this."

"Deen probably got the guys to work for free," Clint Hemet said. "They might even have paid for the privilege. I doubt the girls worked for nothing, especially that Cazzoli broad. They must've been paying her a chunk of dough."

I noticed Hemet had not included Helen. MacDonald was not as diplomatic. "I figure they were paying the men, too. It looks like Cazzoli was working for money. But we didn't find anything unusual about the Cotrell girl's finances. Unless she was stashing the money someplace under another name, she had to be doing it for some other reason."

"You're damn right," I said, and they all turned to stare at me as though they wished I wasn't there. "She had to be...doing those things because she was forced to. I don't know what they had on her, but she'd never do something like that unless they had a gun at her head."

"I agree," Herb Stax said quickly. "I've known her since she was a kid. Besides, we couldn't get her bonded if she wasn't as clean as the cheeks of a Dutch girl's ass."

"People change," MacDonald said. "Maybe she was into drugs or booze. Most hookers are."

I felt a rush of anger that brought me out of my chair, struggling for words of denial. Herb put his hand on my arm, pushing me back. "You've got no reason to say that," he said and now his voice was firm and hard. "You've got no proof she was a hooker, or into drugs or anything else."

"That's right," Hemet said. "There might be no connection between this and the alcohol you found in her blood. Anybody can take a drink. There's no reason to think her death was connected with this."

"That's right," Herb Stax said. "There's not one shred of evidence to connect her death with either the alcohol or this tape. Maybe this was the only one she made. We might never know why."

"Money." MacDonald's voice was cold and cynical. "It doesn't matter how much you've got, you always want more."

"I don't believe that." My voice sounded flat, dead. "I don't know how they made her do it, but I do know she'd never make that film unless she had to. She was going to blow the whistle on them, so they killed her."

"Now wait a minute," Clint Hemet yelped. "We just got through agreeing there might not be any connection. Colton Labs isn't necessarily involved—"

"Colton Labs is involved whether you like it or not," I snapped. "Harry Deen and Hooker are your employees. They used your facilities and your equipment. And she was murdered on your property by one of your people. Don't give me that crap about not being involved."

Herb Stax was on his feet behind me, his hands on my shoulders, pushing me back in my chair. "Hold on, Ben. Clint didn't mean it the way it sounded. He's got a job to do, that's all. You'd be saying the same thing if it was you."

The anger drained and I slumped in the chair. Herb Stax was right. Hemet was probably scared to death about his job. Harry Deen was making porno films right under his nose and he didn't know anything about it. As head of plant security, that wasn't going to look good on his record. Add that to Helen's death and his record was really tarnished. He wasn't just looking at a pornographic movie; he was looking at his career exploding with the bitter suddenness of a bullet in the head.

MacDonald got up and took the tape out of the VCR. "This whole conversation doesn't mean a damn thing anyway," he said. "All we've got so far is a video tape that was illegally obtained. Am I right about that?"

I squirmed uncomfortably. "I don't want to say anything that would damage a court case. So let's just say I obtained the tape from unknown sources."

"All right," MacDonald said. "Let's say that for now. But if it does get to court, you'd better have a damn sight better story—like somebody gave it to you."

"What do you mean 'if'?" Herb cut in. "When you pick up Deen and those people in the film, they can tell you exactly what happened. If Helen Cotrell's death wasn't an accident, I'll bet they had something to do with it."

"Pick up Harry Deen for what?" MacDonald snorted. "You don't have one shred of evidence he had anything to do with this. Hooker either. Except for your word, we don't even know for sure the damn thing was shot here. And if we pick up the others, what do we charge them with? Participating in a porno film? Hell, in this state if we arrested everybody who was in a porno, we'd have half the population in jail."

A wave of rage and frustration hit me. He wasn't going to do a damn thing! "But you saw the background in that set, That was here. I saw that set. That proves Deen was involved."

"You saw it. Who else? You, Herb?"

Herb Stax looked totally disgusted as he shook his head. "No. I've never been in that studio."

MacDonald looked at Clint Hemet whose face had regained some of its color. "You, Clint?"

Hemet looked almost happy as he said, "Not I. I only go in that studio if it involves security."

MacDonald raised his eyebrows at me. "If that set is still there, I can make a move. If it isn't, I haven't got one thing to go on except your word."

"My word should be enough to pick him up," I snarled. I was so angry I had trouble controlling my voice. "Then we can find out the truth about Helen."

"We don't use rubber hoses any more," MacDonald said. "He'd be on the street in an hour, probably with a lawsuit."

Herb Stax stared hard at me, his eyes pleading for me to back off. The idea of a lawsuit had boiled away his anger in a hurry. "MacDonald's right, Ben. We really have no proof. And I'm sure Deen won't talk unless you can really put the pressure on him. If it was me, I sure as hell wouldn't."

Who would? Certainly not Harry Deen. He'd be a fool to say anything. "Maybe it isn't too late," I said. "Let's take a look. If that office set is still up, that'll prove it. We can match it with the one in the tape."

"And if it isn't," MacDonald said, "all you'll do is let him know you're on to him. He'll pull in his horns and we've got nothing."

"I'll go take a look," Clint Hemet said, and his sense of relief was evident in his calm voice. Without proof, he was also off the hook. "He won't be suspicious of me."

"No," I said. "You said yourself you rarely go in that studio. If you start poking around, he might really get suspicious. I'd better go."

"What makes you think he won't be just as suspicious of you?" MacDonald asked.

"I've known Deen for years," I answered. "And I was just in there. That's how I recognized the set up. He won't think anything about it if I drop in again."

"That makes sense," MacDonald said. "How long will it take?"

"Twenty minutes. Maybe less."

"Okay. If that office set is still up, I'll get a court order. We'll pick them up."

"And if it isn't?"

MacDonald shrugged. "Then we're back to square one."

"You get me something I can take to management," Clint Hemet said, "and I'll clean out that whole department."

"And if there's nothing," I said bitterly, "we just forget the whole thing."

"Now, now, Ben," Herb interjected, "I'm sure Clint wants to cooperate. We all want to get to the bottom of this."

"That's right." Clint Hemet's smile was tight. "You go look. If that set is what you say it is, you'll see how fast we can move."

I stared at their tense faces, wondering how they could sit calmly and consider letting Deen and Hooker slip away. I felt a burning resentment of their rationality. I wanted to run screaming through the corridors, challenging those two bastards to try to kill me again. I wanted to escape this civilized, antiseptic discussion and begin hurling stones and spears. Because I knew! I knew!

Then I lost the feeling in a tide of dejection. They believed me. They had to. They wanted to know the truth. I had no reason to believe any of them were holding back, even though Hemet's loyalties had to lie with the company. And Deen was part of the company.

And Herb Stax? Could he be objective? Or did he visualize a lucrative contract slipping away. As for MacDonald—He couldn't move without evidence that would indicate a crime had been committed. Just because Helen had been in the porno picture did not necessarily mean it was tied to her death.

I got up feeling empty but anxious to leave. "Okay. I'll be back in a few minutes."

"You'd better clean up your act before you get down there," MacDonald said. "If Deen or Hooker see you with that expression, they'll know something's wrong."

"I'll get it together," I said. I went out and closed the door.

I had to fight an urge to run as I hurried through the halls of the office section, through the double doors leading to the shop area, and along the corridors. I needed time to cool down, time to put on the actor's face and to plan my attack. Besides, speed was not important. There was no reason for Harry Deen to be suspicious, and therefore, no reason for him to strike the office set. It was still more than an hour before quitting time, so even if Samantha Cazzoli went straight home and immediately discovered the film missing, it would be too late to warn Deen.

I almost stopped in mid-stride. Hanna Carbo. She must've known about the porno operation. That's what she was going to tell me. Had she been killed to keep her mouth shut? If so, then Harry Deen already knew something was wrong. I might already be too late.

I almost ran down the last corridor to the photo shop entrance.

Before going inside, I paused to rehearse my story. I had to convince Harry Deen my visit was strictly social, or that I was still investigating Helen's death, but with no link to him.

I assumed what I hoped was a pleasant expression and walked into the photo department. I'd planned on walking directly though the office to the studio, but Harry Deen was sitting with his feet up on his desk talking on the telephone. He was wearing his usual worn blue jeans and thick-soled hiking boots.

Dean looked up when he saw me, winked and waved me to a chair. If he was suspicious, he gave no indication.

He was talking to a video lab, something about how they'd have to check the color balance before they ordered release tapes. I sat on the edge of a chair and stared around the office. Anything to keep from looking at Deen.

He finally hung up and leaned back in his chair. He picked up a cigarette smoldering in an overflowing ash tray and sucked it into life.

"Hi, Ben, baby," he drawled. "You're out of uniform."

"Yes," I said. "I haven't changed yet."

"You're still pulling guard duty?"

"For another night or two."

Deen's face pulled into a frown. "Say, I'm sorry as hell to hear about your other guard. What was her name?"

"Carbo. Hanna Carbo." It took a massive effort to keep the anger out of my voice.

"I hear it was an accident. Leaking gas."

"That's the theory."

Deen sucked deeply on the cigarette and spoke with the chemicals still in his lungs, each word punctuated by a tendril of smoke. "Damn bad luck. Two of your best guards. They'll be hard to replace.

I stared at him, fascinated. How could anybody deliberately hold those carcinogens inside his lungs? As I watched, he let the smoke curl up from his mouth. His eyes didn't even blink.

"We've got it under control," I told him. "The office has lined up a replacement."

"Tough," he said. "I lost an aunt that way a couple'a years ago. Lived in Wisconsin, or was it Michigan? Anyway, she went off an' left the gas on. Came home an' turned on a light or somethin'. Made a spark. Boom! Blew the roof right off the house. Burnt the damn thing right to the ground. Funny she didn't smell the gas.

"Nothin' like that could happen ta me. I c'n smell gas a mile off. If I'm sleepin' at night and a pilot light, for God's sake, goes out, I c'n smell it. I wake up like that." He snapped his fingers with a hard, sharp pop. "If I walked in a house where the gas'd been on, for Christ sake, I'd sure as hell know enough not to turn on any friggin' lights."

Listening to him, I could almost smell the faint, pungent odor of natural gas. "I'm like that, too. Maybe women haven't developed their sense of smell like men did when they were the hunters."

"Like hell," Deen snorted. "They c'n smell perfume a mile. If they made gas smell like Chanel Number Five, she'd still be alive."

I turned my head so he couldn't read the disgust and hatred in my eyes. He was probably the bastard who'd killed her, and here we were playing our roles better than Hoffman and Cruise. Well, maybe he could keep up the act, but I couldn't. I had to get a look at that studio and get out before I came apart and tried to decorate the walls with his bones.

"You're right, Harry," I said. "Say, did you by any chance find a key in your studio? I lost one the other day and I've looked everywhere except here."

Deen's eyes blinked and his eyebrows lifted. "A key? What kind of a key?"

"Schlage house key. Like an idiot I had it loose in my pocket."

Deen shook his head. "Nope. No key."

I was already moving toward the inner door. "Mind if I take a look around the studio? If you're not shooting anything."

"Hell, no." Deen dropped his feet to the floor with a heavy thud. He stood up and ground out the cigarette in the filthy ash tray. "I'll give you a hand."

"Okay, thanks," I muttered. I didn't care whether he did or not. All I wanted to do was get a quick look at that movie set.

He led the way past the dark room into the studio. There was nothing reluctant about his movements. If he was trying to hide anything, he certainly was a better actor than I thought possible. Up to this point he'd been the same old Harry Deen, full of bull and willing to spread it around. And he certainly hadn't hesitated when I'd suggested going into the studio.

Then I saw why. The office set, the one used in the movie, was gone. In its place was a set designed to represent a conference room. The office flats had been replaced with flats painted to resemble paneled walls. The flat with the window had been moved to the other side of the room and its backdrop repainted to show blue sky. The desk had been replaced with a long conference table ringed with chairs. The big couch, where the heavy action had taken place in the movie, had been replaced with a book case containing engineering manuals.

I stared at the set in dismay. Every article that could be used as identifying evidence was gone. I became aware Deen was watching me, his expression blank. I wondered what he had interpreted from my own uncontrolled look of anguish. I covered as best as I could by saying, "Very neat. Ahhh...what happened to the office set?"

"Oh, we struck that yesterday," he said almost absently. "Now, let me see. We were standing over here."

He began scanning the floor where we'd been standing. I moved beside him and pretended to search the area as I said casually, "Say, Harry. I really admired that big couch you used in that set. Where'd you rent it? Maybe I can make them a deal."

"No way," he replied. "That was mine." He looked at me and grinned. "So was the desk."

"I see. That way you pick up a little change for the rental fee."

"Sure. I make up a few invoices with fake names. If there's anything we need I can supply myself, I bring it in and send accounting an invoice. A company as big as this, they don't know what the hell is goin' on in a piddly photo studio."

"Yeah," I said. "I'll bet they don't." And, I thought, it also helped you cover up its real use and make it nearly impossible to trace. But I had to get that couch or I'd have nothing. I continued my pretended search as I added, "There must be a lot of ways you can pick up a little change here and there."

"You know me," Deen said with a dirty grin. "I've been around this business long enough to learn a trick or two."

The anger surged back, hot and strong. I knew Harry Deen all right, which was why I had no doubt he could run the porno operation and was probably looking around for other ways to pick up some tax-free money. And if he had to kill someone to protect his income, well, that was the price you paid.

But if he'd kept that couch, it might be the piece of evidence we needed to nail him.

"You're sure about that couch?" I said, wondering if I was pushing the subject too hard. "That gold color would really fit in my living room."

"Gold?" Deen straightened and stared at me. "You color blind? That couch was green. Come over to my place. I'll show you."

I almost exploded in a bitter laugh at my own stupidity. If Harry

Deen had realized the necessity of pulling down the office set, he sure wasn't going to leave an incriminating piece of furniture that could be identified. Either it wasn't the same couch or he'd had a fast upholstery job done on it. Which left me with zilch. Now the only way we were going to prove Harry Deen and company were making porno movies was to catch them in the act. That meant never. Deen was too smart to keep the operation going when both the police and I were investigating two deaths.

Or was he? Harry Deen was smart. But he was also greedy. There was a chance he might try to grind out one or two more of the money-making flicks if he thought we didn't know about his operation. Maybe if I gave him enough rope, he just might hang himself by his scrawny neck.

I sadly shook my head. "I guess it's gone. It wasn't that important anyway."

Deen straightened and put his hand in the small of his back. "Damn. Must be getting old. Sorry about the key. I didn't see anything when we struck the office set. Maybe Eddie picked it up. I'll ask him."

Eddie? At the thought of the slob, my stomach roiled again with a nauseous wrench. There had to be a way to make that s-o-b pay. But how? All my evidence had vanished.

"Where is Eddie?"

"He's shooting stills in the software lab," Deen said. He looked at his watch. "Should be back any time. I'll ask him."

He led the way back into his office and searched through the stale cigarette stubs in his ash tray until he found the still-smoldering butt. My stomach almost erupted when he brushed it off, put it in his mouth and relit it.

"About the couch," he said after taking a long drag on the cigarette. "Maybe we can make a deal."

"Nope," I told him. "Can't use green. Well, thanks for the help."

"Any time." He flopped in his chair and leaned back with his hands behind his head and his feet up on the desk, the broken cigarette dangling until I was afraid it was going to set his beard on fire. His half-closed eyes gleamed with arrogance. He had no worries. There was no way anything could be pinned on him. I had to get out before I really was sick.

But at the door I turned back. "I was just thinking," I said, "with two experienced guards out, we're going to be spread a little thin for a couple of nights. Probably won't get over this way much. I'd appreciate it if you'd make double sure everything is locked up."

"Sure thing. We do anyway. Everybody wants to steal a camera or some lenses. They can fence 'em easy, no questions. You'll find this place locked up tighter'n a virgin's ass every night."

Yes, I thought. I'll bet. Especially if you're bootlegging movie deals inside. Maybe I should add a little sweets into the list. "I think I'll move Ron Renbourne over to this building. I'll handle the office area. He and Ed Emblem can work out some kind of a route that'll cover both their territories."

"Sounds okay. You don't have to check here. Guaranteed. That'll take a little off the load."

My smile was terribly sincere as I said, "Thanks, Harry. That'll help."

His eyes had closed and his lips were smiling when I went out and closed the door fighting an impulse to go back and beat the truth out of him.

Green, hell! That couch had been gold.

On the way back to Clint Hemet's office, I tried to piece together a plan that would make sense to MacDonald and would not seem like entrapment. With the office set gone, I had no evidence the movie had been shot in Harry Deen's studio. The fact that three of the actors—four if you counted Helen—worked at Colton Labs meant nothing, except that they were oversexed and short of money. MacDonald could drag each of them down to the station and give them a thorough interrogation, but it was doubtful he'd learn anything that would tie them in with Helen's death—if they could be made to talk at all.

However, if they were caught in *flagrante delicto*, they just might fall apart. One thing was certain—it was the only way MacDonald and Clint Hemet were going to be convinced.

But would Harry Deen take the bait and resume operations? Or would he pack it in for a few weeks or months—or forever? If he did, I might never be able to prove he'd murdered Helen.

Chapter 14

MY KNEES WERE beginning to hurt. If I didn't make a move soon, my joints would be frozen permanently. How long should it take to set up and film a pornographic scene? The thought kept running through my mind as I waited, half crouching behind a massive Matursa machining center in the machine shop. Nearby Clint Hemet and Cal MacDonald also waited, concealed behind silent machines. MacDonald had enough experience with stakeouts that he was sitting on the smooth concrete floor with his back against the wall, completely relaxed. Besides, he had a warrant that said it was legal to enter the photo studio, and if necessary, to make arrests.

Hemet grunted as he shifted to a more comfortable position. I had the feeling that if he could do it without being seen, he would be pacing. Out of the corner of my eye, I saw him check his wrist watch again.

"Seven-thirty," he whispered hoarsely. "I'll give it fifteen minutes more."

Now I really began to worry. When I'd talked Hemet and MacDonald into setting the trap, I'd assumed filming would start shortly after the end of the work day. That way the actors wouldn't have to leave the plant, then return, making them more likely to be noticed. On the other hand, they might simply hide somewhere until midnight or later. Except then they'd have to sign out and that would look suspicious. They couldn't very well claim they were pulling a little overtime on some project if they didn't leave the plant until four or five o'clock in the morning.

I was wiping away a film of nervous perspiration on my forehead when I froze. Footsteps. And coming toward us. MacDonald and Hemet heard them, too, and I saw them tense. I doubted it was a janitor or a workman putting in overtime. The steps were too fast, almost as fast as my heart beat.

We only got a glimpse of him as he moved past our hiding place, but it was enough to jolt me with a powerful shot of adrenalin. Bill Holtz. He was walking rapidly and glancing behind him as though he was worried about being seen.

We heard him open the door to the photo department and go

inside. So Harry Deen hadn't locked it as he'd promised. The trap was working.

I looked at MacDonald and Hemet with a satisfied nod. MacDonald had resumed his relaxed posture, waiting for the other actors to arrive. But Hemet had almost collapsed. He was slumped back against the leg of a workbench, looking old and haggard. This had to be a tremendous shock to him. Until this moment, he'd been able to dismiss the accusations, to reject the idea Helen might've been murdered, but the single brief glimpse of Bill Holtz had changed everything. The truth was tangible and could no longer be ignored.

He was still staring at the floor, his hands hanging limply. We heard laughter and he looked up, his eyes hollow with defeat. I raised my head for a quick peek. Ron Renbourne was walking toward the studio accompanied by a pretty girl who looked more like a secretary than one of the factory assembly workers. He moved confidently, laughing and joking with the girl. He knew there was no chance of being seen by the guard—he was the guard.

When the photo department door closed behind them, I turned to MacDonald. "There should be one more, I guess."

His voice was bored as he said, "What makes you think so?"

"Well, two guys, two girls. We've only seen one."

"Two guys, one girl." He opened one eye and stared at me. "Saves overhead."

Two men? The arrangement didn't seem quit fair to the girl—unless she was getting double pay.

"Give 'em twenty minutes," MacDonald said. "That should put them in the middle of the heavy action."

"Twenty minutes?" I said. "If I know Renbourne, he'll be finished in five."

"Can't be," MacDonald said. "They've got to get set up and focused. And there's retakes and—"

"Retakes?" I couldn't believe that. "How can they do that? How many retakes?"

MacDonald opened both eyes and looked at me. Then his eyes sort of rolled back and he closed them again. "Twenty minutes," he muttered. "Call me."

I settled back to wait. There were no sounds from the photo studio. Except for the faint rush of the air conditioning system and the intermittent whir of electric motors, the building was quiet. Not even one machinist or tool-and-die maker was working overtime. Apparently, Harry Deen kept close tabs on overtime schedules so he'd know when the area was going to be clear. Actually, it wouldn't have mattered. The shooting stage was soundproofed to keep out factory noises. Anything could be happening in there day or night and no one would know.

I tried to keep from imagining what could be going on. Instead, I focused on the implications. If we could prove Helen had been forced into participating in their operation, it would provide the motive for her murder: to keep her from informing. That would make it very easy to implicate both Hooker and Deen. One of them would certainly confess, probably Deen. I was sure he'd plea bargain everything to save his own hide.

I was taken by surprise when MacDonald stood up and stretched. "It's time," he said. "Let's go."

Hemet looked drawn and tired. For a minute I thought I was going to have to help him up. But he used the workbench to pull himself to his feet. Then he sort of reached inside himself and grabbed a handful of resolve. He straightened, his face grim. There was a good chance he'd be losing his job and his reputation. And if they went, so would his life style.

"Okay," he said. "Let's do it."

I followed him and MacDonald to the photo department door. MacDonald tried the knob, but it was locked. He nodded to Hemet who produced a set of keys, selected one and unlocked the door.

Before we entered, MacDonald said, "If there's any trouble, let me handle it."

Hemet frowned. "You think there'll be trouble?"

"No. Porno operators aren't the violent type. They like to make love, not war, as the saying goes. But you never know."

He pulled the door open and went inside. Hemet looked at me, his eyes tired. He sighed and followed MacDonald.

It was semi-dark in the outer office, but I'd given MacDonald a detailed sketch of the area and he moved straight to the studio door. He tried the knob and it turned easily. He pushed the door open and quickly stepped into a blaze of light, Hemet right behind him. I stepped inside, ready for anything—except that!

A macabre scene flashed into my brain as though seared by a burst of lightning. The girl was naked on her hands and knees on the thick carpet, her nude body almost hidden by the writhing nude bodies of Ron Renbourne and Bill Holtz. Eddie Hooker was peering through the view finder of the Ikegami camera talking as he filmed the scene.

"Come on, Connie, give! Give, damn it! Shake your ass. You're supposed to be having fun, for Christ's sake. Come on! Ron, get your ass outta the way."

For an instant that seemed to go on forever, I pictured Helen in place of the girl and my knees went weak with shock. As much as I'd prepared for what I might see, I was totally unprepared for the harsh reality. Under the brilliant studio lights, the scene was as sharply etched as a diamond.

How could anyone perform sexually under such conditions? With the staring, impersonal eye of the camera watching every move, every expression, only an animal in the middle of the rutting season would be able to perform. But it didn't bother Renbourne or Holtz. They were both using the girl like a pair of bulls, uncaring about spectators or surroundings.

And the girl? Was she really enjoying it? Would Helen have enjoyed it? Could she have allowed herself to be used in the glare of the piercing lights, grotesquely smiling at the camera while Eddie Hooker yelled, "Give, baby, give!"

Suddenly, I wanted to kill him and the snarl that came from my throat caused Hooker to jerk his head away from the camera and the actors to freeze in an obscene tableau, their faces angled toward the unexpected sound. I had the impression of Hooker's startled look as I charged past MacDonald and smashed my fist into Hooker's face, feeling a surge of joy when I felt the crunch of flesh and bone. He grunted and fell backward like a slow motion picture.

Then MacDonald grabbed my arm and spun me away. "All right!" he snapped. He turned to the actors, still locked in their erotic *ménage á trois*. "I'm the police. You're under arrest."

If I'd been able to erase the thought of Helen being in the studio, the scene would've been comical. Ron Renbourne and Bill Holtz pulled away from the girl as though she'd suddenly developed AIDS. The move was so fast and violent she gasped and fell. Both Renbourne and Holtz leaped toward the only other exit in the room and tried to wrestle the door open. Unfortunately, it was a door built into the conference room set and when they charged through, they ran into the real studio wall.

"Come on out," MacDonald said calmly. "You're not going anywhere."

There was a long silence. Eddie Hooker sat up and held the side of his face. The girl lay face down where she had fallen as though hoping we wouldn't see her. Then Bill Holtz put his head around the edge of the door frame looking as though he was on the verge of crying. "Can we—can we put on our clothes?" he stammered.

"Yeah," MacDonald said. "Make it quick. I've got to read you your rights."

When they came from behind the set, Holtz had his hands over his genitals and walked looking at the floor. Renbourne had decided there wasn't any use playing coy and he strode across the room with his usual arrogance and began taking his clothes from the back of a chair.

MacDonald moved into the pool of light and pulled the girl to her feet. "You, too," he said. "You want your clothes on or not?"

She turned on him so fast I thought she was going to attack. "What the fuck are you bustin' us for?" she snarled, and what I'd thought was a pretty face and lovely body was suddenly ugly. "Why aren't you bustin' real crooks? There's not a damn thing wrong with this. We aren't hurtin' nobody! But you stupid cops, you let the real crooks run around loose. I can't even walk home without gettin" mugged or raped!"

"Well, you'll be safe tonight," MacDonald said. "Get your clothes on."

While they dressed, MacDonald read them their Maranda rights. Bill Holtz's hands were shaking so violently, I thought he was never going to get his pants on. The girl continued to snarl invectives at MacDonald while she dressed. I'd always thought there was something stimulating about watching a girl remove or put on her clothes, but there was nothing sexy about the way this girl yanked on her clothing. I wondered if she was an employee of Colton Labs and how they'd managed to recruit her. Maybe she really enjoyed sex with more than one man at a time. Would she enjoy making love if there was no money involved? Would Helen?

Hemet crossed to Eddie Hooker who'd slumped into a chair. "Where's Harry Deen?"

Hooker looked at him sullenly. A purple bruise was already appearing on his cheekbone. "Deen? How should I know?"

"He wasn't in on this?"

"In on what?

Hemet glared at him, his fists clinched. "Listen," he said. "Don't get smart. You're in enough trouble."

Hooker refused to answer. He turned his head away and put his hands in his pockets.

Hemet repeated, "Listen, scum. Was Deen in on this?"

Hooker shook his head without looking up. "No. It was my idea."

"Bull," Hemet snarled. "You don't have the brains. Where's

Deen?"

Hooker's head came up and he glared at Hemet. "I don't know." Then the fire went out of his eyes and his head drooped. "It wasn't his idea anyway."

"Yeah," MacDonald said, moving closer. "Whose was it?"

Hooker started to answer, then snapped his jaw shut as though he'd already said too much. "Somebody. I don't know."

MacDonald put his fingers under Hooker's chin and gently forced it up until he could glower into his eyes. "Who?" he said. His voice was soft, but it had the power of an ugly threat.

Eddie Hooker licked his lips. "I don't know. The guy who buys this stuff." He jerked his head away from MacDonald's hand. "He said there was nothin' illegal about it."

"He did, huh?" MacDonald said. "Who is this guy?"

"Shit, I don't know. He never told me his name."

"How do you contact him?"

"I don't. I send the stuff to a post office box. He sends me the money."

"Cash?"

Hooker had regained some of his confidence and he sneered. "No. He writes me a check."

MacDonald looked at Hemet and me. "You don't have to give your right name to rent a post office box. We'd have a hell of a time finding him unless Deen knows something."

"Deen's got nothin' to do with it," Hooker said. "Hell, he's too stupid to know what's goin' on."

"Looks like a dead end," MacDonald said.

"At least it ends here," Hemet said. "God, can you picture what would happen if it came out that Colton Labs was making porno films."

I'd been listening to the conversation impatiently, wondering when they were going to ask the most important question, but neither MacDonald nor Hemet approached the subject. I took a deep breath to get control of my voice and said, "What about Helen Cotrell?"

Hooker gave me a blank look. "Who?"

"Helen. The girl you killed."

"Hey, wait a minute!" Hooker looked at MacDonald. "What the fuck is he talkin' about? I didn't kill nobody."

MacDonald grabbed my arm and practically yanked me aside. "Ben, stop it! If they did kill her, you'll screw up the case."

I realized immediately what he meant. The lawyers, the courts would use any technicality to let a crook go. A confession could be repudiated in court. But now Hooker was scared and he might say something we could use. If we let him get with a lawyer, he would never talk.

MacDonald knew it, too. But he couldn't let me work on him. That, too, could be used by a lawyer to get an acquittal. Not to mention a possible lawsuit against me.

But I had to know! To hell with the litigation. This bastard knew who'd killed Helen even if he hadn't done it himself.

I grabbed Hooker by his shirt front with one hand and gripped his ear with the other. I gave it a vicious twist to let him know I was serious when I snarled, "Who did it, you creep? Who killed her?"

Hooker surprised me by twisting down and away, almost yanking his ear off in the process. His foot snapped up in a karate kick that would've crushed my windpipe if I hadn't blocked it. Then Hemet and MacDonald were between us, wrestling me aside.

"Stop it," MacDonald said sharply. "Go on, Ben. Wait outside."

I glared at Hooker who was holding his hand over his ear. "I'll talk to you later."

MacDonald herded me toward the doorway. On the way I passed Renbourne and Holtz who were finishing putting on their clothes. Renbourne couldn't meet my eye when I said, "I'll be talking to you, too, Renbourne."

Outside the studio, I walked slowly through the echoing shop area, feeling cheap and dirty, as though I'd had a part in the hellish scenario. I wondered what we had accomplished by shutting down the porno operation.

Was Harry Deen involved or not?

I couldn't see how it could go on without his knowledge. But what had been the purpose of killing Helen? It was difficult to believe that the operation was worth risking murder, considering all the complications that were sure to follow. Yet, Helen had been involved. And she was dead. And what other reason could there be?

Chapter 15

IF THERE IS anything good about being an orphan it is that you don't have to attend many funerals. I hate funerals so much I would've avoided them in any case. There are enough depressing things in life without deliberately subjecting your psyche to a hype of grief.

Early Saturday afternoon I estimated there were at least three hundred people jammed into the small chapel at Pacific View Memorial Park. Except for the muted sound of an organ playing 'Abide With Me' and a few stifled coughs, there was no sound, all voices stilled by the open casket at the front of the chapel. I was glad I couldn't see inside the casket from my seat near the middle of the room. Staring at Helen's pale, stone-like face throughout the service would be more than I could take.

I was deeply grateful when the music shifted to Brahm's 'Lullaby.' A minister, whom I assumed to be Methodist, began a tribute about Helen as though he knew her, but it was obvious he was reciting a canned speech, simply changing the name. I knew Helen's parents had been active church members, but I couldn't recall a time when Helen had attended a service. She might have gone to church without telling me, but that did not seem likely.

When we'd first begun going together, we sometimes talked for hours as though we could bring ourselves closer by becoming part of each other's life, and she'd never displayed any deep religions convictions.

She had told me, however, that her mother was especially devout. I watched Claire Cotrell, a thin faded woman sitting in the front row with the other close family members, sobbing softly. I regretted that I'd never bothered to know her better. The one time Helen had invited me to dinner at their home the atmosphere had been cold and strained. Her mother had tried bravely to establish some sort of conviviality, but her father had been grim, his conversation perfunctory, his attitude hostile and withdrawn. Helen and I hadn't really minded. We were lost in each other at the time and all we wanted was to get out of the house and go somewhere we could be alone.

Now Lou Cotrell sat stiffly next to his wife. He was dry-eyed, staring fixedly at the casket. I wondered what was going on in his mind.

He was probably blaming me for what had happened. I could almost feel hate radiating from him. I wondered again, as I had so many times, why Helen had refused to follow the path he'd laid out for her, and instead, had elected to quit school and come to work for me. That had almost killed him. They must have had some bitter fights.

Lou Cotrell was not a man to take rebellion without becoming nasty. And yet, Helen had told me more than once how much she admired her father. So why had she gone against his wishes? I assumed it was because she wanted to be near me. But if she loved me that much, why had we drifted apart?

I would never know. It was over. Forever.

Looking at Lou Cotrell, I hoped he'd never know how guilty I felt. It would give him too much satisfaction.

Near the end of the service, a line was formed to begin the ghoulish ritual of filing past the casket for one last look, as though the happy memories should be suffused by a pale, waxen image representing all the empty tomorrows.

As a friend of the family, Herb Stax was up near the front of the line. I was back with the S&R staff. I'd have preferred to be at the very end of the line. In truth, I didn't want to look at Helen. I hated death. I hated funerals. The peaceful dead filled me with a sense of loss, not for myself, but for them. They'd lost the sun and the rain, green leaves against a blue sky, scented flowers and wind playing in fields of wheat. They'd never again know the pleasure of being with those they loved. That was one of the advantages of being an orphan. You'd never have to attend the funeral of your mother or father, brother or sister. I often wondered whether it balanced out with never knowing their love either.

In a slow shuffle, we moved inexorably toward the open casket. When she reached the casket, Claire Cotrell stood a moment before she turned away, sobs shaking her body. Lou Cotrell did not look at his daughter. He kept his face turned away as he put his arm around his wife's shoulders and led her away, his own face composed, his eyes dry and hard.

Approaching the casket, I gradually I became aware that many of the people were surreptitiously watching me, and I tried to make my expression blank.

But when I looked at Helen lying so dreadfully still, I could feel my chest tighten and my face begin to come apart. It wasn't right that she should be dead while so many bastards were still living. Her life was just beginning. It just wasn't right.

Tears that had began to gather were burned away by an anger

deeper than any I had ever known. Somebody had taken her life from her, had taken away her right to have children, to have a home, happiness, everything. Oh, God, I wanted him! It wasn't right he should be enjoying the pleasure of his life after taking hers. I wouldn't call the death of such a bastard vengeance; I'd call it justice.

The people watching must have mistaken my grim expression for grief because they moved aside without protest as I rudely pushed my way to the door. But it wasn't grief. It was an ugly, burning hate.

Outside, I stood in the hot, harsh sunlight well back from the group while the anger drained away into an empty helplessness. It seemed that everyone was dismissing Helen's death, hoping to bury the questions with her casket. They were so anxious to avoid a connection between the pornography setup and her death. Despite what we'd discovered last night, they still wanted to let it drop. Everyone wanted it to remain an accident or suicide. Murder was ugly. It splattered on everyone. An accident was clean and neat, nobody hurt, nobody punished.

In a few minutes, pall bearers brought the closed casket from the chapel and slid it into the open end of the hearse. I hadn't been invited to be one of them. They were friends of Lou Cotrell, not of Helen.

Herb Stax, Kim Fuji, Judd Proctor, Mrs. Davis, Ed Emblem and Ted Olds were standing in a small group near the chapel in the shade of newly transplanted palm trees. They looked toward me and Kim started to come over, but Herb said something to her and she stopped. Instead, Herb walked over to stand beside me.

"You going out to the grave site?"

The thought of seeing the gaping hole in the raw earth, knowing it was there to entomb Helen for eternity was more than I could stand. "No." I knew my reply was short and blunt, but it was all I could say.

Herb caught the inflection. "Okay," he said. "Come into the office when you feel like it. Don't push it."

He began to turn away, but I caught his sleeve. I didn't feel like talking, but I couldn't keep my despair bottled up any longer. "It's all wrong," I told him. "Herb, it's all wrong."

He looked at me carefully. "What is, Ben?"

"They wouldn't have killed her. Not just for those pictures. They wouldn't have killed her for that."

"You're right. Nobody killed her," Herb said patiently. "They think it was self-inflicted, probably because of guilt about what she was doing."

"She wouldn't do that." I knew I sounded stubborn and petulant, but I couldn't let it go. "She wouldn't kill herself."

"You're wrong, Ben. I know her family. I know what they meant to her. She couldn't face them after those things she did. Especially her father."

"Then why did she get involved?"

"The same reason some people take drugs, I suppose. Somebody talks them into trying it. Then they find they're hooked. And all of a sudden, they don't want to pay the price."

"Not Helen. She couldn't."

Herb put his hand on my shoulder. "Ben, it's over. Let her go."

I looked at the worry in his face and the age that was showing without his big smile. This had to be tearing at him almost as much as it was me. I had no right to hang my guilt on him. Maybe he was right. It was over. Let her go in peace.

"Okay, Herb," I said, and the taut lines in his face smoothed. "You and the others go ahead. I'll see you at the office."

"That's better." His smile was already back as he patted my shoulder. "Accept it, kid. You'll feel better—and so would she. I know."

The anodyne grated on my raw nerves. Why did he have to spoil his sincerity with the phony salesmanship? But that was Herb. I remembered something he had once told me "—The secret of success is sincerity. Once you can fake that, you've got it made." I guess he just couldn't help himself. He'd always give it that last little pitch.

He went back to join the others, talking even before he arrived. I stayed in the sun for a moment, letting the thought that it was over burn in like the summer heat. But there was no warmth, no feeling of peace.

I couldn't face anybody at the moment, so I walked to my car. Maybe a ride or a long swim would help me accept the inevitable. I was fumbling with my keys when someone put a hand on my arm and I flinched in surprise. I turned, startled, and stared into the wide, dark eyes of Samantha Cazzoli. Her face was pale, strained, her beautiful eyes red veined.

Her sensuous lips parted and she said, "I mus' talk to jou."

Seeing her so beautiful, so vital and alive so soon after looking into Helen's still face, remembering who she was and what she'd done, was like looking at an obscene image and I felt the bitterness building. She'd helped kill Helen. She'd helped put her in front of those damn cameras! My God, how could she be here now?

"Go away" I snarled. "You have no right to be here."

She shook her head. "No, no. I don' come for funeral. I come... I wait only for to see jou."

I stared at her, knowing my hatred was naked. "I don't talk to whores."

Her face tightened, but she didn't pull away. "I got to talk to jou. Is important."

"Why? You want to kill me, too?"

"I don' kill nobody. I hear jou arrest Eddie Hooker. He maybe tell big lie about me. I don' want to go to jail. I don' want to lose my job. Jou got to help me."

My barking laugh was bitter. Help her? After what she'd done? Besides, it was too late. Both Hemet and MacDonald already knew about her. Since she hadn't actually been caught in the act, I wasn't sure they could charge her with a crime, but she would certainly lose her job.

"Look, Miss Cazzoli," I said. "I don't want to talk to you—now or ever."

I got in the Corvette and slammed the door. She put her hands on the door and leaned toward me, her breasts straining at the material of her blouse. "No," she said. "Jou got to help me. Somebody is try to kill me."

I was about to turn the key in the ignition. I stopped. I suddenly identified that look in her eyes, the sound in her voice. Fear. She was scared to death. Or was she? Maybe she was just a hell of an actress. But why? This wasn't going to save her job.

"Who would want to kill you?" I sneered. "One of your johns?"

Her eyes blazed in quick anger and her lips pulled back in a snarl. "Sure. Maybe some john. Maybe same john who kill jour girl."

I caught my breath. Could she be right?

She'd been a part of the porno setup. Maybe somebody really was trying to kill her. Maybe there was something else that had to be covered up. I felt a surge of joy. It was still open. If someone was trying to kill Samantha, then Helen's death could not be dismissed.

I motioned to the seat beside me. "Get in."

She quickly came around the car, and I reached over and opened the door for her. Across the broad expanse of lawn I could see some of the people near the chapel were staring at us. It must've looked as though I was leaving Helen's funeral to go off with another girl.

To hell with them. Let them think what they wanted.

The only place I could think of where we could talk without being noticed was in a bar, so I stopped at the first one that looked halfway decent. Samantha ordered scotch-rocks and I asked for a Bloody Mary.

The name suited my mood.

Samantha took a long swallow of the scotch and I was amazed to see her eyes didn't even water. "I was going to the *tienda*...the store...this morning. I drive my car. Somebody—a man—he try to kill me."

"How?"

"I come down hill on Rigel Circle. It steep hill with turn at bottom..."

"I know the place."

"A *camion*...a truck...a big one, come up behind me. He push me. Push hard. It make me go fast, too fast down hill. I put on brakes. He still push. Almost I don' make turn. Almost I go over cliff."

"What did the truck do then?"

"Do? He push me."

"No. I mean, where did it go afterward?"

"*No sé.* I sit in my car. I cry. Aye, *Dios mio!* I really scared. I figure I lucky to be alive."

"You sure it wasn't just an accident? Maybe the truck lost its brakes or something."

"No, no! When that stinkin' truck push me, I put on brakes an' wave my arms, but he don' stop. He don' blow horn for warning. *Nada.* I hear his motor going hard! *Whoommm! Whoommm!* That son-a-ma-bitch push me on purpose!"

"But why? Why would anybody want to kill you?"

She slumped back in the booth and tears gathered in her eyes. "I don' know. I don' done nothin' to nobody."

"But why come to see me? Why not the police?"

She took another gulp of scotch before answering and her eyes assumed their usual wariness. "I think about jour girl. The one jou ask me about. If somebody kill her on purpose, I betcha is same man who try to kill me."

My hands clinched on the edge of the table and my heart kicked up a notch. This might be the first solid evidence Helen had been murdered. "Then you think she was killed?"

"Before today—" she made a small shrug "—I don' think so. But now? *Si*, I think is so."

"Who?" I held my breath. "Do you know who did it?"

She shook her head. "No."

My elation died as suddenly as it had appeared leaving me feeling even more dejected. Without her identification, I was back where I'd started. "Then why?" I asked. "If you don't know anything, why would somebody want to kill you?"

She hesitated and turned her face away. "I...I have done some things jou don' know about. Bad things, maybe."

She was wrong. I did know about them. If we were thinking about the same thing. "You mean the pornographic movies? The pictures?"

She jerked her head around to stare at me. "Jou know about that?"

"Yes. I suppose you heard what happened at Colton Labs last night." I assumed that if Harry Deen was involved, he'd have called her and told her to keep her mouth shut.

"Last night?" she said without hesitation. "Something happen last night?"

"We made a raid on the photo studio. We picked up Eddie Hooker, my guard, Ron Renbourne, that engineer, Bill Holtz, and some girl. They were shooting another porno movie. We'd already seen one of yours."

"Oh, I hear Eddie Hooker in jam but I don' know why." She sat quietly, her long delicate fingers toying with the glass. "They want me for last night. I...ah...could not do it."

Stupid me, I said, "Couldn't? Why not?"

Her full lips twisted into a rueful smile. "I have bad headache. Lucky, no?"

Headache? I could relate to that. Then it dawned on me why she'd smiled when she said it and I felt my face flame. "Oh, that kind of headache."

She was staring at me with a full smile as though she couldn't believe anybody could be so naive and my face grew warmer. To change the subject, I asked, "Ah...what do you know about Helen's death?"

Her fingers closed on the glass convulsively and again she turned her head so she would not have to look at me when she answered. "Did jou know...she make those kind pictures?"

I felt the familiar pain of an old wound being torn open. "Yes," I said. "I found out about that."

Surprise arched her eyebrows. "When? When jou find out?"

"A couple of days ago. That's also when I found out about you."

"Oh."

Did I really want to ask? I steadied my hands by flattening them on the table. "How man...How many of those films did Helen make?"

She saw the pain in my eyes and moved her hands in a negative gesture. "*No sé.* I don' know. Three, four maybe. I not there all the time, jou know."

"But it was more than one?"

"Oh, sure. We make two together. She very good."

She instantly realized she'd twisted a knife in my gut, and she put her hand gently on my arm. "I am sorry. But jou should know. She did not like it."

I grasped the thought desperately. "How do you know?"

She laughed, a short chop with no mirth. "I know. She smile, yes, like we supposed to. She make moves. Very good. Like pro. But it was fake." She smiled again, this time broadly. "Not like me. Me, I really enjoy."

Yeah, I thought. I'll bet. My throat was so tight I could hardly get the next question out. "Why then? Why did she do it?"

She raised her thick, dark eyebrows and stared at me as though I had asked a very stupid question. "For money. Jou know guards don' make *mucho dinero*. Jour boss—what his name? Stax? *El cheapo*."

That stung. We paid our guards more than the standard for the industry, which wasn't a hell of a lot. But Helen hadn't become a guard for the money. Her family would give her all she wanted. She had taken the job to be near me. Hadn't she?

I shook my head. "She didn't need money," I said. "It had to be another reason."

"If not for money, an' she don' like do it, then why?"

It sounded odd to hear someone else ask the question I'd ask myself a thousand times and the feeling of dread grew deeper. "I was hoping you might be able to tell me."

She pulled her mouth down in an exaggerated frown. "No. She don' like it much. She don' need money. Then *por que?*" She looked up at me, her eyes wide. "Somebody make her do it."

What other answer could there be? "I wouldn't be surprised."

Her face cleared as though she had suddenly been born again. "*Por supesto!* I never think she was girl who would do it. Jou can tell. She was good. She very good. But she do it because she have to. She was good girl. I knew it."

"But if she did what they wanted, why was she killed?"

Her expressive face pulled into a puzzled frown. "That good question." Suddenly the fear leaped back into her eyes. "And now they want to kill me. Why? I do everything he asked, too. Everything with everybody."

"Who? Who asked? Eddie Hooker?"

"Sure. Eddie Hooker."

"What about Harry Deen? Was he in on it?"

"Don' know. I never see him aroun'. Only Eddie."

"Then maybe Deen didn't know what was going on. But why kill Helen? And why try to kill you? Especially now? It's over. We've broken up the operation."

"*No sé*. But I scared. *Aye, Dios,* I don' want leave town. I got good house. Almost paid for. I got good car. Almost paid for. Ho boy. Where I get extra money now?"

An idea struck me and I wondered why I hadn't thought of it before. "Those men—You said there were many. Who were they?"

"Well...jou know two—that guard, Ron, he not so bad. *Muy quapo.* Handsome. No like those others."

"Renbourne and Bill Holtz," I said impatiently. "Who were some others?"

She shrugged. "Different guys Eddie get. Sometimes old guys who I think pay him."

"Older guys? Did you recognize any of them?"

"Me? No. All stranger. Some wear mask. Eddie say he get a lot of calls for rape stuff by guy who wear mask. We don' care. Mask, no mask. The part that count all the same."

"We? Not Helen."

She paused and looked down at her fingers plucking at the tablecloth. "Yes."

"With the masked guys?"

"One I know about. He always ask for her. I think he last guy she do it."

I felt the familiar drain of energy and I was suddenly weary, my stomach churning. How she must've hated it. I wondered if there was any way to identify the older men. One of them might know something.

But who were they? If we only had a picture... Wait. Maybe we did.

"Do you have any of those tapes? The ones with the other men?"

She cocked her head and looked at me out of the corner of her eyes. She raised an eyebrow. "Jou want see me with no clothes on?"

Again my face heated and her smile broadened. "It isn't that," I blurted. "I'd like to see if I can recognize any of the men."

"Sure," she said, but she held her wicked smile. "I got tape. When jou want to look?"

"How about now?"

"In middle of day? Jou sure jou don' want come over tonight?"

"Now," I said and got up.

"Okay," she agreed. She was sliding out of the booth when she stopped and her smile slid away. "I better tell jou," she said. "I got tape with jour girl in it."

There was no reason to tell her I'd broken into her house and taken the tape. If she couldn't find it, she might assume it had been lost somewhere. In the mess she called a closet, it could easily happen.

"Okay," I told her. "We'll skip that one."

I drove Samantha back to the funeral chapel where she retrieved her car. Then I followed her back to her house. I experienced a brief pang of irritation when I thought of the curious stares I'd have to face tomorrow at the office. I could attempt to explain, or I could ignore everybody until I had something concrete. In the end, I might not have to explain at all.

When we entered her house she said, "Don' look. Is kind of messed up. I wasn't expectin' no company." She closed the front door, then stood staring across the living room toward the kitchen. "Jou smell somethin' funny?"

The entire house smelled funny to me, like a laundry hamper full of damp dirty clothes that hadn't been opened for a long time. Still, there was an overriding cloying odor I couldn't place.

Samantha walked into the kitchen and her hand went to her mouth as she made a sharp hissing sound of dismay.

I moved to peer over her shoulder, ready to duck. Then I saw one of her cats, the mean one, lying on the floor. Its head was misshapen and blood from its nose had formed a pool on the dirty linoleum.

"Lobo!" Samantha cried, and started to move into the kitchen. I caught her arm and pulled her back.

"Wait! Let me check."

She understood the implication and quickly stepped back into the living room. I paused to listen, standing out of sight of the kitchen. The cat obviously had been dead a couple of hours; it was unlikely whoever had done it was still around. But if they were after Samantha, they could be waiting.

There was no sound except Samantha's ragged breathing. I checked the kitchen, then moved slowly down the short hallway to her bedroom and cautiously pushed the half-open door back against the wall. The other ugly cat was crouched on the bed staring at me. The room was a mess. Clothing was strewn across the bed and on the floor. The drawers of the dresser had been pulled out and their contents dumped haphazardly, then the empty drawers tossed aside. The closet door was open and I could see that it had been thoroughly ransacked.

I picked my way through the mess and looked on the shelf where the photo album and tapes had been stored. As I expected, they were gone.

I called to Samantha and she came in from the hall. When she saw the condition of the room, her face tightened, but she didn't say a word. She was one controlled lady.

"The tapes," I said. "Are they gone?"

She glanced in the closet. "Yes."

"Those were all you had?"

She nodded, unable to speak.

"Did any have the masked guys in them?"

"*Si,*" she whispered. "Two, I think."

"Oh, damn." Now I really wanted to see those tapes. But somebody had made sure that would never happen.

"That why they try kill me," Samantha said. "They think I know those men." She clutched my arm hard as though to convince me she wasn't lying. "I don' know them. I don' know none of them."

"Helen did," I said. "Or they thought she did. We'd better go to the police."

She shook her head violently, her dark hair flying. "No, no. No police. They put me in jail."

"No, they won't," I assured her. "They have nothing on you. You're going to need their protection."

"I protect myself. I don't go to no stinkin' police."

I considered forcing her to go, then I discarded the idea. I'd prefer her cooperation. Arresting her, even holding her as a material witness, would only cause her to become so resentful we'd never learn anything else she might know.

"Okay," I said. "No police. But you'd better not stay here. Have you got a friend you can stay with?"

She thought a moment, then shook her head. "No. I don' got many girl friends."

I could understand that. What girl could compete with a Samantha Cazzoli? "What about a boy friend?"

"No. Right now, nobody especial."

"Well, okay. We'll get you a motel room for a few days. You'd better get some clothes."

"No. I don' stay in no motel," she said firmly.

"Why not?"

She picked her cat up off the bed and hugged the beast to her breasts. "What I do with Toto?" she wailed. "He cannot stay here alone."

The beast stared at me insolently with its big, yellow eyes. I ignored him.

"Sure, he can," I said. "Cats are survivors. They could exist in the middle of the Gobi Desert. Just leave him some food and water. He'll be okay. I'll bury the other one."

She clutched the beast so tightly I thought she'd crush its ribs. "No." Her mouth set in a stubborn line. Then a sly look crossed her face, and she ducked her head to look up at me with an expression I'm sure she'd practiced. "I stay with jou," she said. "I be safe with jou."

For some reason, a tingle shot through my loins. She was every man's fantasy—beautiful, incredibly sexy, fun-loving. But she was also amoral, cold as a cobra and infinitely more dangerous. Besides, the deal would also include her cat, which was probably harboring colonies of ticks and fleas.

"No," I said emphatically. "You can't do that."

"*Como* no," she answered. "Maybe I think who are men in mask. I tell jou right then."

I hesitated, trying to think rationally. What would the neighbors think? What would Jack say? That was no defense. I knew what he'd say. And she did need a place where she'd be safe. It was possible that with the right questioning she might be able to remember some of the men in the videos. Logically, the positives outweighed the negatives. Besides, there was always a hot shower, and flea and tick powder.

"Okay," I said, and she smiled with the same sly look as the cat. "I'll have to find Jack another place."

"Jack?" Her mouth dropped open. "You live with a man?"

"Not the way you think," I said hastily. "He's a friend, a visitor. He's staying with me until he can line up a place of his own. You'll like him."

"Oh." She began to smile, then pulled her plump lower lip between her small, feral teeth. "He *quapo?* Handsome?"

I returned her smile, thinking of Jack's expression when he'd first see Samantha. "Sure," I lied. I wiggled my hand. "A little long in the tooth, but very handsome."

"Long in tooth?"

"Older. But not over the hill, I don't think."

"Oh." Then her shoulders slumped. "If he is guest, I don' want make him to leave."

"Don't worry about it." I had the distinct feeling I'd been trapped the instant she'd made the suggestion. Betrayed by my stupid hormones. "I just wonder what the neighbors are going to say."

She came over, still holding the cat, and took my hand, leaning against me so one soft breast pressed against my arm. The cat dared me to make a move. "They say jou lucky man. What else?"

"Oh, Jesus." I abandoned all resistance. What the hell. If somebody really was trying to kill her, I had to protect my only real witness. "Okay. I'm going to be working tonight, but you'll be okay."

"Tonight. At Colton Labs?"

"Yes. We're short-handed."

"But today is *sabado*."

"They need guards on Saturday, too."

Her lovely face assumed a look that was both puzzled and concerned. "But when jou sleep? It already afternoon. Jou don' sleep, jou get sick."

I wished she hadn't brought that up. It had been on my mind the last two days. How long could I go on burning the candle at both ends? But I knew the answer—as long as it took. "Don't worry about it," I said. "I can handle it."

"Sure," she said. "You big an' strong. But while you guard Colton, who gonna guard me?"

I thought about Jack and smiled. "Don't worry. Jack can keep an eye on you."

"But jou say this Jack is old man. How he gonna take care of me?"

"Believe me. You'll be safer with Jack than anyone else."

She backed a step and thrust out her lips in a soft pout. "An' jou leave me with him?"

"I don't have much choice."

She gestured with her free hand, palm up. "Okay. Jou nice guy. But jou kind of dumb."

While she was packing a bag, I had time to consider her remark. She was right. But not for her reasons. I had the feeling that if somebody really was trying to kill her, she could be more than just trouble, she could be dangerous. And if they weren't trying to kill her, she was still dangerous.

Chapter 16

IT WAS LATE in the afternoon when I walked into Cal MacDonald's office. My eyes felt as though they had been forced to watch reruns of Apocalypse Now all night. My body had lost its fine tuning and was limping along with clogged fuel injectors.

Mac was sitting at his desk in front of an old Royal Standard typewriter, concentrating on typing a report with two fingers and looking pained at the effort.

"Why don't you use a computer?" I asked.

He looked up and grimaced. "I can do it better and faster on this."

He resumed typing, pecking out the letters with the speed of long practice.

"But with word processor software, you could format it for those reports. By boiler-plating some of that text, you could save yourself a lot of time. You could also get a good grammar and spell checker."

MacDonald's typing did not pause. "You know how long it took me to learn how to change a ribbon on this machine? How long do you think it would take me to learn one of those damn computers? Shit, the instruction books alone weigh ten pounds."

"You could do it. In the end, it'd be a lot quicker and easier."

There was a pause while he finished typing a line. He ripped the page out of the typewriter which protested with an ugly whine. "Before you start in on the NBPD," he said, "you'd better do something about Jack Blucher—" he snapped a finger at the sheet of paper "—before this gets any longer."

I stared at the paper. It was almost filled with closely-spaced typing. "Jack? What does he have to do with this?"

"Who knows? He's a loose cannon. Fortunately, nobody's pressed charges—yet."

"Charges? For what?"

"Assault with great bodily harm for one thing. He's also involved with those beach commandos. That could be trouble for him and for us."

"Commandos? What's that supposed to mean?"

He looked up at me with a faint smile. "You don't know? I mean commandos. Mercenary wannna-bes. A lot of them hang out around here. As long as they behave themselves, they're just so many tourists. But your friend, Blucher, has been getting them all charged up. You tell him this isn't Asia or Africa. We're in charge here. *Comprendo?*"

"I'll tell him," I promised, even though I knew it'd be like asking a leopard to change its spots. Mercenaries, for God's sake. In Newport Beach. I'd dumped a magnet in a bunch of iron filings.

MacDonald slipped the paper into a file folder and placed it in an out tray. He indicated a chair beside his desk. "What now?"

I sat down and considered a way to achieve my purpose without getting MacDonald any more agitated. "I've got some information for you," I said, which seemed like a good opening gambit. "And I'd like to talk to Eddie Hooker."

"Can't," MacDonald replied with his usual joie de vivre.

"Why not?"

"Bailed out."

"Oh, damn." That was a possibility I hadn't considered. Not so soon anyway. "Can you get him back?"

MacDonald looked up at me, his eyes inquiring.

"I think I've got proof he was involved in Helen's death."

MacDonald stared at me. "You still on that?"

"That's part of the news. I think Eddie Hooker or somebody killed Helen because she recognized one of the men she...ah..." I stopped, unable to say the words.

MacDonald grimaced, but he swiveled his chair so he was facing me. "That's a damn flimsy motive for murder."

"Maybe it is. But that same person tried to kill Samantha Cazzoli."

For the first time since I came in he looked half-way interested. "Cazzoli? The bimbo in the film?"

"That's right. She came to see me. She was scared. Some guy in a truck tried to run her down this morning."

"Could've been an accident."

"She didn't think so. And when I took her back to her place, it'd been ransacked. The rest of her tapes were gone. They killed one of her cats."

"Guard cats?" He still wasn't taking the whole thing seriously. I raised one shoulder, and he looked toward the door as though he expected Samantha to walk in at any moment. "Where is she?"

I couldn't look him in the eye. "At my place."

MacDonald almost smiled. "Your place?"

"She was afraid to come here. She thought you'd put her in jail.

She's afraid to stay home. And," I added in response to his silent stare, "she has another cat."

MacDonald made a noncommittal "hmmm". He picked up his pipe from the desk and began the slow ritual of lighting it. Between slow puffs, he said, "Why would somebody want to kill her?"

I watched the direction the air conditioning was wafting the noxious cloud of smoke and moved my chair to the other side of the desk. "For the same reason they killed Helen. She might recognize one of the men."

"Might?"

I got the familiar uncomfortable feeling. Again I had no proof, only a string of 'maybes' and 'ifs'. For me, they added up to proof, but for a policeman looking for evidence that would hold up in court, they probably added up to paranoia. "Some of the men wore masks," I said. "She says she doesn't know any of them."

"Then she can't tell us much."

"I guess not. But the point is that if somebody is trying to kill her, it means Helen's death might not have been an accident or suicide."

"That's a big if."

"Well, what about Hanna Carbo? She was going to tell me something. That means her death was no accident either. It's part of the pattern."

MacDonald stared at me coldly, sucking on the pipe as though he was determined to inhale enough carcinogens to commit suicide within the next few minutes. "We have no proof there's a connection."

A surge of frustrated anger caused me to explode, "Jesus, Mac, why can't you see it? Two people dead and another one somebody tried to kill. They even tried to kill me!"

"For a piddling porno operation? You think some civic leader is going to risk killing three people because one of them *might* recognize him? And him wearing a mask? Come on, Ben."

The anger faded to a dull resentment. He was either too lazy or too busy with more important things to spend time on something as nebulous as a possible connection between the porno operation and Helen's death. "All right. But if I'm right, he might try to kill the one person who can really identify him."

"Eddie Hooker?"

"That's right. Samantha said he did the recruiting. If he did, he should know the identify of all the men."

MacDonald shook his head. "I had a long talk with Hooker. He's strictly a small-time con man. You're barking up the wrong tree." He began shuffling through papers on his desk, hinting that I was taking up his valuable time.

My jaw locked in grim resignation. I hadn't expected rejection after I told him about Samantha. But pushing MacDonald wasn't going to get me anywhere. "Okay," I said. "Maybe I'm wrong. But I'd like to talk to Hooker anyway. Can you give me his address?"

He sighed and fished a file folder from the papers on his desk. He flipped it open and took out a paper. "1932 Jefferson." He snapped the file shut and tossed it to the side as though he were dismissing both Hooker and me.

I picked up a message pad from his desk and wrote down the number. I got up, working at controlling my anger. "Thanks," I snapped and turned to the door.

"Ben," MacDonald said and I half-turned back. "I'm up to my neck in a dozen other things," he continued. "I just don't have time to go full bore on a case that's mostly speculation. But I won't wrap it up. You bring me something solid, something that ties these things together, and I'll go after it. I promise you that."

"Sure," I said. "I'll do that."

I left him peering at me through a cloud of smoke. He was breaking a city regulation by smoking in the office, but who was I going to tell?

On the drive to Hooker's place, I sucked in deep drafts of salty ocean air while I tried to think what I'd say when I found him. He couldn't very well deny he was involved in the porno operation, but unless he was a total fool, there was no way he was going to allow himself to be trapped into admitting Helen had been part of the operation.

I could try to beat it out of him. He didn't look like the type who would stand up to heavy physical abuse. The information might not be admissible in court, but it would give me the leads I needed. And to hell with the courts. If a creep like Hooker could get away with murder, why couldn't an honest pillar of the community do the same? The answer was obvious—prosecutors and big lawyers feasted on community pillars. It was the little miscreants who only got their wrists slapped.

Jefferson Street ran through a gerrymandered area of the city on the west side bordering Costa Mesa. As I drove, I noticed the character of the area gradually changed from small shops and homes to an old industrial area that had gone to seed. The closer I got to Hooker's address, the dingier and more rundown the neighborhood became. It was as though I were entering the nest of an army of rats who were working their way outward from a central point, nibbling away at the architecture of civilization; leaving obscene rubble of filth and decay where people moved like dead and dying creatures, unable or unwilling to expend the energy to stop the slow destruction.

The address was on an old apartment building with raw places in the stucco like open sores. I walked to the dim, smelly entrance where a row of mailboxes lined one wall. Most were identified by layers of names where each tenant had scrawled his name over that of the previous one until it was almost impossible to distinguish one from the other. I found the name Hooker heavily marked on number five as though he wanted to make sure his important mail would not end up in the wrong box.

Apartment five was upstairs off a balcony facing an open court. I went up the stairs quietly since I didn't believe Hooker would be particularly happy to see me. The sagging screen was open, but the door was firmly shut and locked, probably triple locked if Hooker owned anything remotely valuable. I knocked on the door. I'd have preferred the advantage of seeing him before he saw me, but it was too late for that.

When there was no answer, I knocked again, louder. Still no answer, not from inside.

"He ain't home," a gravelly voice shouted from the downstairs patio. "You don't have to wake up the whole damn building in the middle of the night."

I looked up at the bright sun. "Sorry about that." I moved to the rail and peered down into the patio, searching for the owner of the voice. "You know where he went?"

"How the hell would I know? Now get the hell out of here."

The voice belonged to a misshapen, fat creature with matted gray hair wearing a voluminous dressing gown. I couldn't tell if it was male or female. "Does he have a car?" I asked quickly. If his car was still here, he might be holed up inside his apartment.

"Hell, yes," the creature snarled. "You crazy? Everybody's got a car."

"What kind does he have?"

"That red Camaro out in front. Wakes the whole damn place every time he starts it, the stupid creep."

I remembered seeing the car. It was parked in front of a fire hydrant directly in front of the apartment. Only it wasn't a Camaro. It was a TransAm, probably an '88 or '89.

"I saw that car out front. He must still be home."

"Naah, I seen him go out. He's in the Goddamn bar again, gettin' drunk."

"What bar is that?"

"Goldy's. Where else? Only place you c'n walk back from without gettin' mugged."

"Where is it?" I was already starting down the stairs.

"Next-fuckin'-door. Where the hell else?"

Outside the building I saw that Hooker's TransAm was still parked in front of the fire hydrant. Other cars were parked in red zones and on the sidewalk like an Italian city street. Apparently, nobody cared about parking tickets. Maybe the police had other things to worry about in this neighborhood, such as staying alive.

Goldy's Bar looked as appealing as a cesspool. Inside, I had to stand for a moment to let my eyes adjust to the gloom and my nose to the odor of stale beer. To my right, the bar ran the length of the wall. There were battered booths along the wall on the other side. There were only two customers hunched over the bar. Both belonged in the neighborhood.

In the back, under a pool of yellow light, two other guys were playing pool, taking time out between shots to swig from open cans of Coors. One of the guys was Eddie Hooker. He hadn't shaved, and in the dim spill of light, he looked big and mean, almost as big and mean as the guy with him.

I waited until Hooker was concentrating on lining up a tough bank shot before I walked up to stand beside him. When he missed, badly, and muttered "shit," I said, "Hello, Eddie. Glad to see you're out."

He stiffened, but didn't whirl around. He moved both hands to the middle of the cue stick and looked back over his shoulder, ready to swing or punch with the stick's butt end if he didn't like what he saw. Then he recognized me and relaxed a little, but kept his grip on the cue stick.

"What the shit do you want?" he growled.

"Nothing much." I kept my voice pleasant and my body relaxed, seemingly vulnerable. Jack Blucher had once told me that when you're dealing with animals try not to look threatening. But be ready to move, fast. "I just had a couple of problems you might be able to help me with."

"Yeah?" He turned to stare at me and I gave him a big smile, acutely conscious that replacing teeth was damn painful and incredibly expensive. Behind Hooker, the other guy started taking shots. "What kinda problems?"

"It's about those porno films. Were you the casting director?"

His body tensed and his hands shifted on the cue stick for a better grip. I got ready to move. "I told the cops already," he said. "I don't know nothin' about no porno stuff."

"You were there. You were running the camera."

"One time only. An' I didn't even know that's what it was gonna be. I thought it was gonna be another stupid sales film."

The other guy missed his shot and said, "Your shot, Eddie."

Hooker stared at me a second, then turned his back and studied the table. But I wasn't going to be dismissed so easily.

"Who told you to be there last night?"

Hooker didn't answer. He crouched and lined up a shot, his mouth drawn into a grim line.

"Who did the casting, Eddie?" I insisted. "That's all I want to know."

"I can't remember," he muttered. "Bug off."

He straightened and leaned over for his shot. I reached past his shoulder and picked up the cue ball. He straightened and snapped around to face me.

"What the shit?" he snarled. "Put that back before I break your face." He lifted the cue stick chest high like a drill sergeant demonstrating hand-to-hand combat with an M1.

"Sure," I said. "Don't get mad."

Jack Blucher said you should always try to get the jump on your opponent when you knew there was no avoiding conflict. Another lesson was to disable your opponent so he couldn't function at full capability, especially when he was bigger and stronger than you. I reached out as though to put the heavy plastic ball on the table, a little amazed at the steadiness of my hand. Then, moving with as much speed as possible, I smashed Hooker in the temple with the ball.

His eyes glazed and his knees buckled. The cue stick fell out of his hands and I caught him under the arms and held him bent back over the table. His mouth was open and he sucked air in ragged gasps. I hoped I hadn't given him a concussion. That was something I wouldn't wish on my worst enemy.

Except he might be the bastard who'd killed Helen. I hoped the headache he was going to have would blow the top of his head off.

But right now I wanted him able to hear me. I put my face close to his and said quietly, but with as much intensity as I could generate, "Names, Hooker. I want the names of those guys in the films, especially the guys in the masks."

His eyes began to focus and his legs steadied. He straightened a little and croaked, "Okay, okay."

I was still holding Hooker off balance, half-bent back over the table when sudden pain flamed in my side and my breath exploded in agony. I'd forgotten about the other guy, and he'd come up behind me and smashed me in the side with a hooked fist. Instinctively, I ducked away. The following punch, aimed at my jaw, glanced off the crown of my head and the man grunted in pain. I hoped he'd broken his damn hand. I stayed in a crouch because the pain in my side wouldn't let me straighten, but I could see the guy's legs and I kicked him in the side of the knee as hard as I could. He yelled and collapsed on the dirty floor, holding his knee with both hands.

I wished he hadn't made me do that. I felt kind of sorry for him. He'd need surgery to get those tendons and ligaments repaired, followed by months of physical therapy. But, hell, I might need surgery myself. He'd missed my kidney but my ribs felt as though they were broken. I couldn't straighten, and now Eddie Hooker would try to finish the job.

I twisted away from the expected blow. When none came, I cautiously turned and looked for Hooker. He was gone. I heard a door slam in the back and I muttered, "Oh, damn!" and broke into a stumbling run, pressing my hand against my throbbing ribs.

In the back of the room was a short hall that led to the rest rooms. There was a door at the end of the hall with a crudely lettered sign above it that said Emergency Exit. I slammed it open and ducked outside, half-expecting to be met by a fist or a brick.

I was in an alley littered with trash and overflowing trash dumpsters. I listened, trying to decide which way Hooker might've run. But the blare of traffic from the street in front drowned all other sounds. Where the devil would he go? To his apartment? Not likely. He'd be trapped there. His car! He'd want to go fast and far.

Gritting my teeth against the pain, praying I wasn't bleeding internally, I charged down the alley toward the street, listening for the sound of squealing tires that would tell me I was too late. I was almost at the alley entrance when I heard the muffled but unmistakable crack of a gun shot. I pulled up quickly, wondering if the shot had been meant for me. If it had, he was a lousy shot because I hadn't heard the bullet. Better yet, I hadn't felt it.

I peered around the corner of the building, keeping low. Half a block away, I could see Hooker's car. The door on the driver's side was standing half open. But there was no sign of Hooker. Maybe he'd opened the door to grab a gun and was now crouched behind it waiting for me, his gun leveled at the alley entrance. I pulled my head back with the speed of a startled turtle, almost feeling the jarring, massive shock of a bullet smashing into my head.

When I realized there'd been no shot, I straightened slowly and listened. There were no sounds except the occasional passing of a car.

Cautiously I peered around the corner again. Nothing had changed. The car still stood quietly, the door still open. But now I could see that someone was sitting in the driver's seat.

I didn't move, staring at the figure. Why didn't he drive away? Why didn't he shoot? Why didn't he move?

I eased from the concealment of the building, ready to dodge back at the first sign of movement. But the figure in the car just sat there, not a flicker of movement. A decoy? Was he waiting for me to move closer for a sure kill? I didn't think so. The Eddie Hookers of this world would run if they weren't cornered. Wouldn't they?

Staring intently, afraid to blink, I began moving toward the car. Now I could see Hooker clearly through the windshield. He was just sitting, looking straight ahead as though he had all the time in the world.

It was a long, long walk to the car. As I moved forward, my gaze riveted on Hooker, I used my peripheral vision to pick out places where I could duck if he came out shooting. It was shadowed inside the car and the windshield grimy, so it wasn't until I'd almost reached the car that I could see Hooker's strangely rigid posture and his staring eyes. Moving around to look through the open passenger window, I saw why Hooker hadn't moved. He was dead.

He was sitting partially slumped in the bucket seat, his head tilted back against the head-rest. The left side of his head was a cavernous mess of blood and tissue. Lying on the seat near his limp right hand was an S&W revolver that looked like a .38 police special. I didn't have to look to know there'd be a small black hole in his right temple. Eddie Hooker had found a way to keep from answering my questions. Or somebody had found a way to stop him.

I didn't know which pained me most, my injured side or my despair. But the real pain was knowing that now Helen's killer would never be found.

Chapter 17

THAT EVENING, THE quietness of Colton Labs seemed to radiate sorrow. The change was subtle, but I could feel it like the cold fingers of a skeleton trailing across the back of my neck. It wasn't the plant. The faint sounds, the odors, the view of deserted machines etched by fluorescent lights were exactly the same. The change was in my perspective. Until tonight I'd been imagining a sinister presence in every shadow, every sound. But tonight, the huge building seemed to have retreated into a languor like a welcome rest after a period of intense activity. Even the on-going environmental tests and experiments seemed to be going through their endless cycles with a cool competence like professionals performing easy routines.

It was over; the illegal operation ended. The building seemed as relieved as I.

The death of Eddie Hooker had closed all the doors. Now there was no one who could positively identify the men in the masks. Cal MacDonald had taken one look and put Hooker's death down as suicide. It was either that or a robbery attempt, possibly a car-jacking gone sour. In that neighborhood, resisting somebody with a gun was the same as suicide.

So I could finally relax. Samantha Cazzoli could not identify any of the men. And if Helen's death had been murder, it had probably been done by Eddie Hooker to keep her from telling about his extra-curricular activities.

The pain in my side had subsided and I walk through my route like a somnambulist. If I could survive the night, tomorrow I could sleep all day.

I came out of my reverie with a start. I was standing outside of Harry Deen's photography studio, staring at the closed door. Some subconscious doubt was holding me, pushing aside the complacency.

How was it possible for Eddie Hooker to carry on the porno operation without Harry Deen knowing about it?

All his expenses had been charged to the lab. The cost of tape, of editing, of making copies had to show up somewhere. And Harry Deen had to approve all photo charges or the company wouldn't pay them. There was the possibility Deen wasn't too conscientious about examining his department's billing before he okayed payment. His department had to do thousands of dollars worth of business every month with outside photo and video labs and post production companies and vendors. It would be possible to hide a few hundred dollars. Deen might've even allowed Hooker to sign the invoices for him.

But over a period of weeks or months, there must've been a lot of extra charges. How could Deen have missed them? He must have had some suspicions.

And if he did know and failed to say anything, why?

There had to be some way to find out. Maybe if I located some of the payment invoices, I could check the signatures. If Deen okayed all invoices, that would prove he knew.

Suddenly my blood was boiling through my tired body like water surging through a canyon after a flash flood. Maybe it wasn't over after all.

I used my pass key to let myself into Deen's dark office and was immediately assaulted by the odor of stale cigarettes. After I closed the door and heard the lock snap, I stood listening. There was nothing to hear except my own shallow breathing. Even the faint sounds of the shop area beyond the door were blocked out. I didn't like the stygian darkness. Unseen people could be moving, closing in on me. I fumbled for the switch and felt a surge of relief when the fluorescent lights came on. Nothing. The office was as deserted as it was supposed to be.

I glanced around the cluttered room. Where would Deen keep his old invoices? From a jumble of papers on his desk I sorted out a few invoices for photography equipment along with a few lab bills, but none had been signed or initialed for payment. What I needed were copies of bills that had been paid.

A logical place to look was in a bank of three steel filing cabinets against the wall. Two of them were fitted with security bars and stickers saying they contained classified or proprietary material. So the unclassified paper work had to be in the other.

After fifteen minutes of leafing through tightly packed file folders, I gave up. There were plenty of papers, letters and invoices signed by Harry Deen and several by Eddie Hooker, but I wasn't knowledgeable enough about the photography business to know if any were significant. All I found out was that either Deen or Hooker could okay a billing.

I closed the filing cabinet and glanced at my watch. I could spare ten more minutes. Then if I didn't find anything meaningful—whatever it was—I'd get back on my patrol.

I went into the editing room and turned on the lights. I considered running some of the video tapes stored on the racks, but decided against it. It was unlikely that anything incriminating would be left where somebody could find it.

The only place left to check was the darkroom. Inside, a dim red light cast an eerie glow. The odor of film processing chemicals was so strong it made me gag.

There was a roll of 35mm film negative hanging from a rack where I assumed it had been hung to dry after processing. Holding it by the edges I turned it so I could see the images against the red light. A tag at the top of the roll said 'Company Classified' which meant the pictures contained proprietary data. Each frame was a close-up picture of something that looked a little like a bazooka rocket with a pointed nose at one end and an exhaust nozzle at the other. Between the two ends was a metal rod with protrusions that looked something like a car's cam shaft.

The pictures seemed perfectly normal to me. Pictures of advanced hardware. They were probably shot for a marketing campaign or a brochure.

I was still looking at the film when I heard the outer door open and someone enter the office. Who the devil would be coming into the studio at this time of the night? And how could I explain my presence?

I heard Harry Deen mutter, "Who the hell left the lights on? Stupid bastards. I told 'em a million times—last one out turns off the friggin' lights. Can't teach 'em a damn thing."

He was coming this way. Frantically, I looked for a place to hide. There was none. The minute he turned on the white light, I'd stand out like a fly pinned on a wall.

The light! I climbed on the chair and partially unscrewed both bulbs in the overhead fixture leaving the dim red light.

I just had time to jump down and crouch in the darkest corner, half-concealed by a stand supporting an enlarger, as Deen felt his way through the darkened light-trap entrance.

In the dim red light, I saw him enter and he snapped the light switch. Oh, Jesus! Did I unscrewed the bulbs enough? Nothing happened. Deen flicked the switch and cursed in frustration.

"Friggin' lights," he said, and gave up. He went directly to the roll of film. Without examining it, he took it down and rolled and inserted it into a 35mm film canister. Then he turned and left, taking the film with him. In a moment, I heard the outer door close.

I stood up slowly. Why had Deen come into the plant in the middle of the night? What was so critical about a roll of film? He could've picked it up in the morning. And, since it was company classified, it would have to be recorded by document control before it could be taken from Colton Labs for any purpose. Except that at this time of night document control was closed. Which meant that Deen was breaking security. And where was he taking it? Did it have anything to do with Helen's death?

The small room seemed to be closing in on me, the single red light a burning eye staring accusingly. Move. Do something. Don't be immobilized by doubt, as helpless as Shakespeare's Dane. Find out where Deen was taking the film. If there was nothing wrong, I'd just be wasting a little time. And time was running out.

When I walked through the office, I noticed Deen had also left the lights on. So much for economy.

I turned off the lights, let myself out and closed the door softly. Harry Deen was far down the long corridor, heading for the outside door. I hurried after him, my rapid steps sounding to me like pistol shots. All Deen had to do was turn around and he'd see me. I had to get out of his sight.

I turned at a cross corridor and trotted to another exit door. If I hurried I could circle and pick up Deen after he left the building.

Outside, the night chill cut through the thin cloth of my uniform. It was almost two o'clock in the morning and a thin fog had rolled in from the ocean. I hurried to the end of the building and peered around the corner. There was plenty of light from rows of security lights high atop the building. But there was no sign of Deen.

I felt a pang of dismay. How could I have lost him? Hadn't he come out the door? If not, where had he gone? My chest felt as though I'd swallowed a cantaloupe whole and it had lodged halfway down. It was either a bad case of nervous tension or I was having a heart attack. At the moment, I didn't have time for either.

I concentrated on listening. If he'd left the building, I might be able to hear his footsteps. The chill night air would make any sound carry. But with my luck, he was probably wearing moccasins.

Then I heard the faint sound of footsteps. To my right. It had to be Deen. He was heading for the main gate.

Moving as silently as possible, I ran to close the distance. I had to see if Deen signed out. Ted Olds was on duty at the gate. If he was on the ball, he'd make sure Deen signed the log book. However, I was aware that sometimes when the person was well-known, the gate guard ignored procedures.

Ted Olds did. I arrived at the gate just behind Harry Deen and stopped at a point where I was concealed by the foliage of a border hedge. The air was misted by night fog, but I could clearly see the lighted interior of the guard station through its heavy plate-glass windows. Harry Deen walked to the open communications window, and to my stunned surprise, handed the roll of film to Ted.

"This is the last for a while," Deen said. "We're cooling it 'til this stink dies down."

"Why?" Ted Olds said. "They bought the porno deal, didn't they?"

"Don't ask questions," Deen said coldly. "Just make the delivery."

Ted Olds' face relaxed into an expressionless mask. "Sure. Like always?"

"Yeah. Like always."

Deen walked out the gate and vanished into the darkness and fog. After a moment, I heard a car start in the nearly deserted parking lot. The car's lights came on, cutting a swath through the tenuous fog as Deen drove out of the lot and down the street.

I stood in the shadows, the pain in my gut forgotten. Ted Olds? And Deen? And the 'porno thing.' They could only be referring to Hooker's porno film operation. Which meant Deen had known about it all along.

But the film he'd passed to Ted Olds had nothing to do with sex. I hadn't looked at it carefully. But what I'd seen were pictures of an odd-looking electronic device.

Was that what this was all about? Was one of my guards involved in some kind of industrial espionage?

Fighting back a deepening sense of apprehension, I walked to the guard station. Ted Olds was putting the roll of film in his lunch box. He heard me and looked up, his eyes wide.

"Oh, hi, Ben," he said with a nervous laugh. "You scared the hell out of me."

"Who was that just left?"

Olds turned to face me, leaning against the counter, half concealing his lunch box behind him. I could tell he was wondering how much I'd seen and how much he could lie about. He decided I'd seen Deen so he said, "Harry Deen. You didn't see him?"

Instead of answering, I turned the log book so I could read the signatures. "I don't see his name, either in or out."

Olds grinned sheepishly and waved his hand. "You know how it is. I know him. He's in an' out all the time."

"So he could come in and out any time, and there'd be no record?"

Olds shifted uncomfortably. "Well, not all the time. Hell, it's only Deen." He caught my stare and forced a smile. "Besides—I'd remember."

"If you were asked, you mean."

"That's right."

"Was he in the night Helen was killed?"

He licked his lips, the tip of his tongue looking as dry as his lips. "Killed?"

"The night she died. Was he in that night?"

"No," he said. "I'd remember that."

I stared at him, letting him squirm. He knew he'd broken a firm rule, and I let him wonder what I was going to do about it. He was probably ready to admit to such a small infraction if that was all I'd seen. But it wasn't all.

There was no point in asking him about the film. He'd only lie.

"He left a roll of film with you," I said. I held out my hand. "Let's have it."

Old's eyes narrowed, then they began to shift rapidly as he searched for an explanation. His breathing stopped for a second, then began again, deep and rapid. "What film? I don't see any film."

A deep sadness came over me. I was no longer angry. Instead, there was a devastating sense of loss. I'd been betrayed by someone I'd considered a friend. "Ah, come on, Ted," I said and I could hear the sick edge of despair in my voice. "I saw him give it to you. It's in your lunch box."

I took a step closer, my hand still outstretched. He backed away and put his hand on the lunch box protectively, his face mirroring indecision. Then his eyes suddenly shifted to focus on a point behind me and he almost smiled. I started to turn, to see what it was that made him so happy when my head exploded in a red ball of pain that instantly turned to total blackness.

Chapter 18

*I WAS RUNNING so hard my heart and lungs were bursting, my feet
pounding the thick grass that bordered the golf course where Newport
High's cross-country team always worked out. But I should be moving
faster. Why wouldn't my legs respond? And why was the pain burning
inside my head instead of deep in my lungs?*

The vision faded as throbbing in my head became my world. It
was a living force, surrounded by blackness and flashes of red that
pulsed through the darkness like white-hot lances.

I gradually became aware that the pulses of pain were
synchronized with the beat of my heart. Each beat triggered a pulse of
agony that reverberated through my head like the stroke of a giant bell
until the next pulse struck. My heart? I was having a heart attack! God,
why does it have to be so painful? And why was it centered in my
head? That wasn't right. Damn. I was doing it all wrong.

Impossible. It wasn't a heart attack at all. It had to be a stroke. No
wonder I couldn't move. I was probably totally paralyzed. So how
could I be feeling pain in every fiber of my body? Thank God for the
pain. I couldn't be paralyzed.

But wait. Oh, Jesus, maybe paralysis was like that. Maybe the
pain was a part of it. The only way to find out for sure was to move.
Move something. An arm.

I willed my right arm to move from where it was doubled under
my chest. Thank God, it was moving. But so slow. And accompanied
by the sound of groaning.

Then it was free, my fingers feeling the rough texture of a cold
concrete floor. At least my right side was not paralyzed.

But what about the left?

I moved the fingers of my left hand, rubbing them over the
concrete, feeling its pits and ridges. Thank the Lord, I could feel them.

My legs? What about my legs? Oh God, please let them be okay.
They were cold and stiff. But they did have feeling. Come on legs. Pull
up. That's it! They were doing it!

Then I was sitting up, clutching my throbbing head, not yet ready
to open my eyes. Damn, it was cold. Probably caused by brain damage
when I'd been hit on the head. Something to do with destroyed neurons

and synapses. Maybe I was blind. That was why I didn't want to open my eyes. My instincts were protecting me from the truth.

I avoided confronting the inevitable by trying to remember what had happened. I'd been about to get the film from Ted Olds when somebody had clubbed me from behind.

Why hadn't they killed me? Leaving me alive didn't make sense. Ted Olds and Harry Deen had to be working together—using the film somehow to steal company secrets—industrial espionage. There had to be millions of dollars involved. That must've been why Helen was killed, not because of the pornography.

What was it Olds had said? 'They bought the porno deal.'

So the porno operation had simply been a cover, a red herring, to hide something much bigger. And I was the only one who could stop it.

So why hadn't they killed me?

I found myself shivering. Fear? I didn't feel afraid. The immediate danger was over. No. It was cold. Intense, bitter cold. California nights could be chilly, but this was ridiculous.

Using a combination of willpower and an incomprehensible urge to remain alive, I opened my eyes. Then I knew why they hadn't killed me. I was inside one of the big atmospheric test chambers. My gaze focused on frost crystals that spangled the walls. How lovely the way they caught the light. Frost crystals? In California?

Oh, God, I'm inside an atmospheric chamber set for Arctic cold! No wonder I was freezing!

Clinching my teeth against stabbing pain, I turned my head to look around the big room. I was sitting on ice-cold concrete next to an Army 2 1/2 ton truck. Overhead a traveling crane was parked at the end near the large double doors, its dangling cables ending in a hooked block-and-tackle. There was a glass-paneled control room on the far side of the truck, the windows covered with a thin layer of frost. An array of cables snaked up from a large box-like structure in the truck bed and into a cable tray near the ceiling that channeled the cables through a seal into the wall. The structure on the truck undoubtedly housed some kind of an electronic system undergoing testing in a simulated arctic environment.

There was nothing simulated about the cold. It was agonizingly real, deep and penetrating, worse than anything I'd ever experienced on the ski slopes. It had to be several degrees below zero. If I hadn't regained consciousness when I did, I'd soon have been a frozen corpse. But that was the point. That was how they meant to kill me. Except for the lump on my head, there'd be no marks. And if I didn't get out fast, they'd succeed.

My fingers had already lost feeling, but I was able to clutch the wheels of the truck and haul myself to my feet. I stood for a moment, leaning against the truck's fender, letting the pain in my head subside to a thick, pulsing throb.

There were two doors—the big entrance doors under the crane and a small door leading to the control room. I pushed away from the truck, and after taking a moment to catch my balance, I walked unsteadily to the small door. Did it open in or out? The hinges were on my side. It had to open my way. I focused on the metal knob. Metal? If I took hold of it with my bare hands my skin would stick to the sub-zero metal. I fumbled my handkerchief from my pocket and wrapped it around the knob. I grasped it in both hands and tried to turn it. Nothing. It was solid. Locked!

I strained at the knob, pulling and turning in a burst of desperate fear. It had to open. But it wouldn't. The door was as solid as the surrounding wall, either locked or frozen into an immovable slab. It could well be the seal to my tomb.

But I couldn't give up. By focusing on a burning core of hate for whoever had done this, I was able to stagger to the thick double doors that I could see opened outward.

Push! Hard! Lean your weight against them.

I might as well be pushing the Washington Monument. They were firm, weatherproof, their edges sealed with some kind of plastic that would not turn brittle in the killing cold. My legs collapsed and I felt myself sinking to the cold concrete of the floor. My feet were unfeeling blocks and my hands wooden claws. I was aware my breathing had deteriorated to a series of labored gasps. Each time I sucked in the super-cooled air, my chest burned as though the air was on fire. I knew I had only minutes of consciousness. My eyes wanted to close, to escape into a deepening pool of warm darkness. I forced them open.

My God, don't sleep. To sleep now was to die!

I seemed to be outside my body, watching it push painfully to its feet, glazed eyes staring. Staring at what? There was no way out of this wintry tomb. Not without a battering ram.

Suddenly, I was back inside my body. My eyes were focused on the truck and a thought drove through the pain—a battering ram.

Of course! The truck! They had to have driven it in. I could drive it out. If I could get it started!

In a series of drunken lurches, I moved to the door of the cab. I yanked it open, not caring if I left acres of skin on the frozen door handle.

My claw-like hands fastened on the steering wheel and I strained to pull myself into the cab. Now. The key... The ignition... How the hell did you start one of these monsters? No key. There was no key; no place for a key! So how? I couldn't be stopped now!

Frantically, I wrenched the gear shift into neutral and began pressing buttons on the dash with unfeeling fingers, pushing and twisting anything that looked like a starter switch. Nothing. I heard a harsh voice screaming in anguish, then a new sound—a sound! A slow grinding, as though a cement mixer was trying to turn against a load that was far too heavy.

I focused on my hands. Nothing. My foot. It was jamming the accelerator to the floor. The switch had to be linked to the gas pedal. Please, foot, don't move. Please! Please! Oh, damn! Damn! Start, damn you, start!

Instead, the starter slowed, then ground to a labored halt. Silence. Death-like silence. Oh, no. God, no! How long had the truck been in the chamber? The oil in the crankcase had to be almost frozen solid. There was no way I was going to get this thing moving.

With a curious detachment, I watched my foot move from the pedal. There was no feeling at all. It was sort of funny, the way it lay there as though it knew more than I did and had already given up. Funny, funny. Parts of me were giving up. Sending messages to my brain. Telling me it was over.

Come on, brain. Get with it. It's over. You're dead and don't even know it. The bad guys have won.

My brain screamed a protest. The hell they have!

I clawed the door open with unfeeling hands and willed my legs to swing out and down to the floor. Incredibly, I was standing. Swaying on legs with all the feeling of wood, but still upright.

And for what? The effort was a total waste of what little energy I had left. I might just as well have stayed in the cab of the truck and allowed the demand for sleep to take over, simply close my eyes and rest, if only for a moment. Why not? It would be impossible to get the rig moving short of a tow truck. There it was—the perfect battering ram—and no way to move it.

Something—was it a thought?—jerked my head around and I found myself staring stupidly up at the overhead crane. My eyes followed the dangling cable down to the big hook.

What the hell are my eyes trying to tell me?

The hook. What about it?

What could I do with a hook—and a crane? Even if it wasn't too frozen to move, what good would it do to hook it up to the big truck? It still would not be possible to drag it forward at a speed that would ram it into the huge doors. Or would it? Was that what some part of my brain was trying to tell me? But the other part was telling me to lie down, go to sleep. Sleep. Wait to be rescued?

No, there would be no rescue! What the hell are you thinking?! Do it yourself!

The crane controls. Where were they? What was it I remembered about crane controls? Oh, yes. There were buttons in a black box that should be hanging about chest high from a cable below the crane. There it was—the control box. But so far. Ten feet. It might just as well have been a mile.

The thought irritated me. I could go ten feet. Couldn't I? This must be how people with physical disabilities felt. My brain was telling my legs to move, my arms to reach. But they refused to respond, to do my will. They had no purpose, no feeling. They were already dead.

Damn it! I wasn't dead! Not yet. Move, bastards. One step. Just one.

Ha! You see. You did it!

Now another! Go on! Good. Good.

Now another. Come on, arms. Help, damn you! Reach out. Take the control box. Hold on tight. Use it to help support your stupid legs.

The buttons. Which ones? Focus. Read. Yeah, yeah. One was marked 'down.'

Come on, finger. Push it. That's it. That's it! Sound! A whirring, grating sound. Movement. The hook was coming down!

Good. Good. Take finger off button. Push button marked 'reverse.' More sound. Look up. The crane. It was moving, coming back, bringing the hook with it.

Now, stop! The hook was dangling directly over the front bumper of the truck. Down a little. Where's the damn button? There.

Push. Yeah, yeah.

Now, stop. Let go of the control box.

You'll fall, you idiot. So what? Fall then. Crawl to the truck. Work the hook under the bumper. Don't fight me, damn you. Do it! Ha, you son-of-a-bitch. Gottcha!

Stand up now. Stand up, you stupid bastard!

The controls. Hang on to them. The buttons. Up. That was it. Push and hold. Was the front of the truck coming up? Move. Front wheels off the ground. A groaning sound. The truck rolling forward a little until the cable was straight up and down.

Back off a little. Look at it. Look at it, damnit! What do you see? Truck, front end suspended. Twenty feet from the big doors. Crane directly over the bumper. Look up. Focus on the crane's rails. They were supposed to extend all the way to the big front doors.

Oh, God, they have to! Yes, yes. There they were. All the way.

Where's the 'forward' button? There! Jam that lump you call a thumb down on it. Hold it. Was the crane moving? Yes, by God, it's moving! Gathering speed, moving toward the big doors, dragging the reluctant truck with it. Popping sounds as the experiment's cables leading into the truck tore loose. Ruined the damn experiment.

Who cares? Put it on the bill. Roll, damn you. Faster! Good. Now! Crane slams into emergency stops. Truck's momentum slams it into doors. *Bam!*

Christ, they're down. Oh God, they're down. Heat. Warm air, blasting in. Fog. Instant fog when it hits the super-cooled air. Find the stupid door. Crawl. Why are you crawling? Too slow. What the hell, all the time in the world now. Feel the heat. Let it take over. Now you can sleep. Sleep. Knit up the raveled sleeve of care.

Stay closed, eyes. It's all right now. Oh, yeeessss.

Chapter 19

IT WASN'T THE thought of freezing that terrified me, although the penetrating chill was causing my bones to shrivel and the skin of my entire body to tremble and writhe in protest. I could live with that. But I couldn't deal with the rats. I could see their eyes all around me, pinpoints burning in the icy darkness. I stared back, wondering why they didn't leave my concrete cell to find warmth. Maybe their hunger was greater than their pain. And if that were true, how long did I have before they'd attack?

I tried to shout and wave at the circling rats, but my arms were too heavy to move. Sensing this, the rats moved closer.

I was saved by the light.

It started as a dull grayness and gradually cleared to a pearl glow. The eyes of the rats retreated with the advancing glow until, to my immense joy, they vanished.

But the cold and the pain intensified, and with it came dim memory of an environmental chamber that was to be my tomb. No wonder I was freezing. This was no basement room in the orphanage. There were no rats. I was trapped in an arctic test chamber and I'd soon be dead.

But why was it so painful? I'd always heard that freezing was an easy way to die; that you simply felt a warm drowsiness and when the desire to sleep became overwhelming, you closed your eyes and gave up. When you woke up, you were in heaven.

That must have been how it happened to Helen. They'd loaded her with alcohol and left her in one of the cold chambers until she became drowsy and lapsed into unconsciousness. Then they'd put her in that Tempest chamber and turned on the powerful radar. Later, they'd taken her body to the test range to make it look like an accident or suicide. By the time she was discovered, all evidence of freezing had vanished. Which was undoubtedly what they had in mind for me.

Strange how I knew that. Perhaps when you were dying the mind took on an increased awareness, an insight denied the living. And I was dying. There could never be this much pain in living. My entire body felt as though it was on fire. Except for my hands and feet. They were unfeeling blocks of flesh and bone.

Then I became conscious of a sound—a voice. "Hey, man," it was saying. "You really done it this time. Why the hell don't you use the door like anybody else?"

Joe Welts? How could he be here? This was my dying place. Maybe if I opened my eyes he'd go away. There. They were open, weren't they? All I could see was a gray haze.

Oh, God, I was blind. Definitely blind. My eyeballs had probably frozen.

Then, hands were under me, and as I was lifted, the grayness focused and became the cement of the floor. I'd been staring at the floor. Boy, was that stupid. I turned my head and looked up at Joe Welts.

"Pretty stupid, huh, Joe?" I croaked. "Hey, you're working late."

"Yeah," he said. "I've been looking for you."

I struggled to grasp his meaning. Maybe dying didn't make you think better at all. At least, not death by freezing, which probably slowed the flow of blood to the brain. The brain wouldn't like that. It would go into a snit of depression and refuse to think at all. It would certainly refuse to cooperate with the arms and legs. No wonder I couldn't move. Which was okay with me. I didn't want to move anyway. I was too tired. All I wanted to do was curl up on the warm floor and wait for the pain to go away.

But Joe Welts wouldn't let me. "Come on," he insisted. "Time to thaw out."

He tugged at me, forcing me into a sitting position and new vistas of pain wrenched through my body.

"Ah, come on, Joe," I muttered. "That hurts."

"Good," he said. "That means you ain't dyin'."

I tried to resist as he heaved me to my feet and draped my arm across his shoulders. I wondered what was holding me up. I had absolutely no feeling in my legs. Except pain—sharp, stabbing pain.

"My God," Welts said. "You're like a lump of ice. I hope I ain't too late."

Too late? Too late for what? I stared down at the swaying gray cement floor as he half-dragged, half-carried me. Where were we going that was so important? I didn't remember any heavy duty appointments.

We turned and I saw we'd entered one of the spacious men's rooms where the machinists washed up after work. This was a strange place for an appointment. I'd hoped for a nice warm hospital where they'd let me sleep.

Joe Welts eased me down to the concrete floor near a round

terrazzo-cement structure I recognized as a big wash basin where the hot water was activated by a foot pedal circling the base. I stared with interest at Joe Welts' big foot as it pushed the steel bar down and I heard the water splash in the basin. I guess Joe was going to clean up before our appointment. But he could forget about me. My only appointment was with sleep.

A sharp ring of metal on metal snapped my eyes open and I saw that Welts had anchored the steel bar down with somebody's tool box. Naughty, naughty, Joe. That guy who owned the box wouldn't like that.

Clouds of steam were drifting up from the big basin, and when Joe Welts lifted me, I thought he was going to drown me in the hot water and I said, "Hey."

My warning worked. Instead of submerging me in the boiling water, he dragged me to one of the toilet stalls. Oh, God, is he going to drown me in that? I tried to struggle, but he easily lifted me and sat me on the floor in front of the toilet. He flushed the toilet and began pulling off my shoes and socks. I was flooded with gratitude. He was going to drown me in clean water—feet first.

"Put your hands in the water," he demanded. "It's cool. Won't thaw you out too fast."

Thaw me out? Before he killed me? That didn't make sense. But it would buy me more time. Maybe I could think of a way to escape. I put the lumps that were my hands into the cold water. Then I pulled them back.

"Wait a minute. Is this a Tidy Bowl?"

Joe Welts snapped. "Get your hands back in there."

To my surprise, he began massaging me feet. Funny way to kill somebody. It was going to take him hours. So much the better. I put my hands back in the water and stared at them. They were in there all right, but I couldn't feel the water. I undoubtedly had frostbite, but how bad? People had lost toes and fingers to frostbite. Joe was doing the right thing—thaw the affected limbs slowly with medium heat. Where had I read that?

Suddenly a shaft of pain shot through my hands so sharply it made me gasp and jerk them from the water. Instead of subsiding, the pain remained, settling into a constant throbbing agony. It felt as though millions of white-hot needles were being driven under my nails and deep into the flesh of my hands.

I groaned and began pounding one hand into the other, anything to try to diminish the pain. "Oh, Jesus, Jesus," I grunted.

Joe Welts grinned wolfishly. "Hurts like hell, huh? That's good."

"Good," I gritted. "What's good about it?"

"Means the circulation's coming back. Tell me when you feel it in your feet."

It was there already. Like my hands, my feet felt as though someone was ripping the flesh away with a blowtorch. Even my ears and nose, my entire face hurt with a searing agony. I had to grit my teeth to keep from crying out. I couldn't stand sitting. I struggled to my feet and began a lurching, arm-swinging walk around the steaming wash basin.

"Chilblains," Welts said. "I take it you never lived where it gets cold."

"I've been there," I said, each word an effort. "I ski."

"Shit, that don't count. You get a little chill, you run in the club house. I mean, you ever had to work where it was so cold your fingers and toes froze?"

"No. And I'm sure as hell not going to either. Not if I can help it."

"It's gonna hurt like hell for a while. But it'll go away. You'll be okay."

"God," I gritted. "I've hurt before, but nothing like this."

Welts handed me my socks. "Here. Put these back on. Keep your feet off the concrete."

I struggled into the socks, unwilling to stop moving long enough to put them on. I wanted to kick my feet against the wall, the wash basin, anything to relieve the pain. I began hopping from one foot to the other, alternately pressing my pain-racked hands under my armpits and wringing them in spastic agony. Welts had said the pain would stop. But when? When, for God's sake?

Welts watched me, not grinning anymore. "People who never felt chilblains don't know the pure hell. I'd say about as bad as a bad burn. Only it do go away."

He was right. The pain was beginning to wane. The degree was infinitesimal, but it was there. "It's feeling a little better," I said.

"How the hell did you get yourself locked in there?" he asked. "You ain't supposed to be in there anyway, is you?"

I looked at him, puzzled by the question. "I don't know."

He pointed to the back of my head. "That have anything to do with it?"

I put my hand on the back of my head and felt a large lump. It was gratifying to be able to feel anything with my half-frozen fingers, but now I was aware my head had been aching for a long time.

"You back into a door?" Welts asked.

Memory surged back. I'd been talking to Olds at the guard house when somebody had hit me. How long ago?

"What time is it?" I asked. I figured my own watch would be frozen solid.

Welts pulled a wristwatch from the pocket of his coveralls. "Keep it in there so it won't get broke," he explained. "Time is three fifty-seven."

Almost four o'clock. I'd lost almost two hours. I had to find a telephone and call Cal MacDonald. He should get out here before Olds and Deen found out I wasn't dead. They'd have to come back to move my body. Or would they? Maybe they'd planned to make it look as though I'd been locked in the environmental chamber accidentally. It wouldn't be smart to have two guards die of microwave radiation. When I would be discovered by the morning shift, I'd be in no condition to tell anybody the truth.

Then it occurred to me it might be better to call Clint Hemet first. This was really his responsibility, and he might have his own ideas on how to proceed.

"I'd better call Clint Hemet," I told Welts. "He'll want to know about the—the broken door." Then I groaned again. "Damn, I don't have his home number."

"Mr. Hemet? He's here."

I stopped my restive movement. "Are you sure? Clint Hemet? Head of plant security?"

"Sure, I'm sure. Saw him come in 'bout an hour ago."

The information stunned me. Why would Hemet be at the plant at this time of the night? Well, the best way to find out was to ask him. If I could make it that far. The pain in my feet and hands had diminished, but they still hurt like hell and I felt disconcertingly weak.

"You think you might help me get up to his office?"

"Sure. But he ain't in his office. He's with that photography guy, Harry Deen."

"With Deen?" What the hell was happening? Why would Hemet be meeting Deen at this hour? It was even more puzzling since I knew Deen was up to his hairy ears in whatever the hell was going on. Maybe Hemet suspected Deen and had come in to confront him. If so, Hemet might be in real danger. If they'd kill me, they certainly wouldn't hesitate to kill Hemet.

The pain in my hands and feet had subside to a dull aching. My head continued to throb. Possibly due to a mild concussion. Too late to worry about that now.

"My shoes? Where are my shoes? I've got to find Hemet."

Welts located my shoes and I painfully forced them onto my swollen feet. He turned off the hot water and put the tool box back against the wall.

When I tried to walk, I almost fell and Welts steadied me by taking my arm. I stumbled against him and felt the outline of a holstered gun under his sweat-streaked coveralls.

"What the hell," I said, and jerked away from him. He had to be one of them! I tried to run, although I knew I'd never get more than a few steps if he wanted to kill me.

"Wait a minute," Welts said. "I'm not with them."

I stopped, feeling stupid. If he wanted to kill me, he could've done it any time. "So who are you?" I remembered the question I'd asked earlier, which he hadn't answered. "What are you doing here this late?"

"Same thing you are."

I stared at him, wondering how much I should tell him—if anything. He didn't look like a janitor anymore. In some subtle fashion, the aura of being a manual laborer had vanished. Now he looked like a shrewd and very strong fellow who could be equally effective as a corporate executive or a very deadly bodyguard. Even his voice had changed, becoming stronger. And the diction was sharp and clear.

"What's that supposed to mean?" I asked.

"I'm a private operator. I work for the Shelby Agency."

I knew the Shelby Agency. They were among the largest of the private investigative agencies. And they specialized in industrial espionage. All feelings of pain were swept aside by a mounting indignation. If Welts was one of their operators, there had to be something going on at Colton Labs a lot bigger than a porno picture operation.

Who'd hired the agency? Why hadn't we been notified?

"You have any credentials?" I asked. Actually, it was a stupid question. His credential was the fact he hadn't killed me.

He fished a wallet from his pocket and dug out a Shelby ID. Feeling like a fool, I checked his photograph. It was authentic. "I think Shelby should've told me about this? Certainly, Hemet should have."

"Hemet doesn't know," Welts said. "Shelby was contracted right from corporate headquarters."

I handed his ID card back to him, anger seething. If corporate had hired Shelby, it meant S&R Security was not trusted. I remembered seeing Harry Deen handing the roll of film to Olds and my anger receded to a deep depression. No wonder we hadn't been informed about the investigation. S&R must have been under suspicion from the beginning. But Hemet? That was different.

"Why wasn't Hemet told? He's in charge of plant security."

"Because Colton's been losing too many proprietary secrets. Hemet hadn't been able to stop it."

"Well, he's on to something now if he's with Deen. And we'd better find them before Deen guesses what he's up to."

I turned and began limping as fast as I could out the door and along the corridor.

Welts strode along beside me, from time to time grabbing my arm to steady my lurching walk. "What makes you think Deen is involved? I couldn't make him."

"Two things. I couldn't believe that Eddie Hooker could operate the porno setup without Deen knowing about it. So why didn't he say anything?"

"He was probably making money out of it, too."

"I think it was more than that. I think the pornography was a cover for his real operation—selling company secrets."

"Well, a lot of people would pay a fortune for the right software decoding tapes or data on high power microwave technology."

"What was that last? You mean radar?"

"It goes beyond radar. Colton has been working on the cutting edge of electron beam technology. That's about all I can tell you."

It was as though I was building a brick wall of evidence in my head and he had slipped a key brick into place. Maybe Helen's 'accidental' death hadn't been caused by a high-powered radar. Maybe it was some other source of microwave energy. I remembered the pictures I'd seen in Harry Deen's processing lab and another brick slid into place.

"Does this technology use a device that looks a little like a small rocket—or a gun?"

Weltz jerked as though I'd jabbed him with a needle. "How the hell did you know that?"

"I'm not exactly a technology illiterate. My guess is the company's developed some kind of a weapon that uses high energy microwaves. That might even be what they used to kill Helen."

Weltz looked up at the ceiling as he decided whether he should tell me anything more. He made up his mind and nodded. "You could be right. They're developing a device designed to blanket a battlefield with so much microwave energy that enemy radars and other equipment can't operate."

"But wouldn't that kill everybody?"

"Not unless the beam was focused."

"And that's what that device I saw is for?"

"That's right. But not for killing people. It's designed to fire a burst of microwave energy at a vehicle or a weapons system to disrupt its electronics."

"But if the power was high enough, it could kill a person, couldn't it?"

Weltz puffed out his cheeks and blew air between his teeth. "It doesn't have that capability."

"Oh, come on. You wouldn't be here if the damn thing could only blow up engines."

"Not true. The data on such a device would be worth a fortune."

"I can believe it. And Deen was selling the data."

"That's our guess. It wouldn't be a problem for Deen to get pictures of the device and its components. It's part of his work. The problem would be how to get them out of the plant."

"When I got clobbered, Deen was giving a roll of 35-millimeter film to my guard at the gate. He put it in his lunch box."

Welts stopped and gripped my shoulder so hard I winced. "Your guard?" Then he looked pleased as though I'd given him the keys to a new Jaguar. "So that's how they got it out. And here we've been watching every crate and briefcase out of this place for weeks." His face hardened as he looked at me. "This is going to play hell with your company. How many guards do you think are involved?"

I couldn't answer. I hadn't had a chance to think about it and didn't want to do so now. The pain I was feeling was different than the pain of chilblains, but no less intense.

How many of my people had betrayed me? Betrayed Herb Stax?

Faces swam through a fog of doubt. Most S&R employees were personal friends. It was inconceivable that any of them could be part of an espionage scheme. Besides, they were DOD-cleared and bonded. All had perfect records. Until now...

"That depends on who hit me," I said. "Deen gave the film to Ted Olds. Then Deen left, so it couldn't have been him. Olds usually worked the gate so he'd be the logical one to handle the deliveries."

"What about Renbourne? He was involved in the porno operation."

"I fired him. Anyway, I think he got into the porno thing for kicks. Maybe they would've used the pictures to blackmail him into their other operation if they needed to, but I don't think he was into espionage."

"And the Cotrell girl? Maybe that's what happened to her. When she found out about the bigger operation, she was going to blow the whistle, so they killed her."

That was the same thought that had flashed through my mind. As difficult as it was for me to believe Helen would've voluntarily become involved in sex for money, it made more sense than to think she had been killed simply because she recognized one of the men. She'd been murdered, probably by Harry Deen and Eddie Hooker. But then why try to kill Samantha Cazzoli? She couldn't possibly be involved in espionage. It was still a tangle I couldn't sort out. At the moment, the only thing I knew for sure was that if we didn't hurry, Deen would probably kill Clint Hemet.

"Come on," I said. "We'd better hurry."

With each passing minute, my legs were feeling better and I could move faster. Tomorrow gangrene probably would start blackening my toes and fingers, but right now I felt pretty good.

Even so, it took a couple of minutes to get to the photo studio. During the final few yards I was straining to hear the sound of shots. Then I remembered that the studio was sound proof. A war could take place in there and nobody would hear a thing.

The door was unlocked, just as I thought it would be. I was about to open it when Joe Welts pulled me back. "I'll go first. If anything happens, you stay out of the way."

I opened my mouth to protest until I saw he was holding a revolver with a six inch barrel. Damn! How stupid can you get? I'd been about to charge into a room where a killer might be waiting. If I were Deen, I'd be reluctant about surrendering.

Welts eased the door open and stepped inside, his gun ready. I followed, my heart pounding, prepared to duck at the first indication of gunfire.

To my relief, there was no sound—no movement. The office was deserted, the lights blazing.

Welts quickly moved through the editing room as though he knew his way around and went into the dark room. That took guts. Coming from the light into the heavy darkness made him an easy target. I held my breath until he came out and shook his head.

I followed him to the closed studio door. Before he opened it, he motioned for me to stand clear. The motion was unnecessary. I was standing plenty clear.

He took hold of the knob with his left hand, holding his weapon poised in his right. I expected him to ease the door open so we could take Deen by surprise. Instead, he violently shoved the door open and leaped inside, landing in a half-crouch, both hands holding the gun, swinging it to cover the entire room. Then he centered it on something to his left.

"Freeze!" he snarled. "Don't move."

By that time, I was inside the room. I saw Harry Deen standing beside the big view-camera, ready to take a picture of a complex circuit diagram that had been fixed to a wall-mounted easel and flooded with light.

But the real shock was seeing Clint Hemet standing next to the easel holding another diagram. Then the diagram slipped out of Hemet's fingers and fluttered to the floor. The color drained from his face until his heavy tan appeared to be painted on a base of white clay.

"Who the hell are you?" Deen said without moving.

"I'll tell you later," Welts told him. "Right now both of you move nice and easy over against the wall."

"Yeah, okay," Deen said. "Just take it easy, friend. Ben, tell him who we are. We can straighten this out."

Deen must have had a light switch near the camera because, as he slowly began to turn, I heard a click and the easel lights went out, plunging the room into total darkness. The next instant, the blackness was slit by flashes and booming thunder as both Deen and Welts seemed to shoot at the same time. Inside the sealed room the noise was deafening, but I was certain I heard the meaty whack of a bullet striking flesh and someone grunted heavily. Then I heard Welts thud to the floor, followed by a groan of pain. I dropped to my knees and felt for his gun. If Deen hadn't been hit, he'd be coming after me.

I was frantically feeling around the carpeted floor when the lights flashed on. With the stark clarity of a lightning flash, I saw Welts' gun almost under my hand, and at the same time I saw him sprawled on the carpet clutching at a spreading red blotch on his chest. Near the camera Harry Deen was lying on his back with his eyes staring vacantly at the ceiling. Next to him, etched in blinding light, Clint Hemet was in a semi-crouch with one hand on the light switch and the other holding a gun—a flat, ugly automatic. It'd been Hemet who'd fired, not Deen! And the muzzle of the gun was now swinging toward me.

I had to get Welts' gun, but there was no time. Hemet's finger was already tightening on the trigger! I twisted and rolled just as his gun roared and I heard the bullet whack the floor and ricochet off with a chilling whine. I kept rolling, pushing frantically at the unyielding floor, knowing that if I stopped Hemet would have a clean shot. But where to go? The only concealment was the plywood wall of the conference room set.

In one motion, I leaped to my feet and dove through the fake window, the sound of another shot mingling with the shattering of the window's framework.

I landed heavily on the floor between the painted flat and the studio wall, unable to tell immediately whether or not I'd been hit.

Another shot sent splinters flying from the plywood as Hemet fired at the spot where he thought I'd landed. He was close. The bullet kicked off the floor an inch from my head and slammed into the sound-proofing material lining the studio wall.

I rolled again and came to my feet behind the flat. The air reeked with the odor of burned gunpowder and I fought to keep from sneezing. In the sound-proof room even the smallest sound would be magnified into a target. I had a mental picture of Hemet studying the thin plywood flat, debating where to fire. He could either stitch a pattern of bullets through the thin wall until he hit me, or he could simply walk around the open end and put a bullet between my eyes. And there was nothing I could do!

Hemet knew it, too. "Sorry you had to get mixed up in this, Ben." He paused, waiting for my answer and I could sense the gun weaving like the head of a snake, waiting to strike. I wondered how many bullets he had left. Maybe if I gave him something to shoot at, he'd run out. Damn! It wouldn't make any difference if I did remember how many shots he'd fired as long as I didn't know the type of gun. I wasn't a handgun expert, but I did know that some automatics could hold fourteen rounds or more.

I sure as hell wouldn't stand a chance trying to outguess Hemet for that many shots. My only chance was getting Welts' gun. And even if I could get it without getting my head blown off, could I bring myself to kill Hemet? A minute ago I wouldn't have hesitated. Kill before you get killed! That was the way animals survived.

But that instant had passed. Now I was no longer being driven purely by animal instincts. Now I was a rational, thinking human, and even though I knew Hemet would kill me without hesitation, I was not at all sure I could deliberately kill him even if I got the chance.

It was Hemet himself who changed my mind.

"Sorry about Helen," he said. Then he laughed. "I can see why you went for her. She had some body. You should've seen her and

Eddie Hooker." I knew he was baiting me, trying to get me to betray my location, and I struggled with a growing desire to feel his neck between my fingers and to hell with the bullets.

"Good old Eddie," he continued. "He was supposed to be taking pictures, but he couldn't keep his hands off her. I even took her. Only not the usual way. I made her—"

Something exploded inside my head and I lunged at the plywood flat, determined to get to him, if only for a second before I died. The wood splintered and fell in a welter of sound and dust, and I was driving straight ahead, my mouth open and making sounds of pain and rage. I had a split-second image of Hemet with his eyes widening in surprise as he whipped the gun around and fired just as I slammed into him and we both went down hard with the gun pinned between us. There were two more muffled roars and I felt a solid thud just above my solar plexus.

I knew I was going to die any second, but my rage was so strong I easily tore the gun from his hand before he could fire again.

I rolled aside and pushed the gun under Hemet's chin and said, "Now, you son-of-a-bitch. Do it! Do it!" I wanted him to reach for me, to touch me. Just touch me, and I'd blow his head off.

But he lay impassively, his breathing ragged, his eyes closed. Then he gasped, and there was no breathing at all.

I got to my feet and moved away so he couldn't grab me if he was faking. But he didn't move, and I could see a spreading red blotch in his rectus sheath area. I stared down at him, feeling cheated. The shots must have penetrated his diaphragm and angled upward directly into his heart.

Had he taken both shots? Or had I been hit? I felt no pain except for the lumps I'd taken. But that didn't mean anything. I could be numb from shock and wouldn't feel the real pain until it was too late.

But maybe it wasn't too late. There was a charred spot on my shirt caused by muzzle blast. That might have been from the shot he'd fired when I was charging him. Where the devil was the hole?

I pulled aside my shirt. No blood. Maybe the bleeding was all internal. I could blackout any second. Except there was no hole. I hadn't been hit. The blow I felt must have been the gun's recoil. I guess I wasn't so unlucky after all.

I knelt beside Hemet and checked his pulse. There was none. I couldn't believe how quickly he'd changed from a living person to a lifeless shell. How could such a metamorphosis take place so quickly? I could still hear his voice—and his words—words that had wiped out years of friendship. If he'd ever been a friend.

I heard a gasp behind me. Welts! Oh, damn. I'd forgotten the man who'd saved my life. I turned to see him trying to sit up and I quickly crossed to his side. "Lie still," I told him. "I'll get an ambulance."

He coughed. "Are they dead?"

"I think so."

"Damn. Now we might never know."

"Know what?"

"Who was—telling them what—to do."

As I was calling the police, using the office telephone, I wondered what he meant. Hemet and Deen had been behind the scheme.

Hadn't they?

Chapter 20

SLEEP WENT BADLY for me. I was laying dreadfully still, unable to move, gripped by terror as a dark figure, its face shrouded by a monk's hood, moved toward me in slow cadence. It reached out to me with gangrenous hands and my throat closed in horror. I had to move! I had to break free of its awful power and run.

With a wrench of will-power I broke away, and found myself sitting up in bed, bathed in early morning sunlight, staring at the familiar outlines of my own bedroom, my harsh cry of fright and rage echoing in my ears.

A small, warm hand pressed against my chest and a soothing voice whispered, "No, no, *querido*. Is a dream. Jou're dreamin'."

The hand pressed me back and I allowed myself to relax, turning to bury my face in the pillow. The specter was gone. I wasn't going to die. Nobody could die while delicate fingers trailed over their skin like the wings of butterflies, and while soft breath felt warm and sweet on their naked flesh. Nobody could die with the scent of roses musky in the air. Roses and dying definitely did not go together.

My eyes snapped open. Roses? What the hell was the sensuous aroma of roses doing in my bedroom?

I rolled over, ignoring my protesting muscles, and looked up into Samantha Cazzoli's beautiful, smiling face. She was sitting on the edge of my bed wearing the same tight blouse she'd worn yesterday. A beam of morning sunlight, streaming through a crack in the tightly drawn drapes back-lighted her hair so her face seemed framed in a halo. It reminded me of a scene from an old movie showing a nun who looked like Elizabeth Taylor looking down at an injured child, her darkly beautiful eyes filled with tender compassion. Samantha might be equally beautiful, but she sure as hell was no nun.

As through she read my thoughts, her sensuous lips curved into a mischief smile. "Feel good, no? Want some more?"

I groaned. Who wouldn't want more? But there was more danger in that direction than there had been in my dream. Maybe, concealed in the dark shadow of the monk's hood, the specter's face had been formed of silken skin, warm lips and wide, liquid eyes framed by dark, lustrous hair. No wonder I'd been so desperate to escape its dark embrace.

But this was reality and much easier to resist. I turned over thinking of the painful day ahead. "What time is it?" I asked, although I knew it had to be late.

The sun had been almost up when I'd come from the hospital where they'd taken Joe Welts. Cal MacDonald had listened to my story patiently. He said he would talk to Welts as soon as they'd allow it, but it looked as though the death of Hemet and Deen had just about wrapped up the case.

He'd allowed me to go home with the understanding I'd come in later to make an official statement.

I remembered stumbling through the door and being only slightly surprised to find Samantha and her ugly cat sleeping on my couch. I'd assumed she'd take the bed and I'd sleep on the couch. Jack was nowhere in sight; probably sleeping on the kitchen floor.

I'd struggled out of my clothes and fallen into bed, too tired even to put on my pajamas. At first, I'd fought against sleep, trying to fit together a puzzle that still seemed to have some of the pieces missing. The last thing I remembered was trying to figure out why, after fitting Clint Hemet into the puzzle, there still seemed to be a blank. The missing piece was there, floating in the darkness, the fuzzy image of a man's face. But each time I reached for it, it slipped through my fingers, dissolving like fog.

Samantha told me it was almost noon and I shooed her out of the room and scampered into the bathroom. Basking under the hot needles of the shower, the impression returned that the death of Clint Hemet and Harry Deen was not the end of the puzzle. Even Joe Welts had felt that it went beyond them.

I was still probing for the elusive face when the shower door slid back. I had instant visions of the movie *Psycho* and of being stabbed to death in my shower. I raised my arms to ward off the first slash of the knife, trying desperately to peer through the film of water. But instead of a knife, a small hand holding a bar of soap appeared out of the mist.

"I wash jour back," Samantha said. "It pretty damn dirty. What kind'a games jou been playing?"

I remembered rolling across the floor of Harry Deen's studio and concluded she was right. My back did need a good scrubbing. "Well, okay," I said and turned so she could reach in through the open shower door. But she had other ideas. Naked, she stepped into the close confines of the shower, gasping at the sudden shock of the hot water.

"Holy molio!" she said. "Jou sure like it hot."

"Yeah," I said. "And it's getting hotter."

"Jou want threw me out?" she said with a wide smile. "Where jou gonna grab?"

I really did plan to put her out. Then I made a big mistake. I stopped looking at her face.

I suppose a fantasy lies in the back of everyone's mind of that absolutely perfect hour or two when everything goes exactly right. For me, it had begun. For some reason, during some part of the gentle bliss, poised on the edge of Nirvana, the refrain of Hunt's poem intruded on my totally sedated mind. "Time, you thief, who loves to put sweets into your list, put that in. Say I'm weary; say I'm sad; say that health and wealth have missed me. Say I'm growing old, but add—Jenny kissed me!"

Substitute the name Samantha and from that time forward you could laugh at adversity. You'd already experienced one great joy, your hour of rapture. It was a memory I'd take to my grave—if I lived that long.

I was getting dressed when, lying on the bed, Samantha stretched like a cat and smiled up at me. "Jou had telephone call las' night. She say she mus' talk to jou *pronto*."

Pronto? A chill of apprehension made my skin crawl. I shook the feeling off. I was getting paranoid, thinking every call was going to be bad news. It was probably only Kim Fuji wanting to know about schedules. "Who was it?" I asked, my voice calm.

"Cotrell. Helen's mama. She want see jou."

That brought the chills back. What could she possibly want? "Did she say why?"

"No. She no say."

Claire Cotrell probably thought I had more information about Helen's death. I wasn't sure I wanted to tell her what I'd learned. But it would be more painful if someone else told her. "Okay. I'll swing by this evening."

"She say is important. She sound like it, too."

Important? Well, perhaps to her it was. "Okay. I'll drop by the first chance I get."

I was putting off the confrontation, and I knew it. The truth was I knew any meeting with Helen's mother would be painful for both of us. Why open old wounds? Helen's father already blamed me for destroying his daughter's career and causing her death. Her mother probably felt the same. It was a meeting I would gladly put off forever.

Then I sighed and reached for the telephone. Claire Cotrell

deserved her catharsis.

I'D HAD TO ask Claire Cotrell for the address of her home. When I'd first met Helen, their home had been a fifty-year-old bungalow over in Costa Mesa. But when Lou Cotrell had grown more affluent, he had moved to Newport's ritzy Corona Del Mar district near the Balboa Yacht Club.

The curving streets were broad and lined with palm trees. There were no cars parked at the curbs. That would have been strictly gauche. The homes, although huge and immaculately maintained, were not exactly new. There'd been time for the trees to put forth a goodly bower and for the sweeping lawns to achieve a deep green. The flower beds looked as carefully tended as the hair and nails of the women who owned them—and just as untouchable; women who every day left their perfect homes to their servants while they lunched at a perfect restaurant or enjoyed the Irvine Coast Country Club's golf course or tennis courts, or reinforced their *de rigueur* tan beside the club's perfect pool.

I rounded a long sweeping curve, checking the house numbers stenciled on the curb, and turned into a circular drive behind a meticulously clipped eight-foot tall hedge that almost hid Cotrell's two-story French chateau-style home.

I parked in front of the small portico and went to the richly paneled door. I was about to ring the doorbell when the door was opened by Claire Cotrell.

I stared at her in stunned surprise. She'd aged terribly since I'd seen her at the funeral. I wouldn't have believed such a transformation could take place in a person in just a few days. I knew Helen's death had hit Lou Cotrell hard, but Claire Cotrell looked as though it was killing her. She'd always been slender, but now she was skin and bones. She was wearing a knee-length, short sleeved dress that was clearly expensive, but which hung on her in loose folds.

Her skin had lost its youthful firmness and now seemed to sag in a network of wrinkles like the skin of an apple left too long in the sun. Her ash-blonde hair was beautifully coiffured as always, but it was lusterless and threaded with silver. Her face had retained its Nordic beauty, but now there was a darkness under her eyes and deepening lines pulled down the corners of her lips. Her eyes, once a sparkling blue, had faded to a dull gray. They briefly came alive when she smiled and held the door open for me to enter.

The smile had faded by the time we were seated at one end of a long table in the dining room. I watched silently as she poured each of us coffee from a silver service. Her wrists looked too thin and weak to hold the heavy pot, but they had to be stronger than they looked because she filled both cups before setting the pot down.

"I'm so glad you could stop by," she began, her voice low and controlled. She tried another smile, but it was a struggle. "I hope it wasn't any trouble."

"No, no. I wanted to come anyway." My lips were uncomfortably stiff and my throat dry. I was not good at lying. I cleared my throat, the sound loud in the dead silence of the room. "I wanted to tell you how sorry I am about Helen."

She nodded as though she had been expecting the words. I could think of nothing more to say so I sat quietly, pretending to sip the tepid coffee, wondering why she'd wanted to see me. If it was for recrimination, she was certainly slow in working herself up to it.

She suddenly put down her cup and leaned forward to stare at me. "How much do you know about Helen?" Her voice was flat, almost hard, as though she was steeling herself for the answer.

"You mean in regard to her work or about—us?"

"I've heard stories," she continued, and I recognized the look in her eyes then. It was pain. "Disturbing stories." She paused and her eyes grew vacant as though she was looking inside herself for some answer.

After an uncomfortable moment, I said, "What kind of stories?" But I already knew the answer. Some son-of-a-bitch at the police station hadn't been able to keep his damn mouth shut.

Her eyes focused on me again. "They say..." She turned her head, unable to look at me. "They say Helen was involved in some sort of...of sex movies. Pornography."

I sorted through my options, searching for a lie that would not sound like a lie, or a truth that would not hurt. Finally, I said nothing, letting silence speak for me.

Claire Cotrell's shoulders slumped and she sighed—a small, sad sound. She folded her hands on the table as she faced me again. "Tell me what you know," she said.

"All right." Maybe it would take some of the pain away if I could make it sound as innocent as possible. "There was evidence uncovered that Helen had participated in a...a sex-oriented film."

A tiny pulse at her throat quickened. "How many?"

I tried to make it easy for her. "As far as I know, just that once."

"As far as you know." It was not a question. It was a flat

statement shaded by a twist of irony as though she could not believe such a thing could happen at all. "What sort of evidence?"

"A video tape. Pictures."

Her lips twisted into a bitter smile. "How many men?"

"One," I said quickly—too quickly.

Her expression did not change. "Did they identify him?"

"Yes. As a matter of fact, it was another guard."

Her body abruptly sagged and I realized she'd been sitting as rigidly as a steel bar. I wondered what had been in my answer that had produced such an expression of relief.

I reached across and touched her hand. It was cold and fragile. "For what it's worth, I don't know why Helen got involved. But I'm sure it wasn't because she wanted to"

She stood up, looking as grim and hard as winter ice. With an effort she forced a smile. "Well," she said. "Thank you for stopping by."

I slowly stood up, unable to believe the meeting was over. She also realized how abrupt she was being and made a small gesture toward the coffee. "Perhaps you'd like some more coffee."

"No, thank you. I'm having lunch with Herb Stax. I'll probably be having coffee there."

At the front door, she held out her hand. When I took it she put her other hand over mine. "Ben," she said. "I know Lou blames you for what happened. But I know it wasn't your fault. Don't make the mistake of blaming yourself."

She was asking the impossible. My degree of guilt might be small, but it was still there. "It's hard not to. I'm the one who got her to come to work for S&R in the first place."

Her eyes seemed to grow dull and she wasn't seeing me anymore. "No," she said. "It wasn't you. It wasn't your fault." Her face cleared before I could figure out what she meant and she let go of my hand. "I want you to stop by any time you can. After all, you were almost my son-in-law."

"Yes. That's right," I agreed. We both knew I'd probably never see her again. I stepped out into the sunshine and paused. I had to ask one more question.

"Why? Why do you think she did it?"

She stepped back, her face incredibly sad. "I hope we never know the answer to that." She gently closed the door.

I got in my Corvette and drove away, wondering what she had meant. Probably nothing, except that as Helen's mother, she would just as soon not know the lurid details of her daughter's fall. She would already have to retreat into a lonely world of seclusion for a time, avoiding the snide innuendoes of her enemies and her friends, waiting for enough time to pass so she could once more walk into a room and not sense the sudden shift in conversation—if she ever could. The same thing would probably happen to me. The thought left me feeling depressed and empty.

I drove up the Pacific Coast Highway which angled toward the towering buildings of the Newport Town Center before it swung toward the sea again at MacArthur Boulevard. I waited for the warm sunshine and the wind in my hair to lift my spirits as they always did, but this time good cheer was slow in coming.

I used my cell phone to call the office. Kim told me Herb had already gone to lunch at his usual place. I knew where that was—the Cock n' Bull.

She tried to ask me about what had happened last night at Colton Labs, but I cut her off, telling her to start lining up substitutes who could fill in for the night shift. I also told her to telephone Cal MacDonald. I wanted him to meet me at the restaurant, if possible, so we could go over the situation with Herb. Maybe among the three of us we could figure out what had really been going on at Colton Labs.

On impulse I also called my house. Jack's voice made a gruff, "Yeah?"

"Me," I said. "Everything okay there?"

"Yeah. Where did that bitch learn to play poker?"

I chuckled. "I think she spent time in Las Vegas. She play pretty well?"

"She cheats. But I can't figure out how. You better get back here before I lose your house and boat."

"Why don't you cheat, too?"

"Shit, I am. And I'm still losing."

"Play for ass. She'll let you win."

"Oh, great," he muttered. "If I lose, she'll kill me."

"That's the idea," I laughed. "You'll be afraid to lose." I hung up.

THE COCK N' Bull was a typical California combination bar and restaurant, meaning it had parking for about fifty cars. It was located on the edge of the Bay's turning basin, the far end of the parking lot separated from the water by a low wall of painted concrete blocks. I saw Herb's Eldorado convertible parked close to the entrance.

Reluctantly, I left my 'vette with the valet parking attendant who

I'd have to tip later for driving it about twenty feet. I paused to regroup my thoughts before I pushed open the thick wooden doors. In order to tell Herb and MacDonald what had happened, I'd have to dredge up some painful memories. I could definitely feel an unpleasant emotional experience approaching.

Inside, there was the usual mood of casual friendliness. Also as usual there were ten or fifteen people sitting and standing near the entrance waiting for tables and another twenty or more waiting in the bar drinking white wine or California spritzers. The men's attire ranged from tennis or jogging shorts and tank tops to three piece suits. Several of the bronzed women had also come straight from the courts, but others looked as though they were high-priced executives or even higher priced housewives.

Daniel, the maitre'd, recognized me and gave me a professional smile and a nod as I edged through the crowd and into the dimly lit dining room. I found Herb seated in a booth near the bar. He was sipping Absolute vodka on the rocks and studiously working out a schedule from a list of guards we could press into service at Colton Labs.

He grinned at me, his chubby cheeks making him look like an overgrown cherub. "When they said you didn't have any holes in you, I figured you'd be here."

He beckoned to a long-haired waitress dressed in a tight miniskirt and a low-cut, heavily embroidered peasant blouse and she hurried over. She gave me a strange look when I asked for a Diet Pepsi.

"What the hell happened last night?" Herb asked. "And what's this about Ted Olds?"

I told him what had happened, ending by saying, "Olds also implicated Ed Emblem. They were both working for Clint Hemet. It was Ed who hit me on the head."

"The bastards," Herb snarled. "I never did trust either of them."

"Than you've got better instincts than I have. I had no idea anything was going on out there."

"Me, either. I just didn't like them." He took a sip of his vodka. "What was Hemet up to exactly?"

"I don't know for sure. Some kind of industrial espionage. I asked MacDonald to meet us here. He should have learned something from Joe Welts by this time."

"I'm really steamed about Shelby putting a team in there without informing us. I'm sure as hell going to have a talk with some people about that."

"I'm glad they did," I said. "Or I might be dead."

"Yeah, I guess you're right" Herb licked his lips. "That guy Welts? How much do you think he knew?"

"From what I can gather, he'd been watching Harry Deen. But he had no idea our people were involved. Or Clint Hemet."

"Hemet," Herb shook his head sadly. "That son-of-a-bitch. You can't trust anybody any more."

I saw Cal MacDonald walking slowly between the tables looking for us, and I waved him over. I slid to the middle of the booth to make room for him.

"Too damn dark in here," he grunted. "How the hell do they expect you to see what you're eating?"

"They don't," Herb said. "That way they can charge more."

"How is Welts?" I asked.

"He'll be okay. He was lucky. The bullet was a nine millimeter. It glanced off a rib before it penetrated his lung."

"Was he able to tell you anything?" Herb asked.

MacDonald shook his head. "Not much. But when we put his reports together with what we already knew, we got a pretty good picture. They were making pictures of company blueprints, papers, circuit boards, lines of software, hardware, anything they could sell. The pictures were given to your guards who brought them out."

"Then who got them?" Herb asked.

"Don't know," MacDonald said. "They were put in a special post office box—one of those private ones. We checked. It didn't lead us anywhere. I didn't think it would."

"What about the pornographic operation?" Herb asked. "Why did they screw around with that?"

"Cover. If anybody got suspicious, the investigation was supposed to dead end when they uncovered the dirty picture business."

"And it would have," Herb said, "if Ben hadn't thought there was something else going on."

MacDonald frowned as though he didn't much like the implication he hadn't done his job. "Well," he admitted, "he brought it to a head."

"If they hadn't killed Helen, we wouldn't have found out anything," I said. "That was really stupid."

"Yeah," MacDonald agreed. "She must've been going to blow the whistle on their porno operation."

"I don't think so," Herb said. "I think she found out about the espionage deal, maybe from Hanna Carbo. That's why she was killed."

He took a large sip of vodka, then set the glass down with a solid thump. "You're not going to like this, Ben, but I bet when she found out our guards were involved, she thought you were behind it.

"Especially after your trip to Uganda. Probably looked to her like you were trying to make direct equipment sales instead of using Deen's pictures. She wouldn't turn you in. Not you. Deen or Hemet must have found out how much it meant to her to keep you clean and used it to blackmail her into the porno operation. Probably Deen. He was slime-ball enough."

I sat staring at Herb, feeling the growing excitement of joy. "She did it to protect me."

"That's the way I see it," Herb said.

"Makes sense," MacDonald echoed.

I shook my head, unable to think clearly. It all fit together neatly. Except Helen was not like that. "She'd have asked me. She would've said something. That operation must've gone on for months."

MacDonald shrugged "But how long did she know about it?"

Herb refused to look at me as he said, "We only know for sure she was involved the last few weeks. She probably thought she was protecting you."

"But, damn it!" I hit the table with my fist hard enough to make people look. "There was nothing to protect. I had nothing to do with it. I can't believe she thought I did."

"Maybe she found that out," MacDonald said grimly. "Maybe she found out who really was behind it, so he had her juiced up with alcohol, locked her in that cold chamber until she was comatose, then put her in front of that high-powered radar for a couple of hours so her death would look like an accident."

"Who? Who did she uncover?"

"Clint Hemet," Herb said. "She must've traced the operation to him through Harry Deen."

"No," I said as the thought that had been nagging me came into sharper focus. "Hemet had to be the inside man. He selected the work to be copied and passed it on to Harry Deen. But he couldn't take a chance on recruiting the guards. If one of them had opened his mouth, it would've blown the deal sky high before it even got off the ground. No. He had to be sure of their cooperation before he even started."

"That's what she must have thought," MacDonald said. "The guards had to be planted from the beginning."

"Only two," I corrected. "Ted Olds and Ed Emblem. They alternated on the gate and took care of the log book."

"And Hanna Carbo," MacDonald added.

"Well, maybe. Either she was in it, too, or like Helen, she stumbled onto what was happening. They might have been paying her off. But when they killed Helen, she got scared and wanted to talk to me. They had to get rid of her."

"What about Renbourne?"

"Hard to tell if he was in on it from the beginning or if he got involved later. My guess is that he was only part of the porno deal. And Hooker was running that."

"Clint Hemet got to Emblem and Olds," Herb said. "Damn them! I trusted those guys. I need another drink." He waved his hand and the waitress was quickly at his side. Herb raised his eyebrows at MacDonald and me, but we both shook our heads. He pointed to his own glass and the girl hurried away.

"Just shows to go you," Herb said to MacDonald. "Some guys will do anything for money. I knew those guys almost ten years. It's in the record. Good cops. Both of them. Hell, they wouldn't even take a free donut."

I sat silently, trying to swallow the acid that kept forming in my throat. I knew. The shadowy figure was now in sharp focus.

"Clint Hemet," I said softly, "had no way of knowing Emblem and Olds would be assigned to those duties and at the right time."

"He didn't have to," Herb interjected. "He simply went after the two guys we put out there. He got to them."

I shook my head. "Suppose they'd turned him down? Worse than that, suppose they blew the whistle on him? He couldn't afford to take a chance like that. He had to be certain they were on his team from the beginning, otherwise the whole deal wouldn't have come together."

"If Hemet didn't sign them up," MacDonald said, staring at Herb and me, "who did? Who put those guys out there?

I looked at Herb, waiting for him to speak. But he sat quietly, toying with his steak knife, pressing lines into the clean linen of the table cloth. I felt sick—really sick.

"You should know about the set up at S&R," I told MacDonald. "Herb came to me four years ago and suggested we form a company. I was to handle the finances and schedules. Herb had a lot of experience in the field—a lot of contacts. He'd had his own company at one time. So he handled sales and P.R." I paused, remembering. "He brought in the start-up money. He also brought in most of the guards—people who'd worked for him. Ed Emblem, Ted Olds, Hanna Carbo."

I had to stop for a minute to fight back an awful depression. A sharp pain had begun behind my eyes and threatened to explode into a painful headache. "So Helen was right about somebody from S&R being behind the operation. Only it wasn't me."

I couldn't continue. The depression had become overwhelming. MacDonald stared at Herb who put his knife down and sat with his hands folded looking down at his empty glass. When Herb spoke, his voice was scarcely more than a whisper. "You don't know what it's like to be broke," he said, and I knew he was talking to me. "You never had to beg for a job. You never had to worry about getting old and not having a crying dime."

"I never had money," I said grimly, wondering where he'd gotten that idea. "I worked for every dime I got."

Herb slid out of the booth. He stood over me, his anger so quick and intense I could only stare at him. "You could get it if you wanted to. Easy! You've got the looks. You're young. All those pretty girls. Shit, I never had a girl that wasn't so damned ugly nobody wanted her. Not 'til I got money. Money! That's what you've got to have if you've got nothing else going for you.

"Well, I got it. Now they all want to know old Herb Stax. Who the hell cares if he's fat or old. He's got the green. You think I was gonna let that get away from me? You think I was gonna give all that up?" He gasped for breath, his voice on the ragged edge of hysteria. "Not for some snot-nosed kid. You should've died in Africa like you were supposed to!"

I was stunned, frozen. MacDonald surged to his feet and Herb turned on him. "Get the hell away from me," he screamed. "Get away!"

He shoved MacDonald violently and ran, pushing aside anyone who got in his way. MacDonald had fallen half across the table. He recovered his balance and began walking swiftly after Herb, passed the incredulous people who were staring at Herb as he slammed out the door.

I shoved out of the booth and started after them, my mind burning with the thought that Herb—my friend Herb—had killed Helen! He was the one!

Outside, I had a blurred image of the valet parking attendant just getting to his feet and Herb running madly for his Eldorado clutching his car keys which he must have grabbed from the parking attendant's key-board. MacDonald was running after him, but Herb had a good start and he was in the car and had the engine running before MacDonald got to him.

Herb shot out of the parking spot with smoke spinning off his rear tires. He skidded into a turn, aiming for the lot's exit, but MacDonald had stopped in the middle of the lane. Herb could have run over him. The big Cadillac would have taken him out like a rampaging bull. Instead, tires squealing, it slued to a stop, the heavy front bumper only inches from MacDonald.

I could see Herb's face through the windshield. His eyes were wide, staring. His face was red from exertion and fright, his hair wild. He looked desperate, crazy.

MacDonald started around the side of the car and Herb rammed the gear-shift. I was afraid he was going to smash forward, to kill

MacDonald. Instead, the tires screamed in reverse and the big car bucked and shot backward down the narrow lane, gathering speed, weaving madly as Herb began to lose control, heading directly for the low wall that fronted the deep bay of Newport Channel.

He tried to stop. The tires burned black marks on the asphalt and the front of the car whipped into a spin as the weight of the heavy engine and front-wheel-drive transmission yanked it around. The car was still screaming a protest when it hit the wall and crashed through in a sickening blast of shattered concrete and rending metal. The car twisted and half-rolled, the unloaded engine revving uncontrollably as the wheels spun in the air. It hit the water on its side, bobbed for a second as though fighting to stay afloat, then rolled over and slid beneath the dark surface in a welter of bubbles and foam.

I was already at the shattered wall. Where the hell was Herb? I had to get him out. I had to get him, to talk to him. I had to know.

I cleaved the water, diving, too traumatized to feel the cold. How deep was it here? Several feet. It had to be. Dark. Not much light filtered through the murky channel water. There it was. Oh, God. The big car was upside down, the windshield embedded in the muddy bottom. I tried to reach under it, to lift, to pry.

A hand. Half-buried in the mud. Herb's. Sticking out from under the edge of the upside-down door. Grab it. Pull! Pull! Oh, God, it's useless. Useless.

I let go and struggled to the surface, my lungs burning for air. I could see MacDonald and the parking attendant standing on the bank staring at me. "It's upside down!" I yelled. "Can't get him out. Get help."

I reached the bank in three quick strokes and MacDonald helped me out of the water. "Get help," I repeated. "He's trapped under there."

MacDonald made a gesture of helplessness. "That's a convertible. If he's trapped under it, he's had it. It's already too late."

"No!" I turned to go back, but MacDonald wrapped his arms around me and yanked me back.

"Don't be a fool," he gritted. "He's dead. He's already dead."

I stopped. He was right. Nobody as out of shape as Herb could last more than a couple of minutes deep under water. I looked at the water, so smooth and placid, giving no indication of the horror underneath. Just like Herb. Like poor old Herb Stax. It was hard not to remember him as my friend.

Chapter 21

SATURDAY THE office was closed so I was later than usual for my morning swim. But instead of plunging into the chilly surf, I sat on the sand and stared out to sea, the sun warm on my back. I couldn't stop thinking about Herb and what he had said. It wasn't true. My life hadn't been easy.

But he couldn't know that. I'd never told him much about my early life. I'd never really told anyone, except Helen. And then only the less traumatic parts. I could have told him about some of the problems, some of the loneliness. But no one who had never been an unwanted child could understand the terrible ache of rejection, of being isolated in an uncaring world.

Herb had a deep fear of being broke. He needed money to feel important. What did I need to survive? Not money. What I craved was a caring friend. Who would it be now that Helen was gone?

That was hard to answer. Herb's betrayal had reinforced hard lessons from the past: Don't trust anyone. You are alone and always will be.

Well, not quite alone. Jack walked across the sand and sat down next to me. Jack might have a lot of deficiencies, but you knew he would never betray a friend.

We sat looking out over the sun-spangled water, listening to the surf. There was something immensely soothing in the sound.

"I thought you were keeping an eye on Samantha," I said after a moment.

"What's the point. It's over. Isn't it?"

"I guess so." Herb's tacit confession had closed the book. "Yes," I corrected. "It's over."

Jack picked up a handful of warm sand and let it trickle through his fingers. Whatever he wanted to say wasn't coming easy. "Something I don't understand. How could Stax be the whole thing? You think he had the contacts to move the stuff?"

"Herb had a lot of contacts in high-tech electronics industries. He's been around for years. Without his help, it'd be impossible to trace the pictures after they left the lab. We've cut off the source. That's about all we can do."

"You sure about that?"

"About what?"

"Cutting off the source. You got the guys at Colton. You think Stax might've been working the same scam at other places you've got guards?

The implications made my blood pressure drop another few points. "God, I hope not. I'll have to run a hard check on all our personnel."

After a moment Jack said, "You'll have to change your name."

"My name?"

"S&R—Stax and Roan. Maybe just RS. Roan Security."

"I suppose so. If there's any business left to change. Our credibility can't be in the stratosphere."

"Ahh, you'll be all right. Anybody who knows you has to know you couldn't be connected with what happened."

"Oh, sure. Those hard-nosed plant security officers are going to look into my innocent face and sign on the dotted line."

"Well, you can always close down and come into business with me."

I had to smile at the thought of Jack Blucher being a glad-handing salesman. "What have you got in mind?"

"Those guys I told you about on the beach."

"The ones between jobs? I've got to talk to you about them. MacDonald said for you to stop trying to start a war."

Jack grinned. "I sure as hell could. The only trouble is those guys are losing their edge. You can't keep in shape playing volley ball, for Christ's sake. So that's my plan."

"What plan?"

He started at me as though my brain wasn't operating. "Set up a training camp. Those guys'll pay good money to keep sharp."

My mouth was suddenly parched. "A training camp? For mercenaries? In Newport Beach? Are you out of your mind?"

"Not *in* Newport Beach. Out a ways. In one of those canyons where nobody goes much."

"In Orange County? MacDonald, the mayor, the entire county will have a collective cardiac."

Jack spread his hands, palms up. "So we won't tell 'em."

"You couldn't keep something like that secret."

"Sure I can. I'll tell everybody it's one 'a those places where they play war with paint guns. They're legal."

I pictured the reaction of the county supervisors. "Jack, do me a favor and put it in Riverside County. Or better yet in San Diego. They're conservative enough to go for it."

"Good idea. And if you need a job, you've always got a place."

Somehow the thought was not comforting. "I'll keep it in mind."

The edge of a wave slithered up the wet sand and washed over Jack's feet. He jerked them back with a gasp. "Shit, man. That's cold. You swim in that stuff?"

"Maybe," I said. "I'm not in the mood today."

"Naah, go ahead. It'll do you good–if it doesn't kill you." He stood up and brushed sand from his pants. "Look, I know it's going to take time to get over this—especially about your girl. But it'll pass. It always does. You'll be okay."

I felt a surge of irritation. If people would stop bringing up this horror, maybe I could bury it under a mound of good memories.

"Sure," I said. "I'll be okay."

"Okay. Just a thought." He started to move away, then stopped. "You going to need me to fill in at the lab tonight?"

"If you don't mind. A couple of nights should do it. By that time, we'll have a full crew lined up."

"Okay. Long as you want. If you need any more guys, I know where to find them."

I quickly shook my head. "No. We've got it under control. Thanks."

"Okay." He trotted away, heading for the volleyball court where a group of guys and girls were already gathering. I watched him join them, laughing in the warm sunshine, his wiry body looking out of place among the stalwart guys and shapely girls. Jack wouldn't even think about that. He was comfortable in his own skin.

I made my swim and started toward the boulevard, feeling a little better. My mind might be deteriorating, but keeping in shape would slow the process.

Somebody called my name. I looked across the wide beach and saw Samantha running toward me. She was wearing a bikini bathing suit and parts of her were bouncing in all directions—magnificently— much to the delight of the beach bums.

She yelled again and waved her arms. I sensed the panic in her voice and trotted across the sand to meet her.

She began talking before I reached her. "Ben," she gasped, her eyes wide and frightened. "I see him! On boat!"

"Who?

"Him! The man in mask."

I stared at her, feeling as though she was trying to claw open a wound that was just beginning to heal. I was surprised at how quickly her fear had been transferred to me.

But as quickly as it had gripped me, the tension vanished. This was something different. This was daylight of a new day. That part of my life was over. "So you saw one of them," I said. "So what?"

"No, no," she said quickly, her fear as strong as ever. "Jou no understand. He see me. He see me!"

I put my arm around her shoulders and began shepherding her back off the beach. "Okay," I said reassuringly. "It doesn't mean anything. He was just one of the johns Harry Deen or Eddie Hooker recruited. He'll just have to go somewhere else for this kicks now."

"No," she insisted, but the panic was beginning to leave her voice. "Is more than that. He is man who try to kill me."

"I doubt that. I think that was Deen or Hemet. When the operation began to come unglued, they started getting rid of the people they thought might know, or guess, who was behind the porno deal. That's why they killed Hanna Carbo and Helen." A thought struck me and I stopped. "Unless it was Herb."

The idea started my temples throbbing. Herb might have been up to his ears in stealing company secrets, but I couldn't believe he'd kill anybody. Hell, he hadn't even been able to run down MacDonald when he was trying to escape. Harry Deen was another matter. He would have no compunctions about killing anyone who got in his way. The same could be said about Clint Hemet.

But it didn't matter now. It was over.

Samantha didn't think so. "The man I see in truck no is Harry Deen, not nobody I know. He is man I see now on boat."

Despite the warm morning sun, I felt a sharp chill. Could she be right? Had one of Deen's 'clients' panicked at the thought he might be recognized and linked with the porno operation. If so, Samantha might still be in danger. "Are you sure?"

"*Si*...yes. I know is him."

"But you said the man was wearing a mask. How can you be sure?"

She turned her luminous eyes on me reproachfully as though I had made a very foolish remark. "I don't know face maybe, but I know man's body. I know this one all right. He is maybe fifty, fifty-five. Hard body. Like athletic. Gray hair on chest. Mean eyes like snake."

Some description. It would fit half the men in Newport Beach. "Where did you see him? When?"

At the note of urgency in my voice, the edge of fear came back into her own. "I go out jour patio. I walk on that sidewalk along edge of bay, looking at boats. I see one go pass, on way out of harbor. Big boat. I thinks to myself, man who own that boat mus' be *muy rico*...very rich. So I look at man driving. He is sideways to me and he have on bathing suit only an' white hat like rich sailor wear. And, holy shit, I know him. At firs', I not remember from where. Then I remember an' get cold all over. I have, how you say, goose bumples."

"You said he saw you."

"*Si.* I think he know somebody look at him. He turn his head an' look right at me. I see by his eyes he know me. Then I really get goose bumples. I run. Here to find jou. I tell jou, that man want me dead!"

"But if he was on a boat in the middle of the bay—"

"No, no. Not in middle. Close to side. Very close. Ten, fifteen foots, maybe."

That was possible. Boats headed down the channel between Lido Isle and the Newport peninsula often passed close to the island. The skipper of a power boat, working from the flying bridge, could have been close enough to be recognized. And to have recognized Samantha.

I took her small, warm hand and began walking back toward my place. "I don't think you have to worry," I told her. "Even if he did recognize you, he wouldn't know where to find you. When this thing hits the papers, he'll know he's safe, and it'll all blow over."

She accepted the idea reluctantly. "Maybe," she said. "But I think I stay with jou. We give this blows over plenty time. Maybe couple months."

A couple of months? Could I survive two months of living with a human volcano? But who knows, maybe that nut was still looking for her. No sense in taking chances.

"Okay," I said. "We'll play it by ear."

She grinned up at me. "By ear? Jou pretty weird. But, how jou say, live an' learn."

I was suddenly conscious of her hip against my thigh and I put a little space between us. "Come on," I said. "Let's get some lunch."

We changed clothes and headed out Newport Boulevard toward where we could pick out a good restaurant from the many new ones. I'd taken the top off the 'vette and Samantha was enjoying the way the wind played with her hair. I was sort of enjoying it myself. There's no better way to experience the delight of speed, sun and wind than to have a gorgeous girl sitting next to you in a convertible and obviously enjoying the ride.

At this time of the year, the rolling hills northeast of Newport were covered with golden grass and I decided to take the long, scenic route so I turned off Newport and headed into the hills. We'd moved away from the traffic and were easing along a deserted stretch of a two-lane road between a deep canyon on our right and a steep cut-bank on our left when a big Mercedes sedan came roaring up behind us and swung out to pass. I saw it looming up in my side mirror, so close it startled me. I pulled over close to the shoulder, thinking the driver was drunk or just plain stupid.

Then, as he shot past, he racked over so sharply I thought he was going to lose it. I jammed on the brakes and snapped the wheel, but he still struck my left front fender. The blow from the heavy sedan shook the little Corvette as thought it had hit a stone wall and it flipped up on two wheels. Samantha screamed. She was hanging onto the door, staring down at the edge of the canyon only inches away.

I battled the wheel, trying not to over-control. The proper move was to turn right, into the direction of tilt. Except that there was no room. I was already tearing up the shoulder of the road with nothing to the right but air and a long drop into rocks as big as houses.

But whoever had designed the Corvette was a genius because she came down on her own, hitting the road with a solid thump, instantly under control.

I worked the brakes gently. A spin this close to the canyon could be disastrous. The shoulder widened a short distance ahead and I pulled onto it and stopped. The Mercedes had already disappeared around a bend.

Samantha sat with her hands braced against the dash, her head bent forward between her arms, her shoulders shaking.

"It's okay," I told her. "We're okay now."

She shook her head without looking up. "I tol' jou. I tol' jou he want to kill me."

"That doesn't make sense. Not now. It had to be a coincidence—a drunk driver."

"It was him," she insisted. "I know it was him."

"But how could he know you were with me? There's no way. He only saw you that few seconds on the bay. He wouldn't have time to dock his boat and follow us."

She lifted her head and leaned back. She put her hands over her face and pressed hard. When she took her hands down, she had her fright under control. "He have telephone. He call somebody."

The same thought had occurred to me, but I'd rejected it as implausible. No one would order Samantha killed. Would they? The way the Mercedes had cut into us certainly looked deliberate.

But it couldn't have been. Killing Samantha just because of an indiscretion she could not even prove would be dangerous and stupid. Besides, if both of us were to die at this stage of the investigation, even in an accident, MacDonald would be on it like a spider on a fly. It had to have been a drunk driver.

I was checking the crumpled fender, cursing the idiot who would damage a classic car, when a thought hit me. What if it wasn't Samantha they were after. What if it was me?

I stared up the deserted road, sweat forming on my palms. This must be how Samantha felt—helpless and vulnerable. How could you protect yourself against an unknown killer?

Unknown? He was out there somewhere in a weapon shaped like a Mercedes sedan.

But the road remained deserted, deathly quiet in the dry, California heat. There wasn't even the sound of a bird or the distant growl of traffic.

I shook my head. Ridiculous. Samantha's panic was rubbing off on me. Why would anybody want to kill me now? It couldn't be related to Colton Labs. Cal MacDonald and even Joe Welts knew more about what had been going on than I did. I was the dumbest guy in the whole case.

I got back in the 'vette and started the engine. "We'll go back to the highway," I told Samantha lightly. "That maniac has taken the romance out of this route."

"Is *verdad.*" She stared up the road, her dark eyes wide. "Take me away from this place. Take me where there are peoples, many peoples."

I made a U-turn and drove back along the winding road, feeling for any false movement in the wheel that would tell me the steering system was damaged. But, except for some vibration, the old girl seemed to handle okay. I'd have the wheel alignment checked when I got the fender repaired. My insurance company—

The nerve-wracking sound of squealing tires snapped my concentration. I glanced in the rear view mirror. Oh, no! He was back. The tires of the big Mercedes squealed again as its driver rocketed around a bend, closing fast. This time he made no move to pass.

He charged straight at the rear of the Corvette like an aircraft carrier bearing down on a rowboat. If he'd known what was under the hood of the 'vette, his timing might've been better. I floorboarded the pedal, speed-shifted down at the same time, and the little beast leaped as though she'd been harpooned.

I was still peeling rubber and beginning to pull away when he hit us. But there was no power behind the blow. The Corvette kind of shook her tail and kept right on throwing smoke off her tires.

I shifted up and jammed the gas pedal to the floor. Sixty... Seventy... We were moving away! He couldn't match the Corvette's acceleration.

Vibration.. Damn, the damaged wheel... As the speed increased, the steering wheel almost shook from my grip. I had to ease off or risk a blowout.

I glanced in the rear view mirror. The Mercedes was rapidly closing the gap between us as though it scented the kill.

Even crippled, the 'vette might have been able to out-performed the big sedan if the road had sharp curves, but it had been well-engineered and all the curves were long and sweeping. So it was virtually a straight run. And I was losing.

Unable to go faster, I estimated he'd catch me at least a mile before we reached the main highway. And at almost eighty miles an hour, tires screaming in the gentle curves, all he had to do was give the 'vette a bump and it would take off end-over-end like a tumbleweed in a monsoon.

Beside me, Samantha crouched in the seat, her hands over her face, her hair whipping violently. In the rear view mirror I could see the big sedan closing in. Unless I did something fast, it wasn't going to be a gentle bump. It was going to be like getting hit with a swinging demolition ball.

I had only one thing going for me. At the moment, I was in control. He had to react to what I did. How good were his reflexes? Better than mine? Not with the adrenaline of fear I had coursing through my body. All he had was a desire to kill.

"Brace yourself," I screamed at Samantha. She heard me and gave me a quick, white-faced look. But she reached up and braced her arms hard against the dashboard.

I watched in the rear view mirror until the Mercedes was within inches of the Corvette, lunging like a bull. And like a matador, I sidestepped. I wrenched the wheel over as hard as I dared, at the same time slamming my foot on the brake pedal.

The 'vette screamed and bucked, taking a glancing blow from the fender of the Mercedes as it rocketed past, its own tires squealing and smoking. The 'vette fishtailed, two wheels off the shoulder of the road, and I played her carefully, getting the speed down where I could wrench her into a heart-stopping 180.

I was accelerating back down the road before the heavy Mercedes had even come to a stop. But as I barreled around a bend I saw the big machine beginning to turn. He wasn't going to give up. So now what the hell could I do? It was miles to a crossroad and nowhere to hide in between. He would overtake us long before then. And this time, he'd be ready.

Samantha was making whimpering sounds, her eyes staring

straight ahead, not heeding the hair that lashed her face.

Who the hell was this maniac trying to kill—her or me? If it was her, all I had to do was stop and kick her out. Throw her to the wolves to save myself? Jesus, I must really be scared shitless!

Then I realized it wasn't such a bad idea. With the damaged wheel, I didn't stand a chance against the Mercedes in a running fight. But if I could get him in just the right position...

Frantically, I began looking for a place to lay the trap. The Mercedes was still out of sight, but I could hear the distant squealing of tires as he closed in.

We had reached the same point in the road where the Mercedes had made its first move with the deep canyon on the right and a high cliff on the left. I slowed a little, looking for a place on the left where I could find some concealment. There. On the left. Bushes. Not enough, but it might work.

I braked hard and swung in behind a clump of brush as far as I could go, the front bumper against the face of the cliff. Damn, the bushes were too few and too low! The windshield was sticking up in clear view and the rear of the sportscar stuck out a couple of feet. Even at the speed he was moving, the Mercedes driver could see the 'vette. I needed a diversion.

Samantha was looking at me as though I'd gone loco. "What jou do?" she screamed. "He find us here."

"I know," I yelled back. "Get out of the car. Get out in the road."

She stared at me, frozen with disbelief. "Jou wan' him to kill me?"

"No, no. Make him come after you. Get him over near the canyon."

She turned her head to look across the road at the sheer drop and understood instantly. Without another word, she quickly got out of the car.

"Jou better not miss," she said.

She slammed the door and ran into the middle of the narrow road. We could hear the big Mercedes approaching in a shrieking, roaring rage. I stared at Samantha. I couldn't believe her guts. She was running toward the sound, knowing she had to lure the big Mercedes to the edge of the canyon at the point where he was opposite the Corvette. She also knew if I missed, she'd be dead.

I shifted into reverse and held the clutch down while revving the engine to a hammering whine.

I peered over the top of the bushes. There he was! The Mercedes came with a rush, screaming around the bend. It seemed to hesitate when the driver saw Samantha in the middle of the road, now running back in my direction, apparently in a frantic effort to escape. The Mercedes driver had to believe I'd kicked her out to save my own skin. Trapped between the cliff on the left and the yawning precipice on the right, she was an easy target. He could smash her into oblivion, then resume his pursuit of me.

That was what he was supposed to think.

It wasn't going to work. He was coming too fast!

Then Samantha stumbled and fell, and my heart stopped. Oh, God, no. He's going to hit her before I could make my move!

She was up, running hard along the dirt shoulder of the road on the very edge of the canyon. I yelled with joy as the Mercedes slowed and moved out with two wheels on the shoulder, closing in on her like a hawk after a rabbit.

She was no more than twenty feet in front of the charging Mercedes, running hard, when I jammed the gas pedal to the floor and released the clutch. The 'vette shot backward, its tires clawing dirt and rocks until they bit into the asphalt where they screamed and smoked, hurling the little car backward like a bolt out of a crossbow. If I missed, I'd never be able to stop before I shot out over the deep canyon like an airplane without wings.

Bam!

The tail of the 'vette slammed into the Mercedes' left front fender.

The big car shuddered and jerked sideways. Then I was spinning along the center of the highway, totally out of control. I saw Samantha still running as I flashed past, missing her by millimeters. I caught a glimpse of the Mercedes bearing down on her. But its right wheels were already off the edge, the undercarriage scraping the ground, spraying gouts of rock and dirt. The driver's face was frozen in panic as the big machine leaned farther and farther out over the abyss and almost gently began a long, lazy dive to the huge boulders far below.

I didn't see it hit. But the sound was a rending, rolling ugliness I never want to hear again.

It was quiet for an instant before an explosion geysered a column of black smoke. I was surprised to find I was sitting in the Corvette at a dead stop in the middle of the road.

I looked for Samantha, dread paralyzing my breath. Where was she? Then I saw her. She was standing at the edge of the precipice looking down at the burning car. I couldn't believe her mouth was not too dry to spit. Mine sure as hell was.

The 'vette was badly wounded, but far from dead. The rear looked as though it had been attacked by a herd of alligators, but when I got the engine restarted, the old girl moved, although with a definite limp.

I stopped beside Samantha and she climbed in. She slammed the door and glared at me. "Now jou believe me," she snapped. "I tell jou he will try to kill me."

"The man in the boat? No. That wasn't him."

"Sure, it is. Why you say that?"

My glimpse of the man's terrified face was seared in my memory, and suddenly, I remembered where I'd seen it before. The image blending with other images that slashed at my brain. The adrenaline of fear that had been sustaining me gave way to grief and dull anger.

I saw the gathering fear in Samantha's eyes, the realization that it might not be over and I said, "No. You're right. He's dead. You can relax."

She turned her eyes toward the rising column of smoke. "Was him? Jou sure?"

"Yes," I lied. "It was him."

She collapsed against the seat and her hands began to tremble. "I want to go home," she said. "My home."

The drive took a long time. I couldn't drive faster than twenty-five miles an hour without the Corvette feeling as though it would lose a wheel, but I finally dropped Samantha off at her own house. I knew she'd be safe. The man who was trying to kill her—actually, to have her killed—probably thought we were both dead by this time.

"I'll bring your cat over later," I told her.

She nodded, still in shock. I left her clutching her purse to her chest and staring down at her torn shoes. "*Carrumba,*" I heard her mutter. "*Mi zapatos mejor.*"

On the way home, I stopped at a pay phone to call Cal MacDonald. He wasn't in his office, but when I told the police operator who I was and what it was about, she said she'd relay the message to him right away.

I sat in the battered 'vette while I debated my next move. There had been two attempts on my life and I was sure somebody still wanted me dead. Two attempts? Make that three. I'd been shot at in Uganda. That's what Herb meant when he said I should be dead. It had been a setup. They'd been waiting for me, expecting me. I'd assumed the ambush had been set up by somebody to steal the computer. But it had been a murder mission, designed to get me out of the way so Herb and his partner could run the operation without the fear I might stumble onto their activities. They hadn't needed me any more. The facade was complete. No wonder Herb had sounded so nervous when he found out I was still alive.

Memories of Herb formed a kaleidoscope: Herb and me sharing drinks; Herb and me riding in his Eldorado and laughing our heads off at one of his stupid jokes; Herb and me with our heads together over an organization chart, putting together our company, a company I now knew was nothing but a front for his bigger scheme.

I put my forehead on the steering wheel on the edge of tears. They had to have planned my death from the beginning. I was supposed to die as soon as they were through using me. I couldn't question Herb about it, but I could talk to his partner. The man in the mask. The man on the boat. The man who had killed Helen.

I started the engine, unable to wait any longer. I had to confront the son-of-a-bitch. Now.

Then I hesitated. If MacDonald couldn't be reached quickly—or if he didn't arrive soon enough—I might need some protection. And I knew just where to get it.

The drive back along the Coast Highway and out on the peninsula was agonizingly slow. I found Jack in Michael's, sitting at a sidewalk table, drinking Coors and watching girls saunter by. He'd pulled on a beat-up pair of blue jeans, sandals and a loose Hawaiian shirt.

When he saw me, he waved to a chair. I didn't sit down.

"Can you come with me?" I asked.

Jack stared at my face, which must've looked as grim and sick as I felt because he said, "Sure," He put down his beer and stood up. Not a question of where we were going or what we were going to do. Why the hell couldn't Herb have been a friend like that?

Jack did give a grunt of surprise when he saw the beat up Corvette. "Must've been a hell of a party."

I told him what had happened while we poked along the Coast Highway. I'd gotten used to other cars cueing up behind me while their angry drivers waited for a chance to swing out into the faster middle lane to pass, but I was glad when we turned off the highway onto the quiet streets of Corona Del Mar.

Jack had listened with a heavy scowl darkening his face. When I finished, he asked, "You want me to kill the shithead?"

"No. So far it's all circumstantial. I've got to be one hundred percent sure."

"Then I'll kill him."

"Then MacDonald arrests him. I just want you there in case somebody gets violent."

Jack's scowl deepened. "You're going to give him the first move? That's a mistake."

"I know, but I've got to be certain."

"You'll probably be dead."

I shrugged, feigning a nonchalance I didn't feel. "Then I'll be sure."

"I can get us some backup," Jack said. "We might need it."

I pictured a regiment of cold-eyed mercenaries armed with automatic weapons and commando knives. "No, no," I quickly said. "There won't be any trouble. Besides, MacDonald will be there."

I almost overshot the hedge-obscured driveway. I turned in and cut the engine, hoping oil would drip on the immaculate concrete. Jack followed as I got out and rang the doorbell. The door was opened by Juan. He was wearing a servant's white jacket and black pants. He looked even bigger and his eyes harder than I remembered.

He stared at us without a word, his hand ready to shut the door at the first sign we were not acceptable.

"Would you tell Mr. Cotrell that Mr. Roan is here to see him."

"The Commander is not receiving visitors today." He spoke with a slight accent, but with a heavy layer of emphasis. He was starting to close the door when I put out a hand and stopped it.

"He'll see me," I said. "Tell him."

"No visitors," he snarled, and leaned into the door.

I set my feet and pushed harder, holding the door open, my anger giving me a determined strength. "If you don't tell him. I'm coming in over you."

His answer was to push harder. But his eyes told me I'd damn well better not try. Jack was stepping forward to help when Claire Cotrell said, "Juan, let them in."

He turned his head without letting up the pressure on the door. She was standing slightly behind him, her back stiff, her hands clenched at her sides.

"The Commander said no visitors," Juan repeated.

"These are not visitors," she said sharply, cutting the words like diamonds. "I said let them in."

Reluctantly, Juan released the pressure on the door. Without waiting for us to enter, he turned and stalked away. Mrs. Cotrell stepped forward and held the door open.

"I'm sorry," she said. "Do come in."

We walked out of the sunshine into the cool, spacious foyer. "Thanks," I said.

Claire Cotrell brought her hands together in front of her chest and she began kneading one with the other. "Something is wrong, isn't it?" Her voice trembled in sharp contrast to the tone she'd used with Juan. "Isn't it?"

"I don't know," I told her. "But I've got to talk to your husband."

"Oh," she said and stood staring, her eyes mirroring her anguish as though she had been expecting something terrible and now it was here.

Juan came in from an archway and said flatly, "Commander Cotrell will see you."

He turned and we followed him, leaving Mrs. Cotrell staring after us while her body remained rigid with apprehension.

Juan led us into a large den comfortably furnished with couches and chairs resting on a thick wall-to-wall carpet. The walls were decorated with bookcases and original oils. A big, fire-blackened fireplace occupied almost an entire wall.

Lou Cotrell was seated behind a huge, walnut desk working on papers. His back was to large windows that overlooked a patio garden. His short-sleeved polo shirt was powder blue with a small insignia on the breast. When we walked in, he didn't get up or lift his head. He made a few more notations before he looked up, the pencil poised impatiently. He cold blue eyes shifted from me to Jack, but he didn't ask for an introduction. His lips scarcely moved when he said, "What do you want?"

I stood in front of the desk staring back at him, matching his arrogance. Out of the corner of my eye I saw Jack move so he could keep an eye on both Juan and Cotrell.

"Not a thing," I said. "I came to tell you something."

"So?"

"Your employee, the one you sent to kill Samantha Cazzoli and me, is dead."

He put the pencil down. "What are you talking about?"

"The man I saw in your office that day I stopped by to tell you about Helen. I didn't catch his name. He did work for you, didn't he?"

He leaned back in the chair. "A lot of people work for me." He looked relaxed and confident. His voice was still cynical, but I had his attention.

"The police won't have any trouble finding out all about him. I'll bet there'll be a lot to learn."

"Are you telling me one of my employees tried to kill some woman? And you?"

"You know damn well he did."

He straightened a little and put his hands flat on his thighs. "I know no such thing. If one of my employees has some sort of lover's quarrel with a woman, that's his business. I'm sorry if you got caught in the middle."

I took a step forward and behind me I heard Juan's feet shuffle. I tensed to counter whatever he tried, but Cotrell signaled him off with a glance.

"Look, Cotrell, Cal MacDonald is on his way over here. When he gets here, I'm going to spell the whole thing out for him. How you, Herb and Clint Hemet set up S&R Security. How Hemet got you into

Colton Labs. How you used your own company to handle the transactions and conceal the finances."

Cotrell's mouth had developed a ring of white but he kept his half-smile. "For what purpose, pray tell?"

"High tech secrets. I know how you did it—S&R guards working with Harry Deen. And so does Colton Labs. They're very interested in you."

"If such an operation does exist," Cotrell said slowly and carefully, "it has nothing to do with me. I rather think it was being run by Herb and you, Mr. Roan."

"Except neither Herb nor I had the marketing connections. They had to come from somebody with a lot more international connections than we had."

"What makes you think it was me?" Cotrell's smile widened. "It could've been anyone."

My smoldering anger gave way to a deepening despair. He was right. Lou Cotrell would never leave any hard evidence of his involvement. He could claim his only connection with Herb and Hemet had been social. Boys from the same club. Nice fellows really. Too bad they got involved in crime. The death of the man he'd sent to kill Samantha and me worked in his favor. Now there was no one who could testify against him. Except—except the one person he'd tried to kill.

"Samantha Cazzoli! She recognized you when she saw you on your boat. You knew she would if she ever saw you. That's why you tried to have her killed."

His smile was gone and his eyes were hooded, burning. "I don't know what you're talking about."

"The porno operation. You were involved. It ties you to the whole thing. That's why you had to kill Hooker. He knew you. So did—" I stopped, shaken by a dreadful truth. "My God, so did Helen. You killed her!"

He stood up, tipping his heavy chair back against the wall with a crash. "You crud," he snarled. "Leave my daughter out of this!"

I had him. I couldn't stop. The words poured out of me like venom. "She either had to know your operation from the beginning or she found out about it."

He stared at me, his mouth working.

"I'll bet she didn't know. She found out. And about the porno operation, too. Hell, she couldn't turn you in. Her own father. And she couldn't stop it without pulling you in. That's when Deen got to her.

He made her come in. He must've told her she had to be one of his girls, or he'd spill the whole thing. You'd go to prison. When you found out he was using her, you saw your chance to—"

"Shut up," he snarled. "Shut up!" He clutched the edge of the desk, his face mottled, his eyes slits of fury.

He looked as though he was on the edge of a stroke. And I wanted to push him over the edge. "You did it, didn't you? You saw a chance to screw your own daughter. And you took it. You were the guy in the mask. But she recognized you, didn't she? She knew! How long had you been wanting to fuck your own daughter, you damn pervert?

"No," he said, his voice a strangled moan. He started to come around the desk. "No."

"How many times, you son-of-a-bitch? How many filthy things did you make her do? My God! She had to stop you. She had to. So you killed her!" I was shaking with rage, unable to remember where I was or why I was here. Only that I wanted to hurt Cotrell as much as he had hurt me. "Jesus! Your own daughter. You filthy—"

He lunged with startling speed. His hands locked on my throat, squeezing. I was fighting for breath, trying to pry his fingers loose before my larynx was crushed. Jack leaped forward and smashed Cotrell in the kidneys with the edge of his right palm. Cotrell's hands came loose and I sank to the floor sucking in air. Then Jack grunted in pain as Juan hit him on the side of the head with a heavy revolver.

Jack's instincts took over, and as he was falling, he drove his fist into Juan's groin. The big man made a shuddering sound as he struggled to keep from bending over and retching. He tried to bring the gun up, but Jack was already standing and he hit Juan in the throat with his elbow. Juan dropped the gun and clutched at his neck, his face contorted. He collapsed on the carpet, his heels drumming as he fought for breath.

I didn't see Cotrell scoop up the revolver. I didn't see it until it was pointed at my chest. Behind it, Cotrell's face was a mask of rage and he squeezed the trigger. The sound of the shot was not the roar I expected. It was a sharp, crisp bang that was quickly followed by another, and another, and another.

Bang! Bang! Bang!

Cotrell's body made little jerking movements each time there was a shot and his eyes bulged in surprise. The sounds stopped and Cotrell collapsed as though he had been waiting for the shooting to stop to give him permission to fall.

I turned to see Claire Cotrell standing close behind me. Her eyes slid toward me and she held out an ugly-looking automatic. I took it from her slack fingers. She looked at me as though pleading for forgiveness.

"I knew he did that to Helen," she whispered. "I knew it. I tried to pretend it didn't happen, but I couldn't."

"You knew?" My voice was harsh with disbelief.

"She was such a pretty little girl." Her vacant eyes lighted briefly. "Such a pretty little thing." Then they glazed again with a bitter memory. "He hurt her, you know. She didn't want to do it. I heard her crying sometimes, but I didn't do anything. I just wanted him to stop." Her eyes teared in an agony of remorse. "There was blood on her dress, so I burned it. I couldn't let anybody know." Her eyes focused on me.

"Could I?"

Cal MacDonald came in and took the pistol from my hand. He put his arm around Claire Cotrell's shoulders and gently led her from the room. "No," he said. "You couldn't. You did the right thing, Claire. You did the right thing."

Jack was standing, his hand rubbing a darkening bruise on the side of his head, watching them walk away. He looked down at Cotrell, touched him with his toe.

"The son-of-a-bitch might've gotten away with it if he hadn't had the hots for his daughter." He looked at me. "How old do you think she was? The time his wife was talking about?"

"I don't know," I muttered. "And I hope I never find out."

I walked out of the house into the sunshine, into the clean beauty of a California day.

Robert L. Hecker

ROBERT L. HECKER was born in Provo, Utah but grew up in Long Beach, CA., graduating from high school just as the U.S. entered WWII. Joining the Air Force, he flew thirty missions over Europe where he was awarded the Distinguished Flying Cross and five Air Medals. After the war, he began writing radio and TV dramas, then moved on to writing and producing more than 500 documentary, educational and marketing films on subjects ranging from military and astronaut training, nuclear physics, aeronautics, the education of Eskimos and Native Americans, psychology, lasers, radars, satellites and submarines. He is currently writing several movie screenplays as well as other novels.